I0599354

PUT IT ON THE MOB

LISA AUSTIN

LISA AUSTIN PUBLICATIONS

 Created with Vellum

HEY Y'ALL

Heyyy! Y'all have been looking for this book for a whole year! Finally, here it is! Initially, it was supposed to be a full stand-alone but Jisei and Ezio have a lot to say and even more to go through and grow through. This book basically leaves off where *Pregnant by a Muthafuckin' Don* left off, except it is from the points of view of Jisei and Ezio. If you recall, Jisei was Scarlett's neighbor and Mocha's best friend. Jisei turned out to be Don, Demise Rinaldi's sister. Ezio is Scarlett's cousin and also the sworn enemy of Don because he is the head of the Cuppacio Mob. I won't say much, but this book will have you pulling your edges out at times lol! There are flashbacks and we all know I despise flashbacks! However, they were necessary in this book. Don't skip them! They are entertaining and help you understand the character.

Trigger warning: This book does have a character that suffers from addiction. If this is not for you, please skip this read and pick up one of the other forty books that make up my catalog.

Thank you so much for your patience! I hope you enjoy!

ORDER OF BOOKS

You can read this book without having read these because I did go into detail with the characters' backstories. But, I promise you will want to read the others first. Two of the four books listed above are shorts and won't take you long at all to read.

SYNOPSIS

Everyone in the Rinaldi Mob has a job to do—a role to play—and newly appointed Mafian, Jisei Harper, is no exception.

Jisei is used to slumming it out on her own. From birth, she was dealt a bad hand, but instead of dwelling on it, she smiled, rolled her shoulders back, and played her cards. After years of struggling, she meets Mocha, a rich daddy's girl, and Scarlett, a naïve hoodlum who had it worse off than Jisei. Little did she know, these two new friendships would lead her to the only blood relative she never knew existed, her brother, Demise Rinaldi—Don and head of the Rinaldi Mafia.

Time has passed and now Jisei is no longer a struggling college student but a corporate Barbie with zeroes in her bank account. Leaving the sweet struggling life of a sorority girl behind, Jisei dove head first into a new clan and that was the one she was granted at birth. In The Mob, she mostly sits back, being spoiled by her big brother, listens to her best friends who have been upgraded to rich mob wives, and spends her days partying, shopping, and living the good life. The term rich Auntie that so many wish was their reality really is Jisei's. With all of her friends being mommies and her brother having a new baby, she spoils all of her babies rotten and sends them on their way.

All good things must come to an end, however, and Jisei's good thing is no exception. With so many blessings falling in her lap, a tech is bound to rear its ugly head. That tech isn't ugly though. As a matter of fact, Ezio Cuppacio doesn't have an unattractive bone in his body. The rival mob, The Cuppacios, were perceived to be all wiped out by Don Demise. As the head, Ezio liked for the world to think his family was all in the dirt and took pride in keeping his head down and protecting and providing for his remaining bloodline. Money is good but it could be better, and when he is given the opportunity of a lifetime from his sworn enemy, he can't help but agree.

Jisei, the humbled beauty, just knew life had gotten sweet for her, but when her brother forces her hand in marriage to a man who sees her as nothing but a means to help his people, she then realizes the Mob isn't all shopping sprees and diamond cleaning. Shit has gotten real, and maybe a little too real for Jisei.

PROLOGUE

"Don, wheels are down in the next five minutes, sir."

Pulling my head from my phone, I looked into the face of a fucking clown. With a scowl covering my own, I locked my screen.

"Why in the fuck you talking all formal and shit, nigga? And do I look like my fucking daddy? Fuck is you calling me sir for?"

Taking his seat across from me, he settled in and looked out of the window.

"Shid, with the way you dragged me out of my pussy, I thought I was the fucking stewardess. And I don't know what the fuck Unc's corpse looks like to say if you look like the dead ass nigga, but before you killed his ass, damn right y'all was twinning."

Matteo broke his cloud gazing and placed his attention back on me. The crazed look in his eyes was one that confirmed the nigga didn't have it all upstairs and marriage and kids

1

didn't do a damn thing to change that. It may have made him even more throwed off.

"I brought yo' ass because you my fucking right hand."

"And you got a left hand too. You should have made that nigga Rut tag along."

Waving my hand dismissively, I signaled for the actual stewardess to bring me a shot of the cognac I'd been sipping. I usually didn't handle business while under the influence, but being back in this city gave a nigga PTSD like a muthafucka.

"Rut has a newborn at the house. Plus, this shit is family business. I needed my best man with me and that's you. Unless you lost ya spark?"

Snickering, I accepted the chilled glass that housed a triple shot. The stewardess went to hand Matteo one and he sent her a look that had her flat booty ass running to the corner she'd been tucked in for the duration of the flight. She probably couldn't wait to get the fuck away from our black asses.

When it was confirmed that I had to go back home, I had my wife call up the pilot and I knew this new hoe on the plane was all Dasani's doing. She wanted to make sure the bitch serving me was the opposite of my type. She did damn good, too, because although I was loyal to my wife, I liked some junk in the trunk and melanin in the genetic makeup. I had something for Mrs. Rinaldi though. I kept trying to tell her I was a faithful ass nigga. I didn't even look at these other bitches because when I did, her sixth sense, childish titty ass always knew.

"Rut ain't the only nigga that got some shit at the crib. Scarlett texted me on some other shit because Princess dipped on her ass. She forever over your sister's house like ours ain't good enough. I need to get my household in order. I'on got time to be coming on none of your fucking dummy missions and shit."

Matteo was so fucking aggravated that it was funny. I had to hold my laugh in, though, because I didn't have time to be tussling with this unhinged ass nigga. I loved my cousin with everything in me and there was no nigga on the planet who put fear in my heart, but I wasn't even dressed to play with his ass. Plus, I didn't want to deal with his father—Uncle Reuchie. He didn't play about his only child. That was the problem though. They should have had this nigga a sibling. Teo had only child syndrome bad as fuck.

"That lil shitty ass girl left because y'all done fucked her up. Sour stomach ass. She the only fucking baby I know be around this bitch smelling like a grown ass man."

Matteo's response was a mean mug and he looked just like his damn daddy at that moment. Matteo treated Scarlett's daughter like she came from his nut sack, and you better not tell this nigga she hadn't. He had been hinting at wanting another child, preferably a son, and we were all praying that shit didn't happen. Just like Matteo when he was a jit, I knew whenever he had a son, we were all going to hate to see his ass coming. The nigga was a walking fucking menace back then and didn't need to procreate, ever. Princess was already taking too many of this nigga's habits because, as pretty as she was, her ass was bad as fuck. A fucking Chucky in a pink and green Shrek dress.

"But on some real shit, though, this is family business. I fuck with Rut and he my man a hunnid grand, but since I'm still feeling this shit out, I needed my blood by my side."

Matteo stared me in the face, and I tried to hold his stare off but my eyes were burning like a bitch. I had to blink before I shed a tear.

"If you coming all this way, that means you already accessed yo' feelings on this shit. Just like you been watching from a distance, so have I. Contrary to your belief, I haven't just

3

been sitting back, changing shitty diapers and eating pussy. If you feel like this is the right move, then I back you."

Matteo sat back in his seat and continued to gaze out of the window. His last sentence lingered like cigarette smoke. If nothing else, I knew my cousin had me. When I told him to pack up his shit and come to Jagoda Bay so that I could reinvent the Rinaldi Mafia, he changed not one word. I tried to set Teo up in our new city but he already had a fucking condo and everything lined up. Matteo had a whole life in Chicago, but the moment I needed him, he came running. No matter how many crazy-ass drills I had my men doing, Matteo did the shit with a smile, even though he didn't need training because we'd been trained up in the world of mafia our entire lives. So, if no one had me, my fucking cousin did.

Matteo had been appointed my consigliere. It was the position his father was to my father and though I didn't really use those old ass mob terms and shit, by him being my right hand and blood line, the title was fitting. I was the Don, and my members were made men. That was how I ran my shit. All that Underboss, Caporegime's and shit was irrelevant. Matteo though was definitely worthy of having a proper fucking role. The nigga might talk shit, but he was coming. Plus, I did his ass a solid. He found a bad ass wife, gained a daughter, and had a new baby just by moving to Jagoda Bay. Him having a family though was a blessing and a curse. We secretly called Scarlett the shadow of death because the number of bodies that had been piling up around Jagoda Bay just from this nigga getting wind of another man blinking at her was unreal. I would say love looked good on my cousin but love made him go off his fucking rocker.

When we landed and were settled in the back of the Maybach truck that was waiting on the strip, it took less than thirty minutes for us to arrive at our destination. I'd been here once a little over a year ago, and just like the last time I'd popped up, this nigga had a fucking driveway full.

Stepping out of the car, Matteo crossed his arms in front of him and waited until I got out. Once my custom loafer hit the gravel, Matteo fell in sync with me, placing his hand on the pistol housed in his jacket. I appreciated his caution, but I wasn't worried about shit popping off. This was a friendly visit, depending on the response I received. I was prepared to either end a lineage for good or expand my fucking kingdom. Either way was good with me.

Matteo took the lead as we approached the door, twisted the knob, and gained entry. Looking upside his head, I scowled.

"You not gon' fucking knock?"

Matteo took his gun out of his jacket and pointed it forward.

"Hell nawl. Come on."

Future's "Mask Off" blared through the speakers. The smell of weed invaded my nostrils while I let this Call of Duty, wannabe ass nigga lead the way. Three young niggas sat in the dining area, breaking down weed. Seeing us walking in their shit didn't raise alarm for them. They simply nodded their heads and went back to rolling their blunts.

Pushing his way through the living room, Matteo continued to walk through this shit like he was in an action movie and more half-breed muthafuckas came into view, not even blinking at our presence. From the last visit, I knew this bitch was heavily guarded with cameras and we could have been lit up the moment we were in the driveway. But again, times had changed, and I wasn't even on the shit I was on back then.

"Nigga, you fucking cheating! Hoe ass boy!"

We approached a dice game being held in the hallway, and

if I wasn't here on business, I would break these niggas. The money on the floor was chump change, but still, I couldn't be beat on the dice and liked to flex that shit from time to time. More than a decade in jail had me picking up more bad-ass habits than I'd gone in with.

"Aye, y'all looking for Cuz?"

One of the niggas standing around watching the dice game shot us a glance and pushed himself from the wall. Matteo turned with his Glock pointed while ole boy stood there shirt-less with a blunt dangling from his lip. Mob Shit was tattooed across his stomach. Nigga was marked up like a pissy-ass subway.

Shifting his low, red eyes from me to Matteo, he kept his neutral expression.

"You can lower your pole, Jo. My family in this bitch. We save that gangsta shit for the streets. If you wanna meet on the pavement, cool. My gun bust just like y'all's. Now, if you came here to handle business with my family, we do that shit without fire."

Matteo's finger was itching, so I lowered his arm and gave the nigga across from us a smile. The game was still going on, but it had become a whole lot quieter as if they were waiting for us to make a move. They may have been cautioned but these niggas knew how I was coming. Not only did my reputa-tion precede me, I was always down to send a muthafucka to the Most High. I came here on some nice shit but we could easily turn it into a crime scene. Again, I was cool with whatever.

"Smart choice. That nigga in the back. I'll see you at the family reunion, *in-law*. Tell Scar her big cousin Shio misses her. I'ma send some shit her way soon."

Before Matteo could go straight Mob style on this nigga, I

grabbed his shoulders and shoved him in the direction of the person we were here to see.

"You a mean ass cousin-in-law. Loosen the fuck up, these your people," I kidded.

Matteo looked around at the simple, modern, two-story home with a frown. "You my people. Fuck these niggas."

Coming to the door that I knew the man of the hour was behind, Matteo's ass kicked it open, almost falling into a damn split. Using his palm to separate him from the floor, it brought me back to when I tried kicking in the door on Dasani that time. I almost split my balls. Slick ass shoes.

"You niggas don't know how to knock?"

"Naw. We don't. You tryna teach us?"

I hit Matteo's chest with the back of my hand twice and stepped up. I probably shouldn't have brought the pit bull with me, but what was done was done.

"Ezio Ezee fucking Cuppacio. We meet again."

Placing his hands behind his head, he didn't look enthusiastic to see me nor did he look bothered, so I guess that was a good thing. I didn't give a fuck how he felt. As long as this conversation went in my favor, I could take my ass back to my city without blood on my hands today. I hadn't killed a nigga in a week, and I felt like a saved man. I wanted to keep my streak going.

"You brought this schizophrenic ass nigga with you, so that means he left my cousin at the house with a kid. Gon' state ya business so y'all can head back home."

"Fuck is all y'all so worried about my wife for?" Matteo spat.

Holding my hand up because I didn't have time for this nigga to unleash the beast, I cleared my throat.

"You told me when I found a way to make the merge happen, to get at you, so here the fuck I am."

Ezio scraped the bottom of his lip with his teeth but held eye contact.

I'd wiped out Ezio's entire mafia on some young and turned up shit, so we were now sworn enemies. I fucked with Ezio and not only because Matteo's wife was his family. I saw something in the nigga even though I killed his daddy and shit. So, I wanted to merge our families. Being Don I did a lot of shit that wasn't traditional, and my uncle Reuchie usually looked past it but merging the clans had to be done the right way or his ass wasn't having it. I didn't want no beef with the old ass nigga so here I was.

"Bullshit. A Rinaldi woman gotta marry me. Last I checked, the Rinaldi women are already married or old as fuck. I'm not into cougar bitches."

Drowning out the slurping and gargling sounds that overpowered the tunes blaring from the Bluetooth speakers, I tucked my hands in the pockets of my black suit pants. These bitches were custom and ran me seventeen racks for the entire set. A nigga was getting better and better at this Mob shit. I damn sure always looked the fucking part.

"Lucky for you, my boy, I do have a Rinaldi woman for ya."

"Word?"

"Word. My sister."

"Yo' smart mouth ass ain't got shit to say to that, hunh?" Matteo teased.

"Yo' sister? You an only child."

"Yeah, well, turns out I'm not."

"A sister?" Ezio repeated, almost in disbelief.

"Did my cousin fucking stutter or are you hard of hearing?" Matteo growled. I knew I had to wrap this bitch up because my boy was a ticking time bomb.

"Nigga, pipe the fuck down, damn. We family and shit."

"You got ten minutes to wash the saliva off your dick and

8

meet us outside. I ain't leaving this city without the groom-to-fucking-be."

THE BITCH who had been gagging on Ezio's dick from the moment we kicked down the door tried to let up, but he held her long, black hair in place. She was ass naked, and from her position, we saw the inside of her pussy. She was thick as fuck too. This nigga was caught with his pants around his waist and kept getting his dick sucked like it was nothing. I had something for his ass though.

I turned on my heels, ready to get the fuck up out of here with Matteo in tow, but then paused. Pulling my rugger from my jacket, I sent a silent and single headshot to thickums.

"Aye, what the fuck?"

Ezio jumped up and snatched his shorts up, tossing what was left of the bitch's sew-in. Blood and brain matter was splattered all over his abdomen.

"You trying to shoot my fucking dick off?"

"You belong to my sister, nigga. Cut the hoes loose. If you think me and this nigga ain't got it all, wait till you meet Jisei Rinaldi. You down to six minutes now."

Leaving that nigga to clean up the mess while meeting his countdown, we walked out the same way we came. Just as the sharp winds smacked our faces, Matteo spoke up.

"And you say I got screws loose."

The driver opened the door as I climbed in.

Once we pulled off, Matteo's phone rang, and the nigga almost broke his finger answering.

"I'm on the way, Princess. Tell your auntie to put some Reese's Pieces in your sippy cup, mama... Aye, Jae, make it the same way I used to when she was a baby. I been gave you the fucking steps."

Shaking my head at this nigga, I pulled my phone out to call my woman. I almost snatched the phone to tell my sister what was up, but she would find out soon enough. Right now, I needed to get the fuck up out of Chicago. I couldn't wait to fuck on my wife. It was about time I put another baby in her; she'd been popping her shit way too hard. I just prayed bringing these niggas to my city wouldn't backfire on my ass. I hoped Jisei was single because that nigga Ezio was just as fucked up as we were. It was lights out for his ass if a hair came out of place on my sister's head. Hopefully, they hit it off so we could plan a fucking wedding. Unc said no more simple unions. We were doing this shit the mob way.

CHAPTER 1
JISEI "JAE" RINALDI

Are you single? Because if not, you gotta let that nigga know it's a wrap. Your fiancé won't appreciate that shit. Fiancé? The six-letter French origin word was a title I hadn't seen myself rocking at least until I was well into my late thirties. Maybe even forties. However, one visit from my brother, a brother I hadn't even known existed up until a year ago, came in and changed my entire trajectory. *A fiancé?*

I'd been by myself for so long, I didn't even know what the fuck to do with a man. I used them for what they were meant to be – a dick to ride on. Even with that, I hadn't laid with a man in well over thirteen months, maybe longer. Now, I was supposed to shift my entire world around for a man. A man I didn't even know.

Confusion plagued my face as tense silence surrounded me. I'd turned everything off in my home because I was on my way to see my niece, who had me smitten until my brother walked into my house. Seeing that he had come by unexpectedly had me grinning because I'd already decided I was riding back to his house with him.

Demise lived on the other side of town in a crib that would put a museum to shame. Being that he was dressed in Nike instead of his custom three-piece suit, I knew he wasn't on mob business. Riding with Don and his driver meant I could get shit-faced with my sister-in-law. It had been a long work week, and nothing calmed the mind down like pretty ass drinks in a multimillion-dollar home with staff to wait on you hand and foot. But now, those words that my brother had just voiced – the command he'd just given- were about to have me drinking for an entirely different reason. *Fiancé?*

Snapping from my thoughts and staring into the face of the most feared man in the city, my mouth slacked, growing drier by the second. How could he give *me* a fiancé? Did he have the power to do that? Of course, he had the power to do so! He was the Don! Whatever he said was law. Sometimes he didn't even have to say shit; one look could determine if you lived or died. That was how much power my brother had. But this was *unexpected*. I mean, I knew when it was revealed that my father had been a ruthless mob leader, which was still a shocker. I was going to have to assume some type of responsibility, but an arranged marriage wasn't even a thought.

"Fiancé? I'm not engaged!"

The look on my brother's handsome face had me clamping my mouth closed. I could hold my own but I wouldn't dare go against anything he said. I'd known he was my brother for a little over a year now and he was so damn busy that we'd only really connected within the last month. It was fine by me, though, because over the year, he let his presence be felt from afar. Being that both my best friends were married to Rinaldi Mafia men, I was always in the same setting as my sibling but we'd never talked. He'd bought me a brand new Range Rover, laced my already fat account, and practically changed my life. I would never go against anything he said. I loved him like I'd known him my entire life, so I respected him to no end, as a little sister should. But this shit was left field.

"But yes, I'm single."

My brother gave me a curt nod and sat back on my grey sofa, smushing one of my pink, fuzzy pillows. I was trying not to lose my fucking mind. With my chest swelling and heaving breaths, I felt like I was about to pass out. Mind still swarming, I took a seat on the loveseat with my back straightened. Eyes on my brother, I silently begged him to say this was all a cruel joke. He wasn't marrying me off like I was some locked-away princess who had been kept pure and trained for her husband.

Not long ago, I was a college girl who had grown fond of partying. I'd had a few wild nights like any other college student, was living in the projects, and the most drama I had in my life was those my friends went through. When I wasn't out shaking my ass and letting my hair down, I was working or in the confines of my own home, living vicariously through my best friends. My sorority sisters all moved away after college so I wasn't really active in the sorority life as I used to be. They weren't missed though. I loved my routine. I loved my life and had no desire to add a damn fiancé to it. Just the thought of the word had me wanting to vomit my insides out. A fiancé?

The beeping of my alarm signaled that someone was walking through the door, and since I was planted on the couch that faced the entryway, I was able to see the exact moment the red and brown designer sneaker hit the laminated white oak floors that I'd just mopped and shined. The passion fruit punch scent still lingered.

He was tall. Not so tall that he had to duck when he entered the space but tall enough that he would tower over me. The brown rain jacket with signature Gucci printed stamped all over it featured striped, red sleeves and he had his hood pulled over his head. Since the light was off in my entryway, I couldn't get a good look at his face since it was shadowed by his hood, but his hardened chest was shielded by a white V-neck t-shirt that showed not only a diamond necklace that sparkled in the lack of light but I was able to get a glimpse of his inked skin. *Damn. Damn. Damn.*

The seat of my panties was drenched, and I felt guilty as hell for not only being turned on in the presence of my brother but for wanting to jump a man's bones whose face I couldn't even see clearly.

Suddenly, my thoughts were frozen as I wrung my hands. My body heat rose to a temperature that had my back matching the moisture of my panties and the fluttering in my stomach had me feeling like I needed to take a shit. Still, he took his time making his way into my space, turning his head to check out everything I loved and adored.

"Who is this?" I rasped.

Still, my looks were on the stranger who'd been promised to me. The Rinaldi men kept their women away from their mafia lives unless they needed them. For the most part, they didn't know much, but what I had seen during holidays and random celebrations was that all the men looked good. Even if the looks on their faces weren't there, their persona and deep pockets made them attractive.

Even with me always being in the space of fine-ass, paid men, I wasn't around to try to catch a big fish. My bestie Moke had set me up nicely way before my brother came along by buying me this house and placing seven figures in my account, so I wasn't in the market for scouting a mobster. But if I was promised to one for the rest of my life, I didn't want a man as attractive as Matteo, Lorenzo, or Don himself. Give me a smedium ugly man who treated me like a queen. That was my thought process back then. Now, though, my mind was chanting, *Please don't be ugly.*

He had the swag, the money judging by his threads and diamonds, and the body from what I could see in the way his jeans hugged his curved legs. The face though? The face was still hard to make out as it was concealed by the wet hood of his jacket.

I watched intently as he took the final step that placed him in the room with my brother and me, holding my breath as he lifted his extra light brown hand and swiped it over the top of his head, removing his hood.

"Sister, this is Ezio Cuppacio. Ezio, this is my sister. Y'all getting married and shit."

Oh God. He was so damn attractive that it hurt my fucking eyes. Those eyes. They were the prettiest shade of brown, with an orange ring around them and hints of a deep green around the orange. His strong and chiseled jawline made up a perfect face. The skin covering his bone structure was light with red undertones. It had been raining all day, so a cool breeze had swept through Jagoda Bay and it was probably the reason his nose was red. There wasn't any facial hair, but it didn't make him look childish. I was never a fan of tattoos that were visible, however the ink on his temple didn't even take away from his good looks. I was furious. I didn't know whether I was angry that he was being forced on me or it was because he looked this damn good. Either way, I stood to my feet, damn near breathing fire. The man was so fine that all I could do was counter.

"Hold up! I didn't sign up for this!"

"Everyone has a role to play, Jisei. Welcome to the Rinaldi Mafia."

My brother's statement was dismissive. Don wasn't a man of patience so I knew this shit was final. Instead of arguing my point, I took my eyes away from the unwelcome guest because the way he was staring at me was creepy, but it turned me on too bad. He crossed his arms over his chest, revealing a diamond watch that was just as blinding as the necklace.

My brother stood and straightened his Nike jacket like he was wearing a damn tux. He was always dressed up, so seeing him not in full mob mode was rare.

"Okay, Demise." I sighed.

I mean, what the fuck else could I do? I wasn't trying to get my ass disowned, or worse, killed. My brother had killed our own father, information that he'd divulged to me himself when we had our official talk. Our father deserved it, from the sounds of it, but I wasn't trying to be made an example. I didn't want to meet my father at all, especially if it meant being sent to my death. Aht. Aht. If my brother said I had to marry, then that was what it was.

"Okay?"

Demise raised a brow, seemingly shocked by my answer, and that brought tears to my eyes. Still, I held my tears back. I wasn't weak. Especially not in the room where there was so much power. I didn't know Ezio but his last name was one I'd known. Cuppacio. The rival mob that my brother had killed off. Scarlett's people. She'd married a Rinaldi, so my guess was he needed me to marry a Cuppacio in order to bring peace and unity. I'd read enough dark romance books to be able to put two and two together.

"Yes, Ize. Okay. I'll marry him if that's what you want me to do."

Demise paused, uncertainty in his eyes until I nodded at him for reassurance. Except I wasn't sure. I'd landed my dream job, had my degree, lived in one of my dream homes, had a Kia in the garage and a Range Rover in the driveway, made a six-figure salary, and had more money than I knew what to do with in the bank. My life was complete as far as I was concerned. I didn't want to marry a stranger but my loyalty lay with my only living blood relative. Plus, what Don said was law. Period. Even if it looked like he was giving you a choice, he wasn't.

"Aite. I'll be outside waiting for you. I'll let you two talk."

Don turned to Ezio and they seemed to be talking with their eyes. Before long, Ezio smiled, and Don snarled and walked out the same way he came in. Though me and my fiancé were left alone in the room, I still couldn't place my face back on him His features were a distraction and I hated how they made me feel like I was the luckiest girl in the world to be given this opportunity. One look at him and I forget how much of a shit show this was. *Why in the fuck did he have to be fine? Why?* This shit was all bad. Everything I'd said to my brother was the opposite of how I felt. This shit was not okay.

"Jisei."

The hairs on the back of my neck stood hearing the grittiness of his tone while saying my name.

"That shit sounds Japanese or some shit."

Clearing my throat, I slowly turned my head to face him and I almost had to pound my chest to get my breath back. How could this man look so rough but so well put together at the same damn time? He was trouble on bowed legs and my brother had fucked up big time pairing him with me.

"It is. But you can call me Jae," I spat.

Now that my brother was outside, the attitude I wanted to have, the one I was too scared to have with him, had surfaced and she was ready to spit fire at this man. I didn't know what the fuck he thought I was or who he thought I was, but I wasn't some mafia princess who bowed down to a man because of his looks and status. Had he said or done something in the few minutes that he'd been in my living room? No, but still, he had to know I wasn't the bitch to be fucked with.

He took steps in my direction, shoes thudding on my PVC

floors. I plopped down on the couch, driving my back into the cushion the closer he got, and when there was no way for me to escape due to him towering over me, he kneeled and was damn near nose and nose. The toothpick dangling from his lips moved as he chewed and stayed in place until he removed it from his mouth. Kush and Bond No. 9 was his fragrance and damn it was an alluring combination.

My chest rose and fell, indicating that I was breathing, but still, I struggled to catch my breath.

"You want to cry bad as hell."

I wanted to knock the smirk off his fine ass face. He'd called me out, and not only was I embarrassed, he was correct. I wanted to cry. I wanted to run to my room, push my face into the pillow, and let it all out. I couldn't help but feel like God had finally blessed me by giving me a tribe and financial freedom and that my life couldn't be real. Now, he'd proven to me that my intuition was right. As good as shit seemed, bullshit always followed.

"I don't. Just because we have to get married doesn't mean my life has to change. I can still do what the fuck I want."

Ezio's gaze slowly raked over me, stopping at the print in my leggings. I crossed my legs and cursed myself because I was sure he could smell how turned on I was. Hell, I could smell it. My pheromones were always strong.

"You can still do what the fuck you want?"

"I can."

Licking his bottom lip, he cocked his head like an innocent puppy, and damn, I loved me a dog.

"Is that right? How many niggas you fucked?"

Choking on my spit, I placed my hand on my chest as I calmed myself back down. By now, my skin was just as red as his and I was brown-skinned.

"Excuse me?"

"You heard me. How many niggas done been in that pussy?"

"That's none of your fucking business. Have I asked you how many bitches have been on yo' dick?"

"I wouldn't know the number if you had asked, so the shit would've been a waste."

I was disgusted and the displeased look on my face showed it.

"Yuck."

That made his smile broaden.

"Come lock up, lil crybaby. I'll come scoop you so we can have lunch or some shit."

He slowly stood to his feet like being crouched hadn't put a strain on his knees. I was only twenty-five, worked out weekly, and still didn't have Megan's knees.

He now looked down at me, the sinister grin never wavering as he placed his toothpick back in and chewed.

"Lunch cool, right? Yeah, that shit cool. You good? You need some bread?"

What the fuck was up with these men and money? My brother had just asked the same question before he laid the bomb on me.

"No. Do it look like I need your money?"

Ezio looked around almost displeasingly. "Yeah. It do."

Reaching into his pocket, he retrieved a wad of money and placed it on the ottoman.

"Go find you a ring and shit. If you need more, let Scarlett know. Y'all friends, right?"

He knew the answer to that, so I wasn't giving him a reply. The moment my brother told him I was to be his wife, I knew he'd done an extensive background check. He probably knew down to the day I got my first period in the seventh grade.

"What the fuck do I look like buying my own ring? I'm not doing that!"

Ezio flicked his thumb over his red snout and turned on his heels.

"I guess you won't be wearing one then, on foe nem. Now, come lock up. I got some shit to do."

Then, just like my brother, he was gone, leaving me to sit in my own thoughts. Last year, all I had were my friends, an apartment in the hood, and the hopes that I would land a job good enough to be able to get out of the hood and pay my student loans. I looked forward to my sorority meeting and the campus parties. Now, here I was, promised to a cocky fuck boy. Still, if he thought he was about to come in and regulate a life I worked so hard building, he had another thing coming. And I put that on BOTH MOBS.

CHAPTER 2
EZIO "EZEE" CUPPACIO

One Month Later

"So, this the house where you and yo' wife will be living at and shit?" Vello asked while chalking his stick. The pool table in this house was right up his alley. That nigga lived for pool. You couldn't tell him he wasn't the best out.

"This shit nice as fuck. Thrice as big as the house back in Chicago but I'm fucking with it," Nel, Vello's twin brother, added. He had his eyes glued to the seventy-five-inch flat screen that displayed highlights from the game.

"Shit, for two mills, it better be laid," Shio added. That nigga was posted up against the wall like my furniture had cooties or some shit while not taking an interest in the TV, the pool table, or this blunt. He was always just to him-fucking-self. Always in his head. Plotting and planning.

"Yeah, this shit laid. One day, I'ma own some shit like this. I wish that bitch was for sale. I can't buy it now, but long as shit stays on track, I'll be able to in a few months."

When Demise interrupted me getting my fucking dick sucked more than a month ago, I hopped on the plane with that nigga and came to Jagoda Bay. We chopped it up and I flew my ass back to Chicago because I had some shit I had to finalize. My family was my top priority and I had to see that everyone was comfortable before I took my leave. It took me a month and my folks weren't too far behind.

We'd been born and raised in Chicago, and it was pretty much all we knew. When our fathers were wiped off the face of the earth—freeing our mothers—we made a vow to get this fucking money to make sure we maintained the lifestyle we'd grown up with. I didn't have mob money and what our fathers left behind only stretched so far. All the boys in the family bossed up, grew into men, and had been carrying the Cuppacios ever since.

I'd grown up in a big-ass house but not one of this magnitude. Hell, I'd even bought my own three thousand square foot home back in my city but some shit like this would have for sure been ten million. I didn't own this place, I was only renting it, but a brand-new, custom, six thousand square foot home for two million dollars was a steal. When I told my cousins this was the house I was renting, we all looked up the address and saw what it was worth. I almost hated that I had chosen this house to rent because it was going to be hard as fuck letting it go.

"Nigga, you act like we were some broke ass niggas back home. You could have had some shit like this, you were just content with what you had," Shio added.

He was right though. I could have had this big muthafucka back home but I would have had to show proof of funds and finance it because I damn sure didn't have the bread to put up and cash it out. I wasn't a broke ass nigga but I didn't have them Ms like Don's ass. My people lived well, thanks to the men hustling and keeping shit afloat, but we weren't touching paper like the Rinaldis. Not yet anyway.

"Yeah, you right." I wasn't up for going back and forth with Shio. That nigga could be impractical as fuck at times, and today, I wanted to get high, chill with my people, and get my balls sucked by one of these bad bitches out here. I'd been out here a month and had already had two bitches eat my dick. They were pretty and thick by the dozens in the bay, I ain't lying.

"Back to yo' wife though. How she look?"

Vello struck the ball but he didn't hit his target as he intended. Sealing the blunt closed, I removed the lighter from the coffee table and sat back on the brown leather sofa. What made this house even more appealing was the fact that the owner had it fully furnished. It rented at twenty-one thousand dollars a month, and though that shit was kinda steep, it was convenient. TVs were mounted, each bedroom was fully furnished in a different neutral theme, couches were all up and through each open space of the home, and there was plenty of shit here to entertain my people. A lot of thought and work had been put into the home and the floor-to-ceiling curtains that covered the windows, and carpets that looked Persian screamed twenty-two K a month to rent. There was so much fucking art, I wanted to get some of this shit appraised.

For the last few weeks, we had been in this bitch, planning and scoping the city out. I fucked with Don, but I wasn't sending for my people until I knew this shit was what it seemed. The Rinaldi had been in possession of my cousin, Scarlett Princesspa, and though she lived the good life and they took damn good care of her, I still had a few reservations. I wasn't uprooting my folks if shit didn't pan out. This was the same nigga that had killed our fathers. Though he'd done us a favor, I still had to keep my eyes open.

Thinking back to the girl Don had presented me caused a deep chuckle to erupt. Shorty real life tried to pop it on a nigga, but when her brother was in the room, she was a fucking Yes Girl. She wanted to do everything but marry my ass, and instead of her telling her big brother to go fuck himself, she agreed. She didn't ask any fucking questions behind his decision-making. She bowed to do this shit, just like mob women. That shit kind of had me vexed, too, because she reminded me so much of my mama, aunties, and cousins. What the mafia men said was law and questioning or defying meant their life. Lil Mama just didn't know, I was far from that shit. I was taking the nigga up on his offer because my people deserved to live just as well as Scar had been, but I had no plans to make her submit. Seeing her, though, had me wanting to lock her the fuck up and throw away the fucking key.

Everyone's eyes were on me, waiting for me to answer Vello's question, and the shit had me turning my nose up and shit.

"Fuck y'all want to know about my fiancée for? All these hoes in this new city and y'all worried about mine."

"You been here five weeks and already fucked more bitches than I have this year. Stop acting like you serious about being a fucking husband. Clown ass nigga," Nel cracked.

"Shid, lil cuz nem done fucked more bitches than you. If I didn't witness the shit myself, I would have thought my twin played for the other team."

We all laughed at Vello. Nel was far from a gay ass nigga, though. He was just selective about who he fucked. Shio shouldn't be laughing, though, because that mean ass nigga was the same.

"She straight," I lied through my fucking teeth.

Jisei. Pretty ass name for a pretty ass girl. She had an innocent look about herself and being in the room with her for twenty minutes told me all I needed to know about her. The big, burly ass hair that she had piled in a ball at the top of her head showed off her round eyes With her slender face, her eyes were almost too big for her face, but the way they turned down at the corners made her look like a walking fucking bill. Like anything she blew at, a nigga was inclined to purchase. She was sitting the majority of the time so I couldn't really see her body, but the way her thighs filled out the leggings let me know even though she was slim, Lil Baby had some grip about herself. When she did stand for a moment my eyes were too focused on that pussy print to see much of anything else. She was pressure. I may have been a red-ass nigga, but I liked my bitches chocolate. She wasn't dark chocolate but the Hershey's kisses tone of her skin made my fucking mouth water.

I was used to girls who kept their lace laid with an ass so phat that it spilled from their shorts. Bad bitches. Bad bitches who could fuck and suck the life out of a nigga, go count the money, set a nigga up if I asked, and kept a razor under their tongue to cut a bitch who looked at her wrong. Those were the type of women I kept in my bed back in Chicago, but I was set to marry the total fucking opposite. Still, she had me curious.

Vello pointed his pool stick at me. "This fool lying. He already in love. I see it in the colored ass eyes of his. Be real. She decent?"

Licking my bottom lip, I didn't even deny the shit. Was I really in love? Fuck no. I had never been in love a day in my fucking life. In like? A few times. But the last time I liked a bitch, she drove my car into Don and almost had the rest of the Cuppacios wiped from the earth. Did I fuck with the way she looked though? Damn right. Jisei was a fucking ten and she was sitting down, looking like she wanted to disappear. She had that type of beauty that was dangerous. I could tell Don was head over heels behind his sister. It almost killed the nigga to promise her to me. He'd even asked her if she was sure and that shit was shocking to me.

"What the fuck y'all want me to say? She looks good. Damn good. Did y'all expect her not to? She's a fucking Rinaldi."

Just like the Cuppacio women, the Rinaldi women were beautiful. The Cuppacio men snatched up women of all different ethnicities. My mom was black, Metavello and Renello's mama was Jamaican, and Shio's mama was Somali. We all looked like mixed-ass black niggas and the rest of our family was just an array of the rainbow.

"Damn, you really engaged. You picked out a ring yet?"

Vello was really intrigued by this shit. He had never even had a fucking girlfriend so I didn't even know why in the fuck he cared. He ran through just as many bitches as I did. He and his twin were like night and fucking day.

"The fuck? Only woman I'm picking a ring out for is my mama, gang. I gave her the money and told her to go get it herself."

I heated the blunt with the lighter to be sure it was sealed and dry.

"Hold up, you tossed a fucking Mafia princess some money and told her to go and get her own ring?" Nel was no longer into the game on the screen and was all in my face.

"Fuck you want me to do? This ain't no traditional ass union. This shit is a business transaction. He wants to merge the mafias so we merging that shit. I'm not about to be out here, doing all that sucka shit."

"Picking out a ring for your fiancée is sucka shit?" Nel asked again.

"Hell yeah, it is. This shit ain't real. That spoiled hoe can go get her own shit. You did right by leaving her the money. I would have let her brother pay for the shit."

Vello was tight with his money and didn't do any tricking,

but if he'd seen Jisei, I guarantee he would have emptied his pockets too. She was one of those women you gave whatever to just because of the light surrounding her. That was why I got the fuck out of her girly, fruity-smelling ass spot. The longer I stayed in there and looked in her face, the longer I fell for her ass. That was five weeks ago and she still hadn't left a nigga's brain.

"Aye, don't listen to this dumb ass nigga. He only fucks Shrek-looking hoes anyway. He too cheap for a bad bitch, and if he comes across one, she gon' take his ass for everything he got."

Vello tossed up a middle finger before shifting the pole in his arms.

"Aye."

Shio pushed himself from off the wall so I knew he was about to give us one of his preaching ass lessons. His mama was the same damn way; that was where he got the shit from. She'd gone off and married a prominent preacher in Chicago and he'd also had a heavy ass impact on my boy. Shio was far from a saint though. The boy had more bodies than a tanning bed.

"What's to you, Shio?"

"You asked us to come out here with you so that you could make this merge happen and we changed not one word. We left behind people we love and customers that keep our bellies fed. Don't no nigga pump fear in none of our hearts, but let's not act like Don didn't almost wipe us out. He got some shit we need and some shit we don't have. An army, connections, and riches – that's what this shit is for. The nigga got relations with all things Jagoda Bay. Everybody knows this is the place to be for getting rich. Don't let your love for getting your dick sat on by different bitches over-shadow the fuckin' mission. We out here to feed our people.

Our mamas and aunts been through so much that they deserve to live like queens."

"You think I'on know that?" I spat.

"I know what you know, but I want to make sure yo' ass understands the severity of the shit. He didn't pair you with a random Rinaldi bitch. He paired you with a fucking princess. His princess. Outside of his wife, daughter, and mama nem, she is the most important woman in his life. If you think he gon' let you come out here and play with his sister for the sake of merging mobs, you not the leader I *thought* you were."

Chuckling, I swiped my hands across my nose and Nel scooted over. We all loved each other to death, but we'd come to blows plenty of times. Shio and I were the closest, but that nigga could get under my skin like no other at times.

"Let me handle my fiancée and the Cuppacio mob. By all means, if you feel like you could do a better job, the floor is yours, nigga."

Rightfully, Scar was first in line, instead of me. She didn't want the shit, so it was me, and after me, Shio. Our fathers were dead but the mob principles were deeply embedded in us.

"Nah, that's all you. But as yo' second in command, I'm gon' always call you out on yo' shit. All you niggas." Shio held eye contact with the twins.

"Don don't need us, nigga! He tried to take us out. He doing this shit simply because you came through and lent a helping hand when all the fingers pointed at us. He has the numbers and connections. We don't. He trusting you with his sister, so do right, nigga. You ain't got nothing to lose and everything to gain. Don't let some loose ass pussy blindside you."

Shio and I held eye contact. The room grew quiet with only the highlights playing in the background.

"Preach, preachaaaaaaa!"

We all laughed except Shio. He simply shook his head.

"You play too fucking much, Metavello. Had the shit been up to you, we would have for sure been doomed."

"My brother is the oldest by three minutes. So, it would have never been up to me. I'm thugging."

"You niggas do know when this merger happens, in order to join the fucking round table, you gotta get a bitch, right?"

"Hell, I can just do like Pops and go snatch a bitch up. Problem solved," Vello snorted. The sad thing about it was the nigga was probably for real.

"Mama dropped you on the head. But I don't have a problem with that, Ezee. When the time comes, I'll have had a girl suitable to be my wife," Nel vowed.

"I hope not that ghost you was fucking in the city."

"Nigga, I'ma get me a Jagoda Bay hoe, now what? Play fucking pool and get the fuck out of my business."

I smirked at Shio, ignoring the brothers' banter.

"So, what about you? You gon' be ready? You gon' be ready to drop all these bitches and come home at a decent hour, commit yourself to one woman, and turn into a simp ass family man?"

Shio rubbed his hand down his face and then scratched his beard. Where the twins had long ass locs, they made sure to keep styled differently to help tell them apart, Shio had a low, wavy fade and I kept my shit cut low.

"You damn right I'ma be ready. Long as I got me some' soft and intelligent, I'm going all in. Fucking hoes get old as fuck. I can't wait to have a woman I can spoil, fuck, lick, and suck on without worrying if she was just eating the next nigga up. I ain't gotta get ready because I already trained my mind to be ready. I know what the fuck is at stake. I know the type of life I want my people to live. Ain't no amount of pussy in the world worth me not making sure my family got the opportunity to have the world at my feet. So, like I said, tighten the fuck up and realize who you promised to."

Keeping eye contact, I placed the blunt to my lips.

"I got this, you just be ready to count this fucking money."

Shio swiped his tongue across his top teeth.

"Say that shit then."

CHAPTER 3
JISEI "JAE" RINALDI

"Un unh. What the fuck is wrong with you, acting all stank?"

Shifting my eyes from looking off into space, down to my niece, Delicate, who was slobbering while resting on my knee, I sighed and straightened my posture.

"Gimme my baby before you transfer that energy to her and have her hollering and shit all night."

I swatted Dasani's hand away and my eyes immediately caught on to the large diamond glacier on her left hand. Her ring was so obnoxiously big that I was shocked her hand wasn't weighed down. It was a beautiful ring that most girls would love to have. I wasn't that girl though. I mean, hell yeah, I wanted a big ass ring, but I didn't want that shit any time soon. Sucks that I had no opinion on the matter.

Placing a kiss on my niece's chubby jaw, I continued to bounce her on my knee until the nanny walked in and took her. Delicate Mafia Rinaldi was as unique as her name. My niece was a third Italian, a third Filipino, and the rest African American. The special blend of genetics made up the perfect toddler.

Delicate had been beautiful since birth and had me wrapped around her stubby little finger that in true mafia fashion housed a gold ring.

Dasani was living the life. She not only was a beautiful woman, but she was the Don's wife, had an immaculate home, a gorgeous, chinky eyed baby, and the world at her beck and call. Still, with everything, I knew there were days when my brother was out on business that she grew lonely. Her sister was always traveling due to her being one of the country's top wedding planners, and though Daylani now lived here in Jagoda Bay and was home as often as she could be, I knew my girl yearned for company from time to time. She had Azure, but whenever she called, I was sure to come running, even if I was tired.

I'd just gotten off work where I stayed an hour past the end of my shift. I had leftover salmon pasta in the fridge waiting for me, along with an ice-cold bottle of Guila wine, yet here I was, sitting in my sister-in-law's girl cave while she looked me upside the head with her feet tucked underneath her butt.

"If you were tired from work, you didn't have to come over. I just missed seeing your face. Me and your niece did."

When I first met Dasani, she was a bit reserved, but with a stank-ass attitude. I thought her ass was mean, especially seeing how she was always on my brother's head. Just like the rest of us, she'd been through some shit. After doing six years for attempting to murder a man who had beat on her sister, she became institutionalized. I understood her after that. She was a sweetheart once you got to know her, and funny as shit too. She stayed on my brother's ass. Some days, he had a comeback, while others, he just let her say whatever. All in all, though, I loved their love. My brother couldn't get enough of the Filipino and Black beauty with the sick body that was still tight after having a baby. Dasani's body was naturally what bitches paid for. A baby only gave her a fatter ass.

"I—"

"Hey, bitchessssss!"

I snapped my head up and my chocolate doll of a bestie walked in. Coming behind Mocha was my other best babe, Scarlett. Azure, Mocha's her step mother was in tow as well.

"Aye, you might be married and shit but don't play with me. You not that fucking grown," Azure snapped.

Mocha rolled her eyes, making sure her step mama didn't see it before giving me a hug. Azure wasn't that much older than us, so we all hung out, but there was only so much that she let Mocha say before she was on her about respect. Once I showed them all my love, everyone settled around Dasani's get-ready room that doubled as a closet and a salon. The space was a dream. The pink and gold crown moldings made up the ceilings while a crystal chandelier hung in the middle. I was smitten with the French provincial style. There were also stations set up for the hairstylists and makeup artists, along with the pink pedicure chairs lining the walls. This room was every girl's dream and we all took advantage of it anytime Dasani had us over. It was so girly and I was truly obsessed with it.

"The chef is cooking and the butler will alert us once it's done—"

"Ladies."

Another server brought a tray full of drinks that had smoke coming from them, followed by a server carrying two more trays that were filled with crab cakes and char-grilled oysters. That was another reason I loved coming to the Rinaldi estate. It was like living in a Disney princess movie over here. There were even days I never had to see a salon if my sister-in-law's glam squad was here. Some days, I truly felt like I was dreaming. Well, up until the damn dreams turned into a nightmare.

"You just got off work, Jae?"

Taking a bite of crab cake, I nodded at Scarlett. Just like the rest of the mob wives in the room, her life had been upgraded and she wore her husband's money well. All four ladies were runway-ready with not a hair out of place. Everyone had a different rock on their finger that told a different story and showed off that their husbands had spared no expense. It made me run my thumb over my ring finger, and all of a sudden, it felt bare as hell.

"I did. Are my babies here?"

I was the only woman who didn't have children out of the crew. I loved me some babies and couldn't wait to be a mother one day. I had a special relationship with each child. They were all adorable and precious. Even my baby, Princess, who everyone swore was bad. I had been in her life since she was born, so she held a special place in my heart. All the children did. I wanted a baby more than I wanted a damn man. I'd been alone so long, it was going to feel good having my own little human. One day.

"Yes, they in the basement with their daddies. Don just called the other two nannies in. They have company, something about an emergency round table," Azure divulged and my heart palpitated in my chest.

"I'm so proud of you, freeen. You got the corner office in the city, showing them corporate folk a little black girl can make it. I'm so glad you followed your dreams."

I smiled weakly at Mocha. We'd met freshman year of college and I was instantly drawn to her fashion. She always looked like an IG model and smelled expensive, even from across the classroom. When we were partnered in a study group, we hit it off. I'd always admired my friend. I was the social butterfly on campus, involved in every club, gunning to pledge the moment I completed my first year. Mocha was that bitch who kept to herself, drove a Benz, and clearly had it all. I didn't even find out she had a son until four months after our friendship formed. LJ was my first baby. When she told me his daddy didn't know he existed, I was shocked and intrigued. We were inseparable, and by year two, we were damn near hard to tell apart, even though we looked nothing alike.

My sophomore year in college, I'd secured an apartment in the hood and that was when I met my second bestie. I'd been living in my aunt's duplex before she died until the landlord was forced to sell the place. My new apartment wasn't new at all. In fact, it was shitty as hell and was next door to Scarlett and her mama. My girl was the total opposite of Mocha. Where Mocha was the IT girl from birth and I was the friendly one who talked a lot, Scarlett was meek, shy, and closed off. Then she became pregnant and that was when I knew her then crack head mom had done something.

I was busy with work, school, and the many things I was involved in on campus but I did my best to help my friend. My auntie used to say, *You think you have it worse until you meet your neighbor,* and she wasn't lying. I was just happy that my girl had found a man who loved her and Princess and it just so happened that he was part of the Rinaldi Mafia, like Mocha's man. Both my girls were living the life. I was surrounded by mob wives and just knew that wouldn't be my story, no matter how great it was. Funny how life shifted.

"Yes, I am so proud."

"We all are."

"Right. It's refreshing to see one of us not being tied down by a mobster."

"Hell, she don't got to be tied down. She is the mobster.

Her ass is the sister of the Don. She in this shit just as deep as we are," Dasani pointed out.

Before I could stop myself, I rubbed my temple and placed my drink down. I felt a hand on my knee and looked up into Mocha's porcelain-like face.

"What's wrong, best? You never this quiet. Is it work?"

Work was a lot at times but I loved my job. I was the youngest in position in my firm and that shit made me feel good.

"She been acting stank since she got here. Who the fuck we got to beat up? I haven't gotten dirty in a minute." Dasani took a sip from her drink.

"Right. You know I'm down to tussle."

"It's nothing."

"Girl, please. You would have been all around this damn room, twerking and throwing shots back. Matter of fact, you been off for a while. Every time I call you, it sounds like you lost your best friends and Scarlett and I are still here. Even when them sorority hoes get to hating on you, we still here."

Karen and Heidy were my pledge sisters who both took jobs in different states. Mocha swore they didn't call me as much because they hated on my new lifestyle. Karen was cool as fuck still—we talked over social media—but I hadn't heard much from Heidy.

"Moke," Azure warned.

"Mama, okay. I'm just saying. They was cool when she was living in the projects and shit, but soon as she became a seven-figure chick, they all of a sudden don't call."

"They are busy, Mocha."

"Girl, please, we are too. We got whole husbands and kids and shit we always be on ya line. Anyway, what's up? And don't lie."

Swallowing hard, I replayed my brother's impromptu visit

in my head. It happened more than five weeks ago but it felt like it was yesterday. Every day I woke up, I prayed that when my phone rang, it wasn't my brother springing a wedding date on me.

Looking up to the ceiling, I batted my mink extensions. I wasn't going to cry. I hadn't cried since I got the news and wasn't going to do so now.

"Jisei, are you okay? For real. Tell us what is going on. Are we not spending enough time with you? I can come over more often."

Leave it up to Scarlett to always feel like she was the problem. My friend was so sweet. I loved her so much.

"I wish it was that simple."

Taking another deep breath, I reached for my glass and tossed it back. The drink tasted like pineapple, kiwi, and the white Hennessey burned going down a bit. I immediately felt its effects.

"Don came to my house with... a... request," I choked out.

"My Don? I mean, your brother Don?"

I faced Dasani and nodded.

"Okay, and what the fuck he request? Spit the shit out, Jisei, because I'm getting mad. Your brother be on dumb ass shit sometimes and forget all of us are not built for this shit. So, what's up?"

All the women were on the edge of their seats, afraid of what my brother had requested, but tried their hardest not to show it. The mob life was, in fact, crazy. I hadn't done anything in the organization unless you counted when we whupped Teasha and her sisters' asses a few months ago. That was a funny ass day. Dasani was shocked as hell that Mocha and I could hold our own. Faces were pretty but our hands were lethal.

"He said I had to marry a man. That it was my duty."

Mocha choked on her drink, Scarlett's eyes ballooned, Azure crossed her legs and shook her head while Dasani bounced her leg.

No one was bold enough to speak on it though. He played a lot, but what Don said was law. It was the way of the Rinaldi Mafia.

"Okay? That nigga ain't the Pied Piper. Reject the fucking request. No fucking telling who in the fuck he tryna get you to marry. You worked too fucking hard just to become a nigga's trophy. I mean, we love our lives but that's not what the fuck you wanted for yourself. We wanted this shit. You have a whole career. You don't want one of Demise's unhinged ass made men. Tell his ass no!"

Azure took a sip of her drink while Scarlett sighed. Dasani could speak ill of the Don because that was her husband, but the other women knew to tread lightly. Yes, their men were intricate to the organization but there was an order of protocols.

"Wow, friend. Just wow. I wasn't expecting that shit at all today."

"Ummm ummph," Azure added behind her daughter.

"Do you know who he is? Your... fiancé? What's he like, Jae?" Scarlett asked.

Biting down on my bottom lip, I grabbed another drink that was no longer smoking and took that one to the head too. If I didn't slow down, the driver was going to be taking me home and I was going to have to take a nap in my office at work tomorrow.

"Friend? Do you even know this nigga? Which one? I'm trying to think. Is it Corleon? Pasa? Ohh, Jode is cute—'

"It's Ezio," I spat.

The room grew eerily quiet and my girls were as still as mannequins.

"Ezio who, Jisei?" Dasani placed her drink down and had her hands crossed in her lap. She spoke calmly but her demeanor was everything but that.

"Oh, God," Scarlett whispered.

"Cuppacio. Scarlett's cousin."

"That crazy-ass nigga from Chicago? Oh no, friend, he looks like he beats bitches." Mocha wasn't making things any better.

"So, you told him no, right?" Dasani clarified.

I shook my head.

"No, we all have a role to play. My brother wants me to marry him, so I'm marrying him."

Dasani smiled, then hopped up from her seat.

"Aw, hell." Azure picked up another drink.

I stood and tried to catch her before she ran out of the room, but it was too late. I found myself following her through the halls, her silk kimono that did nothing to conceal her frame flowing behind her. Dasani considered herself dressed down in a fitted, peach-colored bodysuit and Hermes slides on her feet. Nothing she wore was dressed down though. She eluded black wealth no matter how hard she tried not to.

"Dasani, please. I don't want to cause any problems. Sis. It's okay!"

"No the fuck it's not. I'm on this nigga's ass. He done lost his other mind."

Dasani's short ass was fast. Between trying to catch my breath, swallow the fear, and praying this shit wouldn't go left, I didn't catch up to her till she was trudging down the stairs to where the men hung out anytime they were here. I never came down here because I wasn't a made man but the queen of the castle didn't give one damn.

By the time Dasani's feet hit the last step, I was in the room with her, and the other ladies were also on the side of me. The nannies must've come and retrieved the children because the atmosphere before us screamed no kids allowed. There were more than ten men down here, all dressed in street clothing, so you would never know they were deadly mobsters. It almost looked like a speakeasy taking place with its brick and wooded interior. Someone was behind the bar, making drinks, a dice game was being held in one corner, pool was played in the other, and a group stood and watched the game while the rest all rotated blunts. It was a fine, rich man's haven, and out of the twenty-something men down there, my eyes were locked on one. *Him.*

"Demise!"

"Wassup, baby? What's wrong?"

"Please, Dasani," I whispered, but she wasn't hearing that.

"Nigga, are you fucking crazy?"

Just like that, the room grew quiet. I knew I had to do something, so before I could stop myself, I made my way in front of Ezio, whose eyes were so low that he almost looked like he was sleeping. Throwing caution to the wind, I grabbed his wrist and pulled him behind me. His hand grazed my bottom, making me freeze up a bit, but I kept pulling him along until we were in front of the ladies.

"Forgive me, brother, for intruding, but your wife here just thought it was crazy that you hadn't introduced my husband-to-be to them."

Dasani looked at me as if I'd grown three heads.

"Is that right? That's what it is, Sani baby?"

Demise bit down on his bottom lip, eyes on his wife while she and I exchanged glances. She was pissed and was ready to fuck my brother all the way up. I didn't want them beefing on my account, especially for something I had agreed to.

I pleaded with my eyes and Dasani squinted hers.

"We gon' talk about this shit later." She pointed at my brother.

"It's yo' world, baby."

"And, nigga, who the fuck is you?"

"That's my cousin, Ezio—"

"Scarlett, that nigga knows how to talk for himself. Let him handle that," Matteo spoke in the distance.

"Shid, I'm her fiancé."

"Where the fuck the ring at, then?"

I looked back at Ezio and his eyes were zeroed in on my ass in the tan slacks I was wearing.

"Shid, you know a jeweler? I really just moved here and shit. Wassup, Princesspa?" He tossed at Scarlett.

"Hi, cousin. Hey, Metavello, Renello, and Shio."

The other men Ezio were standing by all spoke to their blood.

"As a matter of fact, I do. DON! Give this nigga the jeweler, now."

Dasani looked Ezio up and down as Don pulled his phone out and tapped on the screen.

"I did it, baby. That nigga ain't got no excuse now." Everyone in the room snickered. Well, all the men did. The women were still on edge.

Dasani continued to study Ezio through scolding eyes.

"Let him know that Ezio Cuppacio not sparing no expense, either, the fuck. Come on, y'all, 'fore I act a fool up in this bitch. Fucking arranged marriages and shit like this the 1830s."

Dasani shot my brother one last look before going back up the stairs, women in tow, leaving the mix of their expensive perfumes lingering.

I dropped Ezio's hand with a sigh of relief and the guys' meeting went back in full swing. Just as I walked off, strong arms swooped around me and his face snuggled in my neck.

"I'ma have fun with yo' lil thick ass."

Clearing my throat, I wiggled out of his embrace and faced him. My brother was watching us like a hawk, so I smiled at him, even though this shit wasn't a laughing matter.

When he looked off, I placed my attention back on Ezio.

"You wish you had the chance to have fun with me. You can't even commit to lunch."

"Oh, you tight about that? We can go right now."

Rolling my eyes, I pushed out of his space and stomped up the steps, leaving this walking-ass broken heart standing there. I needed another drink or three. This was about to be a long rest of my life.

CHAPTER 4
JISEI JAE RINALDI

J isei Harper. It was the name on the glass plate that sat on my desk, and before the maintenance guy finally found the time to come and change the name on my office door, it was there too. Jisei Harper. Born and raised in the lower middle-class neighborhood of Jagoda Bay. I knew when I met Scarlett, I was living in the courts as her next-door neighbor, but before then, my aunt rented a two-bedroom home ten minutes away from the projects.

My entire life, I'd been Jisei Harper – Polene's niece, and Jessica and Brian's daughter. I had no memories of my mother and the man who I grew up thinking was my father was as good as dead too. Sometimes when I daydreamed, I saw glimpses of my mother here and there, but they were always so blurry. I didn't know whether they were dreams or simply moments in time. When my mother died, the man I assumed was my father went off grid, leaving Auntie Polene to take guardianship over me. We lived well. Up until she got sick, we had everything we needed and were happy. There were no trips to Disney, or hell, no trips at all because on the salary of a cook down at the Spaghetti Warehouse that was now long gone, Polene didn't have much to spare. By the time my auntie paid the bills, bought groceries, and paid for our public transportation for the month, there wasn't much left. Still, I was a happy child.

Polene Harper was a hard-working woman who was more spiritual than holy. She had a saying for everything in life, and for so long, those words used to come in one ear and go out the other. One thing that did stick with me that my aunt voiced was the importance of education. Polene hadn't even graduated high school, so a cook was the best job she could get. It was what she was good at. No matter how much Aunt Polene had to work, she dragged her behind in all of my Parent Teacher meetings and was active in all of my schools. There were nights she would work a twelve-hour shift but drag me to the library so that she could help me complete my projects. Aunt Polene didn't have more than an eighth-grade education but her mind was as sharp as a tact. Like Auntie Polene, her mother died of Lupus, leaving her to fend for her siblings. The youngest sibling was my mother, Jessica. They had a fourteen-year age gap so Aunt Polene raised my mama up like a daughter. My uncles grew up and moved states, leaving their sisters to figure out the way of the world.

My aunt and mother moved together, and with both of them working, they went half on the two-bedroom home that I had lived in up until I was seventeen. I didn't grieve my mother because I didn't know her to miss her, but Aunt Polene? I cried forty days and forty damn nights. Just like my grandmother had left my aunt and mom before they were legal, Aunt Polene had done the same. My aunt had prepared me though. She'd been diagnosed with stage three Lupus for five years before it progressed. Auntie took out a small policy and made sure she had me set up to go to college the moment I graduated. Even when she was on her deathbed, the sayings didn't stop coming.

"As a woman, one of your best weapons is being able to financially support yourself."

"Auntie, I can just get a rich man and sit home and watch the babies," I kidded.

Auntie scoffed and licked her chapped lips. She was lying in her bed with the covers pulled up to her frail neck. Her skin was wrinkly and she had lost eighty pounds in the last six months. She didn't look like the headstrong woman I was used to but the remarks hadn't stopped.

"If you let a man have that much power over you, you're a damn fool. Look at how your father jumped ship! That domestic life is for some women, but it's not for a Harper. Even when you get a rich man, take your ass to work. You'll be glad you did in the long run."

"Okay, Auntie. My best weapon is my finances."

"I said ONE of your best weapons. A tactical woman has many."

"Ms. Rinaldi... Ms. Rinaldi... Hey—"

Snapping out of the walk down memory lane, I gave Gerald, the maintenance man, my attention. He was a middle-aged black man who had the aura of an uncle that reminded me so much of what I missed growing up. Gerald was such a cool man. I loved to have elevator chats with him.

Gerald shot me a look of concern but I cleared my throat and sat up in my chair.

"I'm sorry. What was that, Mr. Gerald?"

He held up the scraper and smiled. "You're all taken care of. I changed your name on the outside of the door and your new desk plate should arrive within a week. I'm sorry it's taken so long. We are still training the newcomers, and until they know what the heck they are doing, I'm managing everything."

Standing from my desk, I walked around the front of it and leaned against the dark oak wood.

"Mr. Gerald, now you know even when they are trained, you still won't let them do much. I keep telling you to slow it down."

Mr. Gerald's wife came and visited one day and told me about how he had high blood pressure. I promised her I would keep an eye out for her husband's workload. They were a beautiful couple, and at least three times a week, she made her way to the office and had lunch with her man.

Grand and Woods Corporation was in an eighteen-story building in the middle of downtown. So, with over twenty-two hundred employees, we had an entire cafeteria that was set up like a food court, offering almost any food you'd like. Most times, I bought lunch and dinner to take home when I didn't feel like cooking or going to my brother's house.

"Yeah, well, working for the company for thirty years, I've grown some bad habits."

Mr. Gerald turned on his heels and stopped before he got through the door.

"I'm going on time, Mr. Gerald. I just have to look over this report." I knew he was about to scold me about taking lunch as he always did.

"All right now. Don't let these folks work you too hard."

I wanted to say I could say the same about Mr. Gerald but I let him be. I really did have work to get to, and the longer it took me, the longer I would be in this building. As much as I loved my job, I didn't like taking work home. My house was my safe haven. When my brother came in, bearing that god-awful news, I had to make myself a new sage stick and opened every window to let the damn bad energy out. My brother wasn't the bad energy—that damn man he'd paired me with was. No matter how hard I tried, I couldn't get that eerie ass smile of his out of my head.

Closing the door, I admired the view behind my desk as I

went to take my seat. A year ago, I'd applied for Grand and Woods on a whim. I knew all about the firm because my professor had sworn by it, but I knew it was way out of reach. I didn't have the experience and had only just received my bachelor's degree in business administration. I hadn't even toured the building because it was so tall and fancy, I knew it would take at least ten years for my ass to qualify.

After a night of taking shots, I opened my laptop, submitted my resume, being sure to use the last name Harper, and was shocked when they called me a month later. I'd just found out I was a Rinaldi and my brother let me know he was having my name changed. Since I still had my original license and paperwork, I worked under Harper. I knew how much influence Rinaldi had, good and bad, and didn't want that to follow me to work. They would have either blackballed my ass or hired me because of who I was. I hadn't been a Rinaldi long enough to use its perks and privileges, in my opinion. Plus, I'd worked so hard for my degree, I wanted my success to be my own.

Grand and Wood was so many things. We provided support, strategies, representation, and legal advisory to all types of businesses. With nearly twenty locations around the world, working here had been a dream. Almost every few floors featured a different type of person as far as careers went. At the top floor, were the hotshot lawyers, and then it trickled down from there. I was on the sixteenth floor and that was still mind-blowing. Being at Grand and Wood for two months as an entry-level office specialist, I must've made an impression because I'd been promoted to lead business administrator. As the LBA, my role was to ensure the success of some of our top clients by monitoring its business development and marketing efforts. I also guided my department as they made decisions. My days were mostly spent gathering feedback from clients and working with our intelligence teams to implement both process and configuration changes to support the needs of constituents across the firm.

So, I had major responsibilities. My job was a lot of work, but I wouldn't change it for anything. I loved getting up at six in the morning, dressing up, and coming to my big girl corporate job. They paid me well, treated me with respect, and I knew my auntie would be proud. It wasn't often kids out of college landed their dream job so soon. The odds were in my favor and I didn't even have to use the Mob to get here. This was my little slice of heaven. My little accomplishment. Every day I walked into my office, a sense of pride took over me. I loved being here. I loved the fast-paced environment, but as of late, I was ready to leave and go home so I could sulk in my misery.

"Knock. Knock."

I pulled my head from my computer to see who was coming into my office. My team had been emailing me all day, getting on every nerve I had. There were only three hours until my shift ended so I hoped they had it from here.

"Come—"

The guest made their way in before I could grant permission.

"Jisei Rinaldi? That's... new."

A person I hadn't seen since graduation walked into my office. With his dark, bright eyes locked in on me, my brow rose but a smile set on my face. Dressed in a suit that I was sure was more than my next paycheck, the last man to make me cum stood in front of my desk. When he placed his hands in his pockets, I immediately locked in on the tool that I used to crave, being that it was only a few inches away from my face.

"You in Jagoda Bay? That's new."

The smile covering his handsome, chocolate profile was

nostalgic in a way. It made me feel warm, fuzzy, and his stark white teeth had me feeling horny.

Anakin Dreas was what one would call my college fuck buddy. Back in our JBU days, I knew I didn't want to be fucking randoms, especially with me being popular. So, I chose Nak – the engineering major who came from money but seemed to do everything in his power to piss his people off.

Anakin came from a long line of engineers. Literally, all the men in his family, dating back generations, were in the profession. Though we agreed to keep it about sex, Anakin wanted nothing more than for me to be his woman. Another tradition of his family was that all the men married their college sweethearts. Anakin tried to get me to take it to the next level, no matter how many times I told his ass I was cool with the sex.

When we graduated and he took his ass back to Memphis, where his family's company was, I was pissed, but I had no one to blame but myself. The man proposed to me but I told his ass hell nawl. What the fuck did I look like marrying a sneaky link, just so that he could fall in line with tradition? The shit was weird as fuck to me. The dick was good, but not marry his ass good. Now, look at me, engaged against my will. I almost wish I'd taken him up on his offer. At least I knew what the dick was hitting for.

"What are you doing here, Anakin Dreas?"

Crossing my legs to calm my thudding pussy, I leaned back in my chair and silently praised his genetic build-up. Tall, dark, handsome, beard, and a body that should be worshiped was Anakin.

"So, that's what I am now? Anakin Dreas?"

Tilting my head, I planted my elbows on my desk and leaned forward.

"Yeah. That's your name, right?"

"It is, but I can remember a few names you used to call me."

Anakin used to fuck me like it was going out of style. He had this weird thing where he didn't eat pussy until he was married, but the dick sure did make up for it. I didn't give a damn about the head. You couldn't miss what you'd never had, anyway.

"What are you doing in my office, Anakin?"

"You look good. This shit suits you well. I'm proud of you."

Anakin snaked his head around the space that I'd made my own. I was a girly girl, so all things pink and glittery made up my personality. My office, with its breathtaking views, dark oak desk, and matching built-in bookcase that took up the entire far side of the wall didn't need much, but the pink mini fridge, all the girly trinkets I had spaced on the bookshelf, along with my urban fiction reads that should have never made it through the office doors and the pink décor I had flowing throughout the space made my home away from home feel like home. Anakin always made jokes about my pink obsession anytime he was called over to my place back when I was living in the projects, so I was surprised he'd complimented my workspace.

"Thank you. But answer the question, nigga."

"Ahh, I see you found her office! Jisei, this is Anakin Dreas. He is here to get a tour of our state-of-the-art office. Jisei is the best at what she does and will be your business administrator. I'll let you two chat. Come find me before you leave."

Grady, my boss – a blonde trust fund baby - left before I could get a word in. His grandfather founded the company but he was a cool dude.

"So, your company has hired Grand and Wood?"

Anakin took a step forward.

"No, I had them hire you. You think just because I was in Memphis, a nigga hadn't kept an eye on the love of his life?"

Rolling my eyes to the ceiling, I tried holding back the smile that had never really left my face.

"The best fuck of your life? Yeah. Love though? I think that's a bit of a stretch."

Anakin stuck his hands in the pockets of his navy pants and slowly made his way around my desk. I hadn't wanted to take things further with Anakin because I simply wasn't there yet in life and still wasn't. He was a good fuck, a great listening ear, a handsome face, and sometimes a great study buddy. We didn't take the same classes, but anytime we had upcoming tests, we would study together and quiz each other before ending the night swapping bodily fluids.

I scooted my chair a few inches away from him as he sat his firm body on the oak. My hands began to moisten, so I ran them down the front of my slacks. This was the same man I told to get the fuck out of my face when he thought I was going to run off in the sunset of little ass Memphis to be with him. Now that he was in my presence, no longer in the sweats and Jordans he liked to wear around campus, here I was, acting like I'd never been in his presence, let alone came on his dick.

Rubbing his hand down his bearded face, he held eye contact.

"You know like hell you the love of my life. We supposed to be married and shit by now. But I get it. You want to be on your miss independent wave and it damn sure worked out for you."

We engaged in a stare-off that lasted longer than it should and almost had me jumping his bones, so I cleared my throat and picked up a pen that I'd been doodling with.

"I appreciate you. We are glad to have you and your company on board, Mr. Dreas. Now, if you'll excuse me, I have some work to do."

I didn't have any damn work to do, I just needed him to get the hell out of my office. I'd detoxed myself from this man and wasn't trying to get another hit. I was a fucking Rinaldi, who was promised to a Cuppacio. I couldn't drag Anakin into my bullshit. I had a role to play in the mob, so my days of frolicking around were long over. We were no longer horny ass kids in college. We were grown with careers and separate lives in different cities. It would never work anyway, because again, there wasn't shit for me in Memphis.

"You so full of shit, Jae. But I'ma let you get back to work. I'm in town again next weekend, so at least let me take you out to dinner. No funny shit. I just want to catch up and maybe we can go over what I'm expecting of you for my family's company. I also have some buddies that may need your services, too, so bring your portfolio with you so I can take it back home with me."

"Okay, cool. Shoot me a text and I'll meet you there."

Anakin looked me up and down before licking his lips. He then lifted my chin with his finger and even his hand smelled like his cologne.

"You look good as fuck, Jae. I look forward to seeing you next week. Enjoy the rest of your day, beautiful."

It was like I'd been holding my breath until he slipped out of my office and damn near passed out when I let it go. Tossing my head back, I rubbed my temples. I didn't know what type of games God was playing with me but I really didn't have time for this shit here. I knew I was absolutely ending our date on Anakin's dick. I hadn't fucked since him, and these days, a dick-induced orgasm was what the fuck I needed.

CHAPTER 5
EZIO "EZEE" CUPPACIO

Removing the pill from the prescription bottle with the label that had been scratched out, I took it to the head and rinsed it down with a dirty Sprite. Weed was my drug of choice, but the runner-up was Percocet followed by codeine. I wasn't a junky ass nigga but sometimes weed wasn't enough. I'd been pulled in a million directions since before I could remember. My mind was so gone sometimes, that I couldn't eat, concentrate, hustle or fuck. I needed some strong shit, and since I would never put shit up my nose, this was the strongest of the few forms of drugs I partook in.

With the pill settled on my stomach, I took another sip of the dirty Sprite before placing it on the coffee table. Stretching one leg out in front of me, I studied the tattoos that covered my calf. I had to find an artist out here in Jagoda Bay so that I wouldn't get the urge to fly home. I'd been going to the same tattoo artist since I was sixteen. Essex was only three years older than me at the time but he was a beast on the ink. I'd been getting marked up for a decade but I didn't have a bad one. All of my shit was legit.

Running my tongue across my teeth, my eyes lowered, my mouth watered, my body relaxed, and my jaw slacked. I was in my fucking zone. Just as long as I'd been turning my skin into a subway wall, was the same amount of time I'd been getting high. Growing up the way I did, you needed some shit to zone the fuck out. The private schools, the cooks, the nannies, the mansions, the parties – all that shit sounded good but we were really fucking prisoners.

When Don came to a nigga on some Kumbaya shit, I just knew my folks were going to look at me sideways. This was the man who single-handedly took down our entire organization. Not only that, he killed our fucking fathers, leaving us as fatherless children. I knew what the fuck was up back then but it didn't mean the rest of the children did. Take Princesspa, for instance.

Scarlett thought her father was a god. She'd gone her whole life thinking that her mama had just torn her from the family after he was lowered to the ground. The truth was, Tamala did what the fuck a whole lot of the mothers should have done. She got the fuck out of Chicago.

"Man, y'all cheating! That's why I don't like when y'all come over. Go back to your own small, stank ass house!"

I stood, controller in one hand while I pointed the other finger at Vello and Nel. Nel was the second player in the game but Vello was cheering him on, telling him all the moves to make. That twin shit got on my nerves. They acted like they couldn't do shit without each other.

"How you gon' talk about our house? We got maids just like you! Our shit stay clean! Your bed not even made!"

Vello pointed to the full-sized bed occupying my room that Shio was lying back on with the headphones to his CD player covering his ears. He was staring up at the ceiling, ignoring our bickering, listening to that damn Tupac CD. His boring ass never wanted to play the game. I was glad, too, because he always won. He barely even tried and was the winner each time.

"Y'all house do be fucking stanky! Yo' mama be cooking them raw fish! Got the whole house smelling like pussy—"

"Ezio!"

The booming voice coming from behind me made all the hairs on the back of my neck stand. Dropping the remotes to my Nintendo 64, Vello, Nel, and I stood to our feet in a frenzy and faced my father. Niccoli Cuppacio stood at the doorway with a presence as frightening as the disdain displayed on his face. He remained stoic, scanning all of our faces while I peered from the corner of my eye to make sure Shio was on his feet. If one of us was out of line, we would all be punished. For the most part, we stayed on our shit, but ego would get the best of us even at eight, nine, and ten years old. Thankfully, Shio pulled the headphones from his ear with them resting on his shoulders and a blank expression on the man who brought me into this world.

"Yes, Niccoli?"

Our fathers didn't give us clearance to call them dad. The girls were allowed to but us boys were training to be ruthless mobsters from the moment we were pushed out of the womb. The girls were spoiled with endless hugs, air tosses, ice cream dates, and whatever else their pretty little heads desired. Us boys, though, we had to basically get down or lay the fuck down. Luckily, Shio, Vello, Nel, and I knew how to play our roles so it had been a while since either of us had to face punishment.

"That's enough of that game shit. You have training... now."

Niccoli pulled at his suit jacket and moved aside to let us make our exit. My father was a big, burly man. Wasn't shit stocky or built about him. He ate whatever the fuck he wanted, whenever he wanted to. At two hundred and eighty pounds and six feet tall, his weight stretched out for the most part but his fists were just as stubby as his belly.

With our heads up, we all walked past my father, Shio leaving his CD player on the TV stand my game was nestled on. Every other day, there was a series of training we had to go through. Rather it was running in the pouring rain or scorching sun, counting money until our fingers bled, smoking cigars till our barely ripe lungs could take it, or learning how to tell a lie with a straight face, there was always something new. Our fathers and uncles got together and came up with these strenuous tasks that didn't make any sense to me at my young age. As the oldest of the boys, I tried leading by example by not asking questions and just doing as my father asked. Even if I knew it was flat-out wrong.

Our feet didn't stop moving until we got to the backyard and even then, we had to walk beyond the gate where the playground was secured. I rarely spent time on it anymore but that was cool; I liked playing my game anyway. Chicago was living up to its name because the winds were harsh but there was no rain in sight and the air wasn't too cold either. After about three miles of walking, we made it to the center field, which was nothing more than an open grassy land lined by trees and a lake that was west of the grounds. If we walked east, that would take us to Shio's house. North would take us to Scarlett's house, and West would go to the twins' house. Though it sounded close, by feet, it took about thirty minutes to get to each of their homes from my house, which was south of the field.

My uncles, including Shio and the twins' dad, stood a few feet away from us, all dressed as if they'd just left a round table with expressions matching Niccoli's. We stood silent, waiting for instruction because though we didn't see anything but them, we knew something was coming and more than likely it would be something we didn't like.

"Boys. Today we will have a lesson in aim."

Niccoli made his way in front of us with his hands behind his back, belly leading the way as he paced the bright green grass. As

Consigliere he was the one that called the shots when it came to most things regarding the mob since Don was busy majority of the time.

"In our field, there will be plenty of times when you will have to use your weapon. Sometimes you'll have to use it twice a day, other times just every day. So, I need you all to be able to shoot once and make it count."

I was confused because usually when we shot, we were taken to the range on our Don's compound. Out here in the middle of nowhere, there wasn't anything to shoot unless he was sending us to hunt deer and rabbits. We'd had to do that many times and once, Shio was bitten by a snake and nearly died during our training. The twins and I had to carry him five miles to the nearest Cuppacio house and even then, he was barely hanging on to life. We hadn't had to hunt since then so I looked over at Shio to see how he was feeling. I could see sweat lines on his forehead, but his expression remained neutral. I placed my hand on his shoulder and he slowly turned his head to me.

"Hey, I got you. All right?"

Shio's lip trembled but he held back his emotion and nodded in response. I could hear his father scoff but I ignored him. He didn't scare me. None of these men did. Not even my own father. What had me falling in line was my mother. The punishments hurt but it seemed the more I trained up, the more my father went easy on my mom. She would smile and always put on her best face, but I knew better. I'd spent many nights listening to her cry Bloody Mary. I was sick of that shit, so I was doing whatever I had to do to ensure the safety of the lady I loved more than anything in the world.

"Ezio! Since you have him, as you put it, you first... Bring them up!" Niccoli boomed, with his glare still on me. I matched his stare but made sure I didn't add the mug that I was trying hard to keep contained.

Minutes later, all four of our mothers came out, escorted by my father's brother, who had yet to take another wife, so he didn't have children. His last wife died in a house fire but there was no fire because his house was still the same with not a smoke-stained wall in sight.

I could hear one of the twins suck in a wind of air seeing their mother. I gave them hell about that stank shit she was always cooking but I always ate that shit too. Especially the oxtail. All four women were beautifully dressed in expensive threads that I knew they cared nothing about and though we were on semi-soggy grounds, they kept a steady stride in their heels, forcibly pulling them out of the ground with each step.

Staring into my mother's hazel eyes, I did a visual scan over her petite frame to check for anything being out of place. Enri was beautiful even though it was clear that she was afraid. I could tell by the rise and fall of her chest under the lilac dress she was wearing. The fabric of her A-lined dress blew with the wind in the same direction as her long, thick, dark hair. Finding no physical signs of abuse, I still kept my eyes on her. She was the apple of my eye and the only reason I hadn't tried to run away from the cruel life God saw fit to place me in.

My mother puckered her lips twice, which was a way that she was telling me she loved me. About five times a day, she would walk up to me and place a kiss on my forehead and one on my nose. I looked forward to those kisses. They kept me going when my limbs were aching, my soul was crushed and my heart aching.

"Today's training will include our wives."

My uncle snatched my mother to his chest, causing me to take a step up but Shio pulled me back. I couldn't stand Narciso. He was a fucking snake that was always instigating some shit. When he pulled a black vest over my mom's head, trapping her long hair that always smelled minty, he secured the vest and shoved her back in place. She almost fell due to the four-inch Chanel pumps on her feet but held her balance.

"Ezio, step the fuck up, boy."

This time, I didn't hide the mug. I sported it on my face without fear as I walked up.

"Okay. That's close enough."

The man whose nut sack I sprouted from pulled a gun from his forty-four-inch waist and removed the safety.

"Aim. That's the lesson. You will shoot your mother, aiming where you have been taught is the less damaging with a vest on. If you refuse to do so—"

Narciso placed his gun at my mother's temple, causing my vision to blur. Bile tried making its way up my throat, but I swallowed it down. With wet and shaky palms, a thudding head, and a galloping heart, I searched my mother's eyes wishing she could tell me it was a joke. All she had to do was say the word and we could run. Even if they gunned us before we got a few inches away from everyone, at least we would go out together. Death had to be better than this fucking life.

"If you refuse to do so, your uncle is going to blow her brains out while you chop up and dispose of the body."

Gun now in hand, the fat tear welding in my mother's eyes had me blinking back my own. I couldn't do it. I couldn't shoot my mother. At this distance, the bullet would pierce through the vest and judging by the way my father treated her, he would let her bleed out. If I killed my mother, I was turning the gun on myself and going out with her but not before I brought my father too.

Taking a deep breath, I lifted the gun and did one of the most unethical things I'd ever done in my fucking life. I shot my mother.

"Aye. Aye bruh. Aye! Get yo' ass up!"

Shaking my head, I snapped out of the past where I'd ventured and tried focusing on the person in front of me.

"Aye, you slobbering and shit."

Swiping a palm across my mouth, I leaned forward and picked up the bottle of Sprite.

"Aye, you need to slow the fuck down on that shit. I thought you let them pills and shit go?"

Taking a swig, I finished off the bottle, keeping it in my hand. Shio was occupying my space and well on his way to getting put the fuck out if he'd come over to fuck up my high.

"How the fuck you gon' tell me to stop the Percocet's when you on them shits too?"

All the Cuppacios popped pills, smoked weed, and drank lean heavily. None of us were on the white girl so it was cool. With the fucked-up childhood we'd had to endure, I couldn't blame any of us.

"Yeah, but I don't pop them shits like Skittles and shit. Nigga, you in here like a fucking zombie. You didn't even hear me come in. What if I had upped the pistol on you?"

Waving my hand dismissively, a deep burp erupted from my belly as Shio stood, judging me, looking just like his fucking first lady ass mama. Today was one of the rare days he was wearing shorts, and unlike me, he didn't have tattoos on his legs. The deep purple discoloration on his calf could easily be mistaken for a birthmark but I knew better. It was that fucking snake bite that almost took my cousin out of here. Sadly, we'd all had days where we almost lost our lives in training. Those gut-wrenching days still gave me headaches.

Sitting next to me, he bunched his thick, untamed brows together and pulled his phone from his pocket. Shio, much like the rest of us, didn't really fuck with social media, so the nigga was more than likely reading some shit on his phone or texting. I didn't give a fuck what his ass did long as it didn't bring me off my level. Anytime I popped a perc, the little white pill had me not giving a fuck about my circumstances. I venture back in the past from time to time, but the shit didn't really affect me as it did when I was sober. If it was up to me, I wouldn't spend a day sober for the rest of my days.

Sober was too aware. Sober kept me in my head. Sober was pain.

"Just make sure you keep getting them from me. We don't know shit about these niggas out here. They selling fake pills and killing niggas and shit. When we leave this bitch, it won't be from no fucking synthetic pill. It won't be from no fucking Fentanyl."

I slowly nodded my head in response. The pills mixed with the lean had me moving in slow motion. That was why I popped them shits when I was in the comfort of my own home. As the leader, I had to be on point at all times. But in my home, I was laid the fuck back with my feet kicked up. I was able to relax, knowing a nigga couldn't get at me in my space. I didn't have my army with me but the three niggas who had followed me here had my back and front. My youngins were holding shit down back in Chicago and my mama was more than good. I couldn't wait to send for my lady but that wouldn't be for at least another couple of months. In the meantime, I would just keep her pockets laced.

"I would ask you about your fiancée, but you too fucking throwed off right now."

Grunting was my only response as I reached up to rub my head, only to hit air about four times before landing its intended target. My fiancée. It had been eight weeks since I first saw her and about two weeks since she grabbed me at her brother's house. The more I told myself that I was only doing this shit to get put in position, the more her sexy ass graced my thoughts. Jisei was too fucking pretty. That slim, thick figure, brown skin, and plump lips. Them bitches almost looked too big for her oval-shaped face and she slick had a big ass fore-head, but she was still fine as a muthafucka. She was sick as fuck behind having to marry my ass too. Her brother had come and shut her fucking hot girl summer down handing her over to a nigga like me. But I kept telling myself that I wasn't going to come into her world and disrupt shit. I just had to make sure my dick understood.

I didn't have to look over at Shio to see his judgment.

"I ain't worried about that fucking girl. I'm tryna enjoy my high."

That was partially true, I was trying to enjoy my high but I very much was thinking about that girl. Even when the next bitch had my dick down their throat, it was Jisei's pretty ass face I imagined on her knees. But I wasn't trying to go there with her.

"Don't let these pills be yo' downfall, Ezee. You popping them bitches by the twos. We been here two months and you haven't even tried to sit down with Jisei. What the fuck are we doing out here? We just waiting till y'all get a wedding announcement? What the fuck will our roles be?"

Shio was asking too many fucking questions and all that shit was blurring together. Lately, he'd been constantly throwing up me getting high like I still wasn't making shit happen. We were in a new city, yes, but in the two months that we'd been here, the money hadn't stopped. We were still getting paid. We weren't rich, by any means, but all of our accounts were sitting in the six-figure range. I was over him bringing up these fucking pills. That nigga had no room because, on the right day, he was coming just like me. He was the one who got the pills for us.

As bad as I hated to admit it, Shio was right about copping from just anybody. These low-level ass dealers were forever feeding a nigga straight bullshit with the fake pills and shit. Back then, murder led the deaths at home; nowadays, it was from popping pills. We paid top dollars for our shit so I wasn't worried, and if the nigga Shio copped from ever sold us some bullshit that ended our lives, I had some family that would stop at nothing until I was avenged. They would come like the Don and end entire lineages and shit.

"Ask me all that shit again when I'm sober. I got a meeting with Don coming up but I'll hit you with the details later."

I didn't like to talk much when I was high. I just liked to sit in my zone.

"Aye,"

Turning my head, I gazed at Shio. He usually wasn't up for many words but tonight, he just so happened to be quite the fucking chatterbox.

"You a... fucking... pirate now, Jo?"

Shio pulled his head from his phone and curled the corner of his top lip upward.

"I'm about to get me some food. You want some?"

My stomach grumbled in response.

"Yeah... where you going?"

I hadn't much explored Jagoda Bay because I'd been at the crib, making calls and keeping shit back home in line. Trying to run shit from another city when you could only say so much over the phone proved to be harder than I thought but now, shit was good. I couldn't wait to bring my mama and them up here but when I did that, I would hopefully be a homeowner and have enough bread to comfortably be able to put her in her own shit.

What I had done though was eat some good ass food in the city. Uber Eats was a nigga's best friend. I was fiending for a six-piece lemon pepper with mild sauce and though they didn't do it like back home, the food here was cool. I hadn't met a person who had Nel and Vello's mom on the Jamaica cuisine but we'd gone to this spot two days ago that was decent.

"I'on know yet."

Shio stood, and after the second attempt, I met his level in height.

"Where the fuck you going?"

I looked around the basement and staggered, almost falling back down on the couch.

"I'm riding with you. Come on, Shio. I ain't driving and I'm with my right-hand man. I'm hungry... as a bitch though."

Instead of arguing with me, Shio shook his head and led the way. It took me longer than necessary to get up the flight of steps that led to the main level so Shio, frustrated with my antics, kept moving.

By the time I made it out of the black French iron doors, it wasn't until my feet hit the gravel that I noticed I was only in socks. Luckily, the smart lock on the door hadn't secured itself in place because I couldn't think of the lock code. Walking back inside, I stuck my feet into the gym shoes that were in the main entry. I hadn't remembered leaving them there but was glad they were. I couldn't walk up the stairs to the main bedroom if I wanted to.

Instead of unlacing the gym shoes, I twisted my way into each one, and when they were secured, I went right back outside. The night was still. I must've lost track of time because I could have sworn when I poured up, it was broad daylight. Scanning my neighborhood where these mutha-fuckas didn't have blinds and left their curtains open to their tall ass windows, I concluded that all these bourgeois mutha-fuckas were in bed. The thick-ass realtor that helped me secure the rental had let me know that my community housed an array of elite from ball players to producers. I didn't fuck with too many outside of my people so that shit wasn't of impor-tance for me. But at least if I decided to buy in this area, it would be worth the investment. Wasn't just anybody moving over here so the property value skyrocketed.

"You wearing them?

Shio knew damn well I wasn't going back in that house so he was being sarcastic as fuck. The shoes were a bit tight but it was probably because I had these thick ass socks on. Turning the dial on the stereo was my response and Lil Durk hummed through the speakers of my cousin's Ram truck. I don't know why his ass drove this big ass white man pickup trucks over his other cars and I'd almost busted my ass climbing in but this was the only whip he'd brought from Chicago. Bitch had pipes and everything like it was a fucking Lamborghini.

"Trust issues... so confused... it's me and you... fuck the rules... I want to suck yo' toes baby take off yo' shooooes."

I pounded my chest as I increased the radio to the highest it could go as I sang along to Durk's "India Pt. II". That nigga knew he was sprung as fuck off India's lil red fine ass but he was hard. It was embarrassing the amount of times I played India I and II. Smiling at the thought of all the bitches I'd come across in Jagoda Bay asking me if I knew Durk. Hell nawl I didn't know that nigga. When folks found out you were from Chicago, they always thought we knew Durk, Polo G, Herbo, and Von. Shit was comical as fuck.

"You show over there singing the shit out of that love song for a nigga that ain't never been in love before. Boy probably ain't never even ate pussy but talking about sucking some toes."

Shio called me out like a muthafucka but that shit didn't stop me from starting the song over. Grabbing the front of my jeans, I swayed in my seat.

"Oh, oh, oh, oh, oh, oh, oo, oo, oo, oo, ooo, ooo. Ouuu, you know she got it."

"That muthafucka is hard though," Shio added as he bobbed his head.

I bounced my shoulders and continued to rap along.

Rapping and singing and shit was never my ministry so I knew I sounded like a hoarse-ass bird but this shit was hitting. Durk had a nigga feeling all the love he had for India like I'd fucked or something. He put his whole damn foot in this bitch.

"Aite, Smurkio. We here. You want to keep doing the two step in yo' seat or are you coming in?"

Opening the door, the dewy night air brushed my skin. I was chilling around the house before Shio pulled up, doing me, so I was only in jeans and a V-neck. Long as I wasn't looking like no dirty ass nigga, I was good.

Making sure my Glock was secured at my waist, Shio hopped out, leaving the truck running and since Durk was on repeat, the bass rattled the outside of the white truck. We always left our shit running. We might find ourselves in a jam at any given time and a car not cranking wasn't going to stop us from hopping on the e-way to get the fuck on.

The parking lot was full, so Shio was illegally parked on the curb, damn near at the door. The sign above the brick-and-mortar read *The Bottom Spot Bar and Grill*. Looking the bulky-ass security guard square in the eye, I sauntered right past his ass. I even walked around the metal detectors because I knew I was going to set that bitch off if I walked through it. The bar was completely full, so Shio and I stood back, waiting for a spot to open. If we didn't get a vacancy in two minutes, I was going to push a muthafucka down.

"Hey, fellas. Welcome to The Bottom Spot Sports Bar and Grill. Have you been here before?"

A pretty, chocolate, petite girl with big ass hair and even bigger titties appeared, handing Shio and me both menus.

"Hey, Brooke, we haven't been here before, so what do you recommend? I got a taste for some wings and shit. I really want everything in this bitch, on folk nem."

Brook tore her eyes away from me and smiled bright as hell

at Shio. That nigga was mean to us but was soft on these hoes every time. The thing was, he still didn't have a bitch or a steady. He was just a cool-ass nigga and I blamed that shit on his mama with her sing-song voice having ass. If Brooke smiled any harder her face was going to crack, and all this nigga had done was read off her name tag.

"Well... our wings are a favorite. We have whole wings here, but the SPOT is the house flavor. It's spicy with a bit of sweetness to it. I don't know how wings are where you're from but here in Jagoda Bay, our wings are unmatched."

Shio's smooth criminal-looking ass licked his black-ass lips. "How you know we ain't from here, shorty?"

"Well, first off, shorty, we say shawty. And your accent's heavy as fuck. Y'all sound like Durk."

"Well, we ain't that nigga." I gritted.

"No, y'all definitely ain't. I can put you an order in and give you my number too. I get off at eleven."

I had yet to fuck something out here but I did get my dick sucked every other day. I had about nine bitches I'd had the pleasure of stretching their throats and they were all pretty in their own way. I couldn't touch a bitch if she was average. Despite what the fuck my cousin had been talking about, I wasn't just running through bitches. I usually gave them a trial of throat sessions, and if they passed that shit, they could sample the dick. Not one of the nine, no matter how bad, had me wanting to stick my dick in them.

When Don had my flavor of the week killed in Chicago, she'd just graduated from dick-sucking probation. I was excited to fuck on that pussy too. Her people had been sad as fuck behind her death. I wasn't a social media ass nigga, but every now and again, I scrolled on my old page and just so happened to see her people's post. They found her body out west somewhere and I knew it was a closed casket.

These Jagoda Bay bitches not only looked good, but they all had a hustle or job about themselves and were down to fuck upon first meeting. I was going to love it here. Hell, I was already loving it here two months in.

"How 'bout this? You get us a seat and I'll bless your pockets. That way, you can go get a massage and pedicure or some shit tomorrow when you get off."

Brooke's jaws damn near reached her forehead. Her cheeks had to be hurting. I'd never seen a muthafucka that happy to get told *fuck off* a day in my life.

"I got you. Those two ladies on the end were just leaving. I'll spray the seats down and you can take them."

"Just clear the bar top; you ain't got to spray the seats, love."

Brooke's lil short ass melted to the floor but turned and did a damn shimmy before walking off. Her ass was fat as fuck in the lil black leather shorts she was wearing. If Shio didn't want her, I just might take her down. Percs had a nigga fucking all night when aroused, but since I had no plans of adding a tenth to my rolodex, I tried to steer my mind away from pussy.

Our seats were cleared, so we copped a spot. Looking around, my vision was a bit blurred, but the shit looked nice. I would have to come back when I wasn't rolling and check out the ambiance and food because, right now, a fucking seahorse would look good to a nigga.

We both placed orders for wings but I skipped the house kind because I didn't need that shit fucking my stomach up. The downside to Percs; them shits had me runny as fuck the next day. Those sweet and spicy ass wings were going to have me folded up on the toilet like an omelet. Shio passed on a drink but I wasn't that nigga, so I ordered a triple shot of Hennessey.

Brooke, who was also one of the three bartenders, passed me my shot and I took that bitch to the head. Shio didn't say shit because that wasn't the type of nigga he was. We called each other out all day behind closed doors, but in public, we wasn't on that type of time. All that embarrassing a nigga was for goofies. We dealt with our problems within the confines of our territory and this crowded ass bar damn sure wasn't our territory.

Brooke set a basket of fries in front of each of us, letting us know she wanted us to put something on our stomachs since the food would be at least another half hour. Shio didn't even thank her. I guess he had switched off the nice guy shit, but then again, he was busy surveying the bar. I was shocked this low-key ass nigga had picked a crowded spot to come grab food at. But he was strapped just like I was and if a nigga came at us sideways, it was nothing for a nigga to sober up, and quick.

Popping a fry in my mouth, I was impressed that they were seasoned and crispy and shit. Brooke knew something. She just didn't know she was a French fry away from getting this dick down her throat. Real shit, I'd down the whole basket in three point five seconds. Shio slid his in front of me, focus still on his surroundings and I happily took his down too. The DJ was playing Future and had the spot jumping, I didn't know if this shit was a bar or a club, but the owner was getting his money for real.

My seat was the further right so I was able to rest my back on the brick wall and that shit was real brick too. I rubbed my back across the wall. I'd been itching since earlier, a side effect of the codeine. I needed to invest in a back scratcher like a muthafucka but until then, the wall was doing its job. From where I was sitting, I had a clear shot of the door so every time it swung open, my orbs traveled to it. It was a Thursday night but that didn't stop this bitch from damn near being wall to wall.

"Brooke may as well box that shit to go. This bitch getting too packed."

We weren't familiar with the city but no matter where you were, too many black folks, music, and liquor in one spot meant bullshit. If the security let us in without hassle, there was no telling how many other niggas he'd let hoe him.

The door opened again causing my lips to curl. All that talk about me not wanting to fuck nothing tonight went out the window as I scanned over the slim-thick frame of the lil brown beauty who was bouncing her way through the door. Seeing a nigga on her trail instantly had my smile going upside fucking down. There were two seats next to Shio, so that's where she set her sights on. Just as she was about to take a seat, old boy tried grabbing at her. That was the wrong move on his behalf because I was up on my feet, gun in hand, pointing it at his dome.

"Aye, you gon' have to move the fuck around unless you like black bags."

The nigga held his hands up and ran back out the door. I could hear Brooke gasp but I didn't give a fuck. She needed to go see about our fucking food instead of dick watching. Putting my attention back on Shorty, ignoring her buck eyes, I looped my finger in her belt ring and pulled her back to my seat. I staggered a bit and Shio had to grab my arm so that I didn't hit the ground with her in tow but when I was seated, I pulled her in between my legs.

"Why did you just do that? In a bar full of people at that!"

Her cheeks were flushed a warm red that reminded me of real cherries, not the shits they put on milkshakes. Leaning back on the wall, I made sure she stayed standing in between my legs.

"I'on give a fuck about that nigga. He better be glad I let him escape with his hands, let alone his life. What's up with you though?"

Just like the first day I'd met her ass, she was wearing a scowl that didn't do shit but make her look even more attractive. The low-rise jeans on her curvy frame exposed her waist, which featured a dangerous ass dip in the back. She had two diamonds embedded at the curve of her back and that shit was sexy as fuck. The light blue corset type of top made her small breasts look good. Her hair was pulled in a bun at the top of her head, making her oval-shaped head look bigger than what it was, but at the same time, enhancing her innocent ass features. Whatever the fuck scent she was wearing was going to be stuck in a nigga's clothes but I wasn't mad at the shit; she smelled good as fuck.

"Ezio, please let me go. I've had a long day and I just want to get a drink and some food."

Brooke had made me a Long Island but I hadn't touched the shit yet because she was doing too fucking much and had officially worked her way off the throat list. So, I picked the drink up and handed it to Jisei. My fiancée was pretty as fuck. I didn't know if it was because I was zooted but she just looks fucking breathtaking. Staring at her had my chest all tight and shit to the point that I had to rub it to relieve some tension.

I didn't know whether or not she was wearing makeup but her face was glowing and her brows were perfectly arched. Placing her nose to the rim of the glass, she took a sniff before putting the cocktail straw in her mouth.

"Damn, you don't trust a nigga?"

Rolling her eyes but keeping her ass in between my legs, Jisei continued to sip her concoction. I could smell the liquor when I passed it to her so I knew that bitch was strong but she was taking it to the head like it was a Sprite.

LISA AUSTIN

"Um, no, I don't. I need another one of those though."

Jisei placed the glass down that now only consisted of ice and a lemon wedge before turning her body slightly to face Shio.

"Hi, excuse me for being rude. I saw you at the house the other day. I'm Jisei. You're Shio, right?"

She held her light pink manicured hands out that matched her toes and I almost broke her fucking wrist, snatching it away.

"You don't need to speak to that nigga. He knows who the fuck you is. I see... we... gon' have to establish some ground rules... You too fucking friendly."

Jisei snaked her head back to me so fast that I thought that bitch was about to do a 360.

"Nigga, stop putting your hands on me. Plus, I was just being polite with yo' rude ass. I'm not about to walk up on people and not fucking speak, especially when we will be in the same spaces for the foreseeable future."

"Fuck all that shit you talking... Don't shake no nigga hand in my face."

"You don't run shit Ezio. I barely know your fucking name. I know my brother set up this sick-ass arrangement but don't ever try to play me out in public or private. I came here to get myself a ten-piece Spot whole wings fried hard with double ranch, three drinks, and a watermelon and mint hookah and that's what the fuck I intend to do. If I wanted to be monitored and secured, I could have taken my ass to the Rinaldi estates."

Damn. That fucking mouth. I was a professional at knowing if a bitch's top was decent, just based on how they popped off at the mouth. Jisei, with those big ass, glossy lips that had a peachy tint on them could fasho suck a mean dick. Grabbing her hand, I pressed it on my mans and she snatched away before rolling her eyes again.

72

Gripping my arm around her waist, I pulled her into my chest and licked my lips. I wanted to suck her plump, glossed mouth into mine but I didn't know what the fuck Shorty had done with her lips. I'd seen bitches eat dick and then go slobber down their baby daddies with the next nigga's seeds on their tongue.

"You so fucking pretty. I love loving on yo' pretty ass."

Like my mother still did my grown ass till this day, I kissed her on the forehead and then the nose. I did the shit so fast that she didn't get a chance to resist.

Shio chuckled from the side of us as Brooke placed his food down in front of him, followed by mine.

"What the fuck kind of drugs are you on?"

"I love you," I blurted, not meaning it at all, but the pills had me like that sometimes.

"Shio, what the fuck going on with him?"

Shio dug into his food and shook his head. He wasn't going to tell her shit but he was getting a kick out of the scene.

"Here is your food. I didn't know you had someone with y'all. She eating?"

"Hell yeah, she eating, and she got a fucking name, too, love."

"Brooke, get my fiancée a ten-piece Spot whole wings, fried hard with double ranch, two more drinks, and a watermelon and mint hookah."

I repeated her order while keeping my eye on her pretty ass. Her face was still balled up at Brooke and she'd now crossed her arms under her breasts. She was too damn pretty to be fighting in this bitch and I was too damn high to assist. So to defuse the situation, I reached into my pocket and pulled out four twenties. I was sure the shit didn't cost more than seventy dollars but Brooke could keep the change.

"My bad, girl, I'm on it."

"Thanks." Jisei smiled sarcastically.

"Now, back to you. Is it crack?"

Shio couldn't help himself as he belted out in laughter.

"Aye, what the fuck you talm 'bout?"

"Is... it crack? Your fucking orange ass eyes all glossy and shit. You pulling out guns in these people's establishment and about to fall on your ass, all the while putting your hands on me. Oh, and you got those dusty-ass shoes on that look like you been dancing in the mud. They look like they hurt too. Now, I ask again, is it crack? Did my brother promise me to a fucking crackhead?"

"I ain't no fucking crackhead, crazy ass girl. Now, come sit down, you making me itch standing up and shit."

I patted my lap, causing her to turn her nose up. Brooke must've had the hookah on speed dial because she appeared with one of two of Jisei's drinks, the hookah, and my wings.

"No, whatever bitches you fucking on got you itching."

"I ain't fucking nobody, mean ass lady."

"I don't give a fuck if you were. I'm good on you. Have her send my food to the back. Someone's waiting for me back there. Shio, enjoy your night, and make sure you get this man home in one piece."

"Aye, on my grannie's grave, you gon' make me shoot this bitch up! Take yo' ass back to the car or sit here with me."

"I will not be taking my ass to the CAH. By the way, it's car, not CAH. And I don't drive a CAH; I drive a big boy Range Rover. And stop telling people I'm your fiancée and my ring finger empty as fuck. Shit embarrassing and it makes you look cheap and or broke. I'm not attracted to either. Again, you enjoy your night."

. . .

GRABBING HER SHIT, Jisei turned and I couldn't help but to reach out and slap her fat ass. That shit jiggled, too, even in her tight-ass jeans. She looked back and shot me a scowl but kept it moving to her people.

"You said you wasn't worried about who again?"

I ignored Shio, keeping my eyes on Jisei.

"Grab yo' shit, high ass nigga. Can't take yo' ass nowhere."

"Fuck you."

CHAPTER 6
JISEI "JAE" RINALDI

"Aye, aye, aye, aye! Get it, get it, get it! Aye, aye, aye, aye!"

LJ was dancing his ass off, and as his number one supporter, I was recording with one hand while my other hand housed a red cup filled with drunk punch. Mocha had dragged me to a birthday party with her. One of the girls we went to school with was throwing her son a birthday party in the Bricks. I was familiar with the Bricks because the duplex I'd been raised in was only a few blocks over. I hadn't been to the hood in over a year, and being out here felt good as hell.

Mocha's friend, who was throwing the party, had gone all out. Even though it was in the hood, she had three bounce houses, four grills going, a big ass Ninja Turtle cake surrounded by all types of custom treats and all the Ninja Turtles were beside LJ, dancing with him along with the birthday boy and a few more kids. Mocha's detail was hanging in the background, but he was here. The drunk punch had me on my level and laughing my ass off at these kids.

"Get it, son son! Get it, son son! Aye! Aye!"

Mocha laughed so hard, and LJ fed into it too. He was in the dirt, cutting a rug in his brand-new Prada shoes that had no chance at all. Even though the party was in the hood, the birthday boy's folks had money because not only was this shit lavish, but he was in Red Bottoms. They were fucking the designer shoes up.

A text message flashed across my screen, and since the DJ had switched songs, I took a sip of my drink, stopped the recording, and checked my text.

773-542-7744: Drop the lo

Drawing my head back, I responded to the unknown number. Not many people had my number, and those who did, were saved in my contacts. I had been talking to Anakin, and shockingly, our first date didn't end in me sitting on his dick. He had proven that he really did want to catch up with me, and at the end of the night, he even took my portfolio. I knew this wasn't him because his number was saved, and I had just gotten off the phone with him before I arrived at the birthday party.

Me: Ummm, who is this?"

While I waited for a reply, I filled my cup again. I had no idea what was in it, but the lady who introduced herself as Auntie let us know it was drunk punch. The shit had been doing its job too. I didn't know a soul out here, but they all complimented me and treated us like family. The whole block was at the party, and some people were sitting on their porches, just watching the scene. I loved my new home, but lord knows I missed coming home to a full party being held in the courts.

Once my cup was filled, I took my place, leaning against the hood of my truck. I slept a little late from being on the phone with Anakin, so I told Mocha I would meet her here. Plus, I had to stop and get the birthday boy a gift. He was going to be happy as hell with the fifty-dollar Chick-fil-A card. I didn't know him but I wasn't coming anywhere empty-handed. All kids loved fast food.

I'd feasted on a red smoked sausage, baked beans, and the best ribs I'd ever had. This was my second and final cup of liquor because I didn't want to have to go into one of these folks' houses and pee, even though Auntie told me I could.

Being out here took my mind off the bullshit I had going on. It had been a few days since I saw my so-called fiancé at the Spot Bar and Grill. He had absolutely lost his mind, pulling on me and threatening random folks. Then, when I saw the dirty ass shoes on his feet, I knew he had to be throwed off in the head. Granted, all the other times I'd seen him, he was on point. Maybe he had just got done doing his yard and decided to come get food, but he should have gotten his shit to go. He looked too dusty, but I still melted when he kissed my nose and forehead. It was quick and unexpected, but it was so intimate. I had to get the hell away from him before I forgot that he was sent here to ruin my damn life. No way a nigga with bent-up ass shoes was supposed to make you wet. No fucking way.

Snapping out of my thoughts, I scanned the yard and saw Mocha talking to her friend and LJ was now in the bounce house. I hated that I didn't bring Princess, but I didn't have time for her crazy ass daddy. The other kids were too small to come. The weather was just right. Knowing there would be dirt and dust, I paired a light pink mini cargo skirt with a black and pink Barbie graphic tee, and black platform Chuck Taylors. On my ankle was a Cuban anklet and I rocked the matching necklace. The bust down Audemar on my wrist topped off my look and had the young niggas out here eyeing me. If I was anyone else, I would have been thought of as an easy lick. Slim bitch driving a Range Rover doused in diamonds with a Prada bag on her arm, but when one of them called me Lil Rinaldi, I knew I didn't have shit to worry about. Plus, the gun in my purse could easily keep me safe and my diamonds secured. My brother told me I better not ever be afraid to rock my diamonds anywhere and that was all he had to say.

773-542-7744: I hope it's pop in yo' cup.

There was only one nigga I had been around who used the word pop. My brother slipped up and said it every now and then but this wasn't him on my line. It was fine ass Ezio. The current pain in my ass.

"You standing out here rocking six figures worth of jewelry, unaware of your surroundings, and got ya head in your phone. You lacking."

My eyes rolled before I could even pull my head out of my phone. The voice that never used the letter R in any of his words made my panties cream on impact and I hadn't even looked at him. Taking a deep breath, I locked my screen, then locked eyes with him. Today, his eyes weren't red, the natural color of them standing out against the whiteness, and when I gazed down at his feet, his Air Force Ones were stark white like his teeth. Thank God, he'd left the other shoes at home.

Taking a sip out of my cup to calm my hot ass down, I tried to play it cool when really, my heart was thudding in my fucking chest.

"I'm good out here. You know how my folks coming. I can't say the same about you."

For Ezio to be an out-of-town ass nigga, he was comfortable as hell in the hood. I knew how deadly it could be when a newcomer came into one's territory. We were invited and I wasn't a nigga. Plus, my brother's name held weight. On top of that, Mocha's detail was out here with us. I was straight.

"Shid, I'm good in any hood, shorty."

Ezio smirked at me and then turned his head to scope out

the area. I knew, despite what he was saying, he was watching his back and I didn't blame him.

Before I could take another sip of my cup, he took it from my hands and took a sip. His eyes stayed on me while he drank, and then he drew his head back and balled his handsome face up.

"What the fuck is this?"

Shrugging, I took my cup back, careful not to spill it because I didn't want to get sticky.

"Drunk punch. Good to me. And keep your mouth off my shit. I don't know where your lips been."

Getting all in my personal space, Ezio pulled his pants up his slim ass waist and leaned over me.

"I'm tryna put them on you, but you don't text back."

Ignoring the faucet in between my legs, I placed the cup to my lips but held it there.

"First off, how did you get my number?"

"Come on now, you know who I am, love."

"Outside of being the nigga I'm 'posed to marry and Scarlett's cousin, I really don't."

"Merch?"

"What?"

"Merch," he reiterated, further confusing me.

"Boy, what are you saying? Merch? Merchandise?"

"Chicago shit. Kinda our way of saying swear to God or to show us you not lying. Catch up, shorty."

"Well, I'm not from Chicago, so I don't know shit about the city outside of Durk, mild wings, Harold's, and that the Obamas from there."

"I got a lot to teach you, then. Gimme some more of that shit."

"Un hunh. With the way you was acting like it was nasty,

you not about to play in my shit. Plus, I don't know where yo' mouth been."

"I don't know where yours been, and on foe nem grave, if you say it's been somewhere, I'ma rock yo' shit out here." His statement sounded serious but the smile on his face told a different tale.

"My mouth hasn't been on shit, *on folk nem grave*," I mocked.

"Mine ain't, either. They tryna be on you though."

I took a swig of my drink and looked around to see who was watching. Mocha was still in deep conversation and the kids were dancing and playing while the mothers had their asses out, scouting for their next baby daddy. Nobody was stutting us but I needed a distraction.

"You hear me, Jisei?"

"Merch," I copied.

I was drunk, pussy soaked, and if this nigga was saying he wanted his mouth on me, I wanted to see how serious his ass was. I had been celibate for over a year, and even though I had no intentions of giving his ass any pussy, especially when he couldn't even take me on a lunch date, I would let him bless me with some dome if that was what he was on.

Ezio licked his lips and stood back. When he grabbed his crotch, I could have fucking melted right there on the concrete. He was too damn fine.

"Bobbyyyy! Get it! Get it—"

It was like a record player had scratched, snatching me from being ready to take this man up on his offer.

"Bobby, show these young girls how to get it!"

My eyes lit up at the man Auntie and nem were egging on. I watched him for a minute and then he looked up at me. We locked eyes for a bit before he turned and kept on dancing like he didn't know who I was. He was clean, sweat pouring from his head, but I could tell he was still down bad. I didn't even feel the tears pooling in my eyes. I didn't feel them until they rolled under my chin and tickled my throat.

"Jisei! You good?"

Ezio was speaking to me but I was still watching Bobby dance. He looked happy. He looked free. He looked much better than the last time I saw him.

"Yea-yeah. I gotta go."

With shaking hands, spilling some of the punch, I fumbled with my purse to get my keys out.

"Aye, let me drive you to the crib. You can't drive like this."

Ezio led me to the passenger side, helping me in as tears drenched my shirt. When he hopped on the driver's side of my truck and pulled away from the party, I set the cup in the cup holder and pulled my seatbelt on. He wasn't wearing his, so the dinging didn't stop. I bent over as far as the seat belt would let me and let a few more tears out.

"Jisei—"

"Please. Just be quiet."

I hated crying in front of people. I was strong, always had been. I'd been holding me down for a long ass time. I always had it together even when I didn't have it together. But seeing Bobby sent a whole new wave of emotions through me.

When I dried my tears, I sat up straight in my seat, eyes puffy from succumbing to my emotions.

"I was raised by my auntie. Polene. She was my mama's big sister and had basically raised her. Jessica, that was my mama's name."

He shifted his attention from me to the road and I saw that he finally put his seat belt on because the ringing would have never stopped.

"My mama died when I was a baby so I never remembered her. But my daddy—"

"Don Rinaldi?"

I scoffed. "God, no. Never met that nigga. Brian Bobby West. That was the man I believed was my father for years. Up until I was in elementary, he shared custody with Auntie Polene. He loved to dance. He would put it on slow jams and dance with me in the living room. He lived with Aunt Polene, too, because my mama had always lived with her sister, who was more like her mother."

Looking at the street lights that lined the road, my phone vibrated in my purse, but I ignored it. I couldn't believe I was telling a stranger this shit, but I blamed it on the alcohol.

"One day, Aunt Polene and my daddy argued. I was about six, maybe seven. Daddy was holding a letter he found in my mama's dresser. I guess that letter revealed who my real father was. After that, Brian left, hit the pipe, and turned into Bobby."

I was so young, but the pain was still great. I had run into Bobby plenty of times on the street and he acted like he didn't remember me. Especially when I lived in the hood. It was nothing to see him at the store. I would still give him money, even when he didn't know my name. Even when I didn't have shit.

"I know what my mama did was wrong, but why did I have to suffer? I don't have a daddy. The real one was killed by my brother, so that's that. I'll be okay, but seeing him just... hurt."

Bobby was something that I deemed as out of sight out of mind. The only thing that made me feel not so bad was knowing that someone was taking care of him. He always looked clean and neat. Most of the crackheads around the city were starving, dirty, and health looked as if it was declining. Not Bobby though. I didn't know his story but I did know someone somewhere loved him enough to not have him down bad.

"Damn, shorty."

I let my head hit the back of the seat and watched Ezio drive. This was my first time being on the passenger side of my truck since I'd gotten it. I didn't know why I felt so comfortable with this man, but again, maybe it was the liquor. My necklace pinching my skin had me removing it and placing it in the glove compartment. I rarely wore my jewelry, and when I did, it never lasted more than a few hours on my neck. These shits were too heavy and always bruised me up.

"It's cool. I don't too much worry about it until I see him, and now that I live in the burbs, I rarely do."

"So he hasn't come back around since you were a jit?"

I thought about the time when I was fifteen and he appeared on our doorstep. Auntie Polene and I dragged him into the house and forced him to get clean. That was one of the darkest moments in my life. I cried every day seeing the rage in him. I was too embarrassed to recant that story, so I shook my head.

"No. Hey, can you take me to my brother's house?"

I didn't want to be alone. I would rather ball up next to my niece. I would rather wake up to her blasiantalian ass knocking me upside the head with a bottle rather than being alone.

"You can come to my crib. I'm renting a spot out in Crystal Cove."

Crystal Cove. That was where the elite laid their heads. I didn't trust myself around Ezio. Plus, I was still mad at the entire situation. I couldn't spend the night with him.

"My brother's house is cool."

Silence lingered. The new car smell my truck still held filled my nostrils. I'd only had it for a few months and it had been detailed six times, one for every month – compliments of my brother.

"What is going on with yo' pops is fucked up. Because no matter what DNA says, that's your daddy. Some people can't really handle what life throws at them so they go to an outlet – drugs. The nigga you seeing is not your father. When he on that dope, he is somebody else. But you blessed to have your brother in ya life. Real shit."

My brother. The only reason I was going along with this shit is because he was all I had. I loved Demise. He just got me. You would have never thought twenty-plus years had come between us. I would do anything for my brother because in reality – he was all I had. Yes, I had my friends, but they weren't blood. My uncles? I had never had a relationship with them niggas and didn't care too. I would do anything Demise asked because being alone in this world was no fun.

We pulled up to my brother's immaculate estate and my chest swelled. I was so proud of him. I know he'd been through some shit, him and his wife, but he made it out just like I had. If he didn't have anybody else outside of his mama and Dasani, he had me. I stamped that.

Ezio pulled around the roundabout and parked behind Dasani's G-Wagon. The fountain was still running even though it was now dark out. This place was magical. I loved being here and with all the land he had, he could build seventy more houses and still have acres.

"I drink and smoke my hookah but drugs? I don't do. I got addicted to Red Bulls in college and when my heart started racing once, I put 'em down. I don't knock a person who does weed, but anything harder than that is a no-go. Drugs ruined my family."

Ezio shifted uncomfortably in his seat. He picked up the red cup I'd been sipping and placed it to his lips but said nothing.

"You can take my truck, just bring it back in the morning."

"You good. My cousin on the way, shorty."

For him to complain about my drink, he couldn't stop taking it down.

"Well, I'ma go."

"Yeah, aite."

He seemed to have an attitude but I didn't give a fuck. I was in my feelings my-damn-self. Grabbing my purse, I opened the door and walked up the stairs to the entry. The butler let me in, and I set my sights straight on my niece's room. Dasani and Demise were on the couch, doing god knows what because Dasani was giggling.

"Oh my God, Jisei."

Dasani tried to stand, but my brother shook his head and pulled her right back down. I wasn't in the mood to explain. I just wanted to smell that baby scent on my niece and go to sleep.

When I entered her bedroom, which should have been on the cover of every magazine, I walked over to her crib and saw that she was playing with her toes. With chinky eyes, a head full of hair, and chubby cheeks, she looked just like my brother and Dasani mixed. Everyone said she was my twin, but I didn't see it.

Her sleepy eyes lit up when she saw me but I held my finger up. Going to one of the dressers in her room, I pulled a pair of pajamas I kept over here out, went into her bathroom, and changed. Once I was comfortable, I grabbed my phone and my whining niece. She had a queen-sized bed in her room that had to be for me because I was the only one who used it. Pulling the pink and gold covers back, I slid into bed with her lying on my chest. I could tell her mama had just given her a bath because she smelled of lilac.

"I love you, teetee."

She blinked her long lashes as if to return the love and then buried her head in my chest. I loved my boo so much. Half of her overflowing closet was compliments of my wallet. This was my baby.

With my eyes closed, I tried to erase the day. Everything had been so good until I saw my daddy—until I saw Bobby. The bed dipped and the spot beside me that was just empty was now filled.

"What the fuck happened? I see Cuppacio outside in your truck."

My niece squirmed in my arms and I let her go to get to her father. I lost the battle with Demise every single time.

Keeping my eyes closed, I responded.

"No. Not him. I saw Bobby."

Demise didn't respond. Only the coos from my niece were heard for at least three minutes.

"Fuck that high ass nigga. You got me now."

Those words did more to me than he knew.

"Yes, I do. I love you, brother."

"I love you, too, Jisei."

We fell asleep. Somewhere in the night, Dasani joined us. I was so grateful for them. I was strong, but the strong got weak too. Thankfully, my brother had the strength of an Ox. As of late, he'd been there to pick me up when I fell.

CHAPTER 7
JISEI "JAE" RINALDI

T he pile of dirty clothes in my laundry basket that was tucked near the floor-length mirror of my bedroom had me continuing to steal glances at it when I should have been checking out my outfit. The day had come for me to meet up with Anakin for our second date and it took everything in me not to cancel. Yes, the first date was amazing and we had been talking almost nonstop since then. But seeing my father had put me deep in my feelings. I threw myself into work, only making time to hang with my girls and chill with my babies. The only thing that had me pulling the pair of Fashion Nova ripped jeans from the cream velvet hanger in my closet and sliding them over my thong-clad ass cheeks was the fact that there was nothing holding me back.

Outside of hanging with my very married girls, all I did was work, clean, and eat. A casual dinner with an old friend was harmless. Hell, even if I decided to end the night on Anakin's dick, that was my business. I hadn't the first time but I was thinking about it this go round. I worked hard and celibacy wasn't planned but since the last time I'd fallen on a dick, there had been plenty of nights that I went to be with ole faithful aka my rose. I'd had to replace her twice in the last year from burning the battery out due to the amount of times I'd used her. Then, there was Ezio. Since the night that he saw me break down almost a week ago, I hadn't heard a peep from him. I didn't know if Bobby popping up was a sign or what, but I was so close to letting that Chicago-ass nigga get the pussy. Him not even reaching out to me to see if I was okay, let me know I had done the right thing by holding off. The next morning when I went home, my truck was where he left it and my jewelry was still in the armrest. I didn't peg him as a thief, but you never knew. Outside of that, he hadn't texted me.

"Yeah, I look too thirsty in this," I frowned at my reflection but was pleased with what I saw. I wasn't opposed to getting dick but I didn't want to look like I was handing the pussy over on a silver platter.

Along with the jeans that were completely ripped down the front, I paired them with the matching halter. The rips on the halter were down the back though. I'd complimented the edgy look with white, multicolored Gucci canvas platforms and my green Gucci bag was on the vanity, waiting for me.

Yesterday, Dasani called me because her glam team had arrived and demanded I come over for a pamper day. I went down the rabbit hole on TikTok and fell in love with the shoulder-length, jet-black, bed hair look. So, I had Lunar do me a sew-in with leave out and he added a rinse on my natural hair. The dark hair brought my eyes out more, which weren't anything special like Ezio's, but I looked good. Doing a light beat on my face, I added Baccarat oil to my exposed skin and completed a nude gloss look on my lips. *Ezio.* Why in the fuck was he even evading my thoughts when I was headed out with a fine-ass, paid-ass, educated brotha?

The outfit was cute and I added a green diamond in my

belly ring to bring the look all together, but it was giving *come fuck me* vibes. I didn't have time to change, though, because the reservations were at 7:00 and it was already 6:30. The restaurant was a twenty-minute drive from my townhouse so I had to get a move on.

Running my hand over the side bang of my hair to make sure there were no flyaways, I then checked my baby hair, which wasn't too dramatic but looked good with the style.

"Fuck it. If I fuck him, I fuck him. I'm grown and it ain't like he hasn't already had the pussy." Because he had, countless times.

Snatching my purse, phone, and the keys to my Range Rover, I turned the light off in my room and made sure my home was secured before hopping in my baby. My brother had done his BIG one when he bought me this truck. I didn't even think that this was some shit I could afford, especially right out of college. My best friend had made me a millionaire overnight with the two million dollars she'd placed in my account and I still hadn't thought to buy a luxurious vehicle. All my girls drove six-figure cars, but before that, I was just happy to have my own set of wheels. Scarlett had passed me down her Kia, which was practically new, and before that, I'd been catching Ubers, the bus, and cabs for years, so having my own car was good enough for me. Riding passenger in my girls' foreigns when we were out on the town replaced the itch for wanting my own expensive vehicle. Now that I had my Range, nobody could tell me shit. I was so grateful.

Pulling out of my driveway, I honked at my neighbor who was a TikTok influencer on her way to having a million followers. Glow was a food blogger and her videos did numbers. She revealed all the gems hidden in Jagoda Bay and was one of the reasons my bank account was screaming at my ass from always eating out.

When I first met her, I thought EatYoGlow was just her social media handle. When I found out Glow was her real damn name, I couldn't believe it.

The black ice plug-ins that were clipped on the air vents evaded my nostrils and created a beautiful blend when mixed with the fumes in my hair and the scents on my brown skin.

My phone vibrated in the silver and black cupholder. Since it was connected to Bluetooth, I pressed the phone button on the steering wheel and turned the volume up since I was riding in silence.

"Hey, bestieeeee! What you doing?"

I heard LJ in the background, rapping something, and I also heard Mocha shifting, more than likely getting away from my godson.

"On the way to meet... somebody."

I talked all that shit about being grown and having nothing holding me back from seeing Anakin, but who the fuck was I kidding? I was engaged, even though my ring finger was bare as hell and my husband-to-be and I didn't really vibe.

"Hunh? Meet who? Scarlett is at the house with Princess, who has a stomach ache, Dasani visiting her sister, and my mama is at the house. So, who in the hell are you about to meet? I know after you drove off with your husbae, leaving me alone at the party, it better not be him. And that fake-ass sorority bitch bet' not be in town! If so, I'ma pull up on that bitch."

Mocha couldn't stand Heidy. I liked Heidy. She was just out here living out her dreams. Friends grew apart but Mocha didn't understand it.

"No, Mocha. I'm not meeting with them. And is my boo Princess okay?"

"Nawl, whore, don't change subjects. Matter of fact, answer the FaceTime."

Chuckling, I stopped at the red light, pulled my phone from the cup holder, and pressed it against the magnet that was stuck against the dash. Jagoda Bay had a hands-free policy and a ticket was the last thing I needed.

Pressing answer, I pulled my top up as I waited for Mocha's face to grace the screen. When her glowing skin that resembled dark chocolate came into view, her round eyes spread and she stuck her head in the camera as if that was going to help her get a better look.

"Oh, bitch. You got that outfit on I gave you? I knew it was going to look good on you, bestie!"

Mocha was forever shopping her pretty little heart out, and half the shit she had no room for. My bestie had way more curves than me, but she was also shorter than me, so we still wore the same size in most things. I gladly accepted the outfit, and since it was a warm night in Jagoda Bay with a light breeze, the look was perfect.

"Thank you, bestie. What else you got over there that you don't need?"

I eyed her with a smile. Mocha joined us yesterday and had the stylist give her a long, wavy bust down. Her face looked as if she'd just done some skincare, so it resembled glass. My friend was so damn gorgeous. She and her husband both looked like two fine black ass sculptures side by side. Just chocolate-ass goodness. I knew their sex smelled like shea butter, money, and Creed. It had to.

"You don't even wear what you got, but OMG, friend, you look good. Should I get dressed and drop LJ to my parents? You know it's whatever with me."

There was something I loved about all of my friends' marriages, and with Mocha and Zo, it was the fact that they really acted more like girlfriend and boyfriend. He didn't expect my friend to cook, clean, or be in the house, barefoot and pregnant. He let her come and go as she pleased because his ass was in the wind his damn self. If you asked me, they had the perfect marriage. I loved Scarlett and Matteo's union, too, but his ass was stingy with my girl. He kept her ass in the house on her damn back. I always told her she was going to be pregnant soon, but with the way he loved and protected her, I couldn't blame her. I would have been the same way. I let me my freaky, in-love ass friend make it.

"Well, I would take you up on your offer but I'm meeting... Anakin."

Mocha drew her head back and placed her hand over her mouth.

"Come again. Say what? I thought he lived in Mississippi?"

"Memphis."

"Shit, same thing if you ask me. But whaaaaaat? How the fuck?"

"Long story short, he hired the company to manage and represent his family's business. He's in town and wants to go eat."

I left out the part that this was our second date and that we had been talking on the phone consistently. My life was already a mess; I didn't need more reasons for my friends to question me.

Mocha's shock turned into a frown before she rolled her eyes.

"What he needs to be doing is eating some pussy. If that shit ain't on the table, then he wouldn't have been getting a date from me. I ain't forgot. What nigga don't eat pussy, friend? His ass got to be gay."

"There's plenty of men that don't eat pussy. Hell, all the ones that I'd been with never ate the kitty, so it is what it is." I shrugged.

"Girl, you fucked two and a half niggas."

93

"Half?"

"Yeah, that Domo nigga and that toddler dick don't count, so half. Matter of fact, we are going to say two and a quarter. But bitch... I keep trying to tell you, you're too fine to not be stuffing your pussy in a nigga's face. If a nigga not eating no pussy, he needs to get the fuck on. I be mad as hell when my period comes on because that means I can't get miss kitty sucked on. Sex just ain't complete without a good licking."

The trees that lined my neighborhood turned into tall buildings as I entered the downtown area. Just like everything in Jagoda Bay, all it took was a few minutes on the expressway and you were downtown. I could do this drive with my eyes closed, that was how well I knew it.

Monday through Friday, I was fighting the morning rush to get to the parking garage of my workplace, but tonight, I was going to indulge in a few lemon drops and catch up with an old friend. I know he said he wanted to get me out so that we could discuss him working with me, but I knew Anakin. We had already discussed that on the first date and my team had been doing a damn good job with his family's company. Anakin was a pussy hound. He invited me out with the expectation of getting in my pants and I planned on letting him.

"Well, friend, the first time I mount a nigga's head, you'll be the first to know."

The traffic was thick, and though I was only about six blocks away from the restaurant, I knew it was going to take me more than ten minutes to arrive. I had minutes to spare, so it was all good.

Looking around at the brake lights of the nightly rush hour, I smiled at all the whips that were out this evening. The people had their cars out. Thinking about how Ezio said cars caused me to smile. What the hell was a cah? Shaking him from my thoughts because he was irrelevant, I focused back on the traffic. Every car you could think of was jammed into the traffic and the bass from all the different speakers made my truck vibrate as I held my foot over the left pedal.

"But for real, you know I'm the friend that got your back, right or wrong, right?"

I nervously laughed as I waited for Mocha to finish her statement.

"This shit wrong as two left shoes, friend. Your brother ain't just anybody. He told you that you had to marry that fine ass, unique eyed, tatted up, look like he'll slap a bitch ass nigga and you out in his city, about to meet up with another man. You big brave. I'm riding with you, but if we die behind this shit, I'ma be so mad at you in heaven."

Clearing my throat, I tightened my fingers around the steering wheel and tried to hide my nervousness. I told Mocha about how Ezio drove me home because I had seen my father, but I left it at that. She didn't know how I had cried in front of him. I didn't want shit to do with Ezio. Was he fine? Yes, but there was something about him that rubbed me the wrong way, no matter how hard my panties creamed.

Don had far too many important things to be doing than to be out and about, catching my ass on a date with Anakin. I didn't have a detail like the rest of the wives, mainly because not too many knew I was Don's sister, and the ones who did, knew it was a death sentence doing anything to me other than speaking. I loved the fact that I was able to move around freely but I did keep my bitch by my side in case a strung-out ass send out decided to jump froggy.

I'd been licensed to carry since I was old enough to own a firearm. I moved around the city back then using public transportation and I was living in the hood at the time so I had to make sure I was safe.

"Moke, this marriage is fake as hell. I don't even have a

ring. This is just to merge of the organizations. That's it, that's all. I can do what the fuck I want."

My brother most definitely told me that if I was fucking with somebody to shut it down, but damn, I needed some time to process this. I didn't have a ring on my finger, so in the eyes of the law, I was single. Ezio, from the looks of it, was all over the damn place. He was a lot and I was glad that he wasn't forcing this shit. I was just letting the chips fall where they may, but I wasn't going to stop living.

"Okaaaay. If that's what you feel, then I'm rocking with you. If you need me to pop up and break that shit up, just call me. In the meantime, I'm about to join LJ's concert and make myself a drink. I love you, friend."

I smiled at my gorgeous boo as she moved through her beautiful custom home to find LJ.

"I love you. So damn much."

"I hope you get your pussy eaten tonight. That way, if you die, you'll at least know what it feels like. Byeeeee."

The screen went black before I could reply, and all I could do was shake my head.

I pulled up at the restaurant right on time and the valet parked. Anakin picked one of my favorite restaurants as of late. Hibiscus was a Japanese-infused restaurant with a five-star feel, but there wasn't a dress code. My mouth watered for some yellowtail.

Pulling my jeans up my back, I switched through the waiting area that was full to the brim and garnered the eyes of a few who were indeed on dates. Keeping my head high, I stalked to the hostess booth, ignoring the kissing of teeth. Some women gave me props and looked, along with their men, and others turned their noses up. I could appreciate a gorgeous woman. Hell, I was surrounded by them. I loved dishing out compliments just as much as I loved to receive them.

"Yes, I have reservations. My... date should be here already."

The hostess led me through the restaurant, which was packed to capacity, and led me to my area. The smells of the oriental foods had my stomach growling. Paired with the yellowtail I was going to get the fried lobster fried rice and pork and shrimp dumplings. I could already taste the dumplings bursting in my mouth, damn near burning the taste buds off my tongue from being so hot.

"Jae. Damn, girl."

Anakin stood and immediately had me feeling like I should have followed my first mind and changed. He wasn't in a suit like he was on our first date, but he was in tan slacks, a dark brown shirt, and loafers. The monochromatic look looked good on his thick frame, but our setup was opposite from each other. I should have asked him what he was wearing when he texted to confirm but we were here now.

With his arms spread wide and a handsome grin that made the corner of his eyes push upward, I stepped into his space and froze up. The hairs on the back of my neck stood up and my auntie's words disrupted my thoughts. *Your intuition is your seventh sense. Your body will always tell you when some shit ain't right, just don't be a damn fool and ignore it.* Instead of dwelling on the eerie feeling, I offered him a hug and took my seat that he pulled out. Anakin was a gentleman, for sure. Anytime we were out in the past, he opened doors and pulled out chairs. Sitting across from him, I placed my purse on top of the wooden table and scooted my chair in.

"You smell as good as you look. The firm paying you like that?"

Cocking my head, I ran my tongue across my bottom lip, careful not to ruin the nude combo that took me way too long to perfect.

"I do well. But I'm wearing a cheap outfit, Anakin."

"Gucci isn't cheap, but okay, okay. I won't pry. We talked enough about work on our last date. You look great though."

I forced a smile, still trying to shake the feeling that was tugging at me. The waitress came over and took our drink orders. She informed me that the yellowtail was out for the evening so I ordered the Asian chili fried wings as an appetizer instead.

"Would you like blue cheese?"

"No, I only eat ranch, and could you fry the wings hard? Also, I'll take a lemon drop too. You can take the menu. I know what I want, but you don't have to take my order until the appetizer comes out."

I folded the menu and handed it to the waitress as she turned to Anakin. He, too, ordered wings and I was glad because I didn't share food. I didn't give a damn who was paying. He also asked for a Japanese beer, which didn't have me too shocked. In college, Anakin was on beer heavy.

Our drinks came out before the wings, which was fine by me because I needed something to take the edge off. With the way I felt, I was going to be running out of this date sooner than intended.

"So, how has life been after college? You still friends with Mocha and Karen?"

Anakin and I spent a lot of time together, so he knew all of my friends.

Taking a sip from my lemon drop, I nodded.

"Mocha is my best bitch for life, so yes. I just got off the phone with her, as a matter of fact. She's married now. Karen took a job out of town but we still talk over social media."

"What about your neighbor? The one with the cute baby."

I smiled. "Scarlett. She's married, too, and locked in just like Mocha. Baby is still cute too."

"I love to hear that. Marriage is the goal. That's what's up. So you're the single one out of the crew."

My throat began to itch, so I took another sip and changed the subject.

"What about you? How has life been? I know we talk every other night but I feel like it's mostly about surface shit. Which is cool by me."

"Great. As you know, I work for my family's company. Memphis is home so you know I love being there, especially after being gone four years. I've been settling into the company good too. Like I told you the other day, got my own..."

I'd tuned Anakin out so long ago. This wasn't the way I expected our second date to go, but outside of him asking the first question, he hadn't asked me shit else. It was about him and what plans he had with the company. We talked every other night and managed to keep work out of it. Our conversations were usually around his workout routines, what I could do to get on the health track, and the trending topics on social media. Now that we were in person, the energy was different. I wasn't much up for talking, anyway, because my mind was still on my unsettled nerves. Then, my thoughts went back to Ezio.

Seeing him the other night did something to me. He looked too damn good. Every time I saw him, he looked good, even the night he had on the beat-up Air Force Ones. That day, he looked like he had just got done gardening by the feet, but the simple white T-shirt and black baller shorts were enough to make me saturate my panties. When I saw him in the projects, he was picture fucking perfect in a ghetto ass way. I hated like hell I had cried in front of him. Hated even more that I had told him about Bobby.

One thing I noticed about Ezio was his gun. Gun, or pole, as his Chicago ass called it. I'd been around my brother but had never seen him use his gun. Seeing a man so close to death turned me on in an embarrassing way. I went home after the bar and damn near fucked my stimulation up from the number of times I used the rose.

Ezio was a mystery, and though I was pissed that I was pushed into an arranged marriage, at least my brother had given me a fine-ass man. I was certain that Demise didn't put looks as a factor when he chose me to be with Ezio Cuppacio but I appreciated the good looks. I usually didn't go for light-skinned men. I loved dark chocolate but Ezio had it all. The looks, the swag, the smart ass mouth, the heavy pockets, and the way he insisted on eating my pussy still had me wondering if I hadn't seen Bobby, would he have backed his promise up.

"That's crazy, right?"

Rapidly blinking my lashes, I focused back on the fine-ass man in front of me.

"What?"

Anakin took another swig from his beer, and at the same time, the waitress brought out our wings. She placed the wings with the blue cheese in front of me, so I did a quick switch with Anakin. We then placed our order for entrees, another lemon drop and beer, and she was on her way.

"I said, my father thinking I am waiting till I turn forty to get the company is crazy, right?"

"Unh hunh, yeah. Could you excuse me, Anakin? I have to use the ladies' room."

Before he could protest, I stood to my feet and shuffled to the ladies' room.

This was a bad damn idea. I wasn't even hungry or horny anymore. The man that I was set to marry was all up and through my head. I didn't have a date or a ring, nor did I know anything outside of his last name, but I was to be his damn wife. Then I had told him my entire backstory without him giving me shit in return. Instead of balling up somewhere and crying, I was lusting over him and masturbating to his good looks. That was wild to me. I had to get my shit together and fast.

After fake-using the bathroom, I took my time walking back to our table when a familiar face in the VIP room caught my eye. Usually, the doors were closed, but a waitress walking out had me looking inside out of pure nosiness. Those hairs stood again, and before I could walk off, I locked eyes with the one person I wasn't expecting to see.

"Twin!"

Clearing my throat, I skeptically slid the door open and stepped in before sliding it back behind me. Sitting at a round table with damn near every dish on the menu piled on the table was indeed my twin, my brother. The fucking Don. *Great.*

My brother eyed my outfit and frowned.

"What you up to?"

Uh, out on a date with the nigga you didn't promise me to with plans on getting my back blown out by him.

My focus shifted from my brother to the other man sitting at the table. Today, his shoes were brand new, just like they had been in the Bricks, and ironically, he was in a denim-on-denim look. His eyes pierced through mine, and from the looks of it, today, he wasn't full of weed. The tattoo on his face glossed under his moisturized skin, along with the *Cuppacio* emblem engraved in his neck and as the toothpick in his mouth shifted, he smiled, revealing a mouth full of diamonds.

Oh, god damn. Just when I thought he couldn't get any finer.

"Just out with a friend from work. What uh... what y'all doin' here?"

On wobbly legs, I took the seat next to my brother, who was dressed down too. He was always in the latest or the flyest suit and today wasn't any different.

"A friend from work, hunh?"

Demise eyed me and Ezio looked like he wanted to take my ass down, so I focused my eyes on the table and saw at least three servings of yellowtail. The same yellowtail that was sold out.

"Yeap. I didn't know you would be out. You should have called me. I would have tagged along, unless this is business?"

Instead of looking at the fine-ass man across from me that I wanted to devour whole, I looked at my brother. Demise was still looking at me like he was ready to call me out, so I rested my chin on his shoulder.

"This is business. But I'm glad you here with a friend. I was just telling your fiancé that the wedding planning starts soon. I'll have a date for y'all within a week. We need this shit to happen sooner than later. I hired a planner who will be contacting you, Jisei. Unless you want to push it off."

"Yes!"

"Nah."

We both replied at the same time. My brother eyed us, causing me to speak up.

"I meant, yea okay, brother. I won't miss the call. Well, I'll let y'all get back to your evening."

Standing, I didn't even give Ezio a second glance.

"Here. Some bread to pay for your shit."

Demise handed me a wad of rubber-banded money that I would never get used to and I took my leave. Now, I had to think of a way to tell Anakin I had to end our date short. I didn't want to be responsible for him being sent back to Memphis in a body bag. My panties needed changing, anyway.

CHAPTER 8

EZIO "EZEE" CUPPACIO

O ne... two... three... four... five... six... One... two... three... four... five... six... One... two... three... four... five... six. Six. A triple-six at that. Doing a double count of the three pill bottles sitting on the island that was built in the middle of my closet, I once again came up with the number six. Eighteen, to be exact, but there were six Perc thirties in each of the three orange prescription bottles. Shio already told me that he wasn't going back to Chicago to get more because he wanted me to fall back off the shits, but I knew with the way I popped these muthafuckas, these three bottles wouldn't make it through the week. If I smoked back-to-back blunts, I could push these out maybe nine days, but that was stretching it. With the way my thoughts had been getting the best of me, I knew I needed these pills more now than ever. I loved potent weed just like any other weed head, but marijuana could never get me as high as a thirty did.

Removing two pills from the middle bottle, I screwed the cap back on and shook the pair in my hand while walking around my closet. I had yet to fill this muthafucka, but with how massive it was, it would take at least two years. I wouldn't be here for two years because my name wasn't on the deed. Still, this bitch was massive.

Walking to the section that I had managed to fill in, I scanned over the tagged threads. I didn't have much planned today, but after being in the hood last week and chopping it up with one of the made men, I wanted to get the fuck out tonight. He gave me the heads up on our upcoming training and I damn sure wasn't ready for that shit. I needed to get my mind right, so a night on the town was the move.

My cousins were doing their own thing so I was solo for the moment, but I'd planned on calling one of their asses to be my wheels for the night before I left the crib. They'd been living with me but you wouldn't know because the niggas were never there. When it was time to meet up with the Rinaldis, though, those niggas were front and center so that was all that fucking mattered.

A blue jean jacket and matching jeans caught my eye. I'd picked it up from the Galleria a few days ago, and since the weather wasn't too hot, that was the move. I wasn't popping these fucking pills, though, until I was good and dressed. When I woke up the next morning and noticed that I'd stuffed my big ass feet in Nel's shoes, I wanted to beat his ass. I was wondering why Shio and Jisei had been clowning a nigga's shoes. You would think the nigga was part slave with the way Nel's ass was always in the yard, picking and raking shit. Granted, the yard did look good, thanks to him, but his ass should have tossed those bitches in the trash when he was finished. Had me outside looking like a fucking goofy.

Brooke was a bird-ass bitch to even still be grinning in my face, knowing I looked like a fiend by the feet. Fuck Shio too. Yeah, he asked me if that was how I was rolling but the nigga could have elaborated a bit more. I was high but not that damn high. My thick ass fiancée was the one to call me out and I almost broke my ankles getting the fuck out of there once her words finally sank in.

Jisei. Every time I saw her ass, she got finer and finer. Jisei was like one of those girls you had secret magazines of stashed as a child because she was on the cover. Her beauty was nostalgic as a muthafucka. There was something about the way those low-riding-ass jeans hugged her hips that had my dick bricked up. Then, she had the nerve to have a waist that didn't exist.

Seeing her the other night in such a vulnerable state had me wanting to say so much, but I refrained. She'd been through some shit just like I had, but with the way I coped with my shit, it would for sure be a problem in her world.

Her pops was a junkie and it still hurt her to see that nigga like that. I wanted to reach out but shit looked like it was getting too deep, so I pulled back. It was for the best.

I still hadn't fucked shit in the last three months that I'd been out here, outside of the head I'd been getting because I hadn't had the time to put a bitch through trials, but if I was going to keep running into my wife-to-be, I was going to have to take something down and soon. Head wasn't enough, especially when her fine ass had come around.

Jisei wasn't going for it. I could see it in her eyes that she was going to make a nigga work for that shit, and although she was pretty, I wasn't up for clocking in for pussy. Wife or not, if she wasn't trying to fuck, I was going to get my shit off elsewhere. After seeing her at the bar and almost catching a charge from damn near blowing a nigga's brains out, and wanting to wrap her in my arms because of her daddy issues, I concluded that if she wasn't fucking me, it was for the best. I would flirt and shit with her, but that was as far as the shit would go. I had to let her ass go, real shit, because I could see her and I going up in fucking flames.

After getting dressed, I gathered saliva in my mouth and placed my fist to my face. For me to pop pills as much as I did, I hated swallowing them. Shit felt like I was fighting for my life every time I tried, but the euphoria from them being in my system was well worth it. Before the pill could greet my taste buds, the doorbell sounded, and at the same time, my phone vibrated on the dresser in my closet.

Clamping my Cuban around my neck and popping the diamond grill in my mouth that cost me a fucking car, I swiped the phone from the marble and squinted at the nigga at my front door. What were the fucking odds that I was thinking about his sister and this nigga popped the fuck up?

"Yo?"

Sliding my thumb across the screen, I shook the pills in my hand again as I waited for this nigga to reply. I was a bit agitated to see his ass because that meant my high was about to be interfered with, and my body was beginning to heat and twitch, meaning it had been too long since my last pill.

"Yo? Nigga, stop fucking playing with me and bring yo' ass on. I hope you ain't got them dusty ass shoes on, either, my nigga. Get fly."

This crazy ass nigga mugged the camera and turned on his heels, going back to the waiting Rolls Royce that was complete with a driver behind my whip.

Spreading my palm, I eyed the two pills and battled on whether or not I would pop at least one to keep me level-headed. Knowing Don was a nosy ass nigga who seemed to know every-fucking-thing, I grabbed the middle bottle, unscrewed the top, and placed them back where they belonged. *This shit may not take too long. I'll be back for y'all.*

Me: Aye, I'm headed out with Don.

Cuppacio boys: (Shio) Where? I'm pullin' up. (Nel) Well, have fun. I'm getting my dick sucked. (Vello) You always getting yo' dick sucked. Where you at, Ezee? I can be there in ten.

I fucked with my cousins that were more like brothers because, not only were they settling in good, they had my back 100 percent.

Walking through the crib, I typed my reply before shutting the lights off. I wasn't trying to have a thousand-dollar ass electric bill. If I did, I was going to happily make them niggas give me my cut.

Me: Nah, I'm good. I'll text if I need y'all.

Making my way out the front door, I turned my nose up at Nel's dusty-ass shoes. I could have sworn I threw those bitches in the trash, but there they were, posted in my entryway once again.

The cool air of Jagoda Bay greeted me as I locked my door. I patted my pockets while I walked to the car to ensure I had my money, pistol, and wallet. Those were three things I didn't like to leave home without. The wads of money I kept couldn't fit in my wallet and I didn't like my cards and I.D and shit just sliding around in my pocket. It was the quickest way for them to get lost and I despised losing shit.

The driver tried to open the door for me but I shook my head. I didn't like the idea of another nigga opening the door for me, and I'd seen enough of that shit growing up. I respected his profession but I could get my own fucking door. Reaching into my pocket, I peeled off a blue face and slid it to the middle-aged gentleman. Once I was in the back seat, across from Don, the nigga hadn't even given me a glance from texting on his phone.

"Y'all got training starting tomorrow. All my men had to go through it, and y'all ain't no fucking exception."

His face was still on his phone as I processed his statement. Meeting up at Don's house for the last few months had me getting cool with a few of the made men, it was mostly to pick their fucking brains and shit. Coolie, a young nigga with two ghetto-ass baby mamas who lived in the projects served me some weed, and when I went to meet up with him in the Bricks, he put me on game. I didn't respect the fact that his baby mamas lived in the Bricks, but he assured me his main hoe lived in a mansion. Whatever floated his damn boat. I appreciated him for telling me about the training though.

Before speaking to Coolie, I knew I'd have to go through training, but the turning in my stomach didn't take too well to it. When Coolie told me, I kind of brushed it off, but hearing it from the source had me uneasy as fuck. Now I wished I'd popped a pill like I planned to just to ease the anxiety. I didn't need to be thinking about the fucking past, especially while I was in the presence of the Don. Around my people was one thing, and even with the Cuppacios, I really only let Shio, Nel, and Vello see me off my square. Being the nigga that so many people needed weighed heavy on me from time to time. So, my guilty pleasures were warranted.

"Say less."

Don pulled his head out of his phone about ten minutes later, but the entire time, I continued to check our surroundings. There was a car in front of us as well as behind, guarding us like this nigga was the fucking president, but I still wanted to be on my toes. Plus, just sitting there was making me think too much and thinking was never good for me when I wasn't high.

"We here."

The door was opened against my will, but I stood without fuss. I didn't know where the fuck we were at, posted in the back of an alley, but I kept my eyes open and a hand on my pistol. I was in a city where I had no fucking real connections outside of my sworn enemy-turned-family, and though I fucked with Don, I didn't know how these niggas rolled in his city.

When Don walked through the back door that blended in with the brick of the building, I followed him and relaxed a bit, seeing that we were at a restaurant. The owner, a fat Asian man, all but kissed Don's hand and then gave us his best waitresses. Once we were led to our private section, only then did I relax a bit.

"Aye, I want every last piece of yellowtail y'all got left in this bitch, and bring me a bottle of your best. We also want a little of everything, surprise us."

Don looked over at me while I scanned the menu.

"As a matter of fact, bring me two bottles of your best and a pitcher of water. This nigga is sweating and shit. Fuck you wear a blue jean jacket for?"

Handing the waitress my menu, I picked up the napkin that held eating utensils, unrolled it, and swiped my forehead. Yeah, I should have definitely popped my pill because I wasn't hot by a long shot. I was really cold to be one hundred.

"So, I know you ain't bring me out to talk about my wardrobe. What's good?"

Don sat back in his seat, holding eye contact.

"My sister. Where the fuck she at?"

"Hunh?"

"If you can hunh, you can hear. Dasani? She in Houston at a fucking lounge with her sister even though she told me she was staying in. She just placed an order for a bottle even though she'd been pre-gaming with Daylani and don't need shit else to drink. She gon' be sloppy fucking drunk when she gets in and I'ma be right the fuck there, waiting on her."

"How the fuck you gon' get to Houston that fast when we a few states over?"

"Money, that's how, nigga. If I wanted to go back in time and travel, I could do that shit. But my point is, you supposed to know where yo' woman is at all times. I handed my sister over to you a good three months ago, so that means for ninety-three days, she's been yours. So, again, where the fuck is she at?"

Running my tongue across the bottom of my lip, I squared my shoulders but didn't answer because I didn't fucking know. I really didn't care to fucking know but I wasn't going tell this nigga that. She was mine in my presence, but when I wasn't around her, I could give six shits what the fuck she did with that pussy. I had one goal and one goal only. As long as she walked down that fucking aisle when the time came, it was all good.

"You don't know. Every nigga in the mob knows where the fuck his bitch is, down to the second. I even know what color panties my fucking wife got on right now. You know why? Because if a muthafucka snatch her up, I can trace her ass down in a millisecond. Family first. That's the first fucking rule of the Mafia and you know that shit, unless them dead ass Cuppacio niggas did shit differently."

I chuckled. This nigga was a muthafucka.

"Ezio, you know why I want this merge to happen?"

"Nah." I really didn't. We were small as hell in comparison to the Rinaldi, or hell, any mafia. We were mafia by blood but we didn't even operate as one. We got our fucking money, took care of our people, and stayed out the fucking way. We didn't have connections to arms, dope, animals, land, property, or none of that shit. We were regular niggas who got it out of the mud, all hustle, no luck. So, I really didn't know what the fuck a nigga who had tried to kill us off wanted with us. But when he presented the opportunity, I damn sure didn't turn it down.

"Growing up, the Cuppacios were ruthless. We had the money but the Cuppacios used to terrorize the Rinaldis. The Cuppacios had the fucking balls. My father didn't give a fuck about shit but pussy. That's it. He spent his time fucking the staff instead of reigning terror over his enemies. I was a hot head ass nigga back then so I got sick of the shit."

Don made a gun gesture with his hands and pointed it around the room, pulling the imaginary trigger.

"So, I laid all them niggas down. Lil ole me did some shit my pops couldn't do. That nigga was hot about the shit too. So, he had me sent to prison. Fuck him, though, because I sent that nigga with the Cuppacios. Since he was so pissed about the shit. Go die with them fat mothafuckas."

"I'on feel no type of way about you offing them niggas. I was gon' do the shit eventually anyway. You did us a favor." I shrugged.

Demise constantly bringing up how he was gangsta enough to kill our people did nothing for me. He just lightened my load. I had been trying to figure out how I could kill them niggas for a long ass time. If anything, Don did our dirty work.

Don sat up in his seat, leaning over the table.

"And that should have been your answer when I asked you why the fuck you think I choose to make this merge happen. You niggas don't have shit I need *but* the way you would have, without a doubt, killed your father, is why I want you on my team. You take care of your people. Even with the little resources you have, you make sure your folks live well, but with this unity, they will live like fucking gods."

The waitress came in, followed by three others, and began placing dishes around the round table. My mouth watered at all the selections. Once the table was too full to see the wood, Don continued.

"This"—he spread his arms out—"This is nothing. When you become Rinaldi Mafia, it's nothing you can't have. It's nothing off-limits. Your mama will have so much fucking money that she will find herself looking for the fountain of youth to prolong her life so she can live through all this fucking wealth. I wake up every fucking day to a new couple million. This is the life that's waiting for you. For your people. All seventy-four of y'all will be escalated to a new level. The life they dreamed of."

Don grabbed up his chopsticks and stabbed raw-looking fish floating in soy sauce.

"But the fact that you don't know that my sister is in the dining area with her college fuck buddy is why I'm questioning the fuck out of if I made the right decision to bring yo' ass on."

I watched as this nigga ate the raw fish like it was a delicacy and started on the next plate. Hearing Jisei was here in the restaurant had me feeling a bit tight. I hadn't even had a conversation with the girl but was once again ready to march out the room and blow whoever that nigga she was with brains out. Like I said, I didn't give a fuck what the fuck she did in her free time, but when I was in the vicinity, shit was different.

Don turned his head toward the door. "Twin!"

There she was. I pulled at my dick without thinking as I scanned her frame. The ripped blue jeans weren't too much; the shit was just right on her body. I hated when niggas didn't like their bitch to wear certain things but I wanted mine naked. I wanted a nigga to see what the fuck they would never have. That was if I had a bitch.

Don said some shit to her, and I could tell her ass was scared as fuck to be caught, but she waltzed her fine ass in and sat next to her brother. Just like the pretty ass spoiled princess she was, she placed her chin on his shoulder, all in the nigga's skin. Don tried to act like he was annoyed, but he low key loved that shit. I saw the adoration he had for his sister and I couldn't even blame him. If I had a sister as pretty as Jisei, couldn't no nigga get next to her. Ain't no way in hell I was marrying her off.

She looked over at me with lashes that were lengthy but not so long that she looked like Big Bird. The new hair on her really gave her that sexy-ass, girl-next-door look. That was my favorite look on her and I wanted to see it on her every fucking time I encountered her.

Shuffling the toothpick around in my mouth, I gave her a wink and she rolled her eyes before looking down at the table. *Yeah, avoid me, baby. I'm your worst fucking nightmare.*

She stood, ready to get the fuck on and end her date so that he wouldn't be in the news in the morning. Before she could leave, her brother blessed her pockets. I watched her fat ass until she was out of the room.

"She fine, for sho."

Don balled his face up and grabbed the bottle.

"Nigga, I know that. She's the finest. The girl version of me. And you around this bitch acting like you don't know what the fuck I done handed you for free. In three fucking months, I expected you muthafuckas to be drunk in love. But you running around the city, fucking all of our leftover bitches." Don laughed.

Taking a swig of the liquor, I grunted.

"I ain't fucking them hoes. I barely know their names."

It was true. I didn't even have their numbers saved. I mostly pulled up, got my dick sucked, and dipped.

"So getting brain from bird bitches is more important than my sister? More important than yo' fucking life changing?"

This nigga was chewing on that raw fish like it was a filet mignon. He was right though. This was most definitely an opportunity of a lifetime. All the shit he was speaking, Shio and Nel had too. Vello didn't give a fuck, one way or another. He was just ready to ball out.

The Cuppacio Mafia was known for reigning terror. They did more fucking bullying than they did paper chasing and that was the fucking problem. No, they weren't broke. Most Italian men were hard workers and money-makers, no matter how they had to get it. The Cuppacios weren't any different. The problem was, they took that ruthless shit and ran with it. Instead of doing what most privileged, rich muthafuckas did and shopping for a mail-order bride, those niggas were heavily into human trafficking. You wouldn't even think that shit was that big back then, but honestly, I think it was worse than it is now and that's saying a whole lot, being that muthafuckas come up missing every damn day.

The Cuppacios took their hustle and brought that shit home. Every Cuppacio man had a wife who was snatched from the comfort of their own home or the streets. My mom wasn't an exception. No one was there by choice. Most were pulled away from poverty, so being thrust into a life of glitz and glam sounded like a win to some, but that shit was far from it. Not only did the men put these women through hell, but they put the male children they were forced to bear through it too. Some women and children, like my uncle's wife, didn't make it out.

When my father and the rest of his men fell along with their Don, that left all the women and children unattended. Some women had been taken as young as fourteen years old, so they didn't know how to care for or provide for themselves for real. They had no sense of money management since cash was never put into their hands, and most of them didn't know what Chicago looked like outside of the neighborhoods we lived in. They were living in a luxurious prison.

At fourteen, I was forced to step the fuck up. When those sucker ass men were in the ground, I cleared my father's safe. Thankfully, each man had the same code to their safe, which was the year the Cuppacio Mafia was formed: 1772. Clearing all the safes, all we came up with was about five million dollars. That shit wasn't enough for the large ass family the Cuppacios had created. Some of the women fled, leaving their children behind, which I didn't hold against them. If a fat Italian muthafucka snatched me from my house and forced me to push out a baby, I probably would have left it behind too. I wouldn't have wanted any remnants of the life that dragged me to hell, so I got it.

Even if they left, I handed them a parting gift and wished them well. We couldn't sell any of the houses because they weren't paid off so the city ended up foreclosing them, which was cool by me. I would have loved to get the bread from them, but at fourteen, I didn't know shit about real estate.

After splitting the bread up, and getting housing for everyone, which some shared, we went from having a few mills to a couple hundred thousand. That was when me and my folks got in the streets.

Young as fuck and having to prove ourselves, we made sure to feed our families and had been ever since. The opportunity to merge with the Rinaldis was going to give me that level I needed to be on to set my folks up straight. They could live the lives they were meant to. All the bullshit and tragedy we'd faced over the years would be rewarded just by me putting a fucking ring on my finger. That shit was easy. Way too easy. And any nigga would have been jumping at the opportunity to do so. Hell, I was jumping at the opportunity. I dropped everything and came out here, renting a house before I even knew what the fuck Jisei's pussy looked like. I still didn't know what it looked like and it had been three months.

Don paused while cutting his steak and pointed his fork at me.

"I have missed my sister's entire life. Hell, I missed my own fucking life from being in jail all my adulthood. But I love her like I was there every step of the way. I am trusting you to do right by her, Ezio, and I don't trust any muthafucka but my wife, mama nem, Teo, and Rut. Jisei is a fucking gem. She don't really know shit about Mafia life even though all her friends are married to a mafia man. She's a good girl. A college graduate that got it out of the mud and defeated the odds. Take care of my sister, nigga, and when I say take care of her, I don't mean financially. Damn right, you gon' give her whatever the fuck she blinks at, but the way I'm coming behind her, no matter what the fuck you do, it could never top what the fuck I do. I spare no fucking expense when it comes to Jisei Rinaldi.

"You been down here three months and she don't even acknowledge yo' ass in a room. You saw her at her lowest, and instead of her staying with you and letting you calm her, she went and got in the bed with my daughter. My wife and I had to hear her cry all fucking night. It's cool because I'll always be that shoulder for her to cry on, but as her man, you supposed to trump me in most ways. Jisei didn't even blink at yo' ass just now. You think Dasani would have played with me like that? Well, back then, she definitely did, but that's old shit. I wasn't in my right mind at the time."

When was this nigga ever in his right mind?

"I appreciate everything you doing for a nigga. Real shit. But she is yo' sister. I'm a nigga that's used to having my way with these bitches. Getting married and settling the fuck down is a lot. I can marry her and I can spoil her. My people having everything they deserve is more important than anything to me. I really don't even know how to go about pursuing her. Every time I try to come at her, she throws me to the left. I was just gon' let her do her and show up at the wedding venue. As long as I don't see her disrespecting me, she can do whatever."

"So, let me ask you this. Once your name gets to ringing bells around town and the city not only knows who the fuck you are but knows Jisei's pretty ass is your wife, you telling me you okay with knowing she knocking the next nigga off?"

I gave a one-arm shrug. Jisei was fine as fuck, but my feelings weren't involved. Seeing her out made me react because she looked good but I didn't know her, and she didn't know me. I was going to be at the church with bells on because my people needed this but I wasn't no fake ass nigga. I knew this shit was hard for her and I wasn't on no weird ass shit, trying to force myself on her. Me being all mushy with her was just me on some high shit. I didn't know what the fuck I had going on in my head. I just knew when I was near her, I had to be in her space. Shit was complicated, but that was just what it was.

"What the fuck you want me to do, Demise? What the fuck would you do? Like you said, that's your world. She not just gon' lay down and let me come in, wrecking shit. Plus, if shit hit the fan with us, I can't afford to go to war with you. I will go toe to toe with you by myself any day, any time because no nigga put fear in me, Don or not, but my people can't take that hit. I got cousins and shit that's barely sixteen. I rather play the background and let her do her. I'm a dog ass nigga and I can't promise her I'll be the nigga that she come home to, rubbing her feet and shit. Then when I break her ass down like a fraction, you gon' want to cry about it. What the fuck would you do?"

"That shit sounds like hoe shit if you ask me. But I trapped my wife. Hog-tied her big belly ass, and kidnapped her. Then I imprisoned her until she loved a nigga. That's what the fuck I did to Dasani Rinaldi, but if you ever did that shit to my sister, I'd show you just how much you think you not scared of me. Talking 'bout I'ma want to cry about it. Cryyyy? Nigga, you gon' die before I cry."

Smirking, I picked up my fork and stabbed at a few veggies before taking a bite. Shit was decent too.

"I'on got time to be playing matchmaker with you and Jisei but court her. Get to know her and take her shopping and shit. Fly her out. I'on know. Do what the fuck you got to do, but she don't need to be around town with no other nigga. I built this brand with integrity and finesse, and I'll be damned if they say my lil sister is a Jezebel. Y'all engaged. Look past these hoes out here and it's easy, trust. If I can fuck on one pussy every night, yo' young ass can too."

Don acted like he was so much older than me. The nigga had me by a few years, four to five years tops. But we looked the same damn age. Hearing that he snatched his wife up had me confirming what I already knew: the nigga was delusional. Who the fuck did shit like that? But Dasani was fine as a muthafucka with her thick, Blasian ass. When she came down to the basement to confront his ass about his sister's engagement, everybody in that bitch was fighting hard not to look at her. That nigga was in love like a muthafucka, too, because he had a goofy-ass expression on his face the remainder of the time we were there.

"But now that we got that shit out the way, y'all got training starting in the morning. Four a.m. sharp. My men do it and y'all ain't no fucking exception. I gave you three months to get ya dick wet, Cuppacio. I know you got three with you, but after the wedding, the rest of the crew needs to make the transition. You can't be in two places at once. Everyone will be housed, and I'll have my realtor work with them to put them up nicely."

My chest tightened and sheen littered my forehead, but I kept my expression neutral. Training was a concern of mine because my experience with that shit was literal life or death. I wasn't the same kid, but that very training haunted my ass like the fucking boogey man. Still, I nodded.

We finished our food, making small talk, and I filled him in about all the people remaining in my family, information I was sure his ass already knew. I stayed engaged but I was silently watching the clock so I could get home to my fucking medicine.

"Aye, how the fuck you knew Jisei was here with a nigga?"

Don smiled. "That's my baby sister. She may not know it, but her ass is guarded like the fucking Pope. Don't shit get past me. So that brings me to another thing. If it's some shit you don't want me to know, you better handle that shit now because if I get to digging, I don't stop until every deteriorated skeleton is removed."

Taking a sip from my bottle, I placed it on the table and rubbed my chest.

"I'm an open book. I'm sure yo' ass knows everything anyway." *Cap*.

Don eyed me skeptically. "For your sake, you better hope I do."

Reaching into my wallet, I pulled out a wad of money and tossed it. Don caught it before it could fall on one of the platters.

"What's this?"

"Yo' munyun back for what you just handed yo' sister. She my responsibility. Right? I can't sit idly while another nigga hands her bread, brother or not."

The grin on Demise's face was one that looked sinister and amused at the same time.

"I knew I liked you, Cuppacio."

119

Don looked over the knot of money before setting it on the table.

"But if you tryna play big bank take lil bank, you in for a wild ride, my boy."

Placing the toothpick back in my mouth, I intertwined my fingers in my lap.

"Let the games begin, DON."

CHAPTER 9
JISEI "JAE" RINALDI

"Hold up, hold the fuck up. So your brother knew you were at a restaurant with this man, and no one left out in a body bag?"

Dasani's brows shot up while her strawberry mimosa was in her hand.

"I asked her if she wanted me to be her lifeline before she went, and she was like *no, it's just drinks. I'm grown,*" Mocha mocked.

"Ezio didn't say anything?" Scarlett asked.

Thinking back to last week when I was shaking in my fucking jeans seeing my brother and Ezio at the restaurant, I shook my head. I couldn't get out of that place fast enough. I lied to Anakin like I had a stomachache and got the fuck out of dodge. I took my wings with me though.

"No, they didn't come after me. I was halfway expecting Ezio to show up but he didn't." I shrugged, placing the breakfast margarita to my lips. It was sweet, tangy, and strong.

"See, if he was really 'bout it, he should have pulled up, hemmed yo' ass up after killing Anakin, and fucked the shit out of you until yo' ass couldn't walk. I thought Chicago niggas were ruthless." Mocha rolled her eyes. For her to be a spoiled ass rich girl, she damn sure liked rough-ass niggas.

Before she met Lorenzo, her daddy, Big Zan, had been one of the biggest dope boys in the city. She grew up rotten but a lil while in the hood after her daddy came up missing turned her ass out. My friend had a crazy ass story, but no matter how pretty she was, she played dangerous games. I wasn't brave like that. I didn't want any nigga pulling up on me, killing another, but the thought did make me leak.

"Hell, my Chicago nigga is," Dasani told us what we already knew.

"Mine too," Scarlett added.

"Mocha, you watch too much TV. That man is not thinking about me. I'm not thinking about his ass, either."

Azure was home with the kids, so Mocha was able to speak a bit more freely at brunch. We were at our monthly Sunday outing at Bagels with Bad Bitches, a restaurant that was started by none other than Matteo, Scarlett's husband, and Lorenzo, Mocha's husband. Those two were always doing brunch together back then and now owned one of the largest brunch chains in the States.

The blueberry chicken and waffles were my favorite paired with the pineapple breakfast margarita. Scarlett loved the spinach and chicken sausage omelet with the french vanilla pancakes, Mocha loved to treat her sweet tooth by ordering the cookies and cream french toast, and Dasani got the house bagel, which was sausage, bacon, eggs, and cheese on a freshly baked bagel. We often left here drunk, full, and ready for a nap since usually, we couldn't hold our heads up. We always took Dasani's driver, too, and today wasn't an exception.

Everything on the menu was amazing. Matteo and Lorenzo had two locations in the city and many more spread out in all

PUT IT ON THE MOB

other major cities. I was so proud of them and even happier for my girls for being able to leave this legacy for their children. This was my absolute favorite place to come to in Jagoda Bay and the line was out the door, even if it wasn't a Sunday. Those two hit the nail on the head with *Bagels with Bad Bitches*.

"I'm still pissed at Demise for even putting that responsibility on your back. He damn near forced me to be with him, but at least I was attracted to the man and had already slept with him. You don't know shit about Ezio. Have y'all even had a conversation? Scarlett, boo, I know he's your people and I know arranged marriages are common in the mob world, but this is crazy. Demise done outdone himself this time."

"Oh, none taken. I love my cousin but I agree. This is crazy. I mean, I have somewhat of an arranged marriage with Matteo, but it was my choice in a way. I love my cousin, but you having no choice in the matter makes my heart ache for you. How are you really feeling, friend? I know I ask you this every day and you're tired of hearing it, but still. You turned down Anakin because you didn't want to be a wife. It's been three months since the announcement and you really don't talk about it much."

Stirring the straw in my glass, careful not to scrape the rim so that salt or the decorative pineapple wouldn't fall in, I let Dasani's words marinate. I was absolutely attracted to Ezio. I didn't know too many women who wouldn't be attracted to Ezio. Seeing him once again dressed up with perfect jaw structure, light stubble on his face, alluring eyes, and when he chewed on the toothpick and revealed a mouth full of diamonds? I almost passed out from being overly stimulated. I had to get the fuck out of there because the sexual tension I felt made me uncomfortable with my brother in the room. The man was fine. He knew that shit, too, as he should, but again, that made my life harder.

Being married to a man like that had to come with a life-time supply of headaches and heartaches. I didn't know what the fuck to make of this situation, but I did know the attraction that Dasani spoke of was no factor and the way he acted an ass in those bent-up ass shoes at the bar let me know he was attracted to me too.

The day outside the projects. The forehead and nose kisses. He'd even told me he loved me and I knew that shit was a product of the weed he was on, but shit, I came hard as hell for the past few nights, hearing those words over and over again.

"Ladies, I'm fine. Everything will be fine. The wedding is happening. I don't know when, but it's happening. Don told me that a wedding planner would be reaching out to me. I do want the bridal shower to be in y'all's hands though. I can't fathom a stranger having that much control over my special day. Y'all know I love all things pink and girly, so go crazy." I forced a smile.

Most girls would be squealing with delight for their unmarried friend finally wedding, but everyone sat with a look of uncertainty. No matter what, though, I had to see this through. I trusted my brother. He wouldn't pair me with some fucked-up individual who would make my life hell. He loved me just as much as I loved him, if not more. This was simply a union to solidify his kingdom.

Now, I was wrong for being seen out in public with a man when I was promised to another, so if I chose to see Anakin again, it would definitely have to be at my house or his hotel. The thing was, I wasn't really comfortable bringing Anakin to my home because my brother would pop up at any time. And hotels were still very public. I refused to just lay down and roll over for a stranger just because of a fake ass marriage. I was still going to do me, I just had to be slick about it.

My vibrating phone stirred me from my thoughts.

Removing it from the table, I chewed the inside of my cheek.

773-542-7744: Send me the lo

Ezio still wasn't saved in my phone and he had been either calling or texting me every other day. I hadn't responded to his ass. I didn't want shit to do with the nigga and his bullshit. I had to give it to him; he was putting his best foot forward but he wasn't coming hard enough. No flowers, no lunch, no pop-ups, although I appreciated him for not doing that. Just *wyd* and *send me the lo* texts. Ignoring him like I always did, I focused back on my girls.

"Girl, fuck that wedding. I'm not about to let you go through with this shit. Fuck all that. I will beat Demise's ass on everything I love before you sign your life away. A life you had set up before your rich-ass brother came along. Newsflash! Your two best friends had become millionaires and had broken you off with major bread before you found out Demise was your brother. You were damn near already through college before you found out the nigga had any relations to you! You already had life planned out for you before you found out his psychotic ass was your brother. I love my man, I really do, but if you don't want to do this shit, I'm down for fucking shit up."

Dasani was the best sister-in-law a girl could ask for. Despite the slight age gap, she had truly become a sister to me who I adored. The way she always threatened to go upside my brother's head was hilarious, but I would never ask her to do that. Don already wasn't wrapped too tight.

"Yeah, friend, I would love a wedding, but I will ask Matteo to talk to Don if that is something you don't want to do—"

"You not gon' ask Matteo to do shit."

Matteo stood at the head of our table, making us all jump. The sounds coming from the DJ who was there from the moment the restaurant opened until closed had to have masked us being able to hear him creep up on us.

All eyes went to Scarlett, who forked her pancakes.

"I was just—"

"Shut up."

We shut up, even though we were already quiet. As handsome as Matteo's dread-headed ass was, he was mean as a damn rattlesnake. Scarlett usually didn't pay him any mind, but he had caught her off guard today.

"Y'all food and shit good though?"

And just like that, he had flipped.

We replied in unison that it was good before he snatched Scarlett up out of her seat and tossed her over his shoulder. Lorenzo also requested that Mocha come to his office. That was a sign brunch was over and done because they were both headed to get fucked.

"For real though. If you want to back out of this shit—"

"I'm good, I promise."

Dasani squinted her eyes, studying me hard.

"Well, if you're certain, Daylani will organize this wedding for you. You know my sister is the coldest wedding planner in the fucking country. If you're going to do it, do it right and spend all of your brother's money. We not sparing no expense. Ima tell my sister we want the elite package. I wish that nigga would hire anybody else."

773-542-7744: Either you blind or can't fucking read but I can't imagine that you graduated college without being able to spell out words.

Me: Nigga please stop texting me before I block you.

773-542-7744: Merch?

Locking my screen, I faced Dasani, who still had her sleek orbs fixated on me. I gave her a smile that reached my eyes. I hoped I looked a lot more confident than I felt because deep down, I was scared shitless.

CHAPTER 10
JISEI "JAE" RINALDI

Stretching my limbs above my head, my body felt as heavy as a ton after the nap I'd taken. After getting dropped off at home, I stripped out of my shorts and fell asleep in my blouse and panties. Glancing at the clock on my nightstand, the time read 5:47 p.m., which meant I had been asleep a little over two hours. I was happy that I'd woken up early enough to organize my work clothes for the week. The last time we went to brunch, I woke up around midnight and couldn't go back to sleep to save my life. I stayed up all night watching Netflix and didn't get sleepy until it was time for me to clock in. I bought a bottle of melatonin and a box of sleepy tea after that.

With a grumbling stomach, I stood from my bed, scratching my ass in the process. My home was clean due to the early morning session I'd done with Jhene Aiko to serenade me through the three-hour process. I never had overnight guests and rarely had company since I was always at my people's house. Add in with me spending forty hours a week at work, I was barely here enough to keep a dirty home. Even if I was here, with the rules my auntie instilled in me, I had the worst case of OCD.

If your space is sloppy, you are sloppy. You can't think in mess and a nonthinker ain't a doer and a non-doer is a person who will go look for a doer for dependency. You could end up with the damn devil just because you didn't want to keep a sock off the floor.

That stuck with me all throughout college. No matter where I've lived, I kept it spotless. Even when the roaches crawled across my cabinets in the projects, I kept them clean. I'd come a long way from that though.

Ding, dong.

On my way to the kitchen, my doorbell sounded, prompting me to go back to my room and slide a pair of pajama shorts over my bottom. I looked ridiculous in the dressy ass blouse and cotton striped shorts, but with an unexpected guest at my door, I grabbed the first thing I saw in my drawer that was the most accessible.

Cursing because I should have checked the Ring camera on my phone, I glanced through the peephole to see who was at my door, and when it was revealed, I hopped back like it was on fire.

Ezio.

Snatching the door open, I stuck my head out of it, blocking the rest of my house from view like he hadn't been inside before.

"Yeah?"

Was he scrumdiddlyum-yum? Fuck yes. Today he was, once again, looking like the poster board for hood niggas in a Nike set and Air Maxes. My eyes lingered on his tattooed legs, and though that was different on a man for me, he wore them well with the natural curve of his calves.

"I came to take you to lunch and shit."

Unsettled as fuck by his revelation and not doing anything to mask the irritation, I continued to stare at him.

"You mean the lunch that you were supposed to take me on over three months ago?"

Ezio looked off, grabbing the side of his neck before giving me his attention again. His eyes were so low, I could barely see the natural color of them.

"Yea."

Licking my bottom lip, I slowly opened the door so that he could come in. I had half a mind to close the door in his face, but the reality of the situation was we were engaged to be married. We needed to at least talk and get to know each other. Plus, I needed to let his ass know what the fuck I was and wasn't going to put up with, like popping up at my damn house.

His eyes shot to the print in-between my legs, and though my tongue was heavy with sarcasm, I held it in and let him inside. I didn't know what cologne he was wearing but I liked it. He'd been wearing it every time I was around him, and it suited him well.

I felt his eyes on my backside as I led the way to my living room and the beeping of the alarm system let me know he'd locked the door. Doing a scan of my living room to make sure nothing was out of place, I grabbed the pink and silver decorative pillow and moved it aside so that I could take a seat. Like the first time he'd come over, Ezio looked around my space with disdain, like it was beneath him or some shit.

"If my place isn't up to your standards, you're free to get the fuck on, your royal highness."

Stuffing his hands down the front of his pants, which had me crossing my legs on impact, he ran his tongue across his top teeth. Oh shit, he had those shiny ass tops and bottoms in. I hated a fucking grill. It was childish and a very poor display of so-called wealth. I needed a grown-ass man who showed his natural teeth at all times, even if they weren't stark white. But this man looked so damn good in the blinging pop-outs. Hell, I didn't know which version I liked more: the linen white teeth or his hood nigga teeth. Both suited him well.

He still looked around and I continued to watch him like a hawk as he seemed to look as if he was trying to find some shit out of place. He wouldn't though. Yesterday, I almost scrubbed the damn paint off my walls, that was how hard I cleaned.

"Yo' spot decent," was all he offered as he took a seat on my couch, but not before he removed the decorative pillow. I appreciated him. I didn't like my pillows to get flat or dingy looking from someone simply fucking them up.

"Decent?"

"Yeah, meaning shit cool, it's just girly as fuck." A frown etched on his face, followed by the statement as he stretched his right leg out in front of him.

"I mean, I am a girl. Was I supposed to have my space blue?"

Taking another look around my space that I'd invested a plethora of time and money in, he rubbed his hand across the top of his head.

"I mean, anything's better than all this fucking pink and glitter and shit. Neutral colors or some'. Like normal muthafuckas."

Crossing my arms over my chest, I stated matter-of-factly, "Well, I'm anything but normal."

With his light brown orbs that had too many other colors tossed around them, he scanned my body again, lingering on my thighs, making me remember I was in shorts. My cheeks warmed.

"Nah, you anything but normal, Jisei."

Hardly anyone called me Jisei. When I was at work,

they addressed me by my last name, Harper, at first, and now they called me Rinaldi. When I was around friends, I was Jae, unless they were being serious. Hearing my full name roll off his tongue shouldn't have had me so damn hot and bothered but it did. Everything about this man was a turn on and that shit was a red flag in itself. That's it – he was a walking red flag. From the way he lit up the fucking room to the way he commanded the space just by being. There was rarely a person who could outshine Demise Don Rinaldi when in the same setting, but this man sitting next to me gave him a run for his money. Easily. They said girls went after boys like their father and brother. But I wasn't going after this nigga. He just wouldn't go away.

"I don't want lunch. A lunch you are a few months behind on. So, thanks, but no thanks."

I matched his glare and we both looked out of our minds, just staring at each other in a daring sort of way. Here we were, two strangers, but somehow, we had to get married. This was some TV mess and it was a damn shame that it was what my life had become.

"Well, how 'bout we talk or some shit," he suggested.

"Or some shit? Ezio—"

"Aye. We getting married. Ain't no way around that. I apologize about lunch and shit, but I been trying to get my shit straight since moving here. I planned on letting you do what-the-fuck-ever you wanted to do as long as you not in my face disrespecting me because I don't believe in that forced marriage shit. I saw enough of it—"

Ezio stopped himself, a flash of anger apparent in his eyes.

"I just ain't on that type of time. I ain't into forcing bitches into doing shit they don't want to do and I know I make you uncomfortable as fuck. So, the least we can do is get to know each other and shit so it won't feel like you coming into this... situation with a complete stranger."

There was a pensive shimmer in the shadow of his eyes. I felt my composure was under attack and that proved his statement true. I was uncomfortable around him. But I didn't know whether it was because of the circumstances or if it was because I was so attracted to him.

Outside of the physical attraction that was apparent between the two of us, we didn't know shit about each other. I was tense about the entire situation, but I had no plans of telling my brother that I was backing out, so the least I could do was get to know Ezio. This arranged marriage had become the bane of my existence. I could barely focus some days just by thinking about what was to come. Forming some type of understanding with my husband-to-be would make the arrangement a little less... uncomfortable.

Dusting invisible lint off my bare knee, I sighed before meeting his gaze again.

That look. That fucking look he gave me was one that was begging me to hop in his lap and kiss him, and at the same time, screaming, *Run for the hills*. This man was toxic in every sense and though he was handsome, danger lingered in his aura.

"Okay. I can do that. I mean, we can do it. I'm saying we can get to know one another, Ezio."

He was still studying my profile and it made me shift on the cushion beneath me. All of a sudden, I remembered I'd been sleeping prior to opening the door and I worried that there was dried-up slobber on my face. *Oh God, please don't let that be the case.* That nap was heavenly, and I could imagine that I'd more than likely had some remnants of it on my mug.

"The other night, with yo' pops. I know what the fuck that feels like. I mean, my pops was my real pops but I know how it feels to be rejected by the one muthafucka that's supposed to love you and shit."

I didn't want to think about Bobby. I didn't hate him—I didn't want a relationship or a conversation with him. He wasn't biologically my father, so it was better that way. Him being in my presence when I was gone off the liquor had just caught me off guard. I'd hoped the conversation was shifting to Bobby because all I wanted to do was wish the man well.

"Niccoli. That was my sperm donor's name. He used to... the nigga didn't treat us right. Me or my mama. I'on know how much you know about the Cuppacios but them niggas deserved death. I hate that nigga and I'm better off without him."

His voice had drifted to a hushed whisper and his low, red eyes told me that he'd faced too many blunts to count. I swallowed hard, trying to reach a feasible answer. I watched him warily as I tried to lock down my own emotions.

"Why... why are you telling me this?"

Ezio rubbed his hand over his mouth and sighed. "Because I wanted you to know that you not the only person who was handed a fucked-up parent. I feel you. That shit hurt, but it's life. You better off without either of yo' bitch ass daddies."

I sat up in my seat and snatched the blanket that was resting over the back of the couch onto my lap. I didn't want a visible puddle to show up on my shorts because shamefully, he had me ready to consummate our union. That shit he just spoke had me drenched.

"I hear you," I replied softly.

"Good. Now, tell me some shit about you."

"Like what?"

"Like shit I need to know about my future wife."

I clenched my thighs together again but I didn't think the blanket did a good job of hiding it because those exotic eyes of his went straight to my lap, and when he licked his lips, I damn near passed out.

"Um, okay. Well, I'm Jisei. I'm twenty-four years old. I am a proud JBU graduate. I work in business management and I'm the sister of a Don." My introduction ended with the growling of my belly that I hoped he hadn't heard.

"That's it?"

"That's IT."

"Aite, cool."

He sat back in his seat and pulled out his phone.

"Wait! So, you're not going to tell me about yourself? You're just going to get on the phone and text in my face?"

It came out before I could stop myself. I didn't give a damn what Ezio did on his phone, but it seemed as if my mouth did. Ignoring me, he continued to peck on the screen while I sat, twiddling my thumbs.

"You can leave now."

I was over this impromptu visit. I needed to get my clothing out for the work week and check a few emails. Plus, I could feel a thudding headache brewing from one too many pineapple margaritas and I had a bottle of Tylenol on my nightstand that was going to cure that. Ezio could go and get to know someone else. This shit was a bad idea. I should have left his ass on the porch instead of being nice as fuck like I always was. Nice got me in this situation and nice wasn't getting me out. We would be married and that shit was only going to be on paper. I couldn't give a damn about anything else.

"I'm not going no-fuckin'-where."

Ezio slid his phone into his pocket and sat back on the couch like it was his, gripping his crotch. He was always grabbing at his middle, and instead of the notion creeping me out, it turned me on. It wasn't much he did that didn't turn me on and that was another reason I wanted his ass gone. I wasn't doing this with him. I wasn't going to get caught up in his pretty eyes, good looks, and ruggish ways. He was no more to me a stranger than a bum off the street. If I wasn't giving one of them the pussy, I wasn't giving it to him, either.

"Excuse me?"

"Shit, you excused, shorty."

"Out."

"Move that blanket and pull your shorts down so I can see that pussy."

He spoke so casually, you would have thought he was asking me about the weather. Blood pounded in my temples as I processed his statement. An unwelcomed blush crept up my cheeks. My breath quickened and my body warmed all over.

Ezio stood, stretched, and stalked in my direction.

"Ezio. Don't come over here—"

"Shut the fuck up." He bent down and snatched the cover from my legs, making me fold them underneath me.

"So you gon' be childish as fuck like that?"

"Ezio. Sit back down."

"I will, once I see that pussy."

"Why?"

"Why not?"

"Ezio."

"Ji-sei."

Fuck. I slowly removed my legs from underneath me. When my feet hit the bare carpet, I placed my hands on my thighs, feeling awkward as hell, but more turned on than awkward.

Ezio leaned forward, towering over me, and reached for my waistband. His touch sent shock waves over my body as my soaked shorts slid down my legs. Now, I was sitting in my panties while he tossed my shorts aside.

"Lean back."

A vaguely sensuous light passed between us. My whole being seemed to be filled with waiting. Waiting for his touch again. Waiting for his command again. Waiting to feel him—again. I stared at him with longing as I scooted down on the couch, ass almost hanging off.

Ezio eased down and didn't stop until he was face to face with my pussy. His finger hooked the seat of my panties, eyes still on me and his touch made my senses spin. I felt like a breathless ass girl as he exposed my folds, cool air tickling it. My body jerked as his thumb pushed against my nub.

"You wet as fuck. That shit dripping down yo' ass, bae."

"Ummmmmmm."

The circular motions he made had me drilling my elbows into the couch. There was no way this should have felt so good.

I was so caught up in his enthusiasm as we stared at each other, I realized I was moaning like a wounded animal. Studying his lean, light face, my body jerked again.

"When I put my mouth on this pussy, you better keep that shit on lock. Another nigga bet' not even smell it." He continued to bring me pleasure with his hand.

Men always want to be the only one a woman is sexing when all women want to be is a man's first and only romance. Aunt Polene's words rang in my head as I bit down on my lip. Aunt Polene wasn't talking about shit though. I wanted this man, and I wanted him now.

Ezio removed his thumb, and before I could come to my senses, he shoved his face in between my thighs.

"Oh, fuck!"

It was like a rocket taking off into space for the first time. I didn't know whether I wanted to catch my breath, cry, fuck his face, or grab his head. Then he kept his eyes on me as he devoured me whole.

"Ezio. Shit, babyyyyyy."

Mocha was right. The mouth? The mouth was better than the dick. He was making love to my pussy with his tongue and that shit in itself was sexy. Feeling his saliva mixed with my secretion flow down the crack of my ass and into my couch was so fucking nasty and I loved every bit.

My stomach clenched and he had the nerve to take his big ass palm and place it at the base of my stomach. That was it.

"Fuuuuuck! I'm cumminggggg, Ezio!"

My legs shook and my eyes rolled to the back of my head as I came undone. This shit was so good. So nasty. So fucking perfect, and I wanted it again. He'd made me cum in seconds and I wasn't even shamed about it.

"Pussy tastes good too."

Ezio placed a kiss on my coochie and then stood, leaving me looking like a damn fool. I couldn't believe he'd just done that. He really ate my pussy. If I knew he was this good, I wouldn't have been ignoring his ass.

"Get out, Ezio," I breathed. This wasn't supposed to happen. I wasn't doing this with him. If I didn't think this man was deadly at first, I knew he was now.

"You told me all that surface-ass shit about you. Shit I already knew about you. I could see all that shit just by sitting in this fucking Barbie-themed ass living room."

"It's not Barbie-themed." I stood, his gaze appreciating my frame. Scooping up my shorts, I stuck my legs in them and pulled them over my wet ass. Still in disbelief that he'd really done that.

"Shid, even Stevie Wonder can see that this shit is OD every little girl's dream. Grow up, get a good job and deck her place out to look like a fucking Barbie's dream house. You did that. Fasho. But fuck all that."

He waved his hand.

"Before you had me on my knees, eating that pretty ass box, I'd just ordered some food. My cousin was already out, grabbing some shit, so I told him to bring us some by. If you anything like yo' brother, yo' greedy ass eat it all, so I hope you in the mood for whatever the fuck Shio bringing."

"I don't like you." This man was discussing pointless shit while I was still trying to comprehend what had just happened. If it wasn't for me being startled and the pussy juices on his face, you wouldn't know he had just made me his bitch with his mouth on my couch.

"I promise you gon' love me. And when that shit happens, you gon' wish like hell it had happened sooner. Brace yourself, though, I'm fucked up, Jisei."

I wouldn't admit that my panties were pooled and I also wouldn't admit that the statement about him being fucked up scared me. Looks wise, any woman could fall in love. But I didn't need fucked up in my life. I was terrified of fucked up. I'd worked too hard to deal with fucked up. I'd worked too hard to deal with anything that I felt didn't serve me and Ezio looked like he couldn't serve anything but hard dick and lies.

Going to the back, I slammed my door and washed my ass, while still recanting me getting my pussy eaten for the first time. After I was cleaned, I put on a new pajama set and joined him back in the living room. I saw the Spot wings spread on the ottoman and this nigga had gotten comfortable, removing his shoes and T-shirt. Bare-chested Ezio was my favorite. The tattoos and sexy ass build had me wanting to jump his bones, but I wouldn't be fucking this man, no matter how much I loved the head.

Grabbing the remote, I cleared my throat and went to Netflix so I could put it on the first season of *Bridgerton*. It was my comfort show, and anytime it was on, I could easily get lost in it, not caring about anything going on around me. In this case, I needed to morph through the screen.

If I was to be arranged, I would have rather it been a damn duke or future king instead of a gangster with tattoos on his face, admitting that he had mental issues, all the while ready to fuck me over completely. *But the head was so damn good.*

"Aye, don't put it on no girly ass shit."

Ignoring him, I pressed play on season one, episode one, and grabbed a wing. *And he got my order right.* This was my damn house, and if he didn't like what I put on, he could leave. I needed that mouth again though. Was I sprung?

CHAPTER II
EZIO "EZEE" CUPPACIO

One Month Later

"Man, these bitches fine as hell. These are how my hoes gon' look when I grow up."

"Mine too."

With my eyes on the screen, I smirked at the twins as they salivated at the big screen. Our fathers were hosting one of their famous house parties and this time my dad was the host. I'd begged my dad to let my cousins spend the night and since the adults were occupied, I'd put it on HBO After Dark. I grabbed the pillow that was on the couch in my dad's off-limits room, which was a large room with couches, a bar, TV and a pool table. Nothing too fancy, but if my dad knew I was in here, he would beat my ass.

Sitting the pillow on top of my lap did nothing to soothe the throbbing in between my legs. I was old enough to know I had a hard-on and I was pretty sure the rest of my cousins did, too, as we stared at the screen in fascination. The white lady that was riding the black man's dick looked like it felt good. We were all still virgins *and hadn't really thought about sex, but when Nel suggested we sneak into this room, I pressed play on the remote and this came on.*

"They not even using a condom. That nigga probably gon' have AIDS," Shio added in disgust, but he, too, couldn't tear his eyes away from the screen.

"What's a condom?" Nel asked.

"If you don't know what it is, you damn sure don't need to be watching this shit. Cover your eyes, young ass boy."

We all laughed and I tossed the pillow that had been in my lap at Nel. He held up a finger sign at us but the smirk on his face said he wasn't in his feelings over the shit.

"What the fuck are you in here doing?"

My Uncle Narciso busted in the room, powder residue on his nose, which we knew was cocaine. All of our fathers did the shit and I hated the sight of it. It made them meaner, and often, they took the shit out on our mothers.

Fumbling with the remote, I turned it off as fast as I could, but Narciso had already caught us red-handed.

"You little fucks in here doing gay shit? Watching porn together? You niggers in here humping on each other?"

Shio stood to his feet and yelled, "We ain't gay, bitch ass white boy!"

I was right behind him. "Yeah, and don't call us niggers, with yo' racist ass!"

"Oh, so you're tough, hunh? You're not gay? We about to see."

Narciso reached at his waistline and pulled his gun out. We weren't afraid of guns. We used guns, had even had to use them on our own mothers.

"Follow me."

Without hesitation, we followed my uncle to the main room where coke, liquor, and naked women were being passed around. What we were just watching upstairs was nothing compared to the orgy in front of us, and just like upstairs, we couldn't take our eyes off it.

Three naked, grown-ass women stood in front of us, and by now, my dick was about to run out of my pants.

"You not gay? Show me that shit. The first one to make the cunt squirt will be free of training for a month..."

"Fuuuuuuck!" I grunted my sounds of pleasure just above a whisper, due to the gawking sounds being made from my dick disappearing down the deepest throat I'd ever encountered. Gripping the back of her head, I pushed her face so far in my lap that my pubic hair brushed up against her lips. Tears pooled in her eyes while saliva dripped from her mouth, but she kept sucking, never losing her rhythm.

"Eat all this dick up."

Gagging was her only response, which made my thighs tense as her mouth grew wetter. I'd met Olivia at Target when I called myself going to get some sweets and household products. That was about three days after I ate Jisei's pussy. The tissue and paper towels that came with the long-term rental had run its course, so with the need to wipe my ass and cure my munchies, I went to the bourgeois version of Walmart and ran into the thick, bronze beauty. She would have gobbled my dick right there on aisle six but I took her number with the promise to call. Now that she had my fucking toes throwing up gang signs with her impeccable head skills, I'd wish I let her ass take me down that day.

Her shiny, bare ass was on display since she was bent over the couch with her face in my lap, so I gripped it, slapped it, making it wave like a fucking tsunami, and reached for her wet folds. She was fucking dripping. Dipping my middle finger in her slippery walls, removing it, I trailed back to her ass and stuck my now lubricated finger in her exit hole while using my thumb to massage her clit.

"Ummmmmm."

She moaned in pleasure but the vibrations from her throat sent shockwaves to my dick.

"THE FIRST ONE TO *make the cunt squirt will be free from training for a month.*"

With my free hand, I reached for the pills that were wrapped in aluminum foil on the arm of the couch and tossed them back. Shio had come through twice since with the re-up, but now, I had six more pills after this and the thought had me wanting to break out in fucking hives. Shio made it clear that the last time was the last time. Since he wasn't fucking with the pills anymore, I wasn't, either. He wanted me to focus on my bride-to-be.

Since the night I ate her to tears, I'd been on her line, and the fact that she was still pushing me to the left had me tight. How dare she take my mouth virginity and treat me like a sucka? I was off her ass and on to badder and better bitches. I just needed a wedding date so I could get on with this shit. Listening to her brother was the reason I'd pulled up on Jisei that night. I thought when I sucked the pussy and watched fucking *Bridgeton* with her ass all fucking night, she was going to be on a nigga's dick. At least enough to please her brother. I was wrong as fuck though. She took my lil head and threw up the middle finger.

Running my tongue across my teeth, my eyes lowered, mouth watered, body relaxed except for my curling toes, and my jaw slacked. Getting head while the pill kicked in was the best fucking feeling. All the fucking thoughts of my past escaped me.

Olivia's ass hole tightened around my thumb while my ring and middle finger thrusted in her pussy. I knew her nut was on the verge just as mine was due to the way both her holes had my fingers in a chokehold. With the Percs kicking in, I knew I could go all fucking night if I allowed, so I had to speed this shit up. Switching my fingers out, I had more control and it caused Olivia to go wild all over the dick. I loved sloppy ass, uncontrolled head, so with my legs going stiff in front of me, I let Olivia milk me dry while at the same time, she squirted all over my fucking hand.

"Damn, daddy, I ain't never came from a man fingering me. That shit was good."

Olivia stood from her couch, exposing a body that was too perfect to be real. Her tight, smooth stomach, perky, full breasts that were a bit lighter than the rest of her body, bald pussy, and stout hips had my dick bricking back up. Olivia smirked at me ogling over her and licked her lips, making my dick twitch.

"I can suck that right up out of you again, and I would if I didn't have to work."

Olivia turned on her heels and that fat ass that had me ready to say fuck my rules and bend her the fuck over jiggled with each step she took. I heard a door opening, and shortly after, water ran. Looking around Olivia's space, I appreciated her setup. She had chocolate and mint color schemes flowing throughout her home. I didn't make it to the back of her apartment, but the living room, though small, was neat, smelled good, and looked good. The moment I walked through the door, I knew I wouldn't be leaving Olivia alone only if the head was good. She had definitely passed the fucking test with flying colors, so that sealed the deal on me having her at the top of my list. I didn't know what the fuck kind of relationship Jisei and I would have, but I knew it was going to be hard for me to part with that skilled ass mouth of Olivia's.

She came back into the living room, now in an oversized t-shirt, and dropped to her knees. I watched intently as she wiped my dick clean. Her nasty ass had even found some cum on my thigh, and instead of wiping that away, she licked it up like it was her favorite icing. Yeah, she was stamped.

Standing to my feet, I helped Olivia from the floor and wrapped my arm around her waist. It made her shirt rise, giving me another view of her ass that I had no choice but to slap and grip.

"I appreciate you. Come lock up."

Don had me meeting him and the crew at an address that if you typed it on Google didn't bring anything up. I thought after training for the past four weeks, I could at least have my evenings to myself. But it was what I signed up for. I didn't come here for a vacation or time off. I came here to do what-ever was needed to get my people to the finish line. I had to admit, though, the training he had us going through wasn't shit compared to what we faced as children. I mean, I was sore as a bitch and felt like I was training for World War III, but it wasn't any of the degrading shit I'd gone through as a child. Still, as long as the shit aligned with my morals, I was going do whatever to make sure this shit went off without a hitch because I needed this union for my family's sake.

"Call me. I work all night on the weekends at my second job, but during the week, I get off at six," Olivia purred as she pulled her long, black weave from her back and sat it on her right shoulder, exposing the creaminess of her neck. That shit was sexy, for some reason. Reaching in my pocket, I peeled off a few hundred and she happily obliged.

"I got you."

"When you throw a ring around that dick, pass her to me."

LISA AUSTIN

Nel blew out a wad of smoke as I eased into the car. Since we all knew we would be heading to meet up with Don together, we agreed to ride in one whip. Shio was always on his solo shit whenever given the opportunity and this time was no different. He decided he was driving his own shit, so that left me and the twins. We'd just got done riding through the city, checking shit out when Olivia hit me up. We had time to spare, so the twins dropped me off at her crib, and by her shit being new territory, they opted to wait outside versus hitting a block. I wasn't bringing pussy back to the rental, so it was either a hotel or her spot. I hadn't had time to book a room so her place it was. Olivia lived in a nice part of the city, and I could tell the apartments weren't cheap. Still, my folks weren't taking any chances.

"Nigga, you always want somebody's fucking leftovers! It's too much new pussy floating around this bitch to be swapping semen," Vello jeered.

Nel passed me the blunt, but I passed on it. The pills had me just right. I was about to be surrounded by Rinaldi men and wanted to be alert. I wasn't expecting shit to pop off, but I knew that by us being in training, we were in the trial stage. I'd gotten acquainted with a few of the mobsters, and even though they had some shit with them, the niggas were some money-getting ass dudes.

They were cool, but we knew the made men were watching everything the three Cuppacios did. I had no doubt in my mind that they were also watching the rest of us who were posted in Chicago and that was why we did daily check-ins to make sure the other superior Cuppacio were keeping the youngins in line. Four months later, and shit was cool. I missed Uncle Remus and Harolds and my mama but shit had been going well in Jagoda Bay.

"You niggas always bringing bad ass bitches around.

146

Why in the fuck would I not want a sample? You sound 'bout crazy as you look," Nel argued while easing on the e-way. We'd already rode by the location sent to us earlier so that we could get a feel for it and the shit was in the middle of no-damn-where. Outside of a raggedy row of buildings, it was a ghost town. I didn't know if this shit was training again or what, but I wasn't going to be good for shit but busting my gun. These niggas would have to do the physical and mental work. My trigger finger worked all the same whether I was high, drunk, or sober. I could shoot with my fucking eyes closed.

"You shouldn't want shit we stuck our dicks in. We in a brand-new city with new opportunities and that includes new, soft legs. If you haven't got no hoes in four months, you don't need none. It's plenty of pretty hoes out here but you want a bitch Ezio just dicked down."

Vello was smoking in the back seat, the smoke from his blunt floating past my shoulder. Olivia's juices were still on my fingers, but if my cousin wanted her, he most certainly could have her. I was going to fuck her first before I let him get his go. She wouldn't get dick anytime soon because her trial period had just begun, but her lil sexy ass had me intrigued.

"You can have the bitch, Nel. You know it's never no pressure—"

The seat belt pinging had just stopped, thankfully, because it was loud and annoying as fuck, drowning out the music. I was the only one not wearing one because when I was rolling off the pills, the shit made me feel constricted.

"That's why you my fav." I slapped hands with Nel as he continued to navigate through traffic.

"And that's why y'all dicks gon' be itching just the same. Talking 'bout it's not no pressure. It should be pressure about your wife, nigga. Don't forget what the fuck we here for."

Nel looked at his brother through the rearview mirror.

"Aye, don't start that Shio shit. What the nigga do with his dick ain't none of our business. My fav ain't forget about the mission. He be up at four in the morning, doing the drills like the rest of us. He might have been up getting high as skyscraper pussy the night before, but my dawg shows up. Plus, he ain't married just yet."

I slapped my hands with Nel again. I felt Vello's eyes on us with his silent ass judgment. I was doing what the fuck was asked of me. I'd spent time with Jisei, doing whatever her brother asked, even ate her funky ass pussy. It wasn't funky, but still, she had me tight. I didn't have a bitch parading around town on my arm even though Jisei's lil apple-head ass was still creeping around with ole boy. Fuck her though. My people were my concern.

"This nigga," Vello mumbled.

"What you say, Princess? Speak the fuck up so the masses can hear you," Nel teased, glancing in the rearview mirror again.

I was focused on the road in front of us. We were going every bit of seventy miles an hour, but I swear I was able to count every tree that lined the road and I was already up to two hundred and fifty-two.

"You niggas ain't no fucking masses."

Vello's voice rose an octave as he inhaled the contents of his blunt again.

"That girl gon' have you wrapped around her fucking finger. She gon' have your ass so fucking sprung that we gon' have to pull your ass out the pussy."

"Who?"

"Jisei! That's who."

"Ha! My fav ain't even fucked yet. So miss us with that shit, " Nel retorted.

"Nigga, are you keeping tabs on his dick too? And that ain't yo' fav, you dumb ass! I shared a womb with yo' simple ass. I'm ya fucking favorite until we exit this bitch as one."

Nel looked over at me but I was still counting pines. I was up to three hundred and ten now.

"You hear that shit? This nigga jealous. He mad we getting these bitches. Then, we got our first mission coming up so the money about to pile up. You think we worried about being tied down when we about to have so much fucking money that we gon' have to find places to hide that shit? We will leave that lover boy shit up to you and Shio."

"You niggas talking big shit, but watch both of y'all be the ones to fall the hardest. Nel, you so tough but you a whole fucking crybaby."

"Who?" Nel screeched.

"That owl."

"Nigga, I'm a whole gangsta. I kills niggas for fun. I'm the fucking boogey man. I'm the one that makes muthafuckas cry. The fuck you take me for?"

"I take you for the same nigga that cry as soon as Selena gets shot, pussy. You can't even sit through the movie with a dry eye."

"Man, you know that shit sad! I still have flashbacks of her being shot like I was there. Shit was so fucking sad. I still haven't gotten around to putting money on that short, fat bitch's head that killed her. Jealous ass hoe. If a nigga don't cry when Selena on, I judge him immediately."

"Shit was sad as fuck," I agreed.

"Nigga, you put some money on that lady's head, you fasho going Fed."

"Man, get yo' police ass out of my truck. Talking about I'm going Fed. Wait till I tell Mommy you wishing jail time on me. I gots to sage my shit ASAP."

"Anythiiiing for Seleeeena -- goofy ass."

Opening the door, my foot hit the rocked pavement while the twins continued their banter. If it wasn't Shio and I going at it, it was those two. It wasn't a normal day if we weren't on each other's head and it had been that way since way back then.

Today, it was a bit chilly out so I was in jeans, olive Timberland boots, and an olive Amiri hoodie. Chicago could get cold; Jagoda Bay was mild as hell but had its cold moments. I would take this over snowy roads and below-freezing temperatures any day.

Looking up at the building, I staggered a bit and felt hands on my shoulders, pushing me forward.

"Come on, zooted ass Cuppacio. Put ya fucking game face on." Nel had just been joking, but the seriousness in his tone let me know it was no time for being out of my fucking mind. The rows of foreign cars told me, although the place looked like a ghost town, it was very much occupied.

"And find a fucking bathroom as soon as we get in here. You don't need to be up in this nigga's face with another bitch's pussy scent. You engaged to his sister, nigga," Vello scowled.

"Vello, by all means, if you better at this shit than me, you can take the position. Just like I told Shio. We can round table this shit, and I will happily pass the torch if either of you want it."

By birthright, I was next in line for the empire, but being that it wasn't much but a fallen fucking kingdom, I had always voiced that these niggas could take charge. Growing up, there was shit I went through alone that I hadn't ever even burdened them with because I didn't want a nigga feeling sorry for me. I ain't never cared to be the fucking leader. I liked to play the fucking background. I actually preferred it that way but when the Cuppacio men died, everyone was looking at me for answers and I gave it to them. Along with these niggas, I'd kept the family afloat and I would continue to do that, even if one of these other niggas stepped up.

I'd stopped walking and was damn near nose to nose with Vello. He wore a scowl while I wore a blank expression. I meant every-fucking-thing I'd said too. I would support either of my cousins if they saw fit that they could do a better job than me. That was how much I loved my family. That was how much I respected the remaining Cuppacio men.

"Hey, hey, fellas. We good here. Fav, you know Vello and Shio are concerned about you, especially when you on the Percs. Nobody wants your position. That shit is yours by birthright. I'm too childish for that type of responsibility, this nigga too lover boy, and Shio don't know if he wants to preach to a bitch or dismiss her. You be high as a dope fiend but you the only one suited for the job. Now bring y'all ass on so we can see what type of GI Joe shit this nigga Don got for us. Y'all can have a pissing match another day."

Nel was talking but Vello and I were still in a stare-off. Just when I was about to throw a right hook at the nigga, he smiled. I pushed past his playful ass and resumed walking to the entrance.

It was quiet as fuck in the still of the night, so unless these walls were soundproof, everyone inside must've been silently praying. The only sounds that could be heard were the crunch underneath our shoes.

When we got to the door, which was a tall, steel block, a troll-looking ass man was guarding it. The nigga had on a bulletproof vest, a helmet, and a clipboard in his hands. We weren't short by a long shot, but even we had to look up at this nigga.

"Fee-fi-fo-fum looking ass nigga," Nel kidded.

I looked back at him with a snarl that shut him and his giggling ass twin up.

"Aye—"

"Cuppacio men, head on in and walk through the hall, make a left, and go down the stairs. Enjoy, gentlemen."

Troll opened the door, spoke in a mic, and let us through. The door closed behind us when we were granted entrance and the narrow hallway was dimly lit by fire sconce on the wall.

"Fuck this is? Nineteen-seventy-two?"

Nel said what I'd been thinking, but still, I adjusted my eyes and followed the instructions. Troll should have told us that we would be walking five minutes before we got to the first turn. Still, we followed the path and walked down the iron steps.

"I saw a fucking elevator back there. Two, actually, so why in the fuck are we taking the stairs? My fucking knees hurt."

"Cuz we following directions, fav," I mocked.

My legs were burning like a muthafucka, too, but I continued to descend the stairs. Finally, we came to another door and the exact muthafucka that was guarding the outside was now at this door. Either this nigga had magic, was a twin like Beavis and Butt-Head or I was just too damn high.

"Now I know—"

"Enjoy yourself, gentlemen."

The door opened before Nel could say what I was thinking, and stepping in was like walking into Vegas.

"Now this what the fuck I'm talking about. All that fucking training! I was wondering when the fun shit was going to start."

A woman in a sexy ass, short, black and white dress handed us drinks that we all took. Looking around, there were about thirty waitresses serving the countless number of men throughout the gambling halls. Future blared from the speakers that weren't visible, so they must've been built in. Slot machines lined the walls and lined the swirling pattern of blue, burgundy, and tan on the carpet. Though the music was loud, a mix of machines, jackpot chimes, and laughing men filled the air. There was a mixture of blunt and cigar smoke, creating a light fog. I fanned my hand in front of me like that would help with my vision, but truth be told, I was high and just needed to concentrate on my surroundings and I would be good.

Looking around, I tried to see if I spotted any of the men we'd been training with but came up empty. There was a mixture of people, including ones in business suits, ones who looked like they'd just led a world-class surgery and came straight from the operating room, and street niggas such as myself. I thought this was a men's only establishment until I saw a few pretty faces that were hooked on the arms of men, but that didn't stop them from eying us down, choosing like they would rather us swap places with the ones who'd brought them here.

"This shit too live. Glad I brought a bankroll. Let's find a crap table that looks like we can break."

I nodded in response to Vello, who was walking behind me with his right hand on his side. These niggas got on my fucking nerves, but my life wouldn't be shit without them. For real.

"You niggas finally made it?"

Shio crept up on my side with a drink in his hand. I didn't see his car outside, but this nigga may have been in a rental. You never knew with Shio. I slapped it up with my guy before he gave the same love to the twins.

"Fuck that nigga Don at?" I asked.

The casino was bigger than I'd given credit to because I didn't see where it ended, and we'd walked a few minutes.

Shio took a gulp of his drink before setting it on the tray of a waitress walking by.

"There that nigga go right there."

Don stood at the head of a crap table with so many fucking chips in front of him, they damn near matched him in height. I could tell he was talking shit and the nigga was shirtless but in tuxedo pants. To the right of him was his fine-ass wife, who was giggling at his shenanigans and sipping on a pink drink.

Don's eyes met mine and the smile on his face turned into a mug that I instantly matched. Then the nigga smiled and waved us over.

We walked the distance to Don, taking our time and checking out the scene along the way. Don had a whole fucking bootleg ass casino in the middle of nowhere. When he told us to meet him here and dress regularly, I didn't expect this shit here. I could imagine how many men came in here blowing their whole fucking salary and going home, taking the shit out on their very oblivious wives.

"Cuppacios, welcome to Demise's dungeon." Don spread his arms out wide.

Chuckling, I took a look around the table and noticed a nigga I could have sworn I'd just seen on a billboard on the way here. It was some political ass advertisement and here the nigga was, risking his position down here sinning like a muthafucka.

"Baby, take my spot. You know you my good luck charm. Let me holla at these niggas."

Dasani Rinaldi eyed me and not in a way that the rest of the women here had. It was almost as if she was sizing me up and sending a warning at the same time. I knew she was close with Jisei the day she stormed into her husband's basement ready to go to war with his ass over the arranged marriage.

"Good evening, I see the rest of the Cuppacio men made it.

I thought you niggas was gon' be at the house with a heating pad after the month y'all had."

Don had been working us to the extremes, testing the fuck out of our limits. It felt like we were training for the Olympics but we did it without complaints.

"Shit, some' small to us. We grew up on this shit, remember?"

Don smirked. "How could I forget, Cuppacio?"

"This shit legal?"

I wanted to slap Nel upside the head. Don smiled at Nel.

"Nah, but if you want to sing like Tweety Bird, the chief of police right over there." Don pointed to a fat, black man who looked like he was losing his pension.

"Hell nawl. Just curious. Shit dope."

"Well, you know what they say about curiosity. Shit killed the cat."

"Lucky for us, we don't have fur, claws, a tail, or four legs," I assured.

Don gave his attention back to me. "I like you niggas. Y'all get through this shit, you'll fit right the fuck in. But tonight is not about training or mob shit. I had to make sure y'all was built for this shit before I brought y'all to my baby. You're in the room with the most elite. I have anyone in here from the mayor, senators, doctors, lawyers, street niggas, murderers, robbers, down to the niggas that cook the food at your favorite restaurants. This is fucking Switzerland. Niggas from opposite sides of the spectrum come together here to gamble, drink, smoke, and chop shit up. The muthafuckas who need to know you are in this very room. Alliances have been formed, contracts have been made, and a whole lot of fucking money has been earned in here and not just on slot machines. What-ever the fuck you're into, it's a man or woman in this room that can make it happen. Don't underestimate the bitches. This ain't no dick-swinging contest. It's some very powerful women that frequent this bitch too. But just as they are powerful, they are deadly. Be careful." Don placed his attention on my cousins.

"That's just our type. In Chicago, you know we like 'em with a side of Gakirah Barnes. You ain't saying shit."

Gakirah was a seventeen-year-old legend in Chicago. She'd even had a TV character named after her – Lil Snoop from the hit show, *The Wire*. She was a cold-blooded fucking killer, but her ass was a stud. I liked 'em crazy but not that fucking crazy and manly. Nel was on his own with that one. After I had to kill my last bitch, I wasn't fucking with no gangsta bitches.

"Them Chicago bitches don't have shit on these down south ones. But you'll see. They make Kirah look like a fucking angel. Enjoy yourself though. Let me go holler at y'all's mans."

"You niggas lose everything in yo' pocket, don't look at me. You know how you get, Vello."

Vello may have had a gambling habit. He was forever ready to hit a nigga in the dice or bet on some shit. He was in heaven right now. I wasn't a big gambler, but I fucked with the dice and the crap table from time to time. A nigga like me was a sore loser and be ready to snatch my money back, so I try to stay off that shit.

"Nigga, I got money. When I walk up out this bitch with garbage bags full of money, don't try to ask to help me count it."

"Do I look like a hoe ass nigga to you? I'on want to count shit that ain't mine."

Nel stuck a middle finger up at Shio and he and his twin were off to do exactly what Shio said—lose their fucking money.

"You good?"

Shio remained at my side, eyes on the scene in front of us,

alert, gun on hip, ready just in case some shit popped up. Our city taught us to always be ready and our life taught us to never leave home without your pistol. I was glad Troll nem didn't search us because if my bitch couldn't come in, I wasn't coming in.

"Nigga, he good. Fuck you think I'ma do?" Don spat.

Shio gave me a final look before trudging into the same section the twins went to. Don had a nice ass setup down here. The next time I was here, I was coming sober so I could feel some of these niggas out. I could benefit from some of the folk in position, especially since Jagoda Bay would be my new home.

"You got some solid ass niggas. That Shio nigga reminds me of—"

"Matteo. That's why them niggas be at each other's throat during training."

"You been down here four months. I think it's time for you to make some shit shake in the city. What you into?"

That shit was music to my ears.

"Dope."

"Dope?"

"Yeah, that's all we know. Shit been taking care of us for a minute."

Don eyed me. Some shit the nigga always did. I hoped he couldn't tell I was rolling.

"Aite, I got a man. Goal. Head of the Navarro Cartel. He gon' hit you with some brick, but it's on you to get it off. I'll set it up tomorrow."

That shit was like music to my fucking ears. We were getting bread but a cartel plug was going to take us to the next level.

"That's love."

"Yeah, let me get back to my wife."

"Speaking of yo' wife, I'on think she my biggest fan." My gaze shifted to Mrs. Rinaldi, who was losing her husband's money.

"Nigga, my bitch not friendly. Nor is she a fucking groupie. She supposed to not like yo' ass. Worry about my fucking sister liking you, nigga. That's yo' assignment. My bitch don't like nobody but me."

I laughed at Don as he walked away, still talking shit. From the times I've witnessed his wife glaring at him she didn't like his ass either. Love? Yeah. I saw that shit in her eyes, but she looked like the type that had an attitude about everything.

"If I would have known you would be at my job, I would have gone ahead and sucked that second nut up outta you."

Standing in my view was fine-ass Olivia. My brow rose because I definitely wasn't expecting her ass to be here when she said she had to work. The black and white dress that all the other waitresses wore looked damn good on her and barely went down over her ass. The fishnets gracing her thighs did nothing to conceal their juiciness and the floral scent on her skin made my dick hard. Her long, black hair almost made her look angelic when I knew that throat of her was nothing but the fucking devil.

Licking my lips, I pulled her to my chest, making her hold on to the tray of coins that she had hoisted on her shoulder. The pills made me simp as fuck at times, and seeing her pretty ass in front of me had my heart racing. It could have been me knowing I was about to become a very wealthy man that had my ass all touchy-feely, but whatever the case, Olivia was soft as fuck.

A broad smile covered her face but she nervously chuckled while looking around.

"As much as I loved having your dick down my throat, I

can't play around with my coins. I'm at work, Ezee, and my boss don't play that hoe shit. His words."

I laughed because that sounded like some shit Don would say. But I wasn't trying to hear any of that shit she was talking. Olivia was pretty, thick, smelled good, and was cool as fuck. She was definitely getting this dick in her guts, possibly right in this fucking dungeon.

"What you make? I'll pay you if he get rid of ya."

I hadn't even touched a brick yet and was ready to trick heavily. I couldn't believe this shit. I thought Don was going to wait until I was married to his sister to put me on some money shit. I had my own shit going back home and that kept me afloat, but a fucking Cartel plug? Fuck yeah.

Placing her lime green, pointed nails that matched her toes on my chest, she blinked her long ass lashes.

"As bad as I want to believe that, I can't risk it. I didn't even know your real name and I'm supposed to just let you promise me sixty thousand dollars? Because that's what I make in a year only working weekends here. And I don't have to fuck for it. All I have to do is look pretty and serve. I'm not fucking this job up for nobody. Not even a big dick, fine ass man like you."

Grabbing her hand, I placed it on my dick and her chest swelled.

"You ain't gotta fuck me for it, either, Olivia."

"But I gotta suck you for it though? Right?"

"I—"

"Umm umm."

Moving in slow motion, still holding Olivia's wrist on my dick, my heart accelerated seeing Jisei standing next to us with her arms crossed. Her hair was still in that side part style with the loose curls and baby hair that I was really fucking with. She looked like pure fucking money. With another pair of low rise jeans on that I was starting to believe she loved, instead of heels, she was in Dolce & Gabbana sneakers, a Dolce crop top that showed her belly ring, and the matching bag on her shoulder. It was apparent that baby loved showing her hips. On her neck was a thick diamond chain with a diamond tiara hanging from it. I knew it must've been a gift from her brother because I'd seen him wear one with a crown.

Still, as fine as her ass was, her playing me like I didn't have that pussy spitting up didn't sit right with me. So, instead of acknowledging her, I stayed in Olivia's face.

"I'm sorry, Jisei, is there something I can get you, girl?" Olivia asked with a genuine willingness to assist, not even knowing she was for sure probably about to lose her job, according to the scowl her boss's little sister wore. Still, I kept Olivia's hand in place, and she showed no resistance to removing it.

"Can she help me with something, Jo?" Jisei snaked her head around and Olivia gave a frown before fixing her face.

Olivia looked back at me, confusion plaguing her face.

"Who is Jo?"

Licking my lips, I rubbed my hand down my head.

"Yeah, go get her a lemon drop, baby." I cringed as I let that beautiful word drop from my lips. Shit, I was high.

Olivia nodded and leaned in. "You still smell like me, Ezee. I'll call you when I get off so we can finish what we started."

Olivia stood back, removing her hand, and smiled at Jisei.

"I'll have your drink right up, Pretty."

Jisei's scowl never wavered as Olivia switched off. I watched that ass while she walked away too.

"You a real disrespectful ass nigga. You know that?"

Turning back to Jisei, the frown on her face did nothing to conceal her beauty. That girl was too pretty for words, even pissed. But I was wondering why in the fuck she looked crazy in the face.

"Fuck is you talking about, Jisei?"

"It's Jae. And you know what the fuck I'm talking about. You all up on that bitch in my brother's shit, not giving a fuck that I may or may not be here. What the fuck happened to the shit we agreed upon? Did you forget you had your mouth all on my pussy?"

How could I forget? My dick was so hard that day, and instead of her returning the favor, we watched that Victorian times ass show and ate wings. We had great conversation and it was the first time I chilled with a woman without my dick ending up down her throat, but I was the one that had given head and had gotten dismissed.

"What's to' you? I be on yo' line and you ignore me like I'm a fucking goofy."

"Nigga, I got a job. The fuck? I'on got to respond to you. All you do is *Send the lo* and *What you doing* me to death. No fucking substance."

"Come 'ere, you look pretty as fuck."

I grabbed Jisei by her belt loop and pulled her to my chest. The Chanel perfume on her skin couldn't be missed and I made sure to nuzzle my nose right in the crook of her neck.

"Un hunh. Get yo' fucking hands off me. You smell like that hoe's pussy."

Jisei being so close made me feel all warm, fluttery, and shit, but the moment she snatched away, I immediately felt cold and like something was missing. She was addictive, I give her that, but it could be the high.

"Jisei, that's why I fuck with other bitches. I can touch you. You my fucking fiancée. But you act like a nigga got the cooties."

Jisei tossed her head back in laughter.

"Oh, so *now* I'm your fiancée? Ezee, stay the fuck away from me before I lose my cool. Talking 'bout that's why you fuck with other bitches. You enjoy yo' night and don't pop up at my house no more unless you want to get your feelings hurt, my guy."

Before I could snatch her ass up again, she scattered away from me, ass looking just as delicious as Olivia's, except when I looked at Jisei's, my fucking mouth watered. I watched Jisei until she disappeared into the crowd. I didn't know her ass was here, and if I did, it wouldn't have changed shit. This wasn't a real ass engagement. Plus, I hadn't done shit but complimented Olivia. No harm, no foul.

Feeling eyes burning the side of my head, I followed the glare and saw Shio, who stood, shaking his head. Instead of addressing him, I went to find Olivia because not only was my dick hard, I was starting to get cotton mouth. Jisei would be all right. My focus was meeting with the plug and getting this fucking money. Fuck the rest.

CHAPTER 12
JISEI "JAE" RINALDI

Two months later

If you pull out a game board roll and lose the first turn, you better off walking away. If not, a man will play in your face every single time, and more than likely he will win. – Aunt Polene

"So you're just going to shoot me down? You know I can be on a plane in less than an hour and in your city. Your pretty ass has been pushing me aside for months."

Smiling hard as hell, I listened to Anakin try to plead his way to seeing me. This man had been applying so much damn pressure and he lived hundreds of miles away.

"Nak, I told you, I have been busy as hell. Today is my first time getting out. I've been in the house."

I left out the part where I had been in the house trying to dodge not only my brother but Ezio too. In a matter of six months, the nigga that was from Chicago had managed to make his way in everyone's mouth. Everywhere I went, whether it be on social media or at the fucking grocery store, somebody had something to say about fine-ass Ezio. He and his cousins literally went from being the niggas nobody knew to the men everyone wanted to see, fuck with or be. It was quite sickening. I guess the plus side of it all was that my brother nor anyone else had mentioned a wedding. Daylani had for sure been hired to plan our "wedding" but she was waiting for us. As much as I loved Dasani's baby sister, her ass would be waiting because if it were up to me, this whole shit would be canceled.

"Check this out, you go chill with your people tonight, and by the time the party is over, I can be at the hotel, waiting for you, ready to give you something hard to ride on."

My pussy thumped and since I was wearing a dress, I damn sure didn't need my panties to be soaked. Anakin was tempting and he'd really become the best part of my days but I didn't feel comfortable with him being in the city. A wedding may have not been mentioned but I was still very much engaged even without the ring until my brother said other-wise. So that meant Nak and I would just have to keep our, whatever this was, long distance, at least until I could confirm this shit was really off.

Ezio was the man now, he didn't need me anymore. He was rolling with the Rinaldi Mafia heavy, getting money, making a name for himself and all. He didn't need a marriage to get what he wanted and that was some money.

"Anakin, I'ma call you when I get home tonight. I've been sitting in front of this store too long."

"Make sure you don't forget."

"I'm not."

"Aite, handle your business, baby."

Ending the call, I applied a coat of gloss to my lips. The grin above my chin was still there even after the phone call ended. Anakin was different from Ezio in every way. He not only had a successful career and a very bright future, he wasn't with all the fucking games like my appointed fiancé. I hadn't heard a peep from the nigga in months, but with the way his name stayed on these bitches' tongues, I knew my presence wasn't missed.

Pushing the visor closed, I grabbed my purse so that I could run in and grab what I needed. My brother was hosting a kickback at his mansion, and about halfway into the drive, Dasani called me, asking if I could grab two bottles of Hennessey and three Moëts. They hadn't run out but were running low. I wanted to tell her ass to have it DoorDashed or some shit but I agreed.

By the time I was halfway into the commute, I'd remembered her request. Being on the phone with Nak had my mind in a haze. He was the perfect distraction in my crazy world and the fact that he was in another city was a major plus. I had been enjoying my space and silence these past two months and was starting to prefer it.

The weather was okay, so I settled on a denim skater dress that fit at the waist, making my shape pop and was snug at the chest, giving the girls an extra boost. My sew-in was fresh, due to me going to my backup stylist yesterday and the eighteen-inch bundles were curled just right. I loved my heavy side part and the baby hairs framing the side of my face were perfect. On my feet, I kept it simple with white Air Force Ones and the Cuban on my ankle did the simple shoe justice. It wouldn't be me if I didn't rock my ice. Today the Cuban with the tiara dangling from it was my necklace of choice and I left the Audemar at home. I had a delivery the other day and it was a silver Rolex with pink diamonds in the face. I knew it was from my brother, so today, I put that baby to work. She was pretty as fuck on my wrist too. Some days, I couldn't believe that this was my life. I'd gone from costume jewelry from the local beauty supply store to blood diamonds. Crazy how things worked.

Walking inside the liquor store in a nice neighborhood that I was unfamiliar with, I went straight to the aisle where the Hennessey was. You knew you weren't in the hood anytime there wasn't any liquor behind the counter. I'd gotten off on the first exit when I remembered there were things I was asked to grab, and this one was the first to pop up. My GPS told me my brother's house was only seven minutes away so that was a plus.

"Girl, I'm grabbing my liquor now so that I can be good and drunk by the time that nigga gets to my house."

The voice on the other side of the aisle had me envious because when I got home tonight there wouldn't be any dick waiting. Getting head had ruined me. It made me want sex more and knowing I couldn't get it just yet hurt. I just wanted Ezio to stick his face in it one more time but thinking about how the nigga had dismissed me for Olivia had me pissed. The shit was months ago, and I still hadn't let it go. He knew better than to text my phone because I was going to curse his ass the fuck out.

Grabbing what I needed I walked over to the fridge section to get a few more chasers. Dasani had a hired bartender but some of the chasers I wanted ran out too fast for my liking.

"Girl, Ezee is that nigga. When I tell you he be blessing my fucking pockets, I mean that shit. And the dick? Bitch, the dick is so big. I can just have all of his little brown-eyed babies."

The scalp underneath my sew-in heated and my palm moistened as it gripped the handbasket I was holding. Tossing the pineapple juice in the hand basket, I rounded the corner quickly to see who in the fuck was speaking on this nigga. Sucking my teeth, I wasn't surprised to see Olivia. She was bent over with her hand covering her ass. The short black tank dress was almost too small but her tiny ass waist let her pull it off. She must've felt me staring because just as she grabbed what she was looking for, she shot me a glance.

"Oh, hey, Jisei."

Shooting her a toothless smile, I walked right past her ass and paid for my items.

"Let me call you back, girl."

Just as I was swiping my card, Olivia tapped my shoulder.

"You look so cute, boo. You always look cute. I'm trying to be like you when I grow up."

Oh, so that's why you fucking my fiancé?

I had to mentally check myself as Olivia waited for a reply. That girl hadn't done shit to me. It wasn't her fault my fiancé was slanging dick from here to there. She didn't owe me any fucking loyalty. Hell, she didn't even know I was engaged to Ezio.

"Thanks, girl. You be cute too."

"If this nigga I'm fucking with act right, I'ma be on yo' level real soon. I want me some diamond watches, chains, and shit."

Okay, bitch, now you doing too much.

Olivia and I weren't friends, but anytime I was at the Dungeon, she made sure she took care of us and she was always so polite. I'd even asked her who did her braids once and went to the African shop she sent me to. She was a pretty girl who was about her money. She always got good tips from not only us but the other patrons. Like the rest of the waitresses, she was beautiful and had a banging body but she was down to earth. I wanted to kick my own ass because I was the one to hire her. When my brother told his wife he was going to open the Dungeon, he put her in charge of recruiting the waitresses so there wouldn't be any issues and she brought the rest of the mob wives on the judge panel. As soon as Olivia walked in, Dasani said fuck no because she didn't fuck with her vibe.

Me, though, I liked her. She wasn't shy and she had a beautiful body. Of course, I wasn't dating anyone in the mob so I was all for her when the rest of the ladies were ready to pass on her. I thought she was a pretty girl with a nice personality and would be a great addition to the Dungeon. Dasani told me hiring her was going to bite me in the ass and I thought maybe she was being like that because she thought Olivia was going to look at my brother. Now the girl was fucking on my fiancé and there wasn't shit I could do about it.

Grabbing my bags, I turned to make my exit. "Girl, get yo' own paper. These niggas ain't reliable. Enjoy your night, boo. Wrap it up."

Because if you pop up pregnant, I'ma kill you, that nigga, and y'all brown eyed babies. On Folk nem.

Pushing out of the door, her reply was a mumble because of the harsh wind that seemed to come out of nowhere. The clouds were now dark, even though it was only six o'clock. I hopped in my truck and made the quick commute before the rain could come down. I didn't have an umbrella with me, leaving it in the garage by mistake, and didn't want my leave out to be rained on.

I was so lost in my thoughts that I didn't realize I was in the grand entry of my brother's home until Mocha ran up on me, grabbing the bags. Since he had floor-to-ceiling windows, the murky weather from outside poured into his home, casting a grey shield over the walls and floors.

"Friend! You so damn fine! 'Bout time your hard-working ass joined us regular folk!"

Mocha was cute, as always, in a two-piece Emilio Pucci set. Her chocolate skin was made up perfectly and the outfit showed off all of her curves. Instead of sporting diamonds on her neck and wrist, she kept it simple with bling in her ears and on her ring finger. I even loved her long stiletto nails that featured orange diamonds all over them.

"Girl, please! Act like you don't be busy over there being a whole-ass wife. Let me see your nails," Chimo snapped.

I had a backup nail tech and makeup artist just as I did hairstylist for the times Lunar, Bruno, and Chimo weren't available to service us, but Chimo was still the best on the fucking nails. Those three were always on tour with some superstar or hauled away at award shows. I was shocked that they had been available as much as they had been as of late. Don must've been paying them big racks.

"Yeah, I'ma be sick as fuck when he leaves next month. He going on tour with Kitty Kat. I ain't gon' talk too bad because I love me some her, but damn, I'ma miss coming over here and getting pampered. Back to the fucking salons I go."

"Right. I love The Three Musketeers. But you look cute, too, friend. I see it's quiet up here. Who all here? Y'all ate yet?"

I was shooting question after question at my bestie as her fat ass switched in front of me. She was leading me to the lower level where I knew the kickback was being held. My brother only allowed certain members of the mob in his space, which still could be well over a hundred men, and when he did let them come over, their asses were always in the fucking basement. He didn't play that walking through his house shit. I asked him once if he was scared of too many niggas knowing where he laid his head and his reply was, *I ain't scared of shit. Them niggas know not to play where I lay.*

My appetite was gone but the food the chefs were preparing in the kitchen smelled good as hell. I knew they had done their thing.

"Thank you, friend. You know your brother don't play about these niggas being anywhere up here in his house. No, we haven't eaten yet. The servers about to bring the food down shortly, according to Dasani."

Mocha stopped at the elevator, shifted the liquor in her hand, and turned to face me as she waited. I knew her ass wasn't taking the stairs down with those four-inch heels on her feet.

"If you want to know if your man is here all you got to do is ask me that."

"Girl, I am not worried about Ezio. He is not my man, boo."

Mocha twisted her plump lips. "Yeah, he's not your man, he's your fiancé. Now, come on. He not here."

We walked onto the elevator, which featured a mirror for the entire back wall. I checked my appearance as the doors slid close and fixed my hair the wind had blown out of place. By the time the doors opened again, I was on point with glossed lips. Hearing Ezio wasn't in the building ignited rage. If he wasn't here, he was on his way to that hoe Olivia. The possibility had me ready to turn around and find out where she stayed but that nigga was for everybody. Fuck him. I was going to enjoy my night and keep my impending thoughts of Ezio Cuppacio at a minimum. *Or at least try.*

"Ayeeee, we partying with the fucking money team in this bitch!"

Marijuana smoke clouded the entire basement to the point I had to fan in front of my face. I knew my hair was going to smell like pure weed before I left tonight. Just like at the Dungeon, servers were walking around in black catsuits serving drinks. The DJ had the space jumping and all the fine-ass, paid-ass men in the Rinaldi Mob crowded room—some of blood relation to me but most of them not sharing DNA.

A few of them had their women on their arms or dancing in front of them while others stood on a couch, showing their wealth. My brother had turned this basement into a real-life club, with white couches, illuminating blue lights, a dance floor, and the whole nine yards. He had too much money and had proven time and time again that she just be doing dumb shit with it. The lack of budget he put in place for the fake ass wedding that I had yet to get with Daylani about was proof. This kick back was further proof. The party could have been thrown at a rented-out club, or at the Dungeon.

Hitting a few head nods and side hugs as I followed Mocha, we dropped the liquor off at the bar and headed to where I assumed the rest of the ladies were.

"Ohhhh, I can't believe you got out the house tonight!"

Dasani, Scarlett, and two other ladies that I recognized as being mob wives were in a roped-off section, sipping drinks and looking like boatloads of money. I hugged them all before taking a spot sandwiched between Mocha and Scarlett.

The DJ had the spot jumping and the setting would put any club in Jagoda Bay to shame. Three men walked by and I must've been staring a little too long because Dasani leaned over Scarlett and whispered in my ear, "That fine, grey-eyed nigga is Goal Navarro. He is head of the Navarro Cartel. The younger one that looks just like him is his little brother but his young ass is still in high school and shouldn't even be down here. The dark-skinned nigga is Jett, his shooter."

My brother did business with all types of men and most of them were fine as hell. That must've been a requirement -- easy on the eyes, big dick energy and loaded pockets in order to get next to Don Demise Rinaldi. I'm sure it wasn't but being that every time I looked up my brother was surrounded by somebody fine, the theory had to hold some truth.

"I heard Goal with Aphrodite. You know that girl that owns the online boutique? The one whose baby died those years ago?" One of the wives chimed in, letting Dasani know she wasn't as discreet as she thought.

"Oh yeah, her clothes be so cute. I said I was going to place an order," Mocha added as she sipped and danced in her seat.

"I love my man, but they all fine as hell," the other wife added.

That they were. Fly as hell, dazzled in diamonds like the rest of the men in the space and walking in the room like they owned this bitch. That Aphrodite was a lucky ass woman.

"Anyway, that is who your weak ass fiancé been copping from. That's who your brother plugged him in with."

Dasani's revelation put the puzzle pieces together. I knew I had heard of Goal. He was fine, but taken niggas weren't my type nor were the ones with colored eyes. I already had one cat-eye nigga on my shit list and had no qualms about adding another.

We all watched as Goal and the guys walked by until my brother appeared out of nowhere, shaking it up with him and then mugging us. We all fell out laughing.

"Don done caught y'all asses." Mocha snickered like her ass hadn't been watching the fine ass men too.

"I'm about to use the bathroom and see if some food came down here. I can't drink on an empty stomach."

I still didn't have much of an appetite but I would rather force down some food instead of having a hangover. Lately, liquor has been doing me bad. It's been putting me on my ass for days at a time and with my workload, I couldn't afford to be in bed for two to three days.

On the way to the bar, I'd almost run into a waitress who looked so much like Olivia, that my heart skipped a beat. I was still on edge about our encounter at the liquor store. She just knew in her heart that Ezio was going to whisk her off into the sunset and spoil her with diamonds, pearls, and whatever else it was that gold digging bitches yearned for these days. News-flash, the nigga was engaged and had gone months without even saying a word to me. Had he given me money since we'd met? Yes. It wasn't shit to brag about though. The money was for me to buy my own damn ring, which he had to be smoking that shit Bobby was if he thought I would do some stupid shit like that.

"A peach lemon drop, please."

I waited as the bartender prepared my drink. I also instructed her to make it with Titos. I was keeping it light tonight. I'd signed up for a Pilates class tomorrow and was already regretting it. I at least wanted to be able to get up at seven in the morning without a headache.

When the bartender slid me my drink, I pulled my phone out, snapped a cute picture for my stories, and licked the sugar around the rim before consuming it. Not only was it cold but she'd made it with the perfect mixture of sugar and tart from the peaches and lemons. The liquor was plentiful, and I knew that one more of these would put me on my level.

Aunt Polene loved her a cute drink. Before she became sick, she would always make her own cocktails at home. Before lemon drops trended, Aunt Polene was on them. She always said, *Heavy liquor does nothing but put weight on you and make you a prisoner to your feelings. Cute drinks make you feel good, and you always want to feel good.* Aunt Polene ain't never lied about that, except I was already in my feelings, heavy.

Before I knew it, I'd ordered another Lemon drop this time holding the peaches adding a double shot and when that one was finished, seeing our section flooded with the husbands, I ordered another. The bar was an open one with the bartender only accepting tips. By the time I was at the end of my third glass, I'd made her fifty dollars richer. So much for not getting drunk. I told myself that I was going to lay off the liquor and that shit went out the window the moment I tasted my first drink. I was just going to make sure I ate some fried chicken and a B/C powder pack before I left.

My thudding bladder reminded me that I really did have to pee, so I stood and walked up the stairs to my niece's room instead of using the bathroom downstairs. I loved her bathroom. She was at the beginning stages of potty training and in addition to a normal toilet, Don had her a training potty added to her bathroom except it looked like a whole throne. It was too cute.

Making my way up the stairs, a waitress passed by me, holding plates of fried wings. I grabbed two from her and prayed that it was ranch in the small plastic condiment cups on the clear plate. The smell of grease and seasonings made my stomach growl. I couldn't wait to dig in. Taking the long walk to her room was a blissful journey. Their house was too big for no reason, but I loved everything about it. Anytime I was here, it made me wonder how life would have been if I had grown up in this mob shit instead of poor with Aunt Polene.

Don't get me wrong, life was good with my auntie, but death, heartbreak, and making ends meet were normal for us. Even after Aunt Polene died, I struggled. No matter how hard I worked or how many scholarships I acquired to cover tuition it was never enough. I was always robbing Peter to pay Paul. I did that shit so much that after a while I didn't even stress out about it. Paying my sorority dues had me taking out payday loans, but back then, having a sisterhood made me feel like I wasn't alone. Sometimes, I thought back to when I had nothing and remembered how much I smiled. I was always everywhere even without a car. Popping Red Bull after Red Bull, I didn't miss out on anything even if I had to pull a triple shift the week before to be able to fund it. Now, I had everything. The watch on my wrist probably cost my entire degree. The painting that sat above my niece's crib more than likely was someone's entire life expenses and this house was a dream that people would only step foot in if they closed their eyes.

After a long life of struggling, I wanted for nothing. There were many days Aunt Polene and I had to walk miles to the bus stop and the whole time, my real father was somewhere stuffing his face with lobsters surrounded by a room full of deadly mobsters. That reality was hard to grasp.

I would be crying over Bobby, who didn't have a dime because he smoked it all, wishing he would get clean and just be my dad, and the entire time, my biological father was swimming in wealth in a whole other state. How in the fuck did my mama even get with him? When did she have time to make me when she was with Bobby? According to Bobby, before he chose drugs, he and my mom were madly in love. I hadn't really met her to get her side of the story, but anytime he spoke of her, you could see the love in his eyes. He loved my mother, dearly. So why in the fuck did she fuck Demise's daddy and make me?

There were so many questions, and no one could answer them because they were in the dirt or high out of their mind. But one question constantly circled in my mind and it was one that I could answer. I smiled so much before all of this and I was living in a roach-infested apartment and taking the bus and now that I drove a six-figure car, I rarely smiled. I had my dream job, made great money, and had a seven-figure bank account. Still, some days I felt like I was drowning. Was this what it was like to be a part of the elite? My thoughts ran wild with what ifs and whys but I wanted to know if I was smiling before to laugh to keep from crying? Was I ever really happy or was I putting on? Was I putting on a smile to hide the scars and to keep myself pushing?

Looking back almost two years ago, it was hard for me to sort out my feelings. Was it all a lie back then and now that I was living in truth, was I self-sabotaging? I worked hard for this. Maybe not for private parties with unlimited booze and more diamonds than I deserved but I worked hard to push myself out of poverty. Why was I not happy? Standing over my niece's crib and biting down on a chicken wing I didn't have the answer but the thudding in my heart did. She just wasn't telling it to me. The only person these days who brought me true peace and happiness was Delicate Mafia Rinaldi.

The creaking of the door behind me should have had me jumping but it didn't. Was it bad that I could sense him before he reached for the gold doorknob? Anytime he was near, my senses went haywire. I could smell from my eyes, see from my nose, hear from my mouth, and talk from my ears when he was in range. It didn't make any sense but that was how he made me feel. Was the attraction artificial? Was I only smitten by his good looks and thuggish demeanor? I didn't fucking know but I did know he made me feel something and the shit wasn't good.

"You can get the fuck out of my niece's room."

He shut the door behind him, while I had my back to him still. Turning, being sure not to face him, I walked over to the changing station and set the plates of chicken down. Nelsa kept this place smelling like fresh lemons. My niece was smitten with her nanny, and I had half a mind to go over to Azure and Big Zan's house and pick my baby up. The kids mostly spent their time over at their house with the nannies and babysitters when there was an event or an outing. Their mansion was like a big ass playground.

"Fuck I tell you about tweaking for?"

His heavy ass sneakers sounded off as he walked toward me and the soft chanting of his jewelry could be heard too. There was a tingling in the pit of my stomach, but at the same time, something in his manner soothed me. Ezio was an ain't shit nigga who should have had me running for the hills and I had been, but anytime he was around, I folded like laundry. I was drunk and in my feelings, so I wasn't even going to fight it. If he wanted to devour my pussy, I was going to let him. I was going to have to help Nelsa bleach my niece's room right after, but I was letting him use his mouth to calm me.

Gripping the wood of the furniture, I pushed my chin into my chest and sighed. I tried to steady my breathing as the growing fire sprawled all over my body, but it was no use. Ezio was right on me, and though his body wasn't pressed against mine, if I moved back an inch, my back would be in his chest.

"You look good." His voice was raspier than usual, and he almost slurred his words. He was drunk, or high, or both. If I turned around to look into his eyes, I would see that the brown, orange, and green were surrounded by red with a heavy lid covering them.

"I know that. Can you leave?"

"Nawl. I can't."

Figured.

"That watch looks good on you."

"I know that too. Big girl shit. Something your hoes wish they had. Something cheap ass niggas like you don't know about unless you doing it for yourself."

"You call me cheap, and I been constantly breaking you off? I'm a lot of things, Jisei, but cheap ain't never been one."

"Yeah, okay."

Just eat my pussy and roll, so when you go over that bitch's house she can smell me on your breath.

"Turn around."

My body obeyed even if my mind didn't want to, and a gasp followed. He was damn near in my skin and looking so fucking good. New money looked damn good on him. He looked like that nigga when he first came around, but he was really holding now. *Oh Lord, no wonder why the bitches were on him.*

Ezio traced his finger from my throat to my shoulder bone, then trailed it down my arm before holding my wrist up. The pink diamond watch sparkled in the dimly lit room, making the bling in his mouth and on his wrist. His watch almost matched mine but was bigger and had clear diamonds. We were glittering up the room with stones that cost no telling how much and the shit aided in my thudding pussy.

"You want me to fuck you so bad."

"You wish. I went a year without dick; you a damn fool if you think I'ma give it up to the new nigga in the city that's a pussy hound. You not fena put yo' demonized spirits inside of me. My life complicated enough." I gasped as he kissed the skin above my watch.

"If shit was different, I would love the fuck out of you. Since it ain't. I'ma just settle for spoiling you and enjoying seeing you cum on occasion."

"Ezio—"

"Shut the fuck up."

My lips clamped as he pushed my skirt up, the contact making my skin burn with desire. When he hooked my panties and thrust them down, the weight from my secretion pushed them to the floor and I stepped out of them and kicked them aside. His hand swept over my bald pussy as sticky goo gathered in between my thighs.

"You always look good and smell even better. Skin so fucking soft and pretty."

"I—"

"Didn't I tell you to shut the fuck up?"

Ezio puckered his lips and placed a kiss on my forehead and another on my nose. He'd done that to me on a few occasions and the simple notion was the most intimate thing I'd ever experienced with someone. I wondered if there was any meaning behind it but was to turned on to ask. A moan escaped my lips as he flipped me around, rough as shit, almost breaking my kneecap when it hit against the changing station.

"Oh, shit!"

Ezio spread my ass cheeks, a zipper was heard, and then he thrust himself inside of me.

"Hold up, shiiiiiit! Fuckkkk, Ezio! Back out some!"

Long. Veiny. Curved. Heavy.

"I ain't even all the way in yet. Take this dick." He grunted.

Not even all the way in? *Impossible.* The way he filled my walls to capacity as my mouth hung, struggling to breath told a different story. His large hand took the back of my neck and held it with a grip. He pushed himself inside of my tightness, and while it was painful, it was also fulfilling. Ezio rammed his way in with a roughness that went with his aura while I moaned all types of obscenities. Twisting underneath him and arching my back, I sought to get free, but at the same time, anticipated the dick he served up. Ezio was so big, so long, so thick. His dick matched his demeanor. Big dick, big pockets, big fucking ego.

Our bodies moved in harmony as he fucked me from behind with bent knees. The thrusting of his force made the changing station scrape across the marble floors, but it didn't go far because it was propped up against the wall. I knew we shouldn't be doing this and I told myself he wasn't going to explore my sacred tunnel but my desire for him overrode everything else. I was so wet for him as I drowned him in my juices and his grunts let me know that I felt as good to him as he did to me.

"Throw this big ass back, baby. Fuuuuck!"

I did just that. There wasn't much room between us, but I threw it back as he wrapped my weave around his hand. My hair was still tight from it only being a few days old, but he wasn't pulling so hard, as if he was ripping the follicles from my scalp. The chant of ecstasy slipped through my lips as passion seeped through my veins. I was roused to the peak of desire as he busted my pussy open with his heavy-ass dick. He had no business being this big. He had no business fucking this good. He fucked with a raw act of possession that left me yearning, even though he was still deep in my taut walls. If this was what his dick felt like, I could clearly see why the bitches in the city, Olivia included, went mad over him. He had the looks that made you act a fool, but he had the dick that would turn you into a straight-up goofy.

Clenching my pussy muscles as my orgasm brewed, I cried out as tears gathered at my lids. I held them in, though, but he felt *amazing*.

"Where you want this nut?"

"Fuuuuuuck! I'on carrrreeeeeee. I'm cumming!"

His pumps grew harder and faster, and it only sped my bliss up. This shouldn't be this way. He wasn't supposed to make me bow down with what he toted in his pants. I wasn't ready to give in to this nigga but with the way my legs were shaking, told him I had lost the battle. He'd won.

"Ohmygosssssshhhhhhhh!"

"Un hunh, gosh sounds too much like Josh and that nigga, whoever he is, ain't fucking you. Ezio is. Tell me you love me, baby."

The table was banging hard against the wall and wouldn't hold up much longer.

"I... fuuuuck... I love you, Ezio! I loooove youuuuu!"

I loved the dick for sure. The dick was impossible not to love. The dick deserved a Nobel peace prize. The dick needed to be cut off, placed on ice, shipped to a lab, and studied. The cloning shit the government did needed to include Ezio's long, veiny, heavy, curved tool and if they pulled duplicating it off, all bitches would be satisfied. Even the ones that loved to munch on pussy.

"Fuck, Jisei!"

I felt him fill me up with his seeds as I caught my breath. This man had fucked me senseless on a fucking changing table.

"And before I pull my dick out you, my cheap ass bought that fucking watch. Stop giving your fucking brother credit for shit that's all me, twin. Keep yo' ass up here, wifey. You full of my seeds so you need to get acquainted with cribs and rocking chairs and shit anyway, Jae Bae."

Ezio removed his dick from my middle, causing me to wince, and slapped my ass so hard I was sure he broke skin. My elbows were still resting on the table as I caught my breath. I wasn't obeying that nigga but my eyes were too heavy to even go back downstairs. I was going to push his nut out of me and take my ass to sleep, praying that this shit would be a nightmare by the time I woke up. Thank God, I wasn't ovulating. This nigga didn't need to breed no more big dick replicas. And who the fuck was Jae Bae?

CHAPTER 13
JISEI "JAE BAE" RINALDI

Days later...

When I got to work, my team had been going frantic, trying to make sure we were on track to reach the quarter goals. We still had more than six weeks left in the current quarter but we needed to have everything aligned for the companies we'd been assigned to so that we could start planning for the next.

The ride home was quiet. Traffic had me on a longer ride than usual, but it seemed as the days went on, Jagoda Bay was becoming more and more populated.

Ignoring the grumbling in my stomach, I pulled into my driveway and killed the engine. I didn't even have the energy to let the garage up. Combining the weekend with today, I was officially beat. After kicking my shoes off in the foyer, I removed my pants, dropped them somewhere on the way to the couch, and fell on the sofa. As of late, my blouse and panties were my favorite loungewear. I'd ignored calls from everyone, including my brother, only sending them texts to let them know I was alive but just busy with work.

After the weekend and waking up on the floor of my niece's room, I was not only embarrassed but realized I had to get a handle on myself. I was losing myself behind this nigga and it was starting to show. I should have never got the dick. The dick and the head combo was lethal, and the fact that the nigga nutted and got the fuck on, leaving me on the carpet said a lot. I'd hoped there wasn't a nanny cam in there because my brother was liable to kill us if he saw the nigga slutting me out while bent over Delicate's shit station. Thanks to Ezio, even before the party, I'd been in my feelings hard as of late, and as a person who was always happy and smiling, I hated that for me.

I regretted to admit that the source of my problems derived from one person—Ezio. He was the same nigga who hadn't said a fucking peep to me in two months, but the moment I got in the room with him, folded like a collar. What the fuck? Shouldn't no nigga have all that power. I was embarrassed. What if, after he fucked me, he went and laid with the next hoe? She was all in the liquor store, talking about how he was on his way to her. Niggas was nasty like that. Sticking their dick in one woman and heading to the next drenched in coochie juices and knocking PH balances off in the process. We hadn't used nobodies condom so I was praying a scent didn't follow in the upcoming days. A man who could make go against all that you stood for was a dangerous man.

Two months ago, when he was smiling all up in Olivia's face, I wanted to knock his ass out. He was the main one saying as long as I didn't disrespect him, he wouldn't disrespect me. He was basically fucking the bitch in my face and then he had the nerve to smell like pussy. When she confirmed that he'd been intimate with her, I wanted to scream. Then seeing her the other night, knowing they had still been kicking it had me seething. Instead of standing on business, I let this nigga bend me over and fuck me silly. That was exactly what I was, a silly ass hoe. I was constantly letting this nigga toy with me. Shit was so humiliating, but I couldn't blame anyone but myself.

I could easily reach out to Ezio and tell him I didn't want him fucking with Olivia, especially when he asked me what he could do to get me to stop tweaking, but I wasn't that girl. This was an arranged marriage, and since he made it clear that he could do what the fuck he wanted by popping his shit all around the city, I could do what the fuck I wanted too. Except, I had no interest in playing get back with my pussy. My girl was not only my temple, but she didn't even get wet for every man just because he was fine and paid. My rose did the job until I found someone to take her spot. I just knew for sure it wasn't going to be Ezio. Until the other night, I had been doing so damn good. I couldn't let his dick enter me again. I just had to tell my pussy that so she wouldn't leak like a busted pipe anytime he was near.

It was absurd how now that I'd gotten the dick Ezio and Olivia being together wouldn't leave my brain. I'd heard he'd been with all types of women in the last few months. Every bitch wanted a piece of the new guy but my sights were set on ole girl. I didn't know Olivia personally and she always did her job, but I saw the way the men fawned over her at the Dungeon. I knew she was fucking with a few of them, and hell, I couldn't blame her. The who's fucking who frequented the spot and could easily change someone like Olivia's life. Hell, she confirmed that she hoped Ezio was that one.

During one of our talks, she told me she worked at a clinic as a medical assistant during the week and did the Dungeon on the weekends. She had been so grateful for me hiring her and voiced it every chance she got. I was salty that she was fucking with Ezio, and I wasn't even sure why I was salty, to begin with, but I wasn't a hater ass bitch. I wouldn't dare play with that girl's job. I'd been a working girl once, just trying to make a way, and would have been pissed if my boss's sister had some one-sided beef with me and played with my pockets. So, I wished them well but that friendly shit we had going on was dead and that nigga and his bipolar ways was dead too. Fuck them both. *Big dick bitch ass nigga.*

My eyes began to grow heavy, and just when I was about to give in to sleep, my doorbell sounded off. Groaning, sleep still weighing on me, I went to the door and snatched it open, not remembering that I wasn't wearing pants until it was too late.

"Ugh. Good thing we didn't have your niece and nephew with us. What if we would have been the Amazon driver?"

Playfully rolling my eyes, I stood aside and let Mocha and Scarlett in. While I had just been dressed in slacks, they looked like they'd just come from a Pilates class in their matching workout gear, but the Chanel sneakers on their feet, perfect hair, and no sweat in sight let me know they'd probably either just left shopping or eating or both. There were plenty of days they asked me to play hooky and ditch work while I ran the city with their married, rich asses, but I declined. I loved my job and I loved waking up every day having something to do and somewhere to go, even if it exhausted me from time to time.

"Y'all both have seen me naked before. Now get in here before I give ole Joe across the street a heart attack."

My neighbor Joe was a retired psychologist. He was divorced and had children my age. They were nice enough and Joe watched my house, so I loved that. Joe and Glow were my two favorites out of everyone on my street. The rest of my neighbors minded their business and hadn't said much to me outside of an occasional wave.

"Please get in the house because I would hate to have to have Renzo and Matteo over here on his old ass head for being a creep."

I wanted to tell them that Mr. Joe had more sex than me with the number of women he had running in and out of his house, but I let it be. I respected the fact that he dated his age and was kind to me and my neighbor, making us feel comfortable with having an older man live near us, even though we were both two single, young girls. He put me in the mind of Mr. Gerald at my job. Older men with their life together, loving on their kids and family always brought me back to Bobby, but with Ezio running rampage in my thoughts, I had no room for Bobby and his crackhead antics.

Taking the lead, I headed to my room to slide on a pair of leggings and a big T-shirt while I heard the girls in the kitchen. It was rare that they came over, but since I'd been ignoring everybody for two days, I knew it wouldn't be long before somebody popped up. I was surprised in the two months I'd been MIA that they hadn't dragged my ass out of the house. It was like since they had seen my face at the kickback, me hiding out was done for. But as long as it wasn't my brother popping in, it was all good. I could deal with Scarlett and Mocha. Hell, I wouldn't even have this house if it wasn't for Mocha buying it and Scarlett was responsible for helping me furnish the place and giving me my first car. My girls could pop up whenever they wanted to.

After getting comfortable, I got my charger from behind my nightstand because, last I checked, it was dead. When I made it back to the living room, Mocha had opened a bottle of wine and had three glasses already poured and Scarlett was setting out three plates of Chinese rice. I must have really been sleepy when I opened the door because I didn't see takeout in either of their hands. I was hungry, so I wasn't complaining, and looking at the house fried rice and egg roll on my plate, I was ready to dive in. I'd planned on ordering DoorDash after my nap if it wasn't too late when I woke up, but the dinner my girls brought was right on time.

I hadn't even taken a full bite before Mocha started her shit.

"So, you got fucked at the party."

Scarlett's eyes bulged and she shoulder-bumped Mocha to get her to shut up, but that didn't stop shit. Mocha kept on.

"Fuck that. She's been acting funny since Friday. I know I seen that nigga head behind her. So, what the fuck we do to you? Or what the fuck he do to you? Y'all fucked in your brother's house, hunh?"

I made sure to take a few more bites while they both waited for me to give them an answer. The anticipation had them on the edge of their seats. My friends were spoiled as hell. They spent their days being pretty and spending money while raising their kids, and while one may have thought that was a full-time job, to a Rinaldi woman, it wasn't. They had nannies, maids, chefs, and their men to make their lives easier. To be frank, my girls lived like princesses and had a lot of free time on their hands, so that meant they spent their free time with me. I couldn't go a day to myself without them being brats. But me getting fucked and ducked definitely was the reason I didn't answer my phone on Saturday when they tried to get me to come to the Dungeon, and Sunday when I skipped brunch.

Picking up the wine glass, I took a sip of the cold, burgundy potency. Giulia wine. It was the best around and Mocha finding out there were restaurants in it's franchise had me excited to fly out and give them a try one day.

"Okay."

"Okay what, bitch? Did y'all fuck?"

"Mocha, let her get it out." Scarlett smiled at me, encouraging me to finish.

"Right, bitch. Let me talk. But work has been—"

"Bitch, miss me. You love that ugly ass job. It don't have shit to do with that. You was just fine on Friday until you weren't!"

"Do you need to take some time off? We can fly out to an island for a week and unwind," Scarlett offered.

My friend was so kind. She'd come a long ass way from the girl who had been pimped out by her mother. There were days when she had to use my phone because she didn't have one on her own but now she was ready to fly me out on a jet to some tropical paradise.

"As bad as I want to take you up on your offer—"

"It's not work, it's the nigga." Mocha stuffed a fork full of rice in her mouth, abandoning her chopsticks. I knew she knew how to use them because she'd been the one to teach me.

"Okay, fine. Me and Ezio did have sex."

Scarlett's eyes grew as she sat up on the couch and Mocha squealed.

"Told you it was the nigga. Was the dick good? Bitch, he broke your virginity!"

"Woah. You know I done had my fair share of dick, so he didn't break shit, but we did fuck. Sorry, Scarlett, if it's weird."

"It is," she admitted. "But you're my friend, so I will just have to keep the visual out of my head," She groaned.

"Fuck all that. Is his dick big?"

My cheeks burned and gave the answer before I could. I could still feel his dick in my guts three days later, so damn right it's big. Too big. So big that I had been popping four Tylenols a day since Friday. Two to start my day and two to end it. It was torcher walking around all day with a numb pussy scraping against slacks. Maybe Mocha was right, he did break my virginity which was impossible. He broke something and I was waiting for the pains to subside, or I would have to buy another bottle of Tylenol.

"Ohhh, my bitch got a big dick, rich nigga. He done turned up in the city! Everybody knows that nigga's name."

"And that's why we not going to work," I spat.

"Wait. So, you aren't marrying him anymore?"

"My brother hadn't brought up a wedding and I hadn't really talked to Ezio in months before Saturday. Like Mocha said, he's the man now. The mob accepted him without having to be married to me so, it is what it is. Scarlett, I know that's your cousin, but I got to keep my distance from him. I can see me now, losing my mind and freedom behind him."

"Gurl, first off, your brother is the Don. You will never lose your damn freedom. Now, losing your mind? You just might do that and it has nothing to do with Ezio. That shit is hereditary. Your brother or his cousin aren't wrapped too tight. Now, the dick? The dick done drove you crazy. It be the thug ass niggas every single time. But I really thought y'all was good. Y'all look so good together. Like some hood mafia royalty. Diamonds blinging and matching watches and shit."

I still couldn't believe he bought the watch. How in the hell did he buy a watch but not a ring? The shit was backward and showed just how much an idiot Ezio was.

"Well, the nigga ain't for me."

"If the dick got you like this, imagine the mouth."

"Girl, I been burnt his head."

"What? When?"

"A while ago."

"The fucking Netflix and chill day?"

"How do you even remember that?" Scarlett asked.

"I don't forget shit. But my bitch legit now. Aw, he ate your pussy? He's really about to be possessive over your ass now."

I almost said the nigga didn't give a damn about me because he was busy fucking the city, but I really had to stop telling them all my damn business. Who was I kidding? I had no one else to tell unless I counted Aunt Polene's tombstone.

"I can't do him y'all. Look, a while back, I saw him all up in one of the waitresses' faces. He's fucking her. I heard her talk about it the other day. He was all over her at the Dungeon, even when she was telling him to let her do her job."

Recanting the shit had me pissed. I didn't know why in the hell I was so upset behind a man I'd only been in the same room with a total of seven times. All seven times this man had turned me on and pissed me off. The seventh time he'd fucked me silly but still, I was over him. A man who could only stand there and be a fuck nigga but had the ability to make you see red for no damn reason was a nigga I didn't want no parts of.

"Okay, friend, and hear me out when I say this."

Mocha took a sip of her wine.

"You know I been working on my maturity and shit, so correct me at any point if I'm wrong."

I nodded for Mocha to proceed. It wasn't like if I didn't nod her ass was just going to shut up. If it was on Mocha's brain, she was letting it come out.

"Okay, I know this is an arranged marriage, but you have expressed that you wanted to continue to do you. You even said you'd started back dating Anakin, which I still can't see how that shit is working because, to my knowledge, you don't want that man and he lives in a whole other city. You and Ezio aren't together. This is just a fake marriage, so why do you care what he does, friend, unless you like him more than you letting on? You fucked him after being celibate for a year, so tell me you not feeling him."

Sucking my teeth, I looked away, taking my attention off my gorgeous friends, and glanced at the mantle above the fireplace. Sitting on the butcher block were framed pictures of me and Aunt Polene, my diploma, and my degree. Also, my promotion plaque was up there. Ezio wasn't lying when he said everything about me, my life was on the mantle. Even pictures of my niece, god babies, girls, and one single picture of my brother and me. It was a selfie I took last fourth of July. I was so drunk I didn't remember taking it. We'd just really found out we were siblings, and I snapped the picture. I couldn't believe he had let me. Don wasn't the type of man that had pictures of himself floating around. There weren't really any of him on Dasani's social media.

"I don't know. I mean. I do like him. I think. But then I don't like him... I really don't know him. He just be making me so mad. I feel like he only fucking with me because he needs me to tie this union. Marrying me will change his life. The nigga don't really know me but always acting like I'm everything in my face but then he goes ghost for weeks like I'm nothing. I feel like he playing me," I admitted.

"He isn't. You just said yourself that he is the man out here now. He was seeing money back home but out here he's really getting it. All this happened and you two still aren't married yet. Don hasn't mentioned a wedding as of late and Ezio is still in your face. That says a lot. I think you both are stubborn and stuck in your ways. Ezio is more of an observer. You may think he doesn't know you friend but he does. That's why he is such a good leader. He takes things in, studies it, and applies it however he can."

"I know the nigga fine. I hate to keep saying that, but all the Cuppacio men are so good-looking. They just come in all delicious ass flavors and that is saying a lot because I very much think my chocolate ass husband is the finest out here. But you're fine as hell too. One of the baddest if not the baddest. There is no reason you are in here dodging the world because he won't text or call. You can have any man you want, friend."

I knew I was good-looking. One of the reasons I'd been celibate was because of who I was attached to, I didn't want to get the wrong man. My brother was everything to me and though men tried to holla on the daily, I felt it was best I cool it on them. I was the shit and I knew it. There was no topping me in my opinion and it had nothing to do with me being a mafia princess. I'd always been that girl even when I was rocking dirty ass Keds. But then, I could maybe be feeling myself thinking every man was attracted to me because with Ezio around he looked straight through my ass at times. One moment he would be all up on me and the next, standoffish. Yes, he complimented me, yes he was touchy-feely, yes he ate my pussy, yes he fucked me hard and raw but what did that mean? He hadn't called, texted, took me on a date, or put a ring on my finger.

"Jisei, I am not making an excuse for him non whatsoever. I know I will have to be very careful on the topic of your new fiancé because he is my blood, and my opinions may not mean too much of shit when it comes to him. However, I will say, I know he has been through a lot. I didn't really tell y'all much about when I ran to Chicago to be with my family that time."

"Yeah bitch, you were dead ass wrong, and you and I weren't even close like that. My mama was missing Princess so bad. "

"I went to stay with Ezio as you know with the hopes of reuniting with my long-lost family. The memories I had of my family were all of us being spoiled, living in big homes, and playing together. In my mind, we had the best lives but that wasn't the case. I don't know all the details of Ezio's life but I know it was nothing like mine. He knew and saw things I didn't and I'm sure many of those things were some he shouldn't have even been exposed to back then. Ezio, Shio, Vello, and Nel all were always the closest. So I know they know what goes on in his head and I know it isn't pretty but he's a good person. He cares so much about his family and has really made a nice life for everyone back home. He is the type that will sacrifice everything just for the sake of the remaining Cuppacios. You both have been through a lot. Him flaunting a woman in your face ain't cool though even if this is just an arranged marriage. Boundaries gotta be set. You be upfront about what you will accept and what you won't accept. Or you both just treat this like what it is. A business transaction. No more sex. That way, no feelings are involved. Marry him for the sake of playing your role in the mob and keep on with your life. Nothing has to change but your last name."

"Hell. That shit sounds like hell. I wish Lorenzo would."

"Yes, I agree it does sound like hell. But the both of you are more alike than you realize."

"Hunh? How so?"

"You both will sacrifice yourselves for the sake of your family. He is doing this for the endless opportunities it will award the Cuppacios and you will stop at nothing to make sure your only living family is happy with you. Honestly, I can think of worse things. Ezio is handsome, protective, smart, and good company. If he wants to see other women, it's nothing you can do if you not tryna put your foot down."

Men only do what you allow. Give him an inch, he gon' take a mile. If he wants to be a fucking inchworm, let his ass be and you go get the biggest snail on the block.

"What the hell you smiling at?"

"Nothing just thinking of something my auntie said."

"Oh, I thought that was your Rinaldi side coming out. But God rest Aunt Polene's soul. I wish I would have met her. She had the sayings for days, chile."

"I guess you right, Scar." I sighed.

I didn't know why I was tripping behind a man when Anakin's paid ass was on my line ready to fly out soon as I gave the word. He was cool people and as of late, he hadn't even been talking about himself. He'd been sending me pictures from the various food places around Memphis and I couldn't lie like the shit didn't look good. I'd been crappy to him because I was too focused on a man that was only marrying me to secure his fucking pockets and I had one whose pockets were already secured. Anakin had a big dick and even bigger pockets. He was established in life, handsome, and college-educated. *But his dick didn't have shit on Ezio's.*

"Yeah just do you. Fuck the shit out of Anakin's corporate ass since the celibacy streak is broken. You can't be around town with him but the fact that Anakin lives in another city is a plus. Get you some dick and let Ezio do what the fuck he does with the waitress. I hope he strapping up because them waitresses is pass arounds. Which one is it? And did y'all use protection?"

"I didn't see her face and hell yes we did. Don't play with me," I lied. I lied so fucking hard that my face hurt from trying to force the expression of offense. I didn't know why I was saving Olivia but she didn't deserve to be treated poorly because my so-called fiancé was a hoe. As far as the raw dick, I had already made an appointment to the clinic. If this nigga had burnt me, on folk nem, he was a dead nigga.

"Umm okay. Don't be pregnant on your wedding day now."

"Who? I bet not ever! And it may not even be a wedding. But you right, Moke, I'm just going to do me. I'll fuck with Anakin. He been begging me, anyway." I licked my tongue out when I was really low key crying inside.

Putting my empty plate down, I picked my phone up and

went to my text threads. Just like clockwork, Anakin was the last to text me.

Anakin: How was work? Would you like me to order you some dinner?

"Listen. Please do not listen to Mocha. I know Ezio will never touch you but he killed his girlfriend in cold blood. The bitch deserved it, for sure, but just as your brother has loose screws and Matteo and Lorenzo, so does Ezio. Just get married and live a beautiful life of celibacy. You did it for a year, you can do it again. It's not worth it, friend."

"Girl, you sound dumb as hell. You getting fucked every night and gon' tell our friend to be celibate. After getting grade A dick from a Chicago baller, she gon' be craving some thug lovin'. Friend is a hard-working, fine-ass, bad-ass, rich-ass bitch. Fuck yo' cousin and his elephant dick. If the nigga can fuck hoes, my friend can fuck 'em too. Matter of fact, let's go to the club this weekend. Fuck that, let's do that shit in another city! We having our fucking way out here! You don't sit up in the house and be sick over no nigga that wants to pass up on the princess just to fuck with the help. You can have any nigga you want, in or out of this city. Fuck him, friend. Where you want to go? Vegas? Cali? Dubai? The fuck! We can do what we want, and you can have who you want. Don't ever forget that shit. You doing this nigga a favor. Without you, ain't no merge!"

Scarlett was right. Ezio was out of his mind. I'd seen him pull a gun out on a random man at the Spot Bar and Grill and he looked like he was definitely going to pull the trigger. Then he fucked me in my brother's house. He had a few loose screws. But where he was crazy, my brother was crazier, so I wasn't worried. I was siding with Mocha this time though. Mocha was talking my language. Scarlett was scared of her nigga anyway, as she should be, but Mocha had a bit more leeway with Lorenzo.

"I can't go out this weekend, but next weekend, I'll be ready."

"What the fuck you doing this weekend?"

Me: Come see me this weekend.

"Me. I'm doing me this weekend."

Anakin: Booking my flight now, beautiful.

Ezio thinks he can just pass me up? Cool. I can trip right on the next man's dick. Fuck what I was spitting earlier, playing revenge with the pussy was the move.

CHAPTER 14
EZIO "EZEE" CUPPACIO

Fighting a yawn, my back was posted on the brick wall behind me. To my left, were the twins, and to my right, was Shio. We were all in the warehouse where our training had been taking place for the last few weeks. I was over this shit, but I would never voice that. Getting up at three in the morning to make it here at four was for the fucking birds. As a matter of fact, the birds weren't even out yet. It was still dark outside, as it had been every day that we'd been training. I'd never woken up this early in my fucking life before this. When I was rolling, there were times I did all-nighters, but sober, I wasn't out the bed earlier than nine.

The training was kicking our asses, but the money had been rolling the fuck in. A nigga had been seeing so much paper that it was almost unreal. Copping from the Cartel was love. It was a street nigga's dream come true. When Don plugged a nigga in, that was all his ass did. I had to put up my own paper, which was cool. My cousins and I all put up bread and copped fifty birds. It damn near wiped us out but we'd made our money back times twenty.

At first, we didn't know where we would slang the shit, but the mob turned out to be our biggest customers. Them niggas didn't sniff the shit but they got it off. I was shocked that Don hadn't put them on to the cartel. So, I was their plug, and those niggas made selling this shit easy as fuck.

"I see you muthafuckas came back."

Don walked in the room and instead of his eyes being on any of the twenty men in the room, they were on me. I know he expected a nigga to break. He expected me to just say fuck this shit, but he didn't know me. I was the nigga who did the impossible. When I set my mind to do some shit, I treated it like it was do or die. I got the shit done by any means. So, if it meant I had to keep coming out here, proving myself to this nigga, then that was what the fuck I would do. I knew in the back of his mind, he still looked at me as a fucking Cuppacio. Which, by blood, I was. But we were the new wave of Cuppacios and we didn't back down from shit.

"I'm everywhere you at, Don," I taunted.

A few of the men around the room who had been placed in training with us laughed, making Don look around the warehouse with a snarl. Every day, all these men who I learned were thorough ass niggas from around the world, given the opportunity to join the Rinaldi Mob, showed up and showed out. I had to give it to Demise; he was building a fucking empire where everybody was eating. That alone had me getting my ass up and coming up here. I'd just climbed out of Olivia's throat less than two hours ago, but here I was.

Don took three steps toward me and sized me up. We damn near mirrored in height and just as I was in the required all-black clothing and black boots, so was he. Don had us showing up every day in all black like we were the fucking omen, but for the shit we'd been doing, black was needed.

"You everywhere I'm at? You sure about that, Cuppacio?"

"Positive."

Don began walking backward.

"I'ma hold yo' ass to that. Everybody, fall the fuck in line!"

"Aye, bring y'all ass on. I ain't for this shit today," Matteo spoke up and I didn't even know his ass was in the room. He, along with Lorenzo, were out here with us every day, too, but they didn't train, they simply watched and assessed. Some days Rut and Big Zan tagged along but for the most part it was always Beavis and Butt-Head. Them niggas argued worse than my cousins and I but I'd noticed they were inseparable. When they mentioned having a business together I concluded then that these niggas were besties. Matteo hated this training shit, saying on more than one occasion that he would be damned if he did this shit again and after day four, I couldn't say I blamed him.

The back door to the warehouse opened and it was more like a docking area, so the door slid up. There on the grassy field were four big-ass helicopters. The blades began to spin and I saw the curious faces of the men around me. I didn't know what the fuck this nigga had up his sleeve, but I kept my game face on and waited to hear the instructions. If he wanted us to jump out these bitches, I would curse the whole way down, but for the sake of my family, I was jumping out of a fucking helicopter.

"Five to a fucking copter. Bring y'all ass on. I got shit to do."

The rest of the Cuppacio clan followed me to copter number one, and of course, Don was the last one to hop in. I'd never been on a copter, but seeing the noise cancelling headphones in the seat, I grabbed them and placed them over my head with my cousins following suit.

"What the fuck is this shit, Don?"

"Last year, we were given a boat of animals to sell. That

199

was my first mission. Today, we are visiting one of the buyers of those animals."

"So we turning into zookeepers?" Nel asked.

"Nah, you niggas turning into Tomb Raider. I'm dropping y'all ass off to his plains, and whoever makes it through his fucking habitat, lives to see another training. I hope you niggas not scared of lions and shit."

"Lions? Nigga, the fuck we look like, some circus masters?"

Don placed the earphones over his head and grinned. "This the jungle, nigga. Let's see if that Cuppacio shit really do run through y'all blood."

The helicopter began to lift, and once we were hovered over the building and our cars resembled Hot Wheels in size, we glided through the air to our unknown destination. The ride was about forty-five minutes, and I couldn't even enjoy the beautiful views, due to me wondering what the fuck this nigga had in store for us. I'd hoped he was joking about us going to rumble with wild animals, but this nigga may kee kee from time to time, but his ass never told a damn lie.

Jae Bae. Jisei made her way into my mind. The fucked-up girl who probably had more daddy issues than I had and wanted a nigga to chase her like I ran the relay was the bane of my existence. She was the only reason I'd gone and gotten my dick sucked by Olivia last night. Jisei's pussy was fucking lethal. I knew she had good pussy by the way that fat mutha-fucka sat in her clothes, but my dick wasn't prepared for how tight, wet, and snug it was.

I'd already let her burn my fucking head without getting pussy, and when I was eating her out, my dick screamed to be buried in her taut walls. Now that I'd sampled the shit, it was going to take whatever the fuck Don was about to thrust us in to get me off her. Jisei had that type of pussy that would make a nigga crash out and forget the fucking mission. Fine as fuck, had her own motion, and the pussy was immaculate; it was a wonder Don hadn't been married his sister off. With pussy like hers, he could bargain fucking world peace and be granted that shit. She had a nigga ready to run straight to the altar after drilling her ass from the back. Still, I couldn't let her fine, thick ass side track me. She would be seeing me again though and real soon.

The pilot announced that we were arriving and I sighed with relief, seeing a big ass black building that we landed on top of. I didn't know why I was expecting us to be dropped off dead smack in the middle of Africa or some shit. Once we got the clear to exit, I removed the headphones and fell in line beside my cousins. With everyone out of the copters and wonder displayed on their faces, Don motioned for us to follow him to the only door on the large roof.

"This is your last fucking chance to turn the fuck around. Once we get in, the only way out is going through the course."

"What's this like some CGI shit? We got this." One of the pending made men, Coolie, who had also been copping from me, stroked his beard. Don held eye contact with him and opened the door.

"You gon' wish this shit was CGI. Let's go."

The potent smell of horse shit invaded my nostrils, and it was strong enough to make my eyes water. The other men felt the same because I heard a few gasps and groans behind me. We descended what had to have been about twenty flights of stairs before making it to a dark, empty clearing. There was a giant screen in front of us that indeed looked like CGI, even though it was blacked out. The smell, though; that shit damn sure wasn't artificial intelligence. Shit smelled like we were in the middle of the fucking zoo.

Sounds of heels against the floor prompted all of us to look to the left and an oversized, white guy with sunburnt skin, who I recognized from being at the dungeon, made an appearance. He was even dressed like a damn zookeeper with his tan bucket hat that was stringed under his meaty chin and khaki utility vest over a white shirt that did nothing to conceal his bulging gut. The heels that were clicking were black, worn cowboy boots and his dingy jeans covered them.

"Good morning, gentleman. Welcome to my oasis. This building cost me over three hundred million dollars to create."

The man opened his arms wide.

"You're standing in the middle of every wildlife lover's dream."

"This empty ass room with the broken screen that smells like a rat's ass?"

Vello nudged Nel with his elbow and Big Stomach continued on.

"It's so much more than an empty space and you'll see that in a moment. How many of you have seen the franchise movies *The Hunger Games*?"

I had, and so had Shio, because we sat through them shits on Netflix one day with our little cousins and I was still mad that Prim Rose died. Weak ass shit.

"So, think of this place as *The Hunger Games*. You won't be fighting each other to the death in hopes that sponsors will send you gifts that can save your life. In fact, no one is saving you but yourselves and you'll be given limited resources. But, we will get to that. This place is all solar powered and artificial intelligence. With computers, I have created direct replicas of the most forbidden, sacred, and breathtaking places in the world. It may be fake, but the wildlife inside as well as the plants, grounds, and bodies of water are all real. Technology has created this, but it's as authentic as it can get."

"Damn, if I would have known that nigga was that rich, I woulda robbed his bitch ass," Nel whispered. I didn't know his ass was racked up like that, either. He was always at the crap table, face red as a fucking beet. like he was gambling away his retirement fund. The whole time, this nigga was *the* retirement fund.

"My name is William Preston, but you can call me Preston You will be divided up into four teams. When you enter the realm, you must make it to your safari trucks. Whatever color your truck is, is the color you represent. There will be a GPS on each truck that will take you to the habitat in which your colored flag resides. Once you successfully retrieve your flag, the GPS will recognize it and give you directions to safety."

"Hell nawl! I know these niggas lying!" another man yelled, but I didn't recognize who it was because I was too fucking busy trying to process this shit.

"Serious as a heart attack. Each truck houses supplies such as sunscreen, food, water, blankets, and two guns. One gun is a tranquilizer, and the other has animal safe bullets."

"What the fuck is animal safe bullets?" Shio asked. I heard the distress in his voice and knew he had PTSD from when he was bitten by the snake.

"Just what it's named. I spent a lot of money on these animals so I don't want them harmed. The tranquilizer will put them down, but you only have three tranquilizers, so the animal safe bullets will merely scare them away so that you can make your escape."

This shit was crazy.

The screen in front of us lit up and the shit wasn't a screen; it was a fucking wall of some sort, and behind it was fucking south Africa.

"Is this shit real?"

"Hell yeah, it's real. Aite, the Cuppacios, y'all are together and Matteo gon' join y'all. Y'all are the blue team. I'ma join the red team, and Lorenzo can join the yellow team. Jim here will join the green team."

"Aye, how the fuck they get the owner? That's like the fucking cheat code! Y'all see this shit? Look! It's zebras and giraffes and shit walking around." Nel was losing his damn mind while I was trying to keep my cool. As the transparent wall lifted, dry heat rushed in, and the blazing sun had me holding my hand to shield my eyes. This all black had to fucking go but I would wait until I got to the truck.

Nel wasn't lying though. This nigga had a real life makeshift Africa in a fucking building. Herds of zebras were running in uniform, giraffe could be seen in the distance, eating from trees, birds flew overhead, and the place looked like it stretched for miles. Across the savanna, I could barely see the safari truck and the walk looked like it would take two hours or more at least.

Everyone went to their appointed group as Don continued to lash out instructions at groups. Matteo stood next to me and my cousins with an annoyed expression. He was vexed, while I was questioning my life choices. I saw trees and lakes and jungles and mountains and shit in the distance so there was no fucking telling what was out there. Then we all had to leave our pistols behind, and when I thought I could sneak mine in, he instructed us that Don would fine us 500 Gs if we brought our shit with us. I wasn't giving a soul five hundred racks, so I left my gun in the bucket Preston pointed to.

"I know you may want to run, but don't. There are things out here that could hunt you down in seconds. Our best bet is to walk in groups so we don't look intimidating."

"That nigga ain't talking about shit. I'm running."

"Nigga, no, the fuck you not. Gon' run so I can tell mama her other son died in Madagascar," Nel snickered, ready to snatch Vello by the back of his shirt if he broke out in a sprint.

Pulling my black hoodie over my head and tossing it on the ground behind me, my cousins did the same, all exposing wife beaters. Matteo removed his as well, but he draped his on his shoulders. Everyone began to walk forward, and I was half expecting to hear African drums. This shit was unbelievable. How did muthafuckas get clearances for shit like this?

"So you really got a man-made Africa? White folk are something else," Coolie stated.

"Not just a man-made Africa, but in the distance, where the rain forest is, a man-made Indonesia, India, and Asia. Depending on your flag, you'll get a trip there, no passport needed."

"Aren't they all like different climates and shit?" Jaggard, another nigga from South Carolina, asked.

"Yes, that's where this baby comes in at." Preston pointed toward the ceiling.

"This dome not only keeps the animals in but is climate controlled. Each habitat is provided what it needs."

"How do they eat?" I asked.

"They feed off the land."

The rest of the walk was quiet because our faces were drenched. Being only inches from the zebras were surreal. Preston advised us not to touch because they were meaner than snakes, so we walked right past their asses. We were so close that I was able to determine that the zebras were actually black with white stripes. Much like the rest of this fucking encasing, they stunk like hell too.

What had to have been two hours in dry heat landed us at our appointed trucks, and by the time we all made it, we were drenched in sweat and about as stank as the fucking animals. It was still hard to believe that all of this was run by technology. You couldn't tell me that we weren't in the motherland. It was mind boggling that this was all being controlled by machines. It had me thinking about how they could be altering our reality. Hell, was life even real at this point? What if earth was just a controlled dome? Wealthy muthafuckas could do anything. This fat ass white man had created an alternate reality and Don thought it was cool for us to train in this shit. On top of that, the screen that turned out to be a wall was sealed so the only way out of this shit was falling through with the plan.

"This some movie shit, for real. I feel like we in Jumanji. Look at this shit," Nel complained.

We'd approached our truck, which was parked under a scarce tree that failed at providing shade. The truck was your typical Safari truck that you saw on TV, except there were parallel blue stripes on the hood. Nel had been rambling in the truck and held up a vest that was similar to Preston's.

"Put this shit on so we can camouflage with the truck. I got a family to get home too. I ain't tryna get ate up in here with you niggas." Teo snatched the vest out of Nel's hand and tossed his pull over on the driver's seat. I took that as the nigga was driving and I couldn't be happier. I hated driving and damn sure wasn't up for driving through Africa. I hoped the fucking truck had air conditioning or our asses weren't going to make it to the flag.

Shio removed the rest of the fits out of the third row and passed them to us. It was basically cargo pants, a vest, and the same bucket hat Preston had on. I had to admit, I felt cooler in the change of clothes, especially since the black had attracted so much heat that it drenched the seat. After tossing all our clothes in the back, Nel grabbed five back packs and passed them to us. Everyone else was starting to drive off in their trucks, so we hopped in with me taking the passenger seat, Nel and Vello occupying the second row, and Shio taking the third row. Teo cranked the car up and the moment the engine roared to life, hot air blasted from the vents but cooled after a few seconds.

"I was about to say, for a four hundred million dollar enclosure, this shit better have cold ass air."

Looking at Nel in the rearview, he pulled his dreads up in a knot. That nigga's neck was soaked and it made me grateful to have a low haircut. It was all good with dreads until your ass was dropped in the middle of Africa.

The safari truck was caged in, even though there were no windows and we could very much still feel the humidity. I was just grateful for air and protection. The entire walk, I kept looking behind my fucking back, thinking King Kong was going to come and pounce our asses. The unknown still had a nigga uneasy, but it felt good knowing if some shit came at us, we had two guns resting on the seat between Teo and I even though it was only tranquilizer and animal safe bullets.

The flatscreen that was plastered in the dash flashed static, and when we thought the GPS was going to show us to our flag, Scarlett's face appeared on the screen. She was dressed like us, hat and all, and Matteo sat up in his seat damn near stuffing his face in the screen, trying to make sure it was her. I was puzzled as to what the fuck she had to do with this, too, but Princesspa had always been infatuated with animals. Her pops fed into that shit too.

"Hello, future mobsters."

"Bro, I know this ain't my bitch."

"Aye, that's Scar!"

"Y'all shut the fuck up so we can hear her. She might be telling us how to survive this shit," Shi spat from the back seat.

"Nigga, fuck all that! Fuck is she doing on this fucking screen? Where the fuck lil gas station at?"

Ignoring Teo, I listened in to Scarlett, who looked like a spokesperson for *National Geographic*.

"Your animal is the lion."

"Aw, hell nawl!"

My mouth went drier than a stale cracker, causing me to reach for one of the bottles out of my bag and guzzling it down. A fucking lion? What the fuck them other niggas get? Teo was still staring at the screen like he wanted to snatch Scarlett out of it like we hadn't been handed a death sentence.

"That's right. The king of the jungle, or in this case, the King of the Savanna. No worries, though, you'll be just fine," She smiled showing stark white teeth against her smooth brown skin.

"Like hell we will be. Her ass is somewhere with her feet kicked the fuck up, talking about we will be just fine."

"Vello, shut yo' stupid ass up! She should have her fucking feet kicked up! My wife not trying to get in the Rinaldi Mob, she is the Rinaldi Mob, nigga."

Waving my hand at Teo and Vello to pipe down, I was focused on my cousin. She knew animals like no other. If anything, she would be the one to help us out of here, especially since our phones didn't work. I'd checked several times while walking and had to power it off because an overheating warning flashed across the screen.

"There are a few Prides that have been born here, but you will be looking for the Nakahoochie Pride."

"The what? Coochie?"

Vello was getting on all our damn nerves.

"The Nakahoochie Pride features about twenty lions, cubs, and lionesses. They are the largest pride here. The males weigh anywhere between three hundred and five hundred pounds whereas the females weigh anywhere between the two hundred to the mid three hundreds. Again, no worries. Lions are one of the laziest animals out here. They sleep anywhere between sixteen and twenty hours a day."

"This some crazy ass shit here, Jo."

"Lion's rarely hunt Man. They will only kill a human after a full moon, which is when they are most desperate because that is when they are typically the hungriest. Lions are ambush serial killers with night vision, so they prefer to hunt at night when it's the darkest. A full moon eliminates their element of surprise. Lucky for you, the full moon isn't for another few days, so you better get a move on," Scarlett had the nerve to fucking laugh.

"Female lions are the pride's main hunters."

Scarlett faded out of the screen and a Lioness took her place. Vello jumped like her ass was in here or something. The lion on screen was tackling a Gazelle.

"Lions are carnivores through and through. They only eat meat to ensure survival. Lions can consume about twenty pounds of meat each day, although some of them can chow through up to one hundred pounds."

The screen diverted to two different lions hunting animals and the way they were tackling them to the ground had me fighting a flinch.

"Lions mostly eat wildebeest and zebras but African buffalo, rhinoceros, elephants, gazelles, giraffes, crocodiles, hippos, impalas, warthogs, baboons, topi, lizards and mice are all no exceptions. Lions will eat any living, breathing source of meat."

Every animal Scarlett named popped up on the screen, and seeing the crocodiles reminded me of Goal. That nigga housed three big ass gators in his warehouse and that shit creeped me out any time I re-upped.

"You want to be quiet if that helps. Lions have sensitive hearing and the ability to turn their ears from side to side, allowing them to catch sounds coming from any direction. Meaning, they can hear prey from more than a mile away.

"Okay, I think you have the basics about lions. The GPS will take you to the Nakahoochie Pride and fingers crossed that they are sleeping. Good luck."

The screen went black and the GPS popped up. According to it, we were a thirty-minute drive from death.

"Aye, we gon' be good. Scarlett said they sleep twenty hours a day and hunt at night," I repeated.

"Nigga, she also didn't tell us shit besides what the fuck they eat, which is everything, including our asses," Vello voiced.

"Only if it's a full moon, goofy ass nigga," Nel spat.

Teo pulled off and Don's red truck zoomed in front of us. That crazy ass nigga was hanging out of the window, shirt off, looking through his binoculars with a fucking grin on his face. He was living for this shit. Ole jungle boy ass nigga.

"What animal they got? The fuckin' koala bear? That nigga a lil bit too happy," Vello pointed out. Don was excited as shit and they were going about a hundred miles an hour. When they turned into the direction of what I assumed was the jungle, the truck was on two wheels.

"It's on the screen. Team Red got the gorilla, Team Yellow got the tiger, and Team Green got the anaconda," Shio informed. He was on the third row and saw the screen from way back there, but that nigga had always had 20/20 vision, thanks to the clear contacts his blind ass wore.

The rest of the ride was quiet, and we'd passed giraffes, buffalos, more zebras, and rhinos swimming in murky waters that Teo was sure to speed past. I saw a video once that informed rhinos would kill a human with no regrets.

The GPS showed that we only had five miles until we got to the coochie pride, but we didn't need to be told that. A loud ass roar that startled the truck was warning enough.

PUT IT ON THE MOB

"Them niggas wide awake! You said they would be sleep, Ezee!"

"Nigga, I said they sleep for up to twenty hours a day. Maybe that was a yawn."

I was starting to wish that Vello had gotten swapped with Jaggard or something. He was too fucking shaky and that nigga wasn't scared of shit.

A row of tall shrubs that were lengthy enough to conceal the truck separated us from the lions. They were most definitely awake, but lounging under the man made, hot ass sun.

"Damn. This shit really real," I quipped.

If anything, the lions on TV and the internet looked small compared to these big ass lions a few yards away from us.

"Okay, look, I see the blue flag. It's underneath the one with the black mane's paw," Shio pointed out.

The A/C wasn't doing shit at this point because I was sweating like a fucking slave. Swiping the back of my hand across my forehead, I squinted and located the blue flag. At the same time, the glared in our direction, making all of us crouch even though we were shielded by the bushes.

"Okay, this is the plan. We let that nigga Ezee go out and get the flag. He got the same eyes as the lions so they may think he part of the tribe."

"Nigga, fuck you. I bet' not do no stupid ass shit like that. We will be sitting in this bitch till the full moon waiting on me," I barked.

Vello was out of his rabid ass mind. He could take his ass out there and get fucked off. I was staying my ass in this truck where it was safe.

"Aite, so what's the plan? This y'all mission. I'm just the fucking driver."

Studying each of the twenty lions, it was amazing to witness them in their element. They were really a fucking community. I could tell which ones mothered the cubs by the way they watched them from afar, but the other lionesses in the pride were also attentive to the cubs. I knew with this pride having so many small babies, they were even more vicious. *Protect the fam.*

The males outlined the circle they were all sitting in with the female and young in the middle. Like how me and my cousins were with the rest of the family, and like us, there was only one thing that could distract them and pull them away from the Pride – eating. We'd come to Jagoda Bay to eat, leaving the women and children back in Chicago. Though they were protected by our youngins, we were the muscles.

"I got a plan," I lowly stated.

"Oh, shit. This about to be a good one."

"Unless you got one, shut up and let him talk," Nel scolded his playful ass brother.

"That last pack of zebras we passed about seven miles ago, we chased them this way. The only thing that will distract the lions is eating. We bring them a whole fucking buffet and we can ride past and get the flag."

I didn't know how we were going to go about chasing the zebras straight into Pride lands that we were sure they already knew about but it was our only shot. We were still about three miles apart from the lions, so they didn't hear us when we backed out and turned in the opposite direction. There were twenty plus lions, five of us, and a tranquilizer and pellet gun. If this shit didn't work, we were fucked. Jisei wouldn't even have to worry about a nigga fucking her life up because I was going to make her ass a widow before we even walked down the aisle. I shook her pretty ass from my mind because pussy was the last thing I needed to be worried about. The predator had become the prey and I'd be damned if a lion was going to be gnawing on my bones before I brought my mama to the city.

It took us less than eight minutes to get back to the zebras, who seemed to double in size. They were majestic, exotic looking donkeys and their teeth were strong but brown. They needed some serious fucking dental work. Preston talking about how many millions this shit was worth and these donkeys' teeth were fucked off to the max.

"Go to the back of the pack," I instructed.

Teo hadn't even drank any of his fucking water and I was damn near on bottle two. Either he was used to the harsh temperatures, or the nigga was too wired up about Scarlett being a part of Preston's project. He needed to chill out. I know cuz clocked a bag for this shit. It was really next fucking level, and I was sure Don set the shit up.

"Damn these zebras funky."

Nel wasn't lying but odor wasn't a concern of mine. I was trying to figure out how we could drive these bad mouth ass zebras toward the lions.

"One of y'all should get out."

"Fuuuuuuuuck no, nigga. We not getting out just like you not—"

ZIP. ZIP.

One of the zebras' heads burst open, and at first, the rest of them didn't move until it fell to the ground. They started barking and broke out in a run. The dust underneath their hooves clouded our vision a bit, but as they trampled over their brother, I patted the dashboard and Teo began driving back in the direction of the lions since they were running that way. We stayed on their ass to make sure they didn't turn off.

"Drive this hoe, Teo," Vello urged.

Teo had his pedal to the metal, and even though I had talked shit about Don, I unlatched the cage, covering the window and stuck my upper body out. For an added layer of protection, I grabbed the tranquilizer.

"Here we go, Cuppacios!"

My basic ass plan worked because the zebras ran right to their fucking deaths, making me hop my ass back in the truck and lock the window just as one of the big cats plunged at me. When I was in the truck safely, heart beating out of my fucking chest, I noticed the lioness was aiming for a zebra that was right behind me. Even the fucking cubs were out hunting, and if the shit wasn't so gruesome, it would be admirable.

When Matteo came up on the flag, the big ass lion that was guarding it jumped on the fucking hood of the truck with a thud, halting the vehicle.

"Ohh, shiiit! We fena die! Mufasa done came for his revenge! Ahhhhhhhh!"

The lion had to be every bit of five hundred pounds. His claws were scraping the hood and blood was dripping from his needle sharp teeth.

"Shio, I'm glad as fuck that you brought that gun in. Shoot this nigga."

Rooooaaaaar.

The lion's roar had all of our asses freezing up.

"Don't fucking shoot him. We already killed the fucking zebra. Use the tranquilizer." Teo's voice was calm but that nigga was shaking in the driver's seat like the rest of us. Without taking my eyes off the lion, I lifted the tranquilizer and shot his ass in the neck.

"That nigga ain't budging. Shoot him again! Shoot him again!" Vello screamed, voice raising six octaves.

Aiming the gun, I shot him two more times and he finally slid off the truck while scratching the hood all the way down. The sounds made my flesh crawl but it wasn't more fucked up than the sound of the zebras crying for their lives. Teo backed away from the lion and I was able to grab the flag. The screen lit up and gave us directions to the exit. It was an hour drive and I prayed we didn't encounter any more fucking lions on the way. This was some off the wall ass shit and I couldn't wait to get the fuck out of Preston's rich ass, fake ass Africa.

"Aye, this shit was decent," Vello cheered.

"Shut the fuck up," we all replied in unison. That nigga did the most but had the nerve to gloat at this fucked up ass training session. I needed the whole damn pill bottle behind this shit here.

CHAPTER 15
EZIO "EZEE" CUPPACIO

I'd never imagined I would have to soak in a fucking ice bath, but me lowering my body in the inflatable tub let me know this was indeed reality. I took it back about the training with Don being a piece of fucking cake. The shit was borderline torture. Then, what made the shit so crazy was the nigga Don was enjoying that shit today. When we got to the finish line, his ass was already there, waving his red flag. His probably didn't even break a fucking sweat. I was starting to believe he was part fucking Greek God. I was going to start calling the nigga Hercules.

Usually, after our 4:00 a.m. training sessions, I came straight back to the house and took a fucking nap until it was time to make a serve, but today, I had Nel stop by Sports Authority to purchase the outdoor tub. It took ten bags of ice to get it to the desired temperature and I just knew my balls would never be the same. On top of being in a near freezing bath, it was cold outside. Not Chicago cold, but it was cooler than it had been in Jagoda Bay during the entire time I'd been here.

I only lasted four minutes in the bath and was damn near breaking my necking trying to run back in the house. Once I snatched the door open, I almost busted my ass on the slippery floor.

"I at least thought you was gon' last ten minutes in that bitch. You barely did half."

Don stood in the middle of the living room, full mob gear in his custom suit, looking like he hadn't just run through the motherland with our asses. I still couldn't believe he had all of us shoved in a helicopter, dropped off to Preston's fantasy land and left for dead. I didn't know whether the shit was a simulation or real life, but it was hot as a bitch. The lions, zebras, hyenas, and all types of wildlife inhabiting the building were still imprinted in my brain. I didn't know how in the fuck we made it to the finish line in one piece but I thanked the Lord.

After this morning, I was ready to say fuck this shit, but I had to keep going. Don was certified crazy though.

"Have you ever sat in an ice bath while it was cold outside?"

I was still shaking where I stood, pissed that I didn't skin one of those lions and make a fur. It wasn't my first time seeing wild animals because our Don had an animal obsession, along with his daughter, but we stayed far away. Plus, he didn't have any shit like that.

Before our dads could put us in the cage with the mutha-fuckas, they were dead, and I was glad because I knew death was coming. Little did I know I was going to have to face animals again. I was still trying to figure out where in the fuck we had gone because the copter ride was only about forty-five minutes each way. We all smelled like giraffe ass the entire ride back.

"Hell yes. I take two a week. That shit is good for not only tense muscles but anxiety and shit too. You should add them to your workout routine."

I looked off because, even though I was naturally slim and fit, I didn't have a fucking workout routine. I jogged and did push-ups here and there when I was feeling bloated, but other than that, I thugged that shit out. The most workout I'd been getting as of late was lifting these bricks and counting bags of fucking money plus these damn trainings.

"Yeah, you got a lot to fucking learn, my guy. I'ma send a trainer over here and a fucking nutritionist. You need to get in shape."

More training in addition to the training we already fucking doing? Yeah, this nigga was trying to send me to an early grave.

"Is there a reason you broke in my shit?"

I needed to get warm, shower, and take the longest fucking nap of mankind. Since it was Friday, we didn't have training tomorrow, which I was happy as shit about. If this nigga was here to tell me that he was having me do some more jungle boy shit, I was going to curse his ass out. I had just re-upped and my cousins were out making serves today, but I planned to join them later on.

"Nigga, you know who the fuck I am. I didn't break in shit. Get dressed. I'm dropping you off somewhere."

Don tossed a dry-off towel at my chest and I caught it before it could hit the floor. Instead of turning around and going back to the car, he sat his ass on the couch and looked at his presidential Rolex as if he was clocking my time.

I was too sore, too exhausted, and way past the time for me to get high to argue. My cousin had been so happy about getting plugged in that he'd taken a trip to Chicago and copped for me despite him swearing he wouldn't. Shio wanted me off the pills but the money was a distraction. Getting richer by the hour had me in a daze too, yet I still found myself popping perc 30s. He'd told my ass to slow down because he wasn't going back any time soon but I didn't listen and ran through those bitches. I only had four percs left and hated to think about what the fuck I was going to do when I was out. This time, the nigga Shio was for real about not feeding my habit. I hinted at being out and he told me to drank some syrup. Ole preachin' ass.

Walking in the closet that I was going to be pissed about parting ways with, the pill bottle that housed my last four was posted on the center dresser. Pausing, every aching limb told me to pop one. I didn't know what the fuck Don wanted with me so I wanted to be in my right mind going out with this nigga. The pills had me sluggish, slow, and sometimes too fucking emotional or immune to empathy. It was never in between.

The day I ran into Jisei at the Dungeon, I was immune to empathy. When I came off my high, I felt a bit shitty with how she looked hurt. But on the other hand, she wasn't my bitch. I didn't have a muthafucka dictating what the fuck I was doing before and had no intentions on starting.

Walking right past the percs took all the will I had, and with each painful step I took, water dripped from my body. I had to shake off the craving. Stopping in front of a section that was product of my latest shopping trip, I ran my hands across the fine fabrics. Not putting much thought into what I was going to put on, I snatched down my outfit for the day, grabbed the shoes and accessories and headed out for a shower. I thought I was going to take a hellhound shower, but the hot water was like fire against my skin. The shock from the ice cold plunge hadn't worn off just yet.

Making sure to scrub the lion juice from my balls, I dried off, brushed my teeth, and began getting dressed. It took me less that twenty minutes to be ready for whatever this nigga had for me. Walking down the hallway, passing a mirror that was plastered on the wall, I stared back at my fucking father. His Italian roots ran through me deep and sometimes I felt like his evil ways did too. A snarl covered his face and his double chin rested on his collar. I wanted to pull my gun out and shoot but knew it was just my mind playing tricks on me. A figment of my imagination. *Bitch ass nigga! I hate you.*

Instead of taking my ass in the living room where Don was waiting, I doubled back to the closet and took one of the pills, using a half drank, room temperature dirty Sprite that was on the black nightstand to wash it down. Running my tongue across my teeth, my eyes lowered, my mouth watered, my body relaxed, and my jaw slacked. Since I only took one pill, I would still be alert, just relaxed a bit more. I could already feel myself loosening up by the time I walked through the hallway and this time, when I looked in the mirror, my own reflection stared back.

"Aite then, you just might know something after all. Another point for the Cuppacio leader."

Don stood as I entered the room, and I saw approval in his expression. I wanted to adjust my fucking balls in these tight ass suit pants but refrained from doing so. There were a few times where I had to dress the part growing up, including my bitch ass daddy's funeral, and I hated that shit then just as much as I loathed it now. If I could go on the rest of my life without dressing like an old Englishman, then that would be all right with me. But with this nigga pulling up at my spot, all fucking dapper and shit, I had to put my shit on.

The other day, I walked past a tailor shop and found myself going in after seeing a bad ass suit in the window. The nigga working the counter let me know that it was his uncle's shop and they'd just opened. By the time I left, I'd spent a fucking car tag on button-down shirts, tuxedos, suits, loafers, and slacks. I knew a million other things I could have been doing with my bread but I deemed looking the part as necessary.

The green, black and gold jacket had a few specs of gold in it and fit me to a tee. I fucked with the green double-breasted jacket and the black pants that were tailored just right. I paired the look with suede green loafers that were slippery as fuck on this floor and snatched the black trench coat off the coat rack in the foyer as we made our exit. I felt naked without my jewelry, just as I did without my tool, so a gold Rolex and a thin, gold necklace were my accessories. If I said so myself, I was out dressing this nigga today. The cold bit me in the ass, and when the back door to the Rolls Royce was closed, I fought the shiver resting on my shoulders.

"I made the decision to bring you into my world—into my city—but before this shit became my world, my uncle taught me a lesson of respect."

"Respect?" I snarled.

"Yeah, nigga, respect. You think I just came in this fucking city and took the fuck over? A city as rich and thriving as Jagoda Bay? You think I just brought my big bad ass here and made the city bow down?"

Rubbing my chin, I nodded. "Shid, yeah."

Don smirked. "As bad as I wanted to, I didn't. My uncle didn't play that shit. Jagoda Bay wasn't free territory that I'd hoped it would be. But then again, I didn't give a fuck. I was willing to make it my territory especially since my uncle all but made my ass start over here. To my surprise, there was already a mafia here."

My brows rose in surprise.

"Yeah, the Mecanio Mafia. Ran by Rio Mecanio. Another half breed muthafucka who stepped into the role behind his father. I was ready to wipe his ass out, especially because his

221

shit wasn't making any noise. But respect. No matter how fucking mighty I am, the mighty can definitely fall. Me, though, I ain't even falling asleep so a nigga can never end my reign. I'm wise enough to know anybody can try to knock my ass off.

"So, I had to sit down with Don Mecanio."

"And that's what you want me to do?"

"No, nigga, that's what the fuck you must do. The Rinaldi Mob is not the only mafia in this city. In order to get to where I am and where I'm trying to go, I had to show my fucking respect. I'm bringing you in so that means even though we will act as one, there will now be a new mob coming to the city. Rio is different but the nigga got knowledge, power, and respect. He was one of the keys to how I was able to scale up as fast as I could. So, you about to go to his fucking party of a mansion, soak up the knowledge, make the nigga like you and earn your place in this city."

The car came to a stop.

"Party of a mansion? What is this nigga like? Coke head rich kid?"

A smile spread across Don's face. "Go in there and see for yourself, Cuppacio. I'ma circle the block."

"You ain't coming in?"

"Do I hold yo' dick when you piss, nigga? Fuck nawl, I ain't coming in. I already met the nigga. Nobody came with me. This yo' time to shine, playboy."

The door opened and I climbed out.

There was a new driver, one Don didn't normally use, but just like the last one, he stood there, still as a statue as I walked up to the mansion. This place on the outside still had perfectly green manicured lawns that looked so good that it had to have been artificial grass.

Careful not to bust my ass on the concrete since the shoes

didn't provide much grip, I approached the black cathedral styled doors. Before I could knock, the door croaked and an old ass butler that looked like he was ready to be turned into an obituary opened the door.

"Don Cuppacio. Don Mecanio is expecting you. May I take your jacket?"

Removing the coat from my shoulders, I placed it in the butler's white-gloved hand. The nigga had a hump in his back and the wrinkles in his face almost looked like it was about to melt away off his skin. Don Mecanio was dead ass wrong to have this nigga working, but my high had kicked in, so I held my tongue. I really wanted to ask this nigga why in the fuck he wasn't in some retirement home with his feet kicked up licking on Geritol pussy.

"You may follow me to the sitting room. Don Mecanio will be right with you."

Walking through the home, I had to admit it was grand. The dwellings looked almost like how our Don used to keep his home with the pricy paintings, statues, crowned molded, twenty-foot ceilings and old ass wallpaper. Then the gold. There was so much fucking gold everywhere. But the floors were so clean that I could see my reflection in them .

Butler *dead ass* led me to the room that we would be meeting in, and instead of taking my seat, I stood, waiting for Don Mecanio. I didn't really know what the fuck I was to do at this impromptu ass meeting, but Don said I had to meet the nigga to basically get his approval, but I didn't need his approval to feed my family. The bricks had been flying out of my fucking hands, and some days, I still couldn't believe I was out here getting it. I'd made more money in the last four months than I had the last two years of my life, and I hadn't even said I do. If this meeting was to put some more money in my fucking pockets, then I was all for it. No matter how this meeting went, I was moving my folks here and earning our place. If not in the mafia, then for sure in Jagoda Bay. If I couldn't earn it, I was taking it. Now that I'd been getting this money and exploring more of the city, I knew it would be perfect for my family. Chicago held too many painful memories. I had to do this for my folks. We belonged here.

"Do these muthafuckas got dicks?"

I was focused on the wallpaper that was glued above the crown molding. Leaning my face into the wall, I concluded that the little angels that were in a stamp and repeat pattern were indeed naked as fuck and had mini dicks as the wings on their back had them suspended in the air. The shit was weird and too fucking Italian for me, but if this nigga liked that, then hey --I wasn't the one that had to look at the shit every day or possibly ever again.

"Don Cuppacio."

Turning on my loafers, I fixed my face but didn't put on a smile. I removed the disgust from the choice of decor from my snout, but before I could paint a neutral expression, a frown found its way back in place.

Two topless ass men in only tight ass briefs and a bow tie around their necks were now in the room, holding trays, skin shining like a motherfucker. Last I checked, it was cold as fuck in Jagoda Bay, so these two being damn near naked serving fruit and wine had me trying to figure out if I was imagining this shit. If I *was* imagining shit, I was going to have to check myself because why in the fuck would I imagine male fucking strippers? I had to blame it on that fucking *Bridgerton* marathon Jisei had me on.

I looked behind me, like there was someone else these two niggas were speaking to, and when I noticed the only thing at my back was the fucking little dick angel walls, I reached for my gun. Both men took a step back, and before I could put a hot one in their asses, the doors opened again, but this time, a man who looked to be maybe a few years older than me stepped in.

"Ezio Cuppacio. My servers have fresh fruit that were harvested from my greenhouse and wine flown in from Milan."

When I didn't say shit, the man who was clearly Italian and black turned to his—whoever these niggas were—spoke soft as hell to them, and they placed the trays on the table and made their exit.

What the fuck kind of place did Don bring me to?

"Hello, I am Rio, Don of the Mecanio Cartel. Thank you so much for meeting with me today."

The long ponytail muthafucka held his hand out, and instead of telling him to go fuck himself, I thought better of it and returned the handshake. I was on his territory and was sure he had this bitch guarded like the president. Trying to break his soft ass hand with a shake, I took my seat after him.

"So, tell me something about yourself. I must admit, I didn't think any of the remaining Cuppacio were interested in the ways of the mob any longer."

My mind was still on the fact that Rio had two half naked niggas in this bitch, serving treats I damn sure wasn't putting my mouth on.

"You a faggot?"

Rio crossed his leg, revealing loose-fitting pants that matched the long, burgundy robe he was wearing. Hugh Hefner came to mind because the shit was a replica of what he wore. I'd been dragged to his mansion as a child once and it was exactly how they painted it to be in the movies.

"What is it with you and Demise and this faggot word? You know, it's offensive in my world," Don Mecanio chortled.

Rio had a heavy ass Italian accent that I'd never possessed. Though I was raised by full-blooded Italian men, that side of

LISA AUSTIN

me never stood out. I've talked like a nigga my entire life, even when my father used to be pissed at me for it.

"Faggot, gay, queer, all that shit the same," I dismissed, not wanting to get into a debate about some bullshit that didn't pertain to me.

"Okay, fair enough, but yes. My intimacy lies with men."

When he revealed that, it was like a blow to the face. I'd been brought up in this shit and had never seen an openly gay Don. Was gay shit going on in the mob? Not likely, but if it was, the men kept that shit nipped tucked tight.

"You were handed the role by your father, and he let a nigga that takes it in the ass run his shit? Hell nawl."

"Oh, he didn't want to at first. He preferred my sister to take on the role, but just as Scarlett wasn't cut out to be the leader of the Cuppacio Mafia, neither is Arianee."

Hearing him use Scarlett's name had my chest tight. My cousin was married into the Rinaldi Mafia, but she was still my family. I hadn't had a chance to chop it up with her in the last few months because her husband damn near had her glued to his hip, but I had wired her a few bands here and there. I had to make some time to go over and kick it with her.

"You're tense. No need. I may be the head of a very small mafia but I keep myself educated. The Cuppacio name precedes itself. You come from some very brutal men."

"Fuck them fat fucks," I spat bitterly.

I had only popped one pill when I normally ate two, so I damn sure didn't need to have thoughts of my father swarming in my head. My stash was too far away from me for this shit.

"Indeed. My father couldn't stand them, either."

"I'on mean no harm, I don't feel comfortable sitting in this bitch where you do gay ass orgies. You want to get to know me to make sure all is good with my folks moving in, but it's not your mob that I'm merging with. I ain't here to step into no muthafuckas territory or go neck to neck over mob shit. I just want to feed my family like I been doing. A dick sucker can't tell me shit."

I was starting to get the fucking creeps thinking about the shit that possibly went down in these walls. Rio looked straight as fuck, and so did the servers, but to see that he was openly gay and had no qualms about prancing his sex slaves around let me know he wasn't somebody I wanted to get clearance from. No fucking way. Who even takes a dick sucking man serious any fucking way?

"Ahh, I see. Because I am gay, you think that my opinion does not matter?"

"Damn right."

"Damn wrong."

I crossed my arms and tucked my fist under my armpits. I almost didn't have the room due to this tight ass jacket.

"What are your plans?"

"What, nigga?"

"Your plans. What are they? I know you are merging with your enemy mob, but outside of that, what are your plans? A man that has held his family on his back for years clearly has a plan outside of depending on Don Rinaldi to feed you. What connections have you made? What do you want to get into? Legally? Illegally, I know you deal with Goal, which is someone Don Rinaldi has connected you with, but outside of selling cocaine, what else have you put in motion? You've been in my city what? Six months?"

Holding my hard gaze, I pondered on what he'd asked me. In all truth, I didn't have no plans. I was making this fucking money, selling these birds and the shit was stacking to the ceiling. I made a living in Chicago, but here in Jagoda Bay, I was already a blink away from being rich. I was going to merge with Don and handle whatever he required of me and my folks. Long as we could keep eating like we were, I was cool with whatever, but saying the shit out loud sounded immature. So, I stayed mute.

"Ah. I see."

Rio reached for his cigar and lit it.

"I love Don Rinaldi. When he came to me more than a year ago, he was just as clueless as you. No, actually, you are more far off than him. He did have the connections. He did have a plan. He was just willing to go about his plans the wrong way. Ezio, my father was a lot like yours. A lot like Demise's too. He didn't want me to run his empire because of my sexuality. But what he fail to realize was, I was always going to be a better man than him because I was a fucking planner. I hope you don't take any offense to this, but there is no way in hell you was supposed to come here on a prayer and a wing. Don is a man of his word, yes. He has proven that by connecting you to the cartel even though you barely look his sister's way. However, he is also a man that wiped your entire lineage out. Joining him will be the best thing you could ever do in life *but* you still have to have yourself."

"You asking me to go against him? That's a death wish."

Don Mecanio was tossing out riddles and shit and it was sounding to me like he wanted me to not trust the Rinaldis. Don hadn't given me a reason to not trust him, even though I always had my eyes open when it comes to a nigga. This nigga here in front of me was for sure on some other shit and I was ten seconds away from blowing him and his booty bandit party off the face of the earth.

Rio blew out a cloud of smoke.

"It's indeed a death wish because if you went against him, you go against me. I will kill you myself and get my dick sucked right after. As I stated, I love Demise. You peg me wrong. Let me reiterate."

Rio leaned forward in his chair, matching my hard stare.

"What I'm saying is, by him bringing you on, you should have already had some things set up here to generate income instead of depending on him to eat. Had he not connected you, you would have still been collecting weekly deposits from your cousins back in Chicago."

Biting down on my bottom lip, I let his stinging words marinate.

"Sometimes things are a test even if you feel like you aren't being quizzed. Okay, you're selling cocaine and it's making you rich. Great. Even with that, how many men at the Dungeon have you spoken with? What are you going to do with your dope money? Jagoda Bay is crawling with rich men and women and what do the rich like to do?"

"Fuck, trick off, and snort cocaine?"

Rio ashed his Cuban cigar and grunted. "They like to invest."

"That's how the rich stay rich. Especially with all the expensive habits they have. They like to fucking invest. So my question is, when do you plan on getting a piece of the pie? After training? After marriage, whenever that may be. As a leader of your people, things like that is what you should be focused on, among other things. Dope money is cool, but selling a few kilos a week won't get you to the top. The higher-ups love and respect me because my mafia lowered the crime rate versus increasing it. Coming into the world of the mafia, you are a businessman first, a gangster second. I told Demise this very thing. The moment your feet touched the soil, you should have been ready to make some connections."

. . .

THE TRUTH WAS, Don Mecanio was speaking some real shit. I wouldn't say that I was dependent on Don to put me on because, back in my city, I was already on. I had family who was still making shit happen in Chicago, keeping this shit going. But here in Jagoda Bay, with the training, getting high, getting my dick sucked, and making these bands, life has been good as fuck. There was no need for me to worry about shit else. Connecting with the cartel was a dream for niggas like me. But shit, hearing another man call you out made you feel like you were a complete fuck up. I wouldn't wear my feelings on my face though. I wasn't giving a stranger the satisfaction.

"Ezio, I like you. It takes a lot to step up at such a young age and carry the burden of an entire family. You were barely out of middle school when you assumed the role of Don."

"I'm not a Don."

"You are. No matter the hatred you hold for your elders, you stepped up and carried the family. You're still carrying the family. Don't come out here and lose sight of that. Being a boss is a never-ending job. You have too many people depending on you for you to settle."

I hadn't settled. I didn't even settle debts, so settling wasn't a word that was even in my genetic makeup. I would call it me playing the field and sitting back to watch how shit was going to play out while stacking this money. When it came to my family, if I had to step down and let the next leader direct me, then that was what the fuck I was going to do. I was a team player, but at the moment, I was the captain of the team.

"I hear you."

Rio leaned forward, still holding his smoking cigar.

"You don't, but it's okay. You will."

The doors opened again, and a different nigga walked in, but this time, his ass was naked. Dick and balls just on display and it made me stand to my feet. Rio was dropping gems, but it was hard for me to receive what it was he was spitting due to all this gay ass activity.

"What the fuck you got going on?"

"About to get my dick sucked. You are dismissed. But I'm not ready to clear you just yet. You have some things you need to work through mentally and physically. You're a good man and have the potential to be a great asset to the Rinaldi Mafia and a keen ally to me. You're just not ready yet. I want you to sit down and analyze your life with a clear and *sober* mind, my new friend. Don't let the fact that you are stuck in your ways be your downfall or the *demise* of those you love and care about."

When Dick and Balls dropped to his knees in front of Rio and snatched his robe open, I was out of the fucking door. Ain't no way I was about to watch another man suck a man's dick.

"I want to see you again soon, Ezio. That isn't a request, either," I heard from behind me. At the same time, gagging sounded off from the walls.

"Fuuuuuck. I love how you swallow me."

Fighting vomit that threatened to rise up my throat, I snatched my coat from Old Man Butler who was at the front door, waiting for me. I couldn't get the fuck out of the mansion quickly enough. This was some sick-ass shit here.

Busting out of the double doors and sucking in icy air, I spotted Demise, who was posted on the Rolls Royce, smoking a blunt with a shit-eating grin on his face.

"How you like Gay Boy Mansion?"

"Man, what the fuck that nigga on in there? You like coming over here?"

"Nigga, do it look like I do? But that dick-licking ass nigga got more connections than the fucking governor. If you don't get vetted by nobody else in this city, you gotta get vetted by him. He got his fucking hands in everything but the docks. He controls the fucking docks, which means—"

"He runs any and everything that comes in and out of here by sea, including the bricks I've been slanging," I finished.

"Exactly. He is the key to how Goal gets his shit in without question. So, even though he sits on the other side of the rainbow, that Italian ass nigga knows his shit."

"He said I ain't ready."

"Shit, do you feel like you ready?"

"I do. I'm here, ain't it? I've been selling more dope than Nino Brown and almost got my ass ate the fuck up by Mufasa. Damn right, I'm ready. But I didn't come here to step on no toes. Nobody knows what the fuck I went through growing up. When them niggas left the earth—when you killed them niggas—they left a lot of shit behind. Shit that I had to take care of. That's what I want to do. I want to take care of my people with no fucking violence on their part. It ain't enough of us to protect all of them. I'll go to war with Satan himself, but I prefer to keep my people out of it."

"That's where the fuck you wrong. You are here to step on toes. You actually here to break some fucking ankles. You here to run that shit up. You here to take if it ain't given to you. You here to make yo' fucking mark in the city. You think I would have given my sister to a weak ass nigga? Hell no. I chose you because I know, given the chance, you wouldn't hesitate to take me the fuck out. Granted, you wouldn't survive that shit, but you would do it, nonetheless."

"So what the fuck I'm 'posed to do? All I know is survival. I'on know shit about the politics of this shit."

'That's why the fuck you got me, nigga. You got me here to pick my fucking brain and guide you through this shit, and when you get that nigga in there to trust you, you gon' have him too. But how in the fuck can you say you ready for everything that come with this shit when you haven't even checked off the first task on the list?"

I already know what he meant. Jisei. That fucking good pussy, slick mouth, fine-ass lady. She was the first person I'd stuck my dick inside of since I'd been out here and hadn't disappointed. I tried calling her ass for a round two and she had blocked a nigga again. That pussy was so tight and wet, it had me spraying all up in that shit with no regrets, and on foe nem I would do it again. But I was done chasing her ass. It was the reason she hadn't heard from me in a few months, but her ass was always on my fucking mind. I just might love the lil bitch for real with the way I was always thinking about her sexy ass. But the nigga she was looking for wasn't me. One minute, she wanted me to buy her a ring, and the next, she was treating me like a broke nigga. Fuck all that.

"I ain't fena force yo' sister to fuck with me. We gon' get married and we gon' respect each other in these streets. That's all I can promise."

"You got another bitch you loving or some shit?"

"Nah."

"So what the fuck is the problem? Nigga, the same way you lead your family, you lead my sister. I shouldn't have to beg you to get on your fucking job. I'm Don, nigga. I gave you an opportunity of a fucking lifetime, and instead of you basking in that shit, you running around this bitch with one of my employees."

Olivia had definitely been my lil boo. I hadn't fucked her yet, but the head was astonishing and she was a cool lil vibe.

"I don't give a fuck what you do with your dick, but don't take me connecting you with Goal as saying you locked in. Nigga, I did that off GP to get you acclimated and to be able to have some real money flowing in your pockets. I know you doing yo' thang and out here eating, but I wanted you to really have the buffet. My sister, though? That's still the fucking mission. Both y'all running my fucking blood pressure up but got the nerve to be fucking in my daughter's room."

Yeah, we were wild for that, but a nigga was drunk and horny as fuck. Shit was worth getting caught too. Jae Bae was different. It was like she had these moments where she was relatable, letting me know she'd been through shit just like me, and then the next, she had her nose turned up at a nigga and diamonds on, letting you know you were beneath her because of who the fuck her brother was. We weren't serious and she knew that. She was cool with the shit, and so was I. I did have to sit down with her and discuss this wedding though. The sooner, the better, so that I could send for my people—all of them.

"Aye, all I can tell you is be a man, drop these lemon drop serving ass hoes that eat more dick than the Chippendales in there, and take care of your fucking business."

Don slapped my chest with the back of his hand and turned to get in the car. When I followed, he paused.

"Nah, you met yo' limit with riding with me." He pointed his finger behind him.

An all-black brand new Escalade with LED blue lights pulled around the roundabout.

"That's your truck and your driver. It's time for you to step the fuck up and fit the part entirely. You ready to go ahead and learn this shit for real? Handle yo' fucking household first, nigga. This is my last time telling you. If I call this shit off, not only will I be looked at as the best brother in the world, but yo' ass is grass."

Demise's driver closed the door, jogged to the driver's side, and pulled off, leaving me standing outside the mansion of dicks.

When the driver of the Escalade got out, I nodded my head

at the older black man and hopped in the truck. Once we, too, were pulling off, I inhaled the leather and new car scent. I bet if the partition wasn't up and I was able to see the dashboard, it would read close to zero miles. This shit was brand new and the dials in the back let me know I could control the radio and the partition from the back seat.

Speaking with both Dons had me feeling like a child who had been reprimanded. I'd always held my own with the help of my cousins. Without them, I still held my own. But even though I had some wild and hot-head moments, I wasn't stupid. I was outnumbered in this city. I thought coming here, training, and learning my place was the way, but according to Demise and Rio, I should have been on my bully shit. I tried to keep that Ezio tucked away, and the percs helped me to do so. These niggas thought they did, but they didn't want me to come in this bitch like a wrecking ball. But I heard them both loud and clear. I was man enough to admit when I fucked up and I truly had. I wasn't doing enough. I definitely should have been all about Jisei first and trying to make connections second. She wanted a nigga to be all for her, but she truly didn't know what the fuck that meant. Reporting to her fucking brother about what the fuck I was doing and who the fuck I was spending my time with was childish as fuck. That shit was almost like playing with my money. I had her though. She wanted a fiancé? Cool. A fiancé was who she was going to get, but I was going to address the shit after I figured out how I was gone cop some more percs. Lions and gay ass mobsters. Boy, this shit was too much for one day.

CHAPTER 16
EZIO "EZEE" CUPPACIO

I'd had so much on my plate as of late that it should have been near impossible for me to even care about getting high. But I cared real bad and though I was pissed, it did feel good to pop a perc even though it was my last one. Sitting back and analyzing, I realized that anytime I left Jisei's space, I didn't have one thought about a pill for at least a few days. After the talk with her brother outside of gay boy mansion, I had blown her phone up from my cousin's phones and burner phones, all for her ass not to answer. Between being pissed at her ass and serving my clients, it wasn't until today that I had a flashback, so I took the last pill in the orange bottle. Shio wasn't giving me shit and though I was desperate, I didn't know these niggas out here well enough to cop from them. I thought about having my cousins back home bring me some but it wasn't that serious. I didn't want Shio to feel like I was falling off the deep end, especially when we were so close to sealing the deal on this shit. Plus, my cousins back in Chicago needed to remain there to make sure shit was straight on the home front.

236

These last couple of months, a nigga had been straight grinding. Between me chasing Jisei's ass, selling this fucking dope and making my people's pockets fatter, the days had been running together. Life was good and I hadn't even said I do yet. Since I couldn't fuck Jisei again, I had to get my nut off somehow. Her good pussy kept me at ease for a few days but now, my dick was standing to full attention, and I knew there was no way I could go home with tight nuts. I sent Olivia a text and she sent back that she was on her period. That was cool by me because I wasn't trying to fuck anyway. I'd been fucking with lil mama for a cool lil minute and still hadn't put my dick in her. I strictly wanted my dick sucked.

Since I had been kicking it with her, she didn't complain about not feeling me in her guts. If I wasn't able to get personal with my own fucking fiancée, what the fuck I looked like getting that way with another bitch? Jisei probably thought Olivia had reign over her, but that shit was a lie. Olivia was fine, had good vibes and an amazing mouth. It felt so good to have a bad bitch from a new city that nobody back home had. Olivia didn't nag me or give me attitude. She didn't ask me questions or give me stipulations. She lived on her fucking knees when I was around. I blessed her pockets and she blessed me with her mouth. That was our arrangement. Nothing more.

Sitting on Olivia's couch, I bobbed my head to the beat of her Alexa that was playing Money Bagg Yo. She was in the shower and promised that she wouldn't be long. My high was starting to fade, and I knew it was because I had only taken one pill. I tried not to think of the shit too much because my Dick would go soft and there would be nothing she could do to get me back hard.

The back door creaked, and Olivia came out wearing a black lace thong, and matching bra. She didn't look like a bitch on her period, and I knew pads and thongs didn't go together.

"I have on a tampon. I usually have my Walmart gown on, but since you want some head, I wanted to look good for you, baby." She answered the question that plagued my thoughts.

Spreading my legs, I drove my back into the couch and waited in anticipation for that warm, deep throat. Olivia turned around and touched her toes, then she made that ass clap, making my dick throb. She was too fucking sexy. They made some bad bitches out in Jagoda Bay on gang.

"Give me one second. I want to take a pain killer so I can be good. Let me grab a bottled water. You want one?"

My throat was a bit dry so I nodded and her thick ass disappeared around the corner to her kitchen. Olivia was cool as fuck. It made me wonder why in the fuck she was single. I was surprised a nigga wasn't in this bitch shacking up. A fine ass woman who had her own shit; usually, niggas saw that as a prize and a way for their homeless ass to hit the jackpot. But then again, Jisei was single. I was sure her brother wasn't having a nigga shacking up and living off his sister so that was probably the reason she was single. Well she was sneaking around with that nigga so I didn't know if she identified as single or not. I had to rub my hand down my face because here I was about to stick my dick down the next bitch's throat and Jisei was taking over my thoughts.

Olivia came back in the living room with two bottled waters. She handed me one, plopped down on the other couch where her Gucci purse was and unzipped it. When she pulled out a Tylenol bottle I started to look off but when she popped the top and poured the pills in her hand, my mouth watered. *Fuck.* I couldn't take my eyes off the pills that had me tweaking from not knowing where I was going to get my next hit. We had codeine by the cases but that drank only made me sleepy and itchy. I needed the percs and Olivia was separating them with her pointed blue nails. She must've felt me staring as she pulled a pill from the container, so she looked up, cheeks growing rosy as fuck.

"I ain't no pill head or nothing like that. I, uh... just really take these for cramps."

"What you takin'? Tabs?"

Lortabs were too weak for me and sometimes made a nigga dizzy so I stayed away from them. I knew they weren't tabs. I could point a Perc out with my eyes closed. I just wasn't trying to appear too thirsty.

"Nah. These Percocet thirties."

"Who you cop from?" I asked before I could even stop my-fucking-self. I didn't like folks outside of my cousins knowing I popped pills like fucking Skittles, but I was out, and though I wasn't fiending at the time, I knew I would be soon. Shio wasn't going to help a nigga, so I knew I needed to find a new supplier and ASAP.

"Umm, my god brother."

"He legit?" I was directing my questions to Olivia but I was locked in on the pills in her hand.

"Hell yeah. His girl is a pharmacist so he gets his shit straight from the source. He the only person I trust. Niggas be out here dropping like flies over fake pills. I love my life too fucking much and got plenty to live for."

She was talking but I hadn't heard shit outside of her folks being the pharmacist.

Olivia placed a pill on her tongue, washed it down, and grabbed another pill before coming over to me. She bent over, getting nose to nose with a nigga.

"Open up, baby."

I obeyed, and when she placed the pill in my mouth, I closed down on her finger and sucked it. She bit down on her bottom lip, and when I let her finger go, she opened my water and placed it to my lips. I drank enough to wash the perc down, and at the same time, she dropped to her knees. Running my tongue across my teeth, my eyes lowered, my mouth watered, my body relaxed, and my jaw slacked.

"You can have all the pills in the bottle, baby. It's twelve in there."

"Aite. I'ma pay you for 'em. Just make sure you can keep 'em coming for a nigga."

Olivia pulled my dick out of my sweats and slapped it against her face. She always rubbed my dick against her flawless skin and I loved that shit. It felt so fucking good. Like she was worshipping my dick or some shit.

"I got you, baby."

She spat on my dick and stuck it so far down her throat, I had to grab the back of her head. I knew she was wearing a wig, so I tried not to snatch that shit off, but damn, it felt too good. Olivia gagged on my dick and opened her mouth so wide, it looked like her lips were about to split. Tears pooled in her eyes and she blinked her long ass lashes to sweep the tears away. If it wasn't for the warm air I felt on my pelvis bone, I would have thought Olivia sacrificed breathing to eat my dick. This girl was a fucking pro at what she did. Supahead didn't have shit on her. She hadn't even started using her hands yet and I was damn near moaning. She could quit both her jobs and make a killing off dick eating. It should be a crime the way she knew how to throat a dick.

Olivia finally let up a little and began working her hands around the base of my mans.

"This the biggest dick I ever had, baby. Shiiiit. I love it!"

"Fuuuuuck," I whispered.

I was happy that Olivia knew how to keep up with a nigga because after I busted my nut, I was still going to be on hard.

She could eat this dick all night and I was going to sit here and let her. Once Olivia started sucking my balls, I grunted and that had her putting the dick back down her throat just in time to catch all my seeds. Once she sucked every last drop, I was ready for another round since the pill had kicked in.

"Aye. This shit stays between me and you, aite?"

"I got you. Whatever you need from me, I got you. My lips are sealed."

"Good. Now unseal them bitches and put 'em to better use. I want to fuck yo' throat all night."

Life was straight, but now that I had a pill plug, it was about to get even better. This lil bitch was decent fasho.

CHAPTER 17
JISEI "JAE BAE" RINALDI

One month later
Men always want to be a woman's first love. Women like to be a
man's last romance.

E zio: *Attachment*

Staring at the very first message I received from Ezio since I'd unblocked his number earlier, disgust yielded quickly to fury. My lips thinned with anger as I tapped on the picture and expanded it so that the picture could be more visible. I was so pissed that I couldn't even think straight. I didn't know what to say in response to the bullshit.

Ezio: Come suck this dick, fake ass fiancée.

Long. Veiny. Curved. Heavy. So heavy. His dick was so heavy that it rested against his thigh. Precum rested at his fat mushroom tip. His length damn near lined his knee and the tattooed leg sprawled out in front of him was enough to leave me drooling. It had been a month. One fucking month since he fucked the sanity out of me, and he had the nerve to send me a picture asking me put my mouth on him. That shit was so disrespectful! No telling what else he'd been sending but since he was blocked all this time, I hadn't been getting anything from him. I was furious. Furious because while his pretty ass light brown dick was easily the one thing about him that I missed the most, seeing it had me wondering who he'd been sticking it in.

My phone rang in my hand and my heart escalated, thinking it was him. I sighed with relief when I saw who the caller was.

"I hate this nigga," I spat, standing from my couch, pacing the floor. He had some fucking nerve. But overall, my pussy had some fucking nerve because why in the fuck was it thudding in my fucking pants?

"Woaaaaah, friend. What the fuck is going on?"

I almost hated that it was Scarlett on the other end of the line because this was her cousin, after all. I knew she had loyalty to him, even though they weren't that close. The fact of the matter was that they were still blood related. I couldn't go in like I wanted to with her but fuck all that, he had the game fucked up.

Pressing the speaker button, I swiped up on the screen so that I could migrate back to my messages.

I knew I couldn't forward her a text of her cousin's dick, so I just exited out of the messages all together.

"He just play with me way too fucking much."

"You're going to be married in the next few months. Y'all gotta stop with all this back and forth." Scarlett sighed.

"I don't got to do shit but stay black and die."

We don't even have a date yet.

"Stay black and Italian and die." Scarlett snickered.

It was times that I forgot I was even half Italian. I didn't look it. My entire life, I was an African American with all the amazing African American features and that was how I identified.

"Friend. What I'ma do with you and my cousin? Y'all already had sex, just make the shit official."

"The nigga called me a fake ass fiancée!"

"He was just playing, friend."

"Look, Scarlett, I know you trying to make shit right, but on God, I'm tired of this nigga and these hoes."

I was lurking on Olivia's IG the other day and the nigga was on her couch, knocked out, looking good as fuck. The bitch gon' say, "Me and bae too high." What type of Whitney and Bobby shit was that? I hoped he was only high off weed because anything else and it was really over with for him. Bobby fucked that up for everybody. I wasn't dealing with no crack head under no circumstances. I unblocked his number only because of that post and I wanted to see if he would reach out. Now I was pissed because he had reached out.

"Y'all have to get married, friend, so maybe it's time to stop the bullshit. Just make it official. Clearly, y'all like one another."

Yes, I knew I had to marry this man. Yes, I understood the situation we were in, but what I wasn't going for was a nigga playing me to the left for another bitch, but behind closed doors, be all lovey dovey, eating my soul out and shit. I had never been an Easter egg and I damn sure wasn't going to let a nigga hide me like one. If anything, I was the golden egg – the money egg. The fuck.

"Okay. So, how about this? You call him and this time, you both have a real conversation. No Netflix and chilling. No sex. Just two adults letting one another know what they really want. Get—"

"Aye, get yo' ass off the phone. You got yo' own dick to handle." Matteo was so close to the phone that you would swear he was on three-way. That was how deep he was in my friend's skin.

244

"Give me a second, Jisei."

I heard the phone shuffle but could still hear their conversation clearly.

"Matteo, back the fuck off. I'm on the phone with my friend. I was up with your baby all fucking night because you done fucked her stomach up by giving her that sugary ass cereal ever since she was a baby. Leave me the fuck alone before I pack my shit up and check into a hotel, leaving you with her shitty ass. Stop fucking interrupting me because your dick hard. Go beat the shit in the shower because I'm not fucking you until I get good and ready. You was just calling me a lil prostitute earlier and now you want this prostitute pussy. Well, I'm not in the fucking mood! I done had enough of you and lil gas station."

I placed a hand over my mouth but said a silent praise. My friend mostly always just let Matteo say whatever, paying him no mind and laughing his shenanigans off. It was rare that she got on his ass, but when she did, I always cheered her on. Matteo was a great husband but the muthafucka was crazy and possessive as hell. He let her move how she wanted, but when he was ready to soak up her time, he didn't give a fuck what it was she was doing.

I all but held my breath waiting for his response, praying he didn't jump stupid because, if he did, I already had my shoes on so it would be nothing to grab my keys and pistol. He'd never put anything but ice and dick on my friend, but the nigga didn't have it all upstairs.

"I'll be in the room when you get off the phone, baby."

"Bye, Matteo."

The phone shuffled again and I heard Scarlett walking through their home. The sound of a sliding door and the traffic let me know that she was on the balcony of their beautiful downtown condo.

"You good, friend?"

I may have been going through my shit, but if my friend needed me, I would stop, drop, and roll to be there for her.

"Girl, yes. Matteo stay having to get his ass roasted. Y'all just don't ever really see it but that tough shit don't hold no weight here. He knows what's up. Anyway, back to you. Call Ezio and put your foot down, friend."

"But do I have a right to do that, though?"

"Uhhh, hell yes. You marrying him and you gave him some pussy! Plus, despite what you say, I know you like him, maybe even love him. Call him over, or you can go to his house. I have the address of the rental he's made his temporary home. I'll text it to you now."

The pecking sounds on the screen let me know Scarlett was indeed sending me this man's address. Did I like him? That was to be determined. I didn't know him to like him. It had been months since I'd first met him and I still felt like I didn't know the man. But the dick? The dick was phenomenal. The dick and tongue combination was lethal. But dick wasn't enough. Was he good looking? Fuck yes. Even if he didn't have the orange, brown, green eyes he would be fine, but looks were irrelevant when the muthafucka they were attached to wasn't shit.

Olivia was the bitch that was constantly popping up, but she wasn't the only bitch he had. Jagoda Bay was the smallest big city in the south. I unblocked the nigga and the first thing he texted was come suck his dick. Yeah, I was over his good big dick ass.

The vibration in my ear let me know the address had been sent but I refrained from looking at it. I had no plans on pulling up to where he laid his head even though he didn't have a problem with doing it to me without an invite.

My line beeped indicating another caller was on the line

and seeing Anakin's name and picture had some of the anger I felt toward this other nigga fading.

"I'll talk to him but I'm not going to his house. Look, go handle your husband. This is Anakin. He's here for the weekend and I need to pack my hoe bag."

"Jae. Don't do it. Especially since you just fucked Ezio. You said y'all used a condom but I bet y'all didn't. Don't turn into an urban fiction novel, bookie. End up pregnant and not knowing who the daddy—"

"Bye, Scarlett. I fucked that man weeks ago. His dick juice been out of my system. And I'll have a bum on the street's baby before I have his."

Clicking over, I caught the line just as it was about to go to voicemail.

"Hey, you," I cooed.

Anakin and I had been damn near falling asleep on the phone nightly. When he wasn't talking about himself or his company, shit was cool. I didn't know if it was the distance but I anticipated our phone conversations. For the last week I'd been coming home to dinner from various steak houses around the city, and like clockwork, after I was fed and showered, Anakin would be on my line. He was supposed to come last weekend but Memphis had a bad thunderstorm so all the flights were canceled. To make it up to me, he sent me dinner every night and it was sweet, considering there were times I didn't feel like cooking or forgot to get food for dinner from the cafeteria.

"I just made it through the gates, baby. I'm walking through the terminal now. I just have to check into my hotel and I'm all yours. What you want to do first?"

I was pissed at Ezio, but I wasn't stupid enough to be seen with Anakin in public. It wasn't even about Ezio, it was about embarrassing my brother. True, my brother hadn't mentioned the wedding as of late but he also hadn't mentioned it being canceled, either. No matter how upset I was, I wasn't going to go against Demise for anyone.

"Okay. I'm going to pack a bag and head your way. You still staying at the Westin, right?" I asked, wedging my phone between my shoulder and my ear. I'd completely ignored his question because we wouldn't be doing anything outside of his hotel. Luckily, the Westin had a poetry club, that doubled as a jazz lounge and three restaurants. That, added in with a spa and indoor pool, there was plenty of shit for us to do to enjoy each other's company.

Once my bag was packed, I waved at my neighbor, Glow, who was outside watering her plants and hopped in my truck. I hardly ever used my garage. The Kia was in there and since my truck was so big, I sometimes had to squeeze into it if I didn't park right. So, it was more convenient for me to just keep my baby in the driveway. Plus, I liked how my big body looked up against my house.

The gas light had me stopping for fuel, delaying my trip by fifteen minutes but I'd finally made it to the Westin. I opted out of valet parking because I didn't feel like waiting on them to get my truck when I was ready to leave. I'd planned on spending the weekend with Anakin and indulging in every-thing the hotel had to offer. This would be my staycation since it had been a minute since I went on vacation. I wanted to take the girls up on their constant offers of going out the city but there was just too much going on right now. I wouldn't be able to even enjoy myself with my racing thoughts. So, I was going to take advantage of my stay. I remember there were times I would dream of spending the night at a five-star hotel back when I barely had bus fare. Now I had enough money to live in a hotel for a year straight if I wanted to. But this here was on Anakin's dime, which made it even more exciting.

Walking through the lobby of the Westin, I gushed over its sleek décor that was not only innovative but warm and inviting. Anakin had already texted me the room number, so I trudged in the direction of the elevators and made my way up to room 9123. The ninth floor would give us amazing views of Jagoda Bay, and if he was a good boy, he just may get some pussy on the balcony.

When Ezio fucked my lights out last month, he woke up a fucking beast. I needed dick and bad. It was all good when you didn't get any, but the moment you did it was like you couldn't live without it. I wasn't worried about turning into an urban fiction novel like Scarlett said because I was going to make sure Anakin wrapped his dick up.

I fucked up by fucking Ezio. Anakin had been the one putting in work. He'd been the one flying in, sending dinner, and making sure I got home after work. So many times, I'd wished I had considered his damn proposal because I damn sure wouldn't be in the predicament I was in now. But fuck Ezio; it was Anakin's turn to fuck now.

Adjusting the leather Louis Vuitton duffle on my shoulder that I may have packed way too heavy, I watched the lobby below through the glass door.

I was nervous. Palm sweating. Heart pounding. Scalp itching nervous. Nervous like he hadn't already been balls deep in the coochie. Anakin hadn't touched me in over a year and was the last man to sample Ms. Kitty before Ezio broke the spell. But he was used to fucking on Jae. Jisei had upgraded and the three La Perla crotchless lingerie sets tucked at the bottom of my duffle were proof. I couldn't wait for Anakin to see and experience the new me.

Ezio talked all that shit but I had his ass screaming all types of I love yous and shit. I was that bitch in and out of the bedroom. Long gone was the Jae that sometimes didn't even shave because I was up to my eyeballs in assignments. When I did have the time to shave, it had caused discoloration and razor bumps down below. Now, the new me didn't miss a month at the wax lady. She been touching my pussy so much, I almost made her my bitch and the lady was a married woman with kids. Those vagacials not only had my inner thighs and vagina the same color as the rest of my skin, but had my girl down below looking and feeling so silky smooth. She damn sure looked good enough to eat, even though this nigga didn't eat pussy. Still, I was just excited to be able to get the dick. I had already had my pussy devoured, and even though I hated him, I was sure there was no nigga who could top Ezio's mouth. I would have to burn another man's head in order to compare but Anakin wasn't budging until I became his wife. These niggas around me needed wives like the family company was on the line or some shit.

Approaching his door, I pulled out my phone to text him just in case he was in the shower and wouldn't hear my knock. As I went to the text app, Ezio's name was at the top of my thread with a new text. I'd forgotten to block his ass again an hour ago when he sent the fucking invitation to swallow his dick. Was I tempted even though he was disrespectful as fuck? Yes. I'd had the dick and it was so pretty it belonged in a bitch's mouth. But knowing Olivia and the rest of the city was getting that dick, I wouldn't dare eat it. Instead of locking my screen, my thumb hovered over the text. I wanted to bypass his text but I couldn't. I clicked on his message to see what the fuck else he was sending to piss me the fuck off again.

Ezio: Come here. Fake ass fiancée

Come here? This nigga had truly lost his fucking mind. What the fuck I looked like? Before we fucked, I hadn't heard from his ass since when? Aw, okay. Then he had the nerve to act like I was the one tripping. I didn't know who in the fuck

Ezio was used to dealing with but he had fucked around and found out.

Me: I started to block you for sending me that bullshit ass *invitation* but I have better shit to do. Ezio not only am I not marrying you, I'm not "coming here" and I damn sure ain't sucking your dick. Go call Oliv—

I deleted the last three words and sent the message. I didn't want his ass to think I was pressed about Olivia's ass. I was silk pressed, in fact, but he didn't need to know the shit. His bobble head was big enough. The bubble on the screen let me know he was replying and my stupid ass was eagerly waiting.

Ezio: You know you ready to marry a nigga. Lying to yourself ain't gon' do shit but keep you in yo' feelings. That pussy though? Shit was supa wet. Come put it on my face.

Shit.

I rolled my eyes so fucking hard that it made my damn head hurt but my pussy was so thick with juices that I needed a paper towel to dry it. This nigga was way too full of himself. That was the reason I didn't do pretty boys. I didn't give a fuck how thug he was; he acted like the typical pretty ass nigga. Anakin had that classic, hardworking, Morris Chestnut type of fine going on. He didn't have a perfectly structured face but his broad nose and thick lips were some of his best features. Ezio was too damn pretty and that was his fucking problem.

Me: Okay I lied. I am about to block you. Get off my line, Ezio. I'm busy with a big dick –

I removed the last four words because again he didn't need to know what the fuck I was doing. I didn't know what the fuck he did in his spare time so I wasn't about to put him in my business. Instead of blocking him, I drove my chin into my chest and stared down at the phone, waiting for his response. The duffle on my shoulder burned my skin due to it's weight so I let it drop to the ground beside me.

Ezio: Oh, so you busy Jae Bae?
Me: Yeap. All weekend so don't text me.

Fuuuck, why did I send that? I held down on the text to edit it but figured that would be lame as fuck so I let it rock.

Ezio: Merch?
Me: Blocked.

This time, I really did block him and as soon as the deed was done, Anakin opened the door, making my pussy thud on sight. *Or was it already thudding from thinking of the way Ezio ate me into oblivion that time?* Steam floated atop his head and the water pellets on his bare chocolate chest confirmed he'd just gotten out of the shower. I could smell his Dove body wash and smiled because he remembered. We always used protection when we had sex, but I still preferred him to use the same soap as me. My auntie used to tell me how a man could knock your PH balance off just by using certain soaps and I didn't have time for an itching and leaking pussy.

"Damn, Jisei, you look good as fuck."

I'd showered and dressed comfortably in navy Lululemon high waist leggings and the matching crop jacket. I didn't wear a jacket because I wanted him to have easy access to the new piercings I'd gotten. I got them more than six months ago with Mocha, and while they hurt sometimes when they were snagged on my loofah, I couldn't wait to feel the sensation of them in Anakin's mouth. He didn't eat pussy but he did suck and lick all over the other places on my body.

Anakin reached down and picked up my bag and stood back to let me in. Like I'd changed, so had he. He was always a beast in the gym but I could see now that he had definitely upped his routine. The biceps, triceps and six-pack had me drooling. I wanted him to melt on my tongue but I wouldn't dare put his dick in my mouth and he wasn't returning the favor. I'd sucked dick with the guy before him and that was stupid as fuck of me to let him treat me like a porn star when he didn't eat my pussy either. You would think my shit stank with the way those niggas didn't eat me out but it was all good.

Ezio proved that my girl was indeed edible. Anakin had a big dick that hit all the right spots and it was good enough for me. *But Ezio's was bigger.* I had to shake that nigga from my thoughts.

Entering Anakin's suite, I all but squealed at the perfect view of the city. *Yeah, we were about to have some fun up in here.* Before the other day, I couldn't believe I had even gone so long without getting dick. Now, seeing Anakin in his lounge pants, looking like every woman's wet dream, I should have been called his ass up. He hadn't said shit about being exclusive or marriage during our nightly talks, and if he had been on this type of time after we graduated, there was no telling where we would be.

"I can get dressed and take you out to get some food and drinks. I just had to wash the funk from the airport off of me."

Anakin dropped my duffle bag on the bed and went to the closet so that he could pull out something to wear. Before he could get too far out of arms reach, I grabbed his arm.

"I was thinking we could bless the room first."

Anakin displayed that panty-dropping smile and looked me up and down.

"That's what you on?"

"Ummhumm."

Anakin grabbed me around my waist and pulled me to his chest. He stood over me by only a few inches but as long as he was taller than me, even with heels on, I was cool with that. I didn't do short men, nor did I do fucking giants. Ain't shit a seven foot four man could do for me.

Placing his lips against mine, Anakin snaked his tongue in

my mouth. I sucked the toothpaste off of his slimy, pink tongue as he rubbed his hand down my backside. My pussy was now leaking, and I was sure he felt the combination of my hardened nipples and piercing.

Ready to get this shit popping, I stuck my hands down the front of his pants, bypassing his damp pubic hairs and grabbing his thick, hardened member. I remember when I showed his dick picture to Mocha, she swore up and down he wasn't the biggest. He was bigger than the last dude and had my ass climbing up the wall and sore for days, so he was big to me. If Lorenzo was bigger than that, I just knew my friend didn't have any walls. That was what I had thought at the time, but now I knew better. Ezio was like two of Anakin.

Anakin began backing me up and when I noticed he was going near the balcony, my heart raced with anticipation. Anakin was an amazing kisser; he'd actually taught me. He'd taught me a few things, like how to ride dick like a cowgirl and I was ready to put those skills to use. It had been a while since I'd had the pleasure of sitting on a dick. *Ezio had bent me over and fucked. Damn that was a good fuck too.*

A vibration between us had him pausing on the kiss, and when I tried pulling him back to me, he backed out of my embrace.

"Baby, your phone. Handle that. I promise I got you."

Knowing it was nobody but Mocha since I knew Scarlett had a mouth full of dick, I grabbed my phone from the pocket of my jacket while continuing to eye Anakin. He winked at me and walked to the mini bar to fix us both a drink. I saw his hard dick from here and was ready to press ignore on Mocha. Without paying much attention to the contact name because I was busy watching my dick for the weekend, I answered the phone.

"Hello?"

"Aye, where you at, Jisei?"

I pulled the phone from my ear because I just knew it was Mocha, but the deep voice didn't match hers. Seeing it was none other than my brother, I cleared my throat and tried to swallow my panic. Anakin looked over at me and grinned. But if he knew the grim reaper was on the line he wouldn't be grinning at all. I turned and went straight for the balcony, sliding the door open and closing it behind me.

"Um, what's up, brother? Wha-what you doing?"

I looked down at the outdoor pool and bar below us and prayed that Anakin didn't bring his ass outside. I didn't know why the fuck I was so spooked when it came to my brother but I didn't want his ass knowing what I was up to. I heard him loud and clear when he told me to cut my niggas off and wasn't trying to find out what the hell he would do if he had found out I hadn't.

"Shit. Chillin'. Aye, I'm 'bout to send a driver to scoop you. I need you to be somewhere."

I swallowed hard, trying to manage a feasible answer. I wasn't home but I wasn't going to tell him my whereabouts.

"Umm, can I come a bit later or tomorrow—"

"Nah. You can't. The driver on the way."

"Brother, you can just send me the address. I was already out getting, um… gas, so I can just meet you at the address."

As the line grew quiet, I closed my eyes and held my breath, waiting for his response.

"I'm sending the address now. If you not out of that hotel room and in your truck in three minutes, I'ma send a nigga in there and he shooting first and snatching yo' ass out second."

I chipped my nail opening the sliding door, running back into the room. Anakin was nowhere to be found but the two drinks he made were on the bar. The bathroom door was closed so I grabbed my bag, one of the drinks and all but ran out the door while the phone was still to my ear.

"I-I'm getting in the elevator now, brother. I'm waiting on the address."

"Aite. Drive safe. I love you."

Only Don would threaten me and tell me he loved me.

Tossing the drink back, I stepped on the elevator as soon as it arrived on the floor.

"I love you too. I just got the address, I'm on my way."

As the doors closed behind me, I rested my back against the glass and tried to catch my breath. How in the fuck did he know where I was? My phone vibrated again, and it was Anakin. I didn't have the guts to tell him I had to leave and why, so I ignored him and clicked on the address my brother sent. I didn't even remember walking through the lobby but I was in the truck, peeling out of the parking lot, on the way to the location. I didn't know why my brother wanted me there or where I was going but I had underestimated his reach and pull. If I was going to fuck with Anakin, I may need to fly out to him. I wasn't trying to be the reason that man met Jesus before he even turned thirty.

IT TOOK me less than twenty minutes to make it to the address my brother sent. One would think in twenty minutes that my heart would have slowed in rhythm, but it hadn't. I even found myself looking in the rear-view mirror more times than I usually did. I was still puzzled as to how he knew exactly where I was. I didn't question it, though, I just got the fuck out of dodge. I wasn't stupid enough to test my brother and his promises. I didn't have a trail like the wives did and felt like since I took my gun everywhere, I was good.

People knew who I was. Back in my college days, I was

popular, so I was used to people recognizing me wherever I went. Plus, I had a nice following on social media, so it was common to be pointed out. Over these last few months it was like the city had found out I was Don's sister, and for that, they treated me differently. Doors opened more frequently, I rarely had to pay for my meals, and if there was a waiting list, I was bumped to the top. Being the sister of the Don came with plenty of perks, but now that someone had snitched on my ass, I wished they still only knew me as the struggling, popular, smart, sorority girl.

Looking up at the house in front of me, I was in awe of its beauty. Between my best friend and brother, one would think I was used to seeing gorgeous homes, but I could never grow tired. There was nothing like a beautiful house.

I killed the engine and left my duffle bag on the front seat. Grabbing my phone and keys, I eased onto the pavement with caution, like my brother was going to come out at any moment and beat my ass. The white and black, modern style home was immaculate, and though it wasn't as grand as the rest of my people's home, especially Don's, it was nice.

I pulled my phone out to call my brother but thought against it. He hadn't given me any instructions besides to come to this address, so here I was. Lifting my hand up to the door-bell, I pressed it twice and then stuck my head to the side so I could see inside. The first thing I noticed were some bent-up ass Air Force Ones that I vividly remembered. Fuming, I went back to my texts, clicked on Scarlett's name, and saw the address she'd sent me. Then, I went back to my brother's name and compared the two.

"He sent me to this nigga's house?"

Pissed wasn't the word I would use to describe the emotion I felt. My scalp was on fire and felt like it was going to sweat out my leave out and my neck itched. My dick appointment was being interrupted for this shit? For Ezio's hoe ass? If I didn't think my brother would go in on my ass, I would turn the fuck around, but I wouldn't dare play with my life like that. The door opened and the same racing heart I had for Anakin was replaced by scolding rage. I wanted to pounce on this nigga and knock his ass the fuck out. Mainly because seeing him reminded me of how damn good that beast was between his legs.

"I see you got some sense after all."

Ezio stood over me, hands tucked in the front of his grey sweat pants, big ass gun with the clip hanging off his slim waist. A wife beater covered his upper half but since his arms were exposed, the tattoos etched on his light skin went on for what seemed forever. Whomever his artist was, they were indeed one of the best around. He was a walking work of fucking art. Even the small tattoos on his handsome face were perfectly placed. The diamond necklace he'd had on when he fucked me to a coma was resting around his neck, but other than that, he wore no other jewelry. I almost had wished I'd worn my jewelry. My brother's latest obsession had been dousing me with diamonds. You would think I was a female rapper with the number of chains, Cubans, and pendants I'd been collecting like infinity stones over the past few months. My shit was drowning his easily. So if he thought I was stressing over a cheap ass engagement ring, he was horribly wrong. The watch he gave me was cute and definitely going to be a staple piece for me, but still. I wasn't pressed about a ring.

"Ezio, I didn't peg you for a snitch."

Crossing my arms under my breasts, I cocked my head as I put it all together. He had called my brother and fucked up my situation. Then, he had the nerve to be wearing grey sweat pants! Stupid ass! He had too much dick those male thot joggers.

"Shit, I didn't peg you for one, either. Do as my wife do. Ain't that what the Bible says?"

"Nigga, that shit ain't nowhere in the fucking Bible. Move, I hope yo' ass got some food."

I pushed past Ezio because I couldn't stare at him much longer. He was too fucking fine and I was still so fucking horny. Demise was a fucking cock blocker, and I couldn't wait to bust him and Dasani's shit up. I tried to stay at my own house because when the girls were over, she paid him no mind, but it was on. Only time he was going to get some action from his wife was when I was at work.

I kept the frown on my face, letting my attitude over-shadow my admiration of the home. Scarlett had mentioned that he was renting it and if I hadn't known, I would have assumed. This shit was too well decorated. It didn't even look like he could pronounce some of the designers that filled the space. The black and white theme on the interior of the home flowed throughout the space on the inside. It smelled good too. I didn't miss the three wick candle that was lit on the entry way table. The teakwood fragrance paired with Ezio's cologne was a heavenly combination, but I kept my nose turned like I was whiffing a pile of shit.

Plopping down on the black cloud couch that sat in the middle of the living room, facing a large plastered flat screen, I crossed my legs at the ankle and kept my nose turned up and arms crossed. Ezio came in shortly after still wearing that ugly ass smug on his face. I was surprised his eyes weren't low or that I didn't smell weed in the space. I was sure he'd been blowing it down despite the no smoking rule the hosts most certainly had. Shit was too nice for them to allow people to stain their walls with weed, cigarettes and whatever it was that this nigga smoked.

"Wifey, what the fuck you got going?"

Ezio stretched, making his shirt heighten, exposing the v-cut that featured a trail of hairs. *Shit.* I should have at least let Anakin stick the fucking tip in. I was so ready to sit on a dick that my eye was twitching.

"You're pathetic, you know that? What? Yo' girl on her period or something? Is that why you interrupted my weekend?" I was showing my feelings, but at this point, I didn't give a damn. I wanted to be back at the Westin, getting folded like a fucking pretzel, testing Anakin's new muscles.

"I'on know. Are you on your period Jae Bae?"

"Nigga, no. Not that it's any of your business." I scoffed.

"Girl, it is my business. In a minute, I'ma know yo' shit like the back of my hand. One of us gon' have to keep up with it with the way you not going to want to stay off the dick. I bet I fucked you so good, I knocked that shit on. Say I'm lying," He smirked.

I tossed my head back and laughed but there wasn't shit funny about the way my walls had contracted. I had to be ovulating. That was the only explanation as to why I was so fucking horny. When I ovulated, my rose couldn't stay off my pussy lips. I wore her ass out.

"We fucked a month ago. Ion even remember. You so fucking full of yourself. I can tell you used to bitches falling all over you and bending to your will because you fine, but newsflash. You not the only fine nigga with money and a big dick. In Jagoda Bay, dudes like you come a dime a dozen. The city is flooded with you, so you can save that cocky shit, dude."

Ezio looked as if he was amused with my disrespect, but I was just pointing out the obvious. If I wasn't so focused on school for the earlier parts of my adulthood, there was no telling how many men I would have run through. I wasn't a righteous ass girl. If I wanted to fuck, I would. I wasn't worried about body counts or no shit like that; I had just been too busy to entertain a man and life only got even busier after graduating.

"Yet you're on my couch."

"On your rented couch. This isn't your shit. You're renting yours. I own mine."

I knew that was a low jab, but I didn't give a fuck. In a fight, nothing was off limits and me and this man seemed to do that best. Fight.

"You talk so much shit."

Ezio's eyes lowered, and he began walking toward me, gun still sticking out of his waist. He looked foolish. Who was I kidding? He looked damn good. Too good. Too fucking cocky. Too fucking fine. I couldn't ever see myself being tied down to him because Ezio for sure was going to have me in a straight jacket fucking with him. I knew his type. Big dick, big pockets, big ego, and even bigger mental issues. All of that equaled to big ass problems. Problems I wasn't in the mental capacity to solve—not now or ever. He was fucked up in the head and he used that shit as an excuse to take a muthafucka on a ride straight to hell. Still, his nearness made my senses spin. I drank in the comfort of his closeness, but at the same time, it made me unwell. The sound of his voice affected me deeply. My heart ached under my breasts.

"Ezio, don't bring your ass over here. Please."

That *please* came out cracked and it did nothing to stop his stride. When he was standing over me, I looked straight ahead, staring at the blank screen and the butt of his gun since those two were in my peripheral. I knew what Ezio was working with in all departments. I needed him to get far the fuck away from me because the nigga wasn't good for me. He was too fucking open.

"You gon' learn to shut the fuck up around this bitch."

"Who? You got me fu—"

Ezio grabbed my neck with enough pressure to startle me but not enough to cut my air supply off. He was looking down at me with those amber eyes and a mug that if he thought was intimidating, he was sadly mistaken. The shit was sexy. Just plain out fucking sexy, and if he wanted the pussy again, then he was trudging down the right fucking path. This was what I did want from Anakin when we fucked. He did a lot of love making and knew how to drill a bitch to the cross, but one day when I asked him to choke me, he hopped out the bed so fast and asked if I was okay. Right after that, he asked to marry me, and I said hell no. Fuck I look like marrying you when you didn't even want to fully explore other shit sexually? Ezio came along and fucked me just how I liked it. He was rough, possessive, and at the same time, attentive.

"You gon' make me fuck you up, Jae Bae." Ezio gritted.

"You ain't crazy."

He applied more pressure and I bit back a moan.

His eyes stared right through me. I wondered who he'd gotten them from. His mama? His dead ass daddy? When he pumped me with his babies, would they be blessed with them? Would I be the first to carry his children? So many fucking questions. Questions that shouldn't even be swirling in my head. *I wasn't having his babies, ever.*

"Fuck you gon' do? Tell yo' brother? I'on mean no harm but fuck that nigga. He don't put no fucking fear in my heart, baby. When I take you from the Rinaldi and make you a Cuppacio, he especially ain't gon' be able to run shit. Whether you like it or not, you mine."

"I'm no ones. I'm mine. You sound stupid, goofy."

I looked stupid, going back and forth with him while he held my neck in his hands without trying to break free.

"I can't wait till I have you 'round this bitch begging me to touch you."

Disgust was on my face. He had the fucking nerve.

"You may have what I want, but you damn sure not what I need. My needs trump my wants. Ezio, you're like a bad ass drug. Was the dick good? Yes, it was splendid. If I'm being honest, it was the best dick I've had. But you're not any good for me. You're not any good for anyone but those bottom of the barrel bitches you fuck with. You're perfect for them. I worked too hard to get to where I am to let you have me around this bitch in a strait jacket. I don't give a fuck who you are or where you come from, that shit isn't worth my mental. You came to Jagoda Bay, got a couple bricks and really started smelling your ass. The worst thing on earth is a troubled ass nigga getting new money. Hell no. So you saying I'm going to beg you, is a damn lie. If anything, you gon' be 'round this bitch begging me for my time. Oops, you have been. For how many months now? You see my brother had to get me over here. Your lil words had no merit even after you fucked me. If it wasn't for him calling me, another nigga's cum would be milking my walls right now. I had you from the moment you laid eyes on my pretty ass. You love me, remember?"

I struggled to catch my breath after I let him know what was on my chest. Ezio's features were one of a kind, but behind his eyes was a sadness that ran deeper than the lakes at Bay Harbor. A sadness I was terrified of.

"Only thing I heard you say was you love this dick. I'm too high to comprehend all that other shit."

Ezio grunted and squeeze me harder till the point that I couldn't really breathe, but it didn't matter. I was good at holding my breath for a long time, ever since I won the swimming competition at summer camp as a small child. Dangerous. He was so fucking dangerous, and no matter how my eyes showed me, what my mind told me, or my heart warned me that he wasn't shit, my pussy couldn't comprehend it. When I felt like I was about to pass out, he pushed me into the cushion, grabbed my legs and snatched my leggings off so fast, I wondered if he had ripped the one hundred dollar leggings I had caught on sale. I hissed because I was fucking pissed, but the pain in between my thighs didn't seem to mind.

I hadn't noticed that my pussy was on display till my legs were suspended in the air, chin to chest and his face was so close to my folds that I could feel the air coming from his nose.

"Pretty ass pussy. I been thinking about this shit. She gripping too."

I couldn't fight back the moan if I wanted to. He wasn't even touching me, besides holding my legs back with his left forearm. When he blew cool air, starting from the crack of my ass and slowly made his way up to my hot box, my legs couldn't help but shake. I squirmed in this awkward ass position and my heart thumped in my chest.

"You smell good as fuck too. She dripping like a muthafucka. That's why you always mean as fuck to a nigga? You want me to put this pussy in my mouth again?"

Fuck!

"Umm hummmm."

He started back blowing ice-cold air on me and went up and down both my folds with it. You would have thought this nigga's name was Jack Frost, with how he cooled my shit.

"I'on know what umm humm means."

"Ye-yessss!"

"Was that nigga gon' fold you up and sop yo' ass up like a fucking biscuit?"

"N...nooooo!"

"I know it."

Then I felt cold, hard steel on my pussy lips. I froze up until he started stimulating my clit. I never knew my life being in danger would feel so fucking good.

"I just want to feed my family, Jisei, and you want to play with me. I came here to fulfill my duties, but you want to take that opportunity away from me. You constantly smiling in another nigga's face. You must tryna marry that nigga? He shows you some attention and you ready to bust it open for him. Is that it? You doing that because you want some attention from a nigga, baby?"

His voice was calm and almost melodic, like a father telling his child a lullaby. You wouldn't even think he was playing in my pussy with an AK47.

"I... I don't," I panted.

"You playing though. Now, in order for me to feed my people, I need to seal this union. I ain't letting nobody get in the way of that. You understand that, baby?"

My legs shook like a stripper.

"I... I understandddddd."

My stomach began to cave in and I knew with the cool air, cold steel and hardness from the gun that it wouldn't be long before I came. I had never felt the buildup I was feeling now and he wasn't even touching me himself.

"So, when we getting married?"

"I... I..."

Whewwwwwwwww.

He blew directly into my pussy, causing me to whimper.

"So, when we getting married?" he asked again.

"N-now!"

I heard him laugh.

"You making a fucking mess on my gun, baby, and it's my favorite one. I done killed a lot of niggas with it. Never knew I was gon' be killing the pussy with it. But nah, as bad as I want to, I can't marry yo' sexy ass now. But are you gon' get right for a nigga and stop yo' bullshit, Jae Bae?"

I couldn't hold it any longer, but damn, I was trying my

hardest. I felt the ugly ass faces I was making, and once the high came down, I was going to be embarrassed as fuck.

"Yessss, I'ma chill!"

I was beginning to see black spots behind my lids since I'd closed my eyes. This shit had no business feeling so damn good. I had never experienced anything like this in my life and I wondered where he'd learned this shit from. Like, how did he know this would feel so good to me? This man knew my body and he hadn't even explored it. That was crazy.

"One more thing and I'ma let you cum. Tell me you love me."

This man was obsessed with the word love and knew nothing about it. Did he love his family? Yes, he was on so-called enemy territory with only three other men by his side who so happened to be his family and still ran around the city like my brother wouldn't renege and blow his head off. He loved playing games and I loved being a piece on his chess board. I also loved the way he made my body feel so I obeyed his command with my legs shaking so hard that my thighs jiggled like a bowl of Jell-O.

"Okay! Okay! I love you! I love you, Ezio! I fucking love you."

"Umm humm. I know you do. Now make that pussy nut."

And she did. She spat up so fucking bad that I'd wished he was wearing a fucking bib. When I felt the liquid shoot from my center, his nasty ass didn't even move and I had to open my eyes to see. He was smiling, showing the pearly whites instead of his diamond fronts, and when my girl spat all over his mouth, directly on his teeth, I wanted to hide underneath the couch. His eyes expanded and his nasty ass had the nerve to lick his lips. Oh gosh, he was nasty. He was so fucking nasty, and why in the fuck did I love it?

Ezio let my legs down and stood to his feet. My limbs fell

like dead weights as I sat in my own juices. I was still trying to catch my breath as he stood tall, looking down at me with a drenched face.

"You say I'm not what the fuck you need but you should have said I'm not what the fuck you want, baby. You're the Rinaldi princess so you deserve to be treated as such. Will I treat you like a princess? Fuck yeah. I'll treat you like a princess, but this dick gon' drive you crazy. You ain't ready for this shit, Jisei. The best thing we can do to keep all parties involved safe and secured is just get married and go on about our business. I told you, I'm fucked up, baby. That square ass nigga you fuck with, he's more your speed. But he can't have you. Not now or ever. It's fucked up but these are the circumstances we were handed. Now, you gon' marry me so I can do this shit for my people. I will scale back with the bitches. I never want to see you out here looking bad, but I demand the same respect. Besides that, we gon' treat this shit like what it is.

"I had every intention of letting my fucking gun rip and sending your ass to meet your father. That's what type of nigga I am when I feel like a muthafucka tryna toy with my emotions and my pockets. You doing both, Jisei. See, I would have had to kill you and your whole damn family, and when I got to heaven, you was still gon' be fiendin' for the dick while everybody else up there mad as hell at us for landing us all in that predicament. You not ready for this, Jisei. You a fucking good girl. A college girl. A nigga like me will turn you the fuck out for the worse. Take yo' ass to work, live your best fucking mob wife life, get grade-A dick from me and be the pretty bossed up bitch you are. That's what the fuck the rest of your life looks like."

I was still trying to catch my breath, but since I was no longer folded, I didn't agree with him. I just glared at his ass, trying hard to keep the tears in. My lips trembled, my pussy was still contracting, and my chest heaved. My heart rate had tripled in speed and Ezio just stood above me as he broke my fucking heart again for the umpteenth time.

He scooped my leggings from the floor and handed them to me. Snatching them from his hands, I turned them inside out, stepped in them, snagging my toenail, and slid them over my ass. He watched my every move too.

Once they were on, I stuck my feet back in my Crocs and pushed past Ezio. This man really had a gun to my pussy and admitted he wanted to kill me. Me? Jisei Rinaldi? Had he pulled the trigger, it was lights the fuck out for me. Who even does shit like that? If I called my brother, his ass would be buried faster than he could blink. He actually had a whole nasty ass gun to my pussy. I was going to have to schedule an emergency vagacial and a yoni steam to get those toxins out of me. No telling where in the fuck his gun had been. He had the fucking nerve.

Before I could get out of the door with shaking hands, I looked back and this nigga was licking the gun. He was licking my fucking juices off the gun and he looked so fucking sexy. Knowing he was standing there covered in my cum and actually tasting me and looking as if he enjoyed it was sultry. X-Rated. I didn't even know what other word to use besides euphoric. Maybe blissful? This man was treacherous, and for the first time since this whole shit started, I was starting to fear Ezio. I didn't fear him in anticipation that he would harm me, despite his confession, but I feared that he had the ability to be my undoing. He had the power to make me not give a fuck about any of what I'd worked for.

I had to make sure I limited our communication for real. No more fucking. No more pussy eating. No more gun play. Ezio was a savage and desperate. He was desperate to put his family on and I was collateral. He would be my annihilation if I let him. My elimination. My means to an end. The destruction of Jisei was what Ezio was. I knew he had that potential because while pulling out of his driveway, I had to fight hard not to turn around and beg him to play with my clit with his gun again. God help me. Because if our lord and savior didn't help me, Ezio Cuppacio was going to be the death of me.

CHAPTER 18
EZIO "EZEE" CUPPACIO

I'd just popped my last pill. A few weeks ago, taking my last perc would have terrified me but, now days I didn't even trip about the shit. Jisei had been my new drug of choice, but when she ran out, I knew Olivia was the one to call for a re-up. I didn't know when the fuck it happened, but Jae Bae hadn't left my thoughts since she left my crib, which was a week ago.

She was so fucking turned on by a nigga placing his gun to the pussy, but little did she know, I really wanted to blow her ass to smithereens. Her mouth was too fucking smart, and she knew what the fuck she was doing by constantly fucking with that nigga and playing me to the left. I needed this union to happen just like I needed air. I'd been blessed to be able to push the dope and bring in more money than I had ever seen but knew once this wedding happened, it would really be up. My meetings with Rio at Gay Boy Mansion had been paying off because even though I hated being there, each time he gave me even more knowledge.

Olivia being my supplier was a Godsend. She was consistent and no matter the day or time I requested a re-up she was there. Her shit was legit too. Sometimes she served me in Tylenol bottles and others were in the normal prescription bottle with the label scratched off. No matter how they came, the pills were the real deal.

After Jisei left, I didn't have one thought about the past four days. It wasn't until today that I had a flashback, so I fell back into my habit. I knew I had to visit Olivia even though I should have been trying to wean myself off just as my cousins had but them niggas had never taken as many as me. I wasn't in a position to be going through withdrawals and shit. But I doubt I was even that far gone to go through withdrawals. I may have the shits for a day or two but would be back to normal, however, I wasn't ready to quit just yet. I wasn't sure I ever would be. The pills weren't bothering anybody and made me feel damn good. The money was pouring in, the city was showing me love, and training, although harsh, was becoming routine.

After washing the perc down with the white cup full of dirty sprite that left a purple ring around the inside of the rim, I went ahead and had the driver take me back to The Bottom Spot Bar and Grill before I went to Olivia for my new prescription. Those drinks and wings were the shit and I had been craving them. No lie, having a driver proved to be useful as fuck. My cousins were always off, doing their own thing, and more than likely had grown tired of driving my ass around. I had learned my driver's name was Kory and he did his fucking job. He didn't ask me no questions and was always right the fuck there when I needed him. Even when I called his ass to bring me some Waffle House one night at three in the morning, he obliged.

271

So, when I requested The Spot Bar and Grill, he was there. Sitting at the bar, in my usual spot, I was happy to see Brooke's ass wasn't at work. I wasn't in the mood for her little ass smiling in my face all night. Shorty was cute, but her grinning in my grill, knowing I had some raggedy ass shoes on didn't sit right with me. If a girl wanted a nigga in fucked-up shoes, it meant her pussy stank. It wasn't up for discussion.

I wanted my wings and drinks and to carry my ass to the crib. Training, though routine, was wild as fuck today and I didn't even want to think about the shit. I was really starting to wonder what type of shit Don had going on in the Rinaldi Mafia. My fucking elbows were sore as shit from crawling in the mud and rain. We had to be training for a real-life war. It felt like a nigga was about to be whisked off for battle. As long as we didn't go back to that fucking Savanna I could push through. I'd even had dreams about animals and shit.

Pulling my phone out to send Jisei a text because she had made her way back in my fucking mind, I went to the thread just as a nigga took up the empty seat next to me. I had half a mind to make his ass get up, but the security was already side-eyeing a nigga when I walked in. I wasn't trying to get banned by the owner for causing bloodshed in this here nice ass establishment. I'd already done enough the first time I was here.

Me: What the fuck you got going gun powder pussy?

That girl was shaking like a preacher in the corner of hell when I had her ass folded up. She was dripping wet but I didn't know her little ass was going to squirt. She had a combo of squirt and cream. I'd experienced her do both and was a fucking fan. I hadn't ever seen a woman's pussy, asshole, and inner thighs be the same color as the rest of their body. It was usually a little discolored. But not shorty. Her shit was perfect. The inside of the pussy was piggy pink and snugged tight on my dick. Shit fit so perfectly that it was scary. Some women had pussy that you would never forget and Jisei was that one for me. She was so damn sexy, that she could sell her appeal and make a fucking bag. With the way her pussy suffocated my dick back at the party, Jisei hadn't been fucking in a minute and as good as it felt, I hated I was the one to break her ass in. From the way she looked at me, I knew she really wanted more from a nigga. But my duty was to my people. That love shit will get you killed. I didn't know why in the fuck I always told her I loved her because I had never come close to loving a woman outside of the women who shared the same last name as me.

When my text went green, I chuckled at the fact that she hadn't unblocked a nigga. It was all good though. This shit was probably for the best.

"May I get your order, handsome?"

I gave the waitress my order, which was wings and two double shots. They didn't have mild sauce but The spot sauce was good so I was going to fuck with that tonight. I'd tasted one of Jisei's the night I chilled at her crib. The waitress turned to the nigga next to me and asked the same question. Dragging my eyes to the side of his face, I immediately recognized him. Having the talks with Rio opened my eyes a bit. So, I started doing research and what better person to start off with than my wife-to-be. Jisei was a mystery in a sense and as much as I tried not to care, she had me tracking down her past. The nigga was all I really wanted to get intel on. It took me no time to find that nigga she called herself fucking with. Well, I had Vello look into it because he was good with shit like that. Anakin. Goofy ass trust fund baby. He was sitting next to me, scanning over the menu while the bartender waited, her eyes still looking over at me. I wouldn't even really care that shorty fucked with dude on the low because I still did my thing, but finding out the nigga really wanted her on a deeper level was threatening to what the fuck I was trying to build.

"My girl isn't answering but she said she loves this place. So, what is the best thing on the menu?" Anakin asked the waitress.

"Well, everything is good. I personally love the Philly but everyone comes to get the wings, specifically the *Spot* flavor. It's a house sauce mix."

"Great. Let me get the Philly. I think that is what she would like."

Wrong. Hoe ass nigga.

"I got you. Everything on the sandwich? Fries or onion rings?"

"Uh, sure. Fries. Yes, fries are cool."

The waitress raised her brow. "You sure? The onion rings are really good. Made in an almost sweet batter."

"Fries will do."

"Alrighty. That's it?"

"Yes, I'm afraid I ate before coming. I'm on a fast. Thank you, though."

This nigga got her order completely wrong and had the nerve to call her his girl. I watched him do another sucker ass thing and couldn't do shit but shake my head. He was a foul ass nigga but Vello's research had already told me that. My shots were placed in front of me and I took them both to the head. Our food came out at the same time, and when he paid for his, he grabbed the thank you bag and walked toward the door. I tossed a hundred-dollar bill on the counter, grabbed my food and left too. Before he could get in his rental car, I was flagging him down, pants sagging off my waist due to my heavy ass gun.

His eyebrows bunched and I could tell he was scared, especially when he saw the gun on my hip.

"Um, yes?"

"The bartender told me you grabbed my food and I grabbed yours."

Relief flooded his eyes and he reached for the bag while I held mine out too.

"I appreciate that. Mr—"

"Mr. Ya Worst Nightmare if you fuck my bitch tonight," I told his ass with a straight face.

He took a step back, sweat forming on his wide-ass nose.

"Excuse me?"

"Take my bitch her food and carry your ass back to your city, Anakin. When I get there tonight, yo' ass better be gone or you gon' find out why me and my shorty love this gun. Except, you won't like it for the same reasons as her. I ain't on that Rio shit."

Anakin cleared his throat, ran to his vehicle, and pulled out of the parking lot at record speed. I held my hand up in a gun position and pointed it at his ass. He looked like he was pissing his fucking pants. I had no plans on going to Jisei's house, but even if I did, I knew his ass wasn't going to be there. He was a straight-up pussy, and it was a wonder that Jisei was even fucking with him. The bubbly college girl shit she put on was a front. Her ratchet ass was a freak. A good girl, yes, but a freak, nonetheless.

I HAD every intention of going to Liv and copping the pill then heading straight to the crib, but when I scarfed down the Philly cheese steak that though it was good, did nothing for me, especially since I had a taste for the wings, my high was in full effect. My dick was at full attention, and I knew there was no way I could go home with tight nuts.

I sent Olivia a text, letting her know I needed service with the serve since I initially told her I was only coming to get my pills. As always she was down. She always begged me to fuck and as tempting as she was, I strictly wanted my dick sucked. Olivia had the type of mouth that you wanted to wake up too. Me though, I wasn't on that. I fucked with her because she kept me high, my nuts drained and she was nice as fuck on the eyes. Olivia was the homie in a wig and I liked coming through her spot on occasion.

Jisei was different in every sense in comparison to Mira, my ex bitch but at the same time, she reminded me so much of her dead ass. They both talked hot shit and had no problem standing up to me. I had fucked with Mira heavy for years. She was my bitch, and even though I fucked with other bitches, she was my main one. I knew her lil ass was crazy because she walked around with her fucking nose up. My mama couldn't stand her ass nor could any of my aunties. I even had a few of them threaten to beat her ass anytime they saw me with a new scratch on my body from us straight-up boxing. I couldn't lie like I'd never put my hands on a woman because that wasn't the case. Me and my ex used to be in that bitch tearing the house up. Of course, I didn't handle her like a nigga, but when she wouldn't stand down and continued to put her hands on me, I had to put her lil ass in her place. Little did I fucking know, she was plotting against me. She almost had my whole fucking family wiped out from being her daddy's errand girl. She used my car to damn near kill Don and his wife, who was expecting at the time. Had it not been for the proof, I wouldn't even be here.

Jisei was educated, pretty as fuck, and had her own shit. She would be any man's dream, but all I looked at when I saw her was a fucking nightmare. I could see myself having to handle her the same way I handled Mira. She was an Alpha female in every way. She had her own money and a brother who gave her the fucking world. What the fuck did she need me for? To keep shit on even playing fields, I was keeping my distance. I had a feeling her and I couldn't even be fuck buddies. That shit had too much at stake. Just as long as she didn't pop out with that goofy in public.

Resting on Olivia's sofa, I waited for her to come from out the back with my pills. Shio was constantly badgering me, asking who had been my supplier, and every time I told the nigga to fuck off. He wasn't trying to get me right so it didn't fucking matter who I was buying from. Long as I had my shit, it was cool. I even saw his ass looking around for my pill bottle but the nigga would never catch me lacking. I had my shit put up.

Ms. Fine Brown Ass brought her ass in the living room and my dick bricked up. Olivia always smelled good and put on some sexy shit anytime I came over. Today, she was in some type of lace one piece that was olive green, looking too good against her skin. I was fucking with it.

"I got your pills in the back, daddy. Let me take care of this dick first."

That was another thing. In all the months I had been fucking with Olivia, I had never seen the back of her house. Hell, I'd barely seen the bathroom. She usually wiped my dick off right here on the couch and went on about her business. She could have a whole nigga in the back, and I wouldn't know because I didn't give a fuck. Long as she gave me what the fuck I needed.

Olivia dropped to her knees, removed my dick from my pants and swallowed me whole. I let my head rest on the back of her couch as she sucked my dick with precision. I opted out of pulling her hair because once I snatched her fucking wig off and she was pissed. I paid for the shit, but she was still mad she had to take off work and get it fixed. I paid her for her missed time too. Long as she could keep eating my dick and keep me high, she could damn near get whatever. Damn near.

When Olivia's hand rested on my pockets, her eyes scanned the hard knot that was there. I removed her hand and pumped in and out of her mouth. When she gagged and her mouth grew wetter, I erupted all down her throat.

"Umm." Olivia held her tongue out to show me she had eaten all of my semen like a good hoe. I know she was so full of my nut that if it had been her pussy, she would have been round and protruding in the front.

"When you gon' let me get some of that dick? You still hard. You always still hard and I know even though my head fire, the pussy would leave you satisfied."

Olivia use the warm towel to wipe me off while blinking her long lashes and tucked my dick back in place.

Instead of talking, I reached in my pocket and pulled out the velvet box. When I popped it open, she gasped, hands shooting to cover her mouth.

"Oh my God—"

"Aye, chill. This not for you, shorty. I don't fuck you because I'm engaged. I ain't even tryna be fucking on you and I'm 'bout to get married and shit."

I flipped the box closed, and I saw what looked like hurt in her eyes. Olivia was cool but we had a good thing going, which was purely transactional. I paid her, she copped my pills, and as a bonus, she blessed the mic. I never led her to believe that this shit was more than what it was.

"You getting married? Since when?"

"Since damn near a year ago." I shrugged.

"Where the fuck yo' fiancée be when you over here, getting your dick sucked?"

"Uh, the crib. Aye, what you on?"

Everybody had been on my head about this funky ass ring and little did they know I had been having it made for months now. When the money poured in, I changed up the order and added more karats to her shit. I didn't have plans to give it to Jisei until the wedding. She wasn't about to have my ring on, flaunting in that goofy ass nigga's face.

I had never seen Olivia look this pissed. Yeah, she was mad when I snatched her wig off that time, but this was different. She was hurt and that shit was dumb as hell to me. I'd been giving her ass so much money that she went part time at her full-time job. I planned on continuing what we had going even after the wedding. She was my supplier and I fattened her pockets and got sloppy top. Shit was too good for her. She didn't even have to fuck for a buck.

"Nigga, I thought you was single!"

"You thought I was single, and I only let you suck my dick? Come on, Olivia, you smarter than that."

Olivia stood there in her lingerie, shocked as hell, like my words had turned her little world upside down.

"For real, though, don't shit really gotta change. You can still suck a nigga up and I'll still pay you for the percs. I have always been engaged, Liv, so this shit ain't new to me, it's just new to you. You wanted to know why I don't fuck and that's why. I wasn't about to lie to you. This dick reserved for my wife."

"Wow."

I was yearning for another pill and ready to get the fuck up out of her spot because she was too deep in her feelings for me. Shit was beginning to make me itch. I thought Olivia and I had an understanding but clearly we didn't. Bitches always did the most. I hadn't kissed Olivia nor had I fucked and she was standing there like the signs weren't there. She couldn't have been that damn ditzy.

"Aye, go get my shit. I got somewhere to be."

Olivia gnawed on her bottom lip before nodding. I watched her fat ass sway out of the room while I counted out a few more bills to add to her money. Any bitch in the city would have been happy with the set-up we had going on. Hell, I knew plenty of Chicago bitches who would love to suck my dick and get paid to supply pills. They were hustlers back home. I thought Olivia was on that same type of time, but I was wrong.

By the time Olivia was back in the living room, pills in hand, she was smiling like her normal self and I was able to visibly relax. I thought I was going to have to cut the bitch off or even worse, kill her ass.

"This is only what I have left in my stash. He won't be ready to re-up until another week. You can get those, though, free of charge."

I stood, placing the money on the small coffee table. I pulled Olivia into my arms and slapped her fat ass. If I was in another situation, she could for sure get the dick, but unfortunately, this was how this shit had to be. At least I actually came to her spot. Other bitches sucked me off at the telly or in the car.

"I will have more for you next week, daddy."

"And I'll have more money for you next week too. Come lock up, with yo' sexy ass."

I didn't even wait until I got out the door before I was screwing the top off my Tylenol bottle and eying the percs. Olivia had come through for a nigga each time, but I still inspected my product. Deciding to just vibe on the one pill that I had swallowed earlier, I secured the top and shoved the white and red bottle in my pocket. My dick was still hard but, I couldn't take my ass back in Olivia's house. She was already on some other shit and I had to fill her ass out to see if we could continue our lil situation.

Climbing in the back seat of the Escalade, I gave my driver the next location.

CHAPTER 19
JISEI "JAE BAE" RINALDI

M r. Onfoenem got on every fucking nerve that I had. I couldn't stand that Chicago mild sauce eating bitch. I was even more pissed that I let him make my pussy spit up using a fucking gun. What type of ghetto King Von ass shit was that? I wanted to kick my own ass because I actually liked the shit. His face was so close to my kitty that I knew for sure he was going to reach in and lick it. That mouth of his was remarkable and I knew the nigga was teasing me by not giving it to me last week.

Today was a new day though. I had been so focused on how bad I hated to be in the predicament I was in that I had lost sight of myself. I missed the cheery, nice, happy, corporate party girl. I'd been so consumed with negativity about some shit I couldn't change. I was getting married to a hoe. That was that on that. I was marrying a nigga that didn't give two shits about me. All he cared about was getting his family out of the windy city. I had to take it for what it was. Hopefully, my life wouldn't change outside of me being married on paper. I could still come and go as I pleased and still live my life as I had done before Ezio blew into town. It was time to get back to me. The first step to doing that was to stay out of my fucking feelings, keep his ass on the block list and make sure I didn't get caught with a man. The latter was easy. Anakin lived in a whole other city. To my surprise, he wasn't really upset about me leaving the room last week. I lied to him saying my neighbor saw smoke coming from my house, and when he asked me about it two days later, I had forgotten and had to play it off. That was why I couldn't lie; it took too much to keep up with one. Thankfully, he had business in the city and that kept his ass occupied while I got my pussy played in with a damn murder weapon. My life was a fucking mess.

Tonight was one of those nights that I was chilling at home. Before all of this, my Friday nights were mostly spent with my girls but I just wanted some time alone. I didn't want to hear any wedding shit or answer any questions pertaining to Ezio. Plus, I didn't want to face my brother. After he caught my ass at the room with a man who wasn't my fiancé, I had to admit, I was embarrassed.

Pressing play on *Bridgerton*, I sat back on my couch with my favorite pink blanket thrown over my legs. My phone pinged, letting me know that someone was at my door, so I checked the camera, and when I saw it was Anakin, I shot to my feet. *What the fuck was he doing here?*

Snatching the door open, I pulled Anakin's stupid looking ass in. Him having my address was never a worry. Initially, I didn't want him to have it, but when he offered to send me dinner and flowers and all that and continued to do so, I'd grown accustomed to it. I didn't think he would be bold enough to pull up. He had offered to come over many times in the last few months and I declined every time. I didn't think he would show his ass up, and frankly, it made me uneasy.

Sticking my head out the door I made sure no one was

outside or that no one had seen him come in. The coast was clear, but the visit had to be brief. My brother knew my every fucking move and I knew I had less than ten minutes before he either called or pulled up on my ass.

"Uh, I know you said you love The Bottom Spot Bar and Grill so I got you food. I hope you are in the mood for a philly and fries." Anakin held the bag of food up and it took everything in me not to scoff.

"Anakin, you came all the way to Jagoda Bay to bring me food?" I asked, dumbfounded.

I had a taste for Spot wings for sure, but not only did this fool pull up unannounced, he also brought the wrong shit.

"Okay, I'm guilty. I missed you."

Anakin was cute, he really was. So fucking cute, and had that grown ass man vibe. Not only did he look good but he smelled good, and to the right girl, he would have been the perfect man. But for me, a mafia princess, he didn't fit the bill. I felt bad because I really did like him, but the men in my life would eat his ass for breakfast and still be ready for seconds. He'd been so nice, and we had really connected on a deeper level with the distance. Still, I couldn't ignore that every time we went to chill together, here comes fate, fucking it up, and by now, I was over it.

I grabbed the food that I didn't plan on eating, but to be nice, I accepted it.

"Anakin, it's something I need to tell you."

"Oh, damn. Are you seeing someone? There was a guy at the bar who told me he picked up my food by mistake, so we switched. Then he told me not to fuck his bitch. I thought he was just crazy, but he knew my name now that I think about it."

The blood began to pound in my temples, and I felt ice flooding my stomach.

"Uh, what he look like?"

"Light skinned, tattoos on his face and these creepy eyes—"

I didn't even let Anakin get it all out before I pushed his ass out of the door.

"Hey, what is going on?"

Biting my lip until it throbbed like my pulse, a raw and primitive grief overwhelmed me.

Once I had Anakin on the opposite side of the threshold, I held my food up.

"Thank you so much for this. I appreciate it. But you have to go now. I will call you later to explain it all."

Anakin reluctantly nodded but got into his rental. I didn't sigh with relief until I saw that his taillights were out of view. I then locked my door and fumbled with the thank you bag. The smell didn't align with a philly cheese steak and it had my stomach growling. Once I was able to open the carryout tray, I gasped at what was in it. Anakin said he had gotten me a philly cheese steak, but in the container were Spot wings, onion rings, and three ranch cups. The person who switched food with his was Ezio. Not only did he match Anakin's description, but he also had my order right down to the condiments. Plus, he was the only weird eye ass light skinned man who would threaten Anakin over me in broad daylight. Well, outside of my brother.

"I told that nigga he better had not been here by the time I arrived or it was lights out. Good to see he follows directions."

I was so startled that I dropped the container, sending wings and sauce splattering all over my floors.

"Ezio! What the fuck!"

With my hand clutching my chest, in an attempt to calm my racing heart, I bent over to catch my breath. This man was really in my house, and I hadn't granted him not a bit of access.

"Why the fuck you keep talking to that goofy?"

"Why the fuck you break into my house? How did you get in?"

"Shit, yo' bedroom window," he staggered.

Now I had a new fear unlocked. I expected him to say the back door or the kitchen window or something, but my bedroom window? I had to invest in bars like the grannies in the projects did back in the day ASAP.

"Ezio, please leave."

"Aye, I'ma be in the shower. Clean this shit up and join me."

This negro dismissed my ass by walking to the back. When I heard my shower run, I took off behind him, leaving the food on the floor. Butterflies swarmed in my belly, and I didn't know whether it was from me being afraid or from me being happy that he was here in my space. One second, I hated this man for coming around and disrupting my peace, and then the next I hated him for not being what a regular fiancé should. I got the news from my brother that I was going to be married months ago and my finger was still fucking bare.

Trudging down the hallway, I pushed the already cracked door open. Steam floated from the door of my en suite bathroom and that further enraged me. He had just broken in my shit, approached Anakin, and had the nerve to come here and get in my fucking shower. From the fumes, I could tell he was using my brand new body wash. The glass to the standing shower was foggy so I could only see his silhouette. Pulling the door open, Ezio's frame was exposed, and it caused me to stand back a bit. The water from the black shower head spurted down on his body, making a mist of water splatter on me. His tattoos under the water made them even more vibrant. The muscles bulging in his back showed how he had really been putting in work doing the training my brother had been putting him through. Ezio was so fucking fine that the nigga should be framed and hung on the wall in a fucking trap museum or something.

My eyes traveled to his lower half and I stumbled and gasped at what was hanging between his legs. *Long. Veiny. Curved. Heavy.* So heavy. He was too damn heavy. Too damn long. Too damn thick. Anakin couldn't hold a candle to Ezio. As a matter of fact his dick was a fucking toddler compared to what Ezio was holding in between his thighs. I couldn't tear my eyes away from him. It was... too much. I had handled it well, but the days I was still sore after he penetrated me. The brand new bottle of Tylenol I'd purchased earlier that I had removed from my purse and tossed on my bed was a reminder that he wasn't shit to play with in the bedroom, or in our case, in the nursery. The nigga had me popping Tylenols like skittles. How was his dick that impactful? It was like my pussy couldn't recover from him. It was probably all in my head but that didn't stop me from taking two pain killers every time I felt a thud below.

"He like to be sucked, not stared at, shorty."

Fuck, then there he goes with that Chicago accent. I acted like I couldn't stand it but I loved to hear him talk. The way he never pronounced the R in anything, and how I damn near had to ask him to repeat almost word he said. Ezio knew he was the shit and I hated it but was turned on at the same time.

"Is you cool?"

I tossed his words back at him and it made him grin.

"You ain't me, G."

"And you ain't me, yet you're in my fucking shower! Using up all of my body wash," I spat.

"I'll buy you some mo'."

"You haven't even bought me a fucking ring!"

"Oh, so that's what got you tweaking? How many times have I given you the money for that ring, Jae Bae?"

I loved when he called me that stupid ass name but was too prideful to show it.

"That ain't the point, nigga! You're supposed to buy my ring! That's your job! What the fuck I look like, walking in the jeweler, asking for an engagement ring? A goofy ass, that's what."

"You'll look like a woman that is picking out exactly what the fuck she wants. You the one got to wear that muthafucka for the rest of yo' life. May as well get some shit you fuck with."

"Ezio, get the fuck out my shower and out of my house. Don't you got yo' own fucking shower?"

"I do, but I just came from getting my dick sucked. Unless you want the next bitch's DNA in yo' walls, let me wash my dick off before I fuck you."

I hated how bad those words turned me on. Him saying he had just gotten head from the next woman who I could only assume was Olivia, should have had me picking up his gun and letting it rip. Especially since he'd told me he was going to chill on the bitches. I could see the shit on the news now: *Ringless fiancée kills her fiancé in the shower of her Shirah townhome.* Instead, I was ready for him to wash that dick and serve it up to me.

"Ezio—"

My head flew back as he snatched me into the shower, fully clothed. The water immediately ruined my brand new sew in. I opened my mouth to tell his ass off, but the penetrating gaze he gave me had me shutting up and staring into his eyes. He towered over me, water dripping from his face into mine. My clothes were drenched and sticking to my skin and the thin fabric of my pajama top exposed my nipples. Ezio grabbed my chin, pulling it upward and then brushing his thumb over my lips. He then swept his hand down my neck, to my shoulder, knocking the string of my top down my arm. My left breast was now on display, along with the pink diamond hearts on my breasts. I'd just changed them out, and seeing the glow in his eyes let me know he appreciated the efforts.

Once he had my shirt completely around my waist, the weight from the shirt tugged at my shorts so I stepped out of them. Standing just as nude as he was, we both stared at each other. The shower fogged around us, and I was constantly having to blink due to the weight of my lashes and water combo.

"You so fucking pretty, Jae Bae."

"T-t-thank you."

I knew I was pretty. Been knowing I was pretty my entire life. But anytime he said it, it caused me to gush like a school girl.

"You said that we need to keep shit mild. Why are you breaking in my house, Ezio?"

"Why not?" he responded.

"You're off your rocker." I moaned as his thumb swept over my nipple.

"I am. I'm out of my fucking mind, baby."

"Just leave me alone, Ezio," I spat out.

"I'm not yo' type. You like goofies, baby. I will ruin you. I'm a jealous ass nigga that ain't wrapped too tight. You know how fucked up I really am? I have tracked down Anakin's entire family, ready to wipe them all out like yo' brother did mine. Except, I ain't keeping a soul alive. That's the type of nigga you marrying. So, I should leave you alone but you know why I can't."

I swallowed hard.

"Well, why are you here? Why did you break in? It's understood we getting married, but we can just stop seeing each other until the wedding planning begins."

"Didn't you hear me say I'm a jealous ass nigga? I wanted to make sure you wasn't giving that nigga my pussy."

"But you said—"

"Fuck what I was talm 'bout. I ain't got it all upstairs, baby."

His eyes were so red and low, they were almost closed. I'd been around him long enough to know that was the norm for him. At this point, I didn't even know if a sober Ezio existed.

"So, what are we doing, Ezio? I can't keep going back and forth with you. It's been too long. Are we getting married and just having the shit on paper, or are we really doing this as a couple? For real? No bitches involved, no goofies, as you call him."

Ezio dragged his finger down my chest and stopped at my nipple. When he toyed with the ring, making it extra sensitive, I moaned in response.

"You don't want me, Jisei."

"I do," I rushed out.

I wanted him. I'd been wanting him. I just hated being thrust into some shit with no control. Then, Ezio came at me hard, and when he fell off with it, it gave me whiplash. Maybe I was wrong for wanting him to continue chasing me, but was it bad to desire being desired?

"Merch it?"

"It's merched."

His lingo was so damn off the wall, but I loved it. Ezio had given me that crash course and I had even found myself using it around the girls. Scarlett fell out every time too.

Ezio wrapped his arm around my back and pulled me up around his waist. My heated pussy rested on his hardened abdomen. His lips caught mine and my pussy leaped with excitement. I felt his arm thudding against my own as our tongues wrestled. A hot ache grew in my throat as he slowly stepped out of the shower, not missing a step, as I held on for dear life. The cool air from no longer being surrounded by steam chilled down my back and when he lowered me onto the thickness of my comforter, I tightened my legs around his back. I didn't want him to move. His nearness was so fucking compelling. The way he played in my pussy with the gun, the way he ate me alive like we were the only people in the room, and the way he fucked me savagely was so fucking addicting and had me craving him on the daily. If this was how Bobby felt I understood why he sucked the glass dick.

"Hold up, baby, I just want to get a good look at you."

I finally let him go. He stumbled a bit and then stood straight. The dick that was already too big for words grew in between his legs while he fawned over me, laying in all my glory. He grabbed at his thick member and slowly stroked it. He had a fat, mushroom tip and there was pre-cum oozing from it.

"Tell me what yo' pretty ass wants."

I wanted it all. I wanted him to fuck me like it was our first time because, with the size of him and the way we were both drunk and in the heat of the moment at my brother's house, we owed it to ourselves. It would surely feel like my first fucking time. I had a feeling that no matter how many times I fucked Ezio, it would always feel like I was losing my damn V-card. I wanted him to bury himself so deep in me that it would take prayer to get him out. I wanted him to kiss me like I was the only one because God knows I wanted to be. I wanted him to use his mouth on every part of my body that he deemed edible and I wanted him to deem it all as edible. Last, I wanted him to love me and only me. I wanted him to say he loved me and for him to be as serious as a heart attack. I wanted him to fall head over heels in love with me and never fall in love again as I had done him. I loved him. I probably loved him since the first day my brother brought him to my home. I wanted it all from Ezio but pride wouldn't let me voice it so I kept it locked up inside of me where I knew it was safe. Safe from rejection. Safe from him not reciprocating. Safe from heartache. I wanted to tell him why I had changed. I wanted him to know why I was no longer the care free sorority college girl from almost two years ago. I wanted him to know my deepest darkest secrets and I wanted to know his. I wanted everything that came with him because I was a fiend off of the drug that was Ezio Cuppacio. Instead of telling him that, I told him what I wanted from him that I really could have. Something that he was willing to give me.

"I want to feel your mouth," I cracked.

Ezio licked his lips, causing my center to thud. I wanted so much more but the mouth would be a great starting point.

"You like when I eat your pussy, baby?"

Him standing there stroking his dick had me squirming, looking crazy as hell.

"Yes."

"Has anybody ever ate yo' pussy like me?"

"You're the only person to ever do it," I shamefully admitted.

But damn, it was an amazing first time.

"I broke your head virginity? That's sexy. I got you, shorty."

Ezio eased down to the side of the bed and buried his face in between my thighs.

"How is your shit so fucking pretty?"

He stuck his nose dead in my folds and took a long sniff.

"I love smelling you. Shit smells as good as it tastes."

The feel of his lips on my second set was heavenly. His mouth was so wet and warm, and the slurping sounds he made as he sucked my clit had me bucking against his face. Getting my pussy ate felt so intimate. I couldn't even blame Anakin or the nigga before him for not wanting to do it to me. Pussy eating, especially the way Ezio skillfully devoured mine, should only be reserved for the one you loved. He was making love to my pussy with his mouth and the exchange of energy made me feel like he loved me.

Grabbing his head, I pushed my legs up and over my head, making them touch the headboard. When his tongue migrated from my lower lips to my anal, I squealed.

"Ohmygossssh!"

He stuck his tongue in my asshole and rocked my body hard, making my ass bounce on his face as he fucked me with his tongue.

"Eziooooo! Shiiiiiiiiiiit! Fuck! Fuck! Fuuuuuuuuck!"

I had never felt something so good before in my life. Getting head was one thing, but getting the groceries eaten was next level. If this man thought he was getting rid of me after this, he had to be smoking rocks, on folk nem.

He let my legs go when it felt like I was about to see stars and grabbed my nipples while making his way back to my pussy. I clamped my thighs around his head, suffocating him, but that didn't stop him from eating me like he was a starved bum. I didn't know why, but tears streamed down the sides of my face. I felt my climax making a grand entrance and all I could do was whimper, look at the ceiling, and let the tears flow. No one should have the ability to make a person feel this good – this vulnerable.

"I'm 'bout to cum!"

Ezio didn't suck harder, he didn't speed up, he kept the same consistency, and that shit was a beauty in itself. Just as I had when he used his gun, I splattered all over his face, making a big ass mess that was going to give me no choice but to wash the sheets when we were done.

My stomach clenched and then caved as my legs vibrated around his head. With my chest rising and falling, he made sure to lick up as much as he could before he moved up my body. His face was drenched, so I swiped my hand down it and he caught my hand, kissing my palm. Everything this man did to me, no matter how small, turned me on.

"You squirting is my favorite thing in life, on bro nem."

Trying to laugh while catching my breath was harder than I imagined. Ezio caught my lips with his damp mouth letting me taste my juices. Feeling him line himself with my front had me bracing and even with me being super wet, he had to push his way through just like the first time.

"You so fucking biiiiiiig."

"You got it. Take it, baby."

Gripping the sheets underneath us, I held my breath until he hit the base and I swore I could feel him in my stomach. I was gathered underneath his warm, wet, hardened body. With each stroke, Ezio was making me fall for him even harder and I thought that shit was impossible.

"This pussy so good. Shit too tight."

His pumps were long, hard and steady. Heat rippled under my skin as I recognized the flush of sexual desire I hadn't felt for months. He was all up in my guts and all over my body, yet I still craved him. His dick rammed inside of my wet folds, fucking me with the same precision as a predator, but I wanted more. I wanted to be in this man's skin. Fuck that, I wanted to be underneath his flesh. When he stuck his nose in the crook of my neck and then placed a soft, delicate kiss there, I wrapped my arms around his neck.

"I love you. I love you so fucking much, Ezio! Shiiiiiiiiiiit."

"I love... yo' ass... too... Fuck, girl."

My nipple piercing scratched against his chest each time he pumped in and out of me. I was filled with an amazing sense of completeness as my heart burst with love and anguish. The air in the room was filled with so much passion that it suffocated me. Fire spread to my heart and a deep feeling of peace entered my being. This was what I wanted. This was what I'd been missing. This fucking thug of a man fucking the lights out of me, filling me with too much emotion that I was barely able to speak.

I'd cum three times in this same position, and he was still going strong. Ezio was the definition of fucking you all night. It had been over an hour and I had come undone so many times. Our bodies had dried, then wet again due to his sweat. If I didn't know any better, I would think he had taken a fucking Viagra. Just when I was about to tap out, he grunted and stiffened, and I sang praises of halleluiah because I was sore and raw.

"I love this pussy! Shiiiiiiiit!"

As he spilled his seeds, I came just off the feeling. Instead of falling on top of me, he rolled to the side, chest rising and falling.

"I hate to make you get up, but I need to change the sheets."

Ezio looked over at me, sweat drenching his tattooed face, and playfully rolled his eyes. I'd just noticed he had his diamonds in which meant he ate my pussy and ass with them in. I was leaking again but was in no position to take him again. Unlike the first time, he took an hour to nut. A whole fucking sixty minutes and if this was his normal, I was going to have to drink a Red Bull to be able to keep up.

He stood, pulling me up and slapping my ass. Turning around, I removed the sheets and the mattress protector from the bed with his help. We tossed the covers in a pile on the floor and I retrieved fresh sheets out of the linen closet that was in my bathroom. When we had fresh sheets and a fresh comforter in place, I slid my robe on and grabbed the pile.

"Aye, bring me back a pop from the fridge."

I nodded and took my pile to the laundry room, which was behind the kitchen. My dumb ass smiled the whole walk even though my insides were screaming. He had officially arranged my shit and the nut crawling down my legs were proof. I had to shower before getting back in the bed for sure. My vibrating phone on the fireplace mantle caught my attention so I grabbed it. When I had made it to the laundry room, I placed my covers on top of the front loader washer. This was a luxury that I still hadn't gotten used to. Since I was a child, all the way through college, I used the laundry mat. Having this fancy set had me not knowing how to act.

Resting my back against the washer, I went to my call log and saw that I had missed calls from Mocha and Heidy of all people. I hadn't heard from her in a minute, but I was guessing she heard the news about me getting married from Karen.

I dialed Mocha back because I didn't want her ass to worry. She wouldn't hesitate to pull up on me.

"Bitch, you got me blocked?" was how she greeted me.

"Uh, no. I had my phone on Do Not Disturb. Anakin pulled up and Ezio broke in. I didn't want him calling me while the crazy ass Cuppacio was here." I didn't remember placing my phone on the shelf above the fireplace but I did remember placing that shit on do not disturb before running to the back. The nigga was unhinged, and I didn't have time for his shit.

A smile graced my face, thinking of all the nasty things we'd just done.

"Biiitch, you got the diiiiiiiick again!"

"And did!"

"Y'all done fucked twice now, it's official. I'm glad, though, because you been having that man chase you forever. I hope he fucked yo' ass to death."

"Did!"

"My friend laying up with something so dangerous, she had to put her shit on double do not disturb. That's what the fuck I'm talking about!"

Holding the phone to my ear with my shoulder, I began pulling the sheets apart so that I could start the cycle. Sleep was making its way in, and I was ready to shower and lay down next to my fiancé. Fiancé. How in the fuck was I going to ride a dick that big that could go that long for the rest of my life? Shit with us was wishy-washy as fuck, but one thing for sure was the dick was A1.

"Girl, and he don't get tired. I gotta build my stamina up. The only reason I'm up is because I had to change the sheets," I bashfully admitted.

"Not he made that pussy squirt!"

"I always squirt with him!"

After the sheets were in the washer, I held the comforter up and shook it to make sure my remote wasn't trapped in it. I washed it once and was pissed that I had to buy a universal one until Samsung shipped me another.

"That's because he that nigga and your fake ass been wanting him forever. I only squirt when I'm extremely turned on and that got to be the case with you too."

A thud and rattle could be heard as I shook the cover and the item fell on the side of the washer.

"Shit, my Tylenol fell. Let me call you back tomorrow, friend. Let's do brunch at Bagels with Bad Bitches this Sunday."

"Okay. Make sure you pull that dick out your ass and come too. Don't make me pull up! You and that nigga so damn confusing that y'all make my head hurt. I need a pineapple mimosa and smiley face waffles."

"I got you, friend."

I ended the call and stuck my arm down the side of the washer. It took me feeling around blindly for a few minutes until I was able to touch the bottle with my fingertips. I pulled it toward me and then gripped it. Lord knows I needed my Tylenol right now. I was going to pop two as soon as I had the brand new bottle in my hand.

Finally, grabbing the bottle, I placed it on top of the dryer and stuck the comforter in the washer. Pouring washing powder in its slot, I added fabric softener and started the load. It took me a while to figure out how to stop my comforter from being so wet after its wash cycle and it was due to me not putting it on extra spin.

Remembering Ezio wanted something to drink, or a pop as he called it, I made my naked ass way to the kitchen with my bottle. It was trifling as hell the way his gooey nut was smeared in the inside of my thighs, and I was going to handle it the moment I took the pain pills. Grabbing a canned sprit for Ezio, I tucked it under my arms like it wasn't ice cold, got a bottled water for me and popped the top on the medication. Shaking two in my hand, I tossed them back and swallowed them down. I was hoping this man didn't want to go another round. I needed time for my meds to kick in. In the morning though we had to have a talk. Me admitting to loving him was for real this time. Somewhere deep down I think it was always real. But now I knew for sure. I was tired of running and tired of the back and forward. I needed this man to choose me and not because his family was on the line. If he opened his heart up to me --demons included, I would do the same. I loved Ezio Cuppacio and was ready for everything that came with him. I just prayed that it wasn't more than I could bear. As crazy as he was, I trusted him with my life and knew above all despite the gun play that time, he wouldn't put me in arms way. The same way I felt around my brother, I felt around him. Safe. This man had me so gone that I had to close my eyes because I felt like I was floating.

CHAPTER 20
EZIO "EZEE" CUPPACIO

Jisei had good pussy, the best if a nigga was being honest but fucking her this time felt --different. Not different in a bad way but right after I busted my nut, I felt unsettled as fuck. It wasn't shit she did. Shorty was perfect. She was fucking my mind and soul up and that was one of the reasons I kept her ass at arm's length. Don had to be still fucked up in the head for handing her over to a nigga like me. A dog ass nigga like me. His sister was un fucking real. I couldn't even blame her ass for running from a nigga and playing games and shit. I would be questioning her if she hadn't been. Shorty was a fucking queen. The cream of the crop. There was no topping Jisei. *Jae Bae.* She made a nigga ---happy. I was happy around my people. I was happy when I made money but that was as far as my happiness went. If I wanted to feel anything as close to happiness I had to pop a perc but Jae Bae had come around and fucked the game up. Just staring at her pretty ass made my fucking heart skip a beat. This shit was more terrifying than any of the shit my father had put me through. *Love.*

My phone vibrated on the nightstand next to me, so I

reached my arm out and grabbed it while lying on the bare mattress. Jisei didn't have not a stain in her pillow top mattress. Some bitches had period stains, piss stains, juice stains but not Jisei. It looked fresh off the show room floor. As a matter of fact her whole house was clean. I didn't even know this bitch had a basement. I hadn't seen much outside of her living room and bedroom but planned on giving myself a tour of her luxurious townhouse in the morning. When I broke in through the window I expected to see it messy because a girl like her looked like she went through a lot of steps to get ready for the day. But not a thing was out of place. The tropical plug in mixed in with the perfume she was wearing hung in the air along with the smells of our lovemaking. *Lovemaking.* I had never done that shit a day in my life. But Jisei pulled that out of me with the blink of her full lashes.

"Aye?"

Shio's face graced the screen as I balanced the iPhone on my bare chest. He could see my mug resting on the headboard behind me so I knew he was about to ask questions.

Before he could start his shit, I looked at the door to make sure Jisei wasn't coming and reached down to my pants, snatching the velvet box out of my pocket. This same box had Olivia sending a million texts to my phone that I hadn't bothered to read. She hadn't ever tripped on a nigga before and I wasn't about to entertain that shit now. She wasn't my bitch.

Flipping the box open, I showed him the two in a half carat natural diamond engagement ring. It was a halo design with one large diamond in the center with smaller stoned circling it while more were engraved in the band. The shit cost me damn near ninety G's but I knew I had to come correct. I still felt like I fell short compared to what her people had on their fingers, but I planned on upgrading her with time. Still this bitch was nasty and the wide as grin on Shio's face told me I had done right by her. Don's jeweler had done his big one. I just hoped his mean ass wife approved. I wasn't ready to be a one man woman but hopefully giving Jisei this ring would let her know I wasn't playing in her face.

"I called to get on yo' ass, but Ima let you make it since you not as dumb as I thought."

"Shut yo' goofy ass up, nigga."

I slid the ring back in my pocket and fell back in place on the bed. My legs were spread, and my dick was resting against my thigh due to Jae Bae's sticky essence and if Shio knew I was but naked he would hang up in my face.

"So, you 'bout to really do this shit? It took you how long to get right? You know what, it don't even matter. I'm proud of you. I know this shit ain't what you planned to do but Jisei a real one. She fine *and* on her shit."

I growled at my cousin and that had him tossing his head back in laughter. Instead of his contacts he was wearing his Malcom X glasses so that let me know he had just got done either reading the paper or a book. I swear he was an old ass man at heart.

"Yeah, Jae Bae pressure."

"Ima let you go cuz I know yo ass naked. But, we gone talk."

Shio held up the pill bottle that his snooping ass found. It was empty because I had the filled one with me but I kept my face hardened.

"Just gone speak yo peace cuz I ain't gone want to hear that shit later."

Later I would be high out of my fucking mind and would be liable to curse his ass out. So, I'd rather hear his shit now why I was only gone off one pill. I wouldn't be no good to a preaching after two.

"She in the room?"

I shook my head no and sat up, slinging my legs to the side of her bed. My Jae Bae had a crazy obsession with Pink. It was everywhere in here.

"You got to get off this shit, cuz. I did. Vello did. Nel did. We got too much at stake to be fucking going out sad behind a perc. You bigger than this. You stronger than this. You fucking better than this."

"It's just a pill, Shio. Everybody get high, nigga."

"But it ain't just a pill and you addicted to that shit. You been so high that damn near a year done flew by and no wedding. I'm glad you bought a ring but come on. Our people anxious and ready. You know why I stopped going home to get the shit for you? Hunh? Cuz I love you too bad to see this shit have you crashing out. We all we got nigga. We been all we had since we were brought in this fucking world."

"I hear you."

"Do you?"

"Yeah. And I know why you do the shit too. To erase the memories but ain't no erasing that shit."

Running my tongue across my teeth my chest tightened as my cousin looked through me.

"H...how I get through the shit?"

"You get through it by making new memories, starting with Jisei Rinaldi. Fuck the merging of the mafias nigga, just do some shit that make you happy for once without the family in mind. I love you, hit me tomorrow and we gone put some shit together to kick you off this shit for good before something happen that you can't come back from. I don't know where you getting that shit from but these niggas out here selling Fentanyl and passing it off as Percocet's. Ain't no coming back from the Fen Fen. Shit taking niggas out bro and I don't want that shit to be you. I refuse to let a bad pill put you in the dirt."

"I love you too."

Hanging up the phone, I tossed it on the nightstand and placed my head in my fist with my elbows resting on my knees. I knew I needed to eventually stop but, I had a handle on mine. I would hear Shio out tomorrow but, I knew for a fact I was gone pop two and wash it down with lean once he was done. Wasn't shit gone happen that couldn't come back from except for me making so much money that I would never go broke again. I knew the difference between a Percocet and Fentanyl. I was good.

Standing to my feet because my mouth was dry as fuck and it was taking Jisei too damn long with my pop, I stretched and peeled my dick from my thigh so it could air out.

Walking my naked ass through her hall, I heard a loud thud. Pausing, because my gun was in the fucking bedroom, I made a turn, snatched it up, along with Jisei's pink fuzzy robe that was hanging on her door and slid it on. The shit was short as fuck on me but, I didn't want to blow a nigga's ass off with big dick and balls out. I ran to the sound of the noise and halted. My heart stopped and gun dropped. My brain followed my heart and for a brief moment, I was stuck. I wasn't breathing, moving, or thinking.

"J...Jae Bae....get..get up...stop playing!"

Jisei naked as the day she was born was sprawled on the floor, looking up at me with buck eyes. She began clawing at her neck like she was trying to scratch something out of it. *What the fuck?* Finally finding my footing, I ran to her side and scooped her head in the crook of my arms. Her wet hair stuck to my skin and her eyes found mine.

"Fuck! Fuck! What the fuck did you do Jisei?"

Rocking her in my arms, I looked around the kitchen floor and saw a sprite rolled under the cabinet, the screen of her phone cracked near the island, and a Tylenol bottle under the fridge. Pills were scattered about causing me to close my eyes and try and steady my heart. It was beating so fucking hard that it hurt.

"Fuuuuuuck! Fuck Jae baby just focus Look at me!"

Her eyes obeyed my command, but it pained me to see the fear in her orbs. She was terrified and there wasn't shit I could do to protect her. I was supposed to protect her. This man had given me his sister and she was in the fucking floor in my fucking arms.

"Jae Bae. Stay focus on me baby. Stay focused. Fight this shit! I got you a ring. I got you a fucking ring Jae Bae! Fuuuuuuck!"

I reached over and snatched the pill bottle up like it could tell me what to do in this case. Seeing the Tylenol warnings that wouldn't help a bit I flung the empty bottle across the room. Fear and anger knotted inside of me as she began to convulse.

"What the fuck going on! Stay with me! Stay with yo nigga, baby!"

Kissing her forehead and then her nose, Water hit my face and when I pulled back, I saw that it wasn't water at all. It was spit. Jisei was foaming at the mouth and her body heated at an alarming temperature. She was dying in my arms. She was fucking dying and I was so fucking confused because this shit wasn't supposed to happen.

"Jiseiiiiiiiiiiiii! What the fuckkkkk!"

Panic like I'd never known welled in my throat. I choked back a cry, frightened and electrified. I stretched my arm to reach her phone, careful not to crush her and paused at the thought of calling an ambulance. *I love you, hit me tomorrow and we gone put some shit together to kick you off this shit for good before something happen that you can't come back from.* Shio's words from moments ago rang clear and sadly they were now my reality. I knew the devil was going to come and collect. I knew death was going to knock at my door, I just didn't think it would be this soon. I didn't think he would use beautiful ass Jisei to bring me to my knees. Or maybe I did know, and it was the reason why I'd been dodging her ass. Shio was right, I couldn't come back from this.

Not even caring about the war that was going to start, I dialed 911 and it took a few attempts due to the cracked screen. I knew the deal was off. I knew my family coming here and having the life they deserved wasn't happening and most of all, I knew Jisei's brother was about to kill me for taking his sister out with my nasty ass habit. Even with all of stream of events that were sure to commence, I waited to hear the operator's voice.

"Hello! Aye! Send some fuckin' help! My fiancée! She... she's fuckin' overdosing!"

Jisei's body bucked, as I wedged the phone between my shoulder and ear. Sticking my finger down her throat with tears blinding my vision, I tried to get her to throw up the bad pill. The fentanyl. It was too fucking late. The damage had been done. I'd been on pills for years and had yet to take a bad pill and Jisei had popped one by fucking mistake!

"Jae Bae! I promise if you kick this shit, its me and you against the fucking world! I swear to fucking God Jae Bae! Fight this shit!"

"Sir we need your address!"

Pressing my forehead against hers, I cried like a fucking baby as she continued to buck and jump in my arms. I'd fucked up and this time I didn't know how to fix it. I placed repeated kisses on her forehead and nose.

"I love you Jisei! I love the fuck out of you girl. Please don't fucking leave me, baby! I ain't gone survive this shit if you do. Yo' brother won't have to take me out cuz I'll do it myself. I can't handle no more fucking pain baby. I can't handle no more losses. Please!"

This shit hurt. And it hurt deep. Just when I was about to try CPR or at least my version of it, time stood slow as her heart stopped. *Love* had me wishing mine had stopped as well.

To be continued...

AFTERWORD

I hope you enjoyed this part one! Initially, this book was going to be a full stand-alone, and book two was going to be about Shio, while the twins took book three but Jisei and Ezio had a lot to say. No worries, you won't have to wait long for book two because it's halfway written. This will be the only book in the mob universe with two parts (I think). I promise it is coming in a few weeks! Also book two of Jisei and Ezio will have more interaction from Don, Matteo, Lorenzo, and the rest of your favs especially since we're down a character (hehe). I just had to weave Jae and Ezio's story first and keep the focus on them. Please don't forget to leave a review and share! Thank you so much for your support. I hope y'all are ready for what is next. Things are about to get crazy!

ABOUT THE AUTHOR

Lisa Austin is an award winning, National best selling, independent Author who often creates tales about the grit and grind of the streets but with a romantic twist. Born and raised in Memphis, TN, the on the rise Author has been penning stories her entire life.

Also By Lisa Austin

Pregnant by a Muthaf*ckin Don 1&2

A Winter Crest Christmas: Pure & Luxe

A Winter Crest Valentine's: Snowy & Sphere

Wealth over riches & bad b*tches

Paradise Bay: Coastal & Bliss

Exhilarated 1-3

Put it on The Mob: Ezio and Jae

www.ingramcontent.com/pod-product-compliance
Lightning Source LLC
Chambersburg PA
CBHW060424030726

47495CB00003B/723